SNIPER ELITE:

ONE-WAY TRIP

A NOVEL

SCOTT McEWEN

WITH THOMAS KOLONIAR

A Touchstone Book
Published by Simon & Schuster
New York London Toronto Sydney New Delhi

Touchstone
A Division of Simon & Schuster, Inc.
1230 Avenue of the Americas
New York, NY 10020

First Touchstone hardcover edition June 2013

TOUCHSTONE and colophon are registered trademarks of
Simon & Schuster, Inc.

For information about special discounts for bulk purchases, please contact
Simon & Schuster Special Sales at 1-866-506-1949 or
business@simonandschuster.com.

The Simon & Schuster Speakers Bureau can bring authors to your live event.
For more information or to book an event contact the Simon & Schuster
Speakers Bureau at 1-866-248-3049 or visit our website at www.simonspeakers.com.

Designed by Claudia Martinez

Manufactured in the United States of America

10 9 8 7 6 5 4 3 2 1

Library of Congress Cataloging-in-Publication Data

McEwen, Scott.
    Sniper elite : one-way trip : a novel / Scott McEwen.
        pages   cm
    "A Touchstone book."
1. Snipers—Fiction.   2. United States. Navy. SEALs—Fiction.   3. Undercover
operations—Fiction.   4. War on Terrorism, 2001–2009—Fiction.   I. Title.
    PS3613.M4355S65 2013
813'.6—dc23   2013010321

ISBN 978-1-4767-4605-0
ISBN 978-1-4767-4608-1 (ebook)

SNIPER ELITE:

ONE-WAY TRIP

PROLOGUE

Sitting with a couple of SEAL Team buddies at Danny's Bar in Coronado, I was introduced to an individual that both of them described as one of the most badass SEALs they knew. I thought to myself: *The two guys I'm drinking with are probably the baddest-ass characters I know, so if they think this guy is badass, he must be.*

About twenty-five years old, 5'8" and roughly 170 pounds, a guy who I will call "Gil" is introduced to me. The conversation starts calmly, as I am introduced as the coauthor of the book *American Sniper*, etc. We have a couple of beers and I am "vetted" by Gil through his subtle yet insightful questioning of my motive. I then found out why Gil was "badass."

Gil was shot more than fifteen times in a single battle somewhere outside the wire. After several more drinks, Gil proceeded to show me the entry and exit wounds that literally covered his body from his legs to his neck. These were not flesh wounds in any sense, but direct hits from 7.62X39-AK-47 rounds. What struck me from the discussion was not that Gil was "proud" of his battle scars, but instead he was proud that he stayed in the fight the entire time before being evac'd for medical attention.

This book is dedicated to the warriors of the SEAL Teams that are always in the fight, even when dealt serious injuries and overwhelming odds. The fictional accounts are based on actual Black Ops missions.

Scott McEwen

1

MONTANA

The horse was a four-year-old gray Appaloosa mare named Tico Chiz, but Navy Master Chief Gil Shannon simply called her Tico. He spent time with his wife, Marie, and his mother-in-law on their horse ranch in Bozeman, Montana, but his true home was the Navy. Most of his life was spent either at the Naval Training Center Hampton Roads in Virginia Beach, Virginia, or off in faraway corners of the globe doing what Marie, a bit too often for his taste, derisively referred to as *serving his corporate masters.*

The life of any camp follower was difficult, but being the wife of a US Navy SEAL was just plain grueling at times, and there was a bitterness within his wife that Gil could see growing slowly stronger with each passing year. The hard truth was that he and his wife shared only a few things in common. They both loved Montana like their next breath, had horse blood in their veins, and they shared a chemical attraction for each other strong enough to rival the force of gravity.

He put his boot into the stirrup and hauled himself up into the saddle as Marie came into the stable dressed in jeans and boots and a maroon Carhartt jacket. He looked at her approvingly, touching the brim of his hat. "Ma'am," he said, his blue eyes smiling.

She smiled back in the same shy way she always did after they'd made love, her brown eyes twinkling, long brown hair loosely braided. She was thirty-six, one year older than her husband, and at the very least his intellectual equal. Crossing her arms, she leaned against a support post cluttered with tack. "You know that horse likely forgot your name last time you were away."

Gil grinned, sidling Tico over to the wall where he took down a Browning .300 Winchester Magnum with a 3 to 24 Nightforce scope. "I ain't all that convinced she ever knew it." He shucked the rifle backward into the saddle scabbard. "Self-centered beast that she is."

"You know there ain't nothing out there gonna hurt you."

"Well, all the same, I like to have it along," he said quietly, never liking to disagree with her, their time together always being too short.

She arched an eyebrow in warning. "You'd better leave my elk alone, Gil Shannon."

He laughed, knowing he was caught, removing a pouch of tobacco from his tan Carhartt and rolling himself a cigarette. There was a Zen to the process that helped keep him anchored whenever he felt the waves of anxiety slapping at his hull. The sad reality was that life on the ranch was too slow for him, too tidy and safe, and he sometimes began to feel as though he might crawl out of his skin. He understood why this was, of course. He'd been raised the son of the warrior, and as a result carried much of the emotional baggage that often came along with being the son of a Green Beret who had served multiple tours during the Vietnam War. He was extremely proud of his heritage, however, having consciously chosen a form of service that meant he would spend most of his adult life far away from the Montana of his youth. Montana would always be there, he told himself. And when he finally grew too old to run, jump, and swim for the Navy, he would retire there and finally settle down with Marie, secure in the knowledge that he had done all that he could to defend this great land.

He smiled at his wife, poking the cigarette between his lips. "Don't worry. Old man Spencer said I could hunt his place anytime I want."

Marie understood that her husband had demons he kept deep inside. She could see them in the shadows that crossed his brow in those painful moments when he thought she wasn't looking.

"I see," she said thoughtfully. "So you're letting out for the high country."

He drew from the cigarette and exhaled through his nose. "I'll stay below the snow line. Don't worry."

"I never worry when you're home," she said, stepping from the post to touch his leg. "I already told you there's nothing out there gonna hurt you. Montana's where you draw your strength."

He leaned to kiss her and straightened up in the saddle. "Have you seen Oso this morning?"

"Out back watching the colts, as usual. He thinks they're his."

Gil gave her a wink and pressed his heels into the flanks of the horse to set her walking out the door. As he rounded the corner, he saw the Chesapeake Bay retriever sitting over near the paddock where two painted colts were kept with their mothers.

"Oso!" he called, and the dog came trotting. His full name was Oso Cazador—bear hunter—named by Gil's late friend Miguel, the dog's original owner who had raised him to go grizzly hunting with him in the high country outside of Yellowstone. Miguel had died the year before of cancer, and his daughter, Carmen, had shown up with Oso at the funeral, asking Gil if he would let the dog come to live on the ranch, claiming that her apartment back in LA was just too small for a 120-pound animal. Before Gil even had a chance to think it over, Marie had taken the leash and welcomed Oso into the family. The arrangement had worked out well, too. Oso kept the coyotes away from the colts, looked after Marie and his mother-in-law whenever Gil was away, and had a keen eye for the movement of game at long distances.

In truth, Oso was something of a devil dog, overly protective of Marie whenever Gil was not at the house, and he had this way of showing his teeth when he was happy, a kind of menacing canine smile that could be hard to interpret. In a way, he reminded Gil of the young SEALs he worked with: fiercely loyal, intelligent, athletic, and fearless, though hardheaded at times. And like those young men, Oso was known on occasion to challenge Gil for his position in the hierarchy. It was through sheer force of will, however, that Gil was able to impress his alpha status upon man as well as beast. It was the iron will he had inherited from his father, and he was more grateful for that than any other trait. He was not the strongest in the DEVGRU teams, or the largest or the fastest, or even the best shot, but during numerous trials in the field, his will alone had enabled him to succeed where men of apparent superior physical prowess had failed.

This was the reason he was so often considered the go-to man.

He reined the horse around and headed off toward the high country at the trot. Oso tended to travel inside the horse's shadow even when the weather was cool, and though Gil wasn't entirely sure, he thought it must be to keep the sun out of his eyes.

Within twenty minutes, they passed through the gate on the western border of the ranch, and Gil stopped to roll another cigarette. As he sat in the saddle smoking, he took a Milk-Bone from his pocket and tossed it down to Oso, who immediately dug a shallow hole with his forepaws and dropped the bone in, using his nose to cover it over. Then the dog sat down and barked, wanting another.

Gil smiled, drawing deeply from the cigarette and tossing down another bone. Oso ate it immediately.

Two hours later, they made the crest of a high ridge where Gil dismounted and stood holding the reins as he overlooked the Spencer Valley below. He knew there were elk down there, moving carefully among the brush. Rut would be starting soon, and they would grow careless, but for now, they were still lying low, and this was when Gil preferred to hunt them. For him, there wasn't much of a trick to shooting an animal hopped up on hormones, bugling its ass off, almost daring you to squeeze the trigger.

A large bull elk stepped from the trees to his left, roughly a hundred yards off down the slope, and Oso lowered himself to the ground to signal that he had spotted their prey.

Gil took the rifle from its scabbard, popping the lens caps and shouldering the weapon for a closer look. The bull was mature and well racked with ten points, chewing a mouthful of grass without a care in the world. He capped the lenses and returned the rifle to the scabbard. At a hundred yards, he could almost take it out with a stone. He never wasted a bullet on game at less than five hundred yards, valuing the challenge far more than the kill itself.

He tied Tico's reins off to a dead tree standing nearby and removed her saddle. Then he poured water into a canteen cup for Oso and cleared a spot on the ground for himself to settle in behind the saddle. When the firing position was prepared, he retrieved the rifle and settled in to wait. He spent his time gauging the slight breeze, unconsciously doing the math in his head for different target areas within the valley. He almost never dealt in actual numbers anymore, the calculations as automatic in his brain as $2 + 2$ equaling 4.

After forty minutes, Oso stood up and stared straight down into the valley.

Gil took up the rifle and searched far below their position, spotting the young, four-by-four-point bull standing broadside at the edge of the tree line a thousand yards off down the 30-degree slope. The scope on the rifle was set to compensate for the drop of the bullet over flat terrain, so Gil knew without even thinking that he would need to aim slightly lower than he normally would, in effect compensating for the preset compensation of the drop. This concept was often one of the toughest for raw SEAL Team recruits to wrap their brains around.

He placed the reticle on the ridge of the bull's spinal column just behind the shoulder blades where he wanted the 7.62 mm round to strike. Then he lowered his aim slightly, as if he were about to engage a target at just over 800 yards instead of 1,000. There was no real way to teach this kind of shooting. This was the kind of precision developed over thousands of rounds fired downrange. Had there been any concern at all in Gil's mind the round would maim the animal or cause it any pain, he would simply have aimed for the much easier-to-hit heart.

As he drew a shallow breath, preparing to squeeze the trigger, it happened again—the memory of his first kill in combat coming back in living color . . .

THE SECOND IRAQ War was only a month old. Gil and his partner Tony had been called into a small town outside of Baghdad to relieve the pressure on two companies of Marines who were being decimated by enemy sniper fire. One of the Marine snipers was already dead, and their morale had begun to flag in a way that only enemy sniper fire can cause. So their CO had called for tactical support, and half an hour later a Cayuse helicopter dropped Gil and Tony in the Marines' rear. It was during their march forward over five blocks of hell that the two SEALs were able to collect real-time intel from the grunts on the ground.

By the time they reached the Marines' forward positions, Tony had marked the locations of all thirteen wounded and dead Marines on his map. He grabbed Gil by the elbow and pulled him into a concrete garage with good cover.

"Okay, look," Tony said, dropping to his knee and laying out the map. "See the kill pattern here? This isn't random. That means one guy, Gil. And he's falling back in a kind of zigzag. See—?" He ran his finger back and forth along the grid to clarify his point. "He's moving corner to corner to maintain a clear field of fire—and all our head-shot Marines are inside this same diminishing kill zone. The fucker's bleeding them out, and by the time these boys work their way to the far side of town, they'll lose ten more. And then this *haji* prick is just gonna fade the fuck away—only we ain't gonna let that *the fuck* happen!" He quickly folded the map away inside his body armor. "So now we gotta find that jarhead CO and get him to halt this fucking advance before the sun starts to set—or better yet—get these guys to fucking pull back a block or two. That'll lure this *haji* motherfucker right back to us. Then you'll step on his dick, and I'll hack it off at the balls!"

As they were stepping out of the garage, a Navy corpsman and pair of stretcher-bearers rounded the corner carrying a young Marine with his face shot completely off.

"Put 'im down!" the corpsman shouted. "I gotta restore his fucking airway!"

Gil stood over the dying Marine, gaping at the shapeless mass of flesh where the boy's face had once been, unable to believe that a man without a face could even still be alive.

The corpsman hurriedly performed a tracheotomy to restore the Marine's airway, then the bearers hefted the stretcher back up between them, and they took off down the street in the direction of the incoming medevac.

"Ruck up!" Tony said, busting Gil on the shoulder, and the two of them took off to find the Marine major in charge of taking the town.

It took some hard convincing on Tony's part before the major would agree to give up two blocks of hard-earned real estate. "Look, major, with respect—*sir*. You called us. Now, I'm telling you how we can kill this *haji* bastard. If you'll withdraw just two blocks, sir, those motherfuckers will think they're winning this goddamn battle. And that fucking sniper of theirs won't be able to resist moving to retake this prime position." Tony indicated the position on the aerial photograph posted on the wall of the command post. "Sir, I'm fucking *positive* that's where he was when he took out six of your Marines in under ten minutes."

"Where do you intend to lay for him?" the major wanted to know.

Tony indicated a tall building in the center of the block south of the suspected sniper position. "We'll take up an elevated position here, sir, with an excellent view overlooking his nest."

The major looked to his captain. "What do you think, Steve?"

The captain looked at Tony. "You do realize that building will go back over to the enemy after we withdraw. You'll be cut off and surrounded."

Tony smiled. "Only for a little while, Captain."

The captain nodded, turning to the major. "If I was in command, sir, I'd take his advice. He seems to know what he's talking about."

"Okay," the major said. "How much time do you need to get in position?"

"Shouldn't take us more than fifteen minutes to get set, sir," Tony replied. "After that, you can begin your withdrawal. The enemy sniper *should* approach from one of these two alleys to reoccupy the position. And when he does, sir, we will bag his ass."

Twenty minutes later, Gil and Tony were in place with a perfect overview of the enemy sniper nest in a corner meat market. They watched from their well-concealed hide on the roof of a three-story apartment building as the Marines were falling back through the position. Within ten minutes, they were isolated and soon to be cut off by encroaching enemy troops now moving to retake the ground they had lost during the first half of the day.

"We could hit a bunch of these guys right now," Gil said, watching the enemy moving toward them along empty streets through the scope of the M-21 sniper rifle he still carried in those days.

"Which is exactly what that *haji* sniper is waiting for," Tony said bitterly, watching through the scope of his own M-21. "He's waiting to see if one of our snipers takes advantage of this fucking duck shoot. Give him time. Keep your fucking eyes peeled for a *haji* carrying a Dragunov. That'll be your guy."

"My guy?" Gil said, taking his eye briefly away from the scope.

Tony grinned. "I can't think of a better prick for you to bust your fucking cherry on, Gilligan."

Feeling his palms suddenly begin to sweat, Gil put his eye to the scope and carefully scanned each new man who came into view, their weapons, their beards and faces, multicolored shemaghs blowing with the breeze as they marched boldly forward. Many of them were laughing and gesturing excitedly, believing they were succeeding in forcing the Marines from the town.

A man dressed in green and carrying a longer weapon than the standard AK-47 darted from a laundry service to disappear beneath an awning.

"Did you see that?" Gil said. "Looked like a guy carrying a Dragunov just ducked under that awning."

The Dragunov was a semiautomatic, 7.62 mm rifle that had been in Soviet service since 1963. Though it had not been developed originally as a sniper rifle, the rugged weapon had since become the preferred choice of snipers in the Middle East, boasting a range of 1,300 meters when fixed with a scope.

"See a scope?"

"No, it didn't have a scope, but the stock was wrapped in cloth."

"Probably just an RPK," Tony said. "Our guy isn't making these shots over open sights."

An RPK-74 was a light machine gun that looked like an over-grown AK-47.

A couple of minutes later, a blur of dark green darted from beneath the awning, and this time there was a scope attached to his rifle. "I got him!" Gil said. He was unable to draw a good enough bead as the sniper darted carefully from shop to shop coming down the alley.

"See what the fuck I told you!" Tony said. "He's moving to reoccupy that fucking position. Just be patient and let him come right into your kill zone. He'll give you his back when he turns to mount that fucking staircase—that's when you take him."

The enemy sniper checked one last time up and down the alley, desperately scanning the rooftops without a prayer of spotting Gil or Tony ensconced among the scattered rubble of the cityscape. With the speed of a lizard, he darted across the street toward the staircase leading up the side of the building he intended to reoccupy.

He mounted the stairs and gave Gil his back at 200 yards.

"Take him," Tony said calmly, watching the sniper through his own crosshairs in case Gil should miss.

Gil centered on the sniper's spine at the base of the neck and squeezed off the round. The enemy sniper was dead instantly, crashing to his knees and falling backward down the stairs.

"Reap the whirlwind, motherfucker." Tony bashed Gil on the shoulder. "When the battle's over we'll find that fucker and get you your boar's tooth."

NOW GIL LAY in his position behind the saddle, watching the elk move gracefully through the grass. The animal paused to test the air. Gil drew a shallow breath and squeezed the trigger. The round severed the beast's spinal cord at the base of the neck just forward of the shoulders, and the elk dropped dead to the ground, never knowing what hit it.

2

AFGHANISTAN,
Nangarhar Province

Warrant Officer Sandra Brux sat beside her copilot Warrant Officer Billy Mitchell in the open doorway of their UH-60M Black Hawk helicopter smoking cigarettes and shooting the shit. Sandra was twenty-nine years old with dark hair and blue eyes, an excellent helicopter pilot beginning her third tour in the Middle East. They watched as a six-man team of US Army Rangers ran through a training exercise, rehearsing a night raid "snatch 'n' grab" presently set for the following week. Sandra and Mitchell were both Night Stalkers, pilots of the elite 160th Special Operations Aviation Regiment (SOAR), which routinely operated with both Army and Naval Special Forces. Known throughout the Spec-Ops community as the best of the best, they were the go-to badasses in the air for the go-to badasses on the ground, and Sandra was the first female pilot to be made a member.

The Rangers were maneuvering through a flimsy plywood village mock-up, working out the timing of their attack. The rehearsal site was considered "secure" as it was located fifty miles from the lines (to the extent that "lines" even existed in this godforsaken place). The snatch 'n' grab was to be carried out against a Muslim cleric named Aasif Kohistani living in a small village in the north of Nangarhar Province. Kohistani was the leader of an Islamist political party called the Hezb-e Islami Khalis (the HIK). The HIK was gaining political influence in the Afghan parliament, and recent intelligence reports indicated that Kohistani was now working with the Taliban to consolidate his growing military power in and around Nangarhar Province in the face of the scheduled American drawdown.

Obviously, American forces would not be able to make their scheduled drawdown work if the HIK and Taliban forces began a resurgence, so it was necessary to remove Kohistani from the picture, lest he become as strong as the already troublesome Gulbuddin Hekmatyar who lead the Hezb-e Islami Gulbuddin faction (HIG) based out of the Shok Valley of the Hindu Kush. Both the HIK and the HIG had made significant gains in parliamentary influence over the past year, and both were violently opposed to Afghan-US relations.

Sandra flicked away the smoking butt of her cigarette and lay back on the deck of the helicopter to close her eyes, smiling pleasantly to herself. She and the Ranger team leader, Captain Sean Bordeaux, had secretly hooked up the night before back at the air base outside of Jalalabad. It had been a much-needed tryst for both of them, each of their military spouses being stationed on the other side of the world. Six months was a long time for anyone to go without, but the nature of their respective jobs was extremely stressful, and this stress had long been exacerbated by the uncommonly strong attraction between them—which was no one's fault but that of Mother Nature. The sexual tension between them was now dispelled, however, and both of them were thinking much more clearly, able to focus their full attention on their respective missions.

"Hey, have you heard from Beth?" Sandra asked.

Mitchell sat squinting into the morning sun, watching as the Rangers retook their positions to begin another "infiltration" of the village. He and Sandra were the only security for the training op. He drew pensively from his cigarette, thinking of his wife who was due to give birth in less than a week.

"Last night," he answered. "She said she could pop any minute. Could be happening right now, for all I know. How come you and John don't have any kids?"

She lifted her head to look at him. "Do I look like I'm ready to have kids?"

He laughed. "Well, I guess it's a little different with you guys."

"You can say that," she said, rising up onto her elbows. "I mean, we only see each other about four months of the year. Sometimes, I wonder why we even—"

Machine gun fire raked the front of the Black Hawk, and bullets went whining off into the air.

"What the fuck!" Mitchell said, grabbing up his M4. "Enemy front!"

"Incoming!" one of the Rangers screamed from the far side of the ersatz village.

The first couple of mortars struck the ground, their telltale *crumping* sounds ripping through the air. Two more rounds quickly fell, and the flimsy buildings blew apart like houses made from playing cards. The nearest pair of Rangers leapt back to their feet and came sprinting toward the Black Hawk. Another round dropped just in front of them and they vanished.

"Jesus Christ!" Sandra scrambled into the cockpit. "Where the fuck did they come from? We're in the middle of fucking nowhere."

"We gotta get this bitch off the ground." Mitchell was climbing into the gunner's compartment behind her. "We're a sitting fucking duck here!"

The four remaining Rangers were still a hundred yards off across the village, running hard for the chopper as Sandra flipped the switches in the cockpit and the rotors began to turn. "We'll be airborne in sixty seconds."

"We don't have sixty—!"

A mortar struck the tail section of the helicopter, lifting the hind end of the bird into the air and causing it to slew wildly around. Mitchell was slammed against the bulkhead, splitting his head open, and Sandra was thrown from her seat to the other side of the cockpit. The sound of small arms fire filled the air. Bullets snapped through the fuselage as she tried to call for support over the radio.

"It's fucked!" Mitchell grabbed for her arm. "We gotta dismount!" A round struck him in the chest and he dropped dead to the deck.

Captain Bordeaux leapt into the bird, grabbing Sandra's collar and hauling her from the aircraft against a hail of gunfire. They were both hit and fell out the open door. The other three remaining Rangers took cover as best they could near the fuselage, but it seemed they were surrounded on all sides, and the cover among the rocks was sparse at best.

"Did you get off a call for help?" Bordeaux asked, firing a few rounds into a coppice of trees to keep the enemy's head down.

"They took out the radio first thing," Sandra said, gasping against the pain in her thigh where she'd taken a round from an AK-47. "I think it's up against the bone, Sean. Fuck me! It hurts like a holy bastard."

Bordeaux grabbed up Mitchell's M4 and jammed it into her hands as he half-carried, half-dragged her toward the rocks where his men were digging in as best they could with the butts of their carbines. "We're in some deep shit here, guys. No cover and nowhere to run."

One of the other men went right to work applying a pressure tourniquet to Sandra's leg. Shock was setting in fast and she'd already begun to fade.

"We'd better think of something fast," one of the other Rangers said. "When they correct fire on those mortars, we're dead."

"They could've done that already," Bordeaux said. "They're maneuvering to take us alive."

"Or her," said a sergeant named Tornero.

"Or her, yeah." Bordeaux spat in disgust. Their radioman had been blasted to hell, and it would be at least another hour, maybe two, before anyone tried to raise them and thought to send another chopper. This was supposed to have been a very secure zone, which was why it had been chosen in the first place. Something was wrong. "I don't know, guys, but it feels like they were here waiting for us."

Tornero was jamming cotton wadding into a shoulder wound. "Yeah, well, the way they've been blabbing about the op back at HQ, it don't fucking surprise me."

"I don't like having a woman in this shit," Bordeaux said.

"Maybe you can trade me," Sandra groaned, fighting the urge to vomit.

Another furious fusillade of gunfire erupted, forcing them all belly-down against the earth as the enemy maneuvered still closer.

"There's at least twenty!" shouted one of the other Rangers, firing away, finally managing to kill one. "They're gonna jerk the noose tight."

Bordeaux knew their time had run out. It was time to surrender or break out across country, and there was no way to break out without leaving Sandra behind.

"Sergeant, you three haul ass for that defilade!" he ordered. "There's no other way. Try to fight your way north toward friendlies. Surrender's not an option here."

Tornero exchanged looks with the other two members of the

team, all of them shaking their heads. He looked back at Bordeaux and grinned. "I think we'll stay, Captain."

"I said haul ass!"

Tornero popped up just long enough to biff a grenade then ducked back down. "You can court-martial us if we live long enough, sir, but we're stayin'."

"Stubborn fuckers," Bordeaux muttered, crawling off for a better look at the defilade to their north. Three of the enemy had already occupied the depression, and they opened fire the second they saw his face. He jerked the pin from a grenade and slung it in their direction before scrabbling back to the others, taking more hits, one to the arm and another to the boron carbide ballistic panel on his back. The grenade went off with a sharp blast, flinging body parts into the air. Bordeaux and his men all sprang into a crouch, firing in all four directions as the enemy continued to maneuver aggressively against them.

One of the Rangers took a round to the face and fell over backward.

Knowing they were down to mere seconds now, Bordeaux fired his M4 until the magazine ran dry then jerked his M9 pistol and turned to aim it at Sandra.

She winked at him and covered her eyes with her hand.

He hesitated a fraction of an instant, remembering the night before, and then squeezed the trigger.

A 7.62 mm slug blew out the side of his head, causing the round from his pistol to strike the ground near Sandra's shoulder as he toppled from his knees.

Sergeant Tornero spun to fire on the man who'd killed Bordeaux, stitching him from the groin to the throat before taking multiple hits to his armor, limbs, and guts. He pitched forward onto his hands and knees, still taking hits, choking blood as he crawled desperately forward to cover Sandra's body with his own.

Sandra was struggling to tug Tornero's pistol from its holster when the shadowy figure of a Taliban fighter blocked out the sun. He stepped on her hand and reached down to take the pistol from the holster, tossing it to one of his men before hefting Tornero's body aside. He spoke calmly in Pashto, pointing at the American weapons on the ground, ordering them gathered up. The Rangers were quickly stripped of their armor and ammunition, their boots, money, watches, dog tags—everything.

Deep in shock, Sandra was vaguely aware of being lifted from the ground and slung over the shoulder of a squat, muscular man. She opened her eyes briefly, seeing the ground passing below, the sandaled heels of her captor moving back and forth as he walked along.

They walked all the rest of the day, taking turns carrying their prisoner toward the foothills near the Pakistan border. Sometime after nightfall, Sandra awoke to feel herself jostling around in the back of a pickup truck as it made its way higher into the mountains of the Hindu Kush. She mumbled that she was cold, and someone in the back of the truck with her must have spoken English because she was covered with a coat a few moments later.

The next time she awoke was to a bright light being shined into one of her eyes. She was carried from the truck on what felt like a sheet of plywood into a dimly lit hut where she felt needles being pricked into her. She screamed aloud when a steel probe was inserted into her leg wound and struggled against the pain. Someone with gorilla-like strength held her down while the bullet was removed and the wound was sutured closed. After that, a dirty brown sack was slipped over her head, and she was put back into the truck and driven away.

Later in the night, the bag was taken off and she was made to drink a great deal more water than she cared to, a bright flashlight being shined into her face the entire time. She coughed and gagged, swallowing as much as she could, and the canteen was finally taken away and the bag replaced. After what felt like an eternity, the truck stopped again, and she was carried into another building where she was tied to some kind of a wooden bed.

She awoke in the morning with her leg fevered and throbbing to find that she was still tied to the bed, but that her boots and flight suit had been taken away, replaced with a kind of dirty white gown made from a coarse cloth. A man of about forty sat beside her bed reading the Koran through a pair of dark-framed glasses that seemed too large for his face. He wore the white *jubbah* of a Muslim cleric, and his neatly trimmed black beard was flecked with gray.

He looked up to see her watching him and slowly closed the Koran, setting it aside on a table. "You are awake," he said in good English.

"I'd like to have my uniform back," was the first thing she said.

He removed the glasses from his face and folded them away into the pocket of his robe. "That's been burned," he replied. "Your leg has been repaired, and you are far away from your people now. Very far away. They will not be able to find you here. I am Aasif Kohistani of the Hezb-e Islami Khalis. I am the political leader you and your friends were preparing to illegally kidnap from my village in Nangarhar."

"Brux," Sandra said. "Sandra J., Warrant Officer. 280-76-0987."

He smiled a humorless smile. "I have that information already." He took from the table a handful of dog tags taken from Sandra's dead compatriots and selected hers from the collection. "You are also Catholic. What else can you tell me about CIA intentions against our party? Are they preparing military strikes?"

"Can I be untied?" Sandra asked, her mouth dry as a sock.

He set the dog tags aside. "It is impossible that you will not tell me what I want to know," he said patiently. "It would be better for you to tell me now. This will prevent great difficulties for you."

"I'm just a pilot," she said. "The CIA doesn't tell us about their plans. I don't even know why they wanted you." And what worried Sandra the most was that this was the truth. She had no idea why the CIA wanted Kohistani or whether or not there were any military strikes being planned.

"You are not just a pilot," he said, taking her Night Stalker shoulder patch from the table. "You are one of these people. We know this name very well. I will give you one last opportunity to tell me what you know. After that I will call Ramesh."

"You really have to believe me," she begged. "I don't know anything! If I did, I would tell you. I don't give a shit about the CIA."

"That is not the answer I was looking for."

"Do you want me to make something up?" she said helplessly. As she lay there trying to think back to the mock interrogations she had undergone during survival school, Kohistani calmly lifted a previously unnoticed wooden rod from the foot of the bed and gave her a sharp crack against the bullet wound in her thigh.

Pain exploded in her leg. She arched her back involuntarily, her entire body going ramrod stiff, barely stifling the cry that threatened to rip from her throat. She gulped air in deep breaths, girding herself for the next blow, but she knew that it was no use. The pain was too intense.

He stood and raised the rod high over his head.

"Don't— I'll tell you!"

He brought the rod down again, and this time with a truly savage amount of force. Sandra screamed in pain, her mind reeling, as the cleric delivered her a third blow. She wailed in agony, sobbing shamelessly as she babbled completely made-up information in a desperate bid to prevent him from striking her a fourth time.

Kohistani stopped short of delivering the blow, tossing the rod onto the foot of the bed with a grimace. "Do you see how senseless . . . how pointless it was for you to suffer?"

She closed her eyes and tried to sob as quietly as she could in an attempt to retain what little remained of her dignity.

"Open your eyes," he ordered, looking down on her. "Do you know why your country will lose in Afghanistan? The fearless capitalists will lose because they send women to fight their war. Now, I will send in Ramesh to learn if what you told me was the truth."

He left the room, and a brutish, angry-looking man came in a few moments later, toting a brown canvas bag, setting it down on the table with a metallic clunk.

Gripped by abject terror, Sandra shut her eyes again and tried to disappear.

3

MONTANA

Gil and Marie were spreading fresh hay in the stable when his mother-in-law called him on his cellular to tell him he had a call on the house phone.

"Be right back," he said to his wife, slipping the phone back into his pocket.

Marie didn't even look at him. She cut the twine on another bale of hay and broke it apart with her foot.

"It's probably nothin', babe."

She stopped and stared at him. "It's never nothin' with the Navy. It's only been a month, and you're supposed to get two. You're telling me their ships won't float without Gil Shannon aboard?"

He grinned, knowing she knew damn well he was no deckhand. "Well, they float well enough . . . but the crews won't go out of sight of land unless I'm aboard."

She shook her head and went back to work, his sarcastic sense of humor no longer holding the appeal for her that it once did.

Gil found the cordless on the kitchen table and took it out onto the back porch. "This is Shannon."

"Gil, its Hal. Something's happened, and I thought it important enough to call. Can you call me back on your sat phone?" Master Chief Halligan Steelyard was a fellow member of DEVGRU (United States Naval Special Warfare Development Group, aka SEAL Team Six) and one of Gil's closest friends. He'd been in the Navy since Chester Nimitz was a baby, and he was something of his own institution among the SEALs.

"Give me one minute." Gil hung up the phone and then went to the bedroom where he kept a secure satellite phone and called Steelyard back. "So what's up?"

"Sorry to bother you at home with this," Steelyard said. "Sean Bordeaux and five of his men bought it yesterday in an ambush here in Nangarhar Province, south of Jalalabad."

Gil had worked with Bordeaux a number of times in the past and considered him a friend, but this loss wasn't the kind of news that rated a satellite call from a guy like Steelyard from halfway around the world. "What else, Chief?"

"A Night Stalker pilot was taken prisoner in the same ambush," Steelyard went on. "Taliban caught the bird on the ground during a Ranger training op, shot everybody up, killed the copilot, and stripped the bodies. It's a problem because the pilot they took is a woman, pretty thing, twenty-nine years old . . . the only Night Stalker female. It's not going to play well in the media, especially if she shows up bleeding on Al Jazeera. I thought you'd like a heads up because I expect it's only a matter of time before you get the call from SOG."

SOG was the CIA's Special Operations Group, a more evolved version of the once infamous and now extinct MACV-SOG (Military

Assistance Command, Vietnam—Studies and Observations Group)
that Gil's father had once been a part of. Though the CIA still recruited through SOG from all branches of the US military—the same
as they had during Vietnam—the modern CIA was no longer permit-
ted its own "in-house" specialists. So operators like Gil Shannon were
often pulled from their assigned Special Mission Units (SMUs) for
the purpose of carrying out one-man operations that were often so
highly classified that no one else in the Special Forces community ever
knew a thing about them . . . at least not officially.

Gil's current, primary unit assignment was to DEVGRU the
same as that of Chief Steelyard. Being so highly classified that the
US government preferred not to admit its existence, DEVGRU was
one of only four SMUs within the United States military. The other
three SMUs were: Delta Force of the US Army, the 24th Special
Tactics Squadron of the US Air Force, and the Intelligence Support
Activity—also under the auspices of the US Army.

Gil patted his jacket pocket for his tobacco. "Are we talking
about Warrant Officer Sandra Brux, Chief?"

"Yeah. Know her?"

"She's flown top-cover for us a couple of times," Gil said. "They're
gonna tear her up, Chief. How'd this happen?"

"It's a CID investigation right now," Steelyard said. CID was
the Army Criminal Investigation Command—originally known as
the Criminal Investigations Division first established under General
Pershing during the First World War. For the purposes of continuity,
the agency was still referred to as the CID. "But I had a talk with
our guy in NCIS who's connected." NCIS was the Naval Criminal
Investigative Service. "He says CID just took some Pakistani intel
guy into custody who's been selling information to the other side. I'm
thinking he may have tipped off the enemy about the Army's plan to
snatch an Al Qaeda cleric who's been making them nervous. Listen,
I'll get back to you in a few days. Sound good?"

"Sounds good, Chief, yeah. Thanks for the heads up."

"You bet."

Gil went back downstairs to find his mother-in-law in the kitchen making sandwiches. "Thanks for calling me in, Mom."

His mother-in-law smiled. "Are you leaving us again?" Her name was Janet, and she was sixty-five years old, short with long gray hair she wore in the braid of a horsewoman, like her daughter.

"No," he said. "That was just an update to keep me in the loop."

"Think Marie will buy that?" Janet asked.

He laughed. "There's not much space between you two, is there?"

She shook her head, offering him a plated roast beef sandwich with potato chips. "Like a beer with that?"

"Yes, I would," he said, wishing in earnest that he did not personally know Sandra Brux. The two of them had shared some laughs one night half a year earlier, swapping stories about the challenges of holding a marriage together.

LATER THAT NIGHT, after his mother-in-law had washed the dinner dishes and gone to bed, Gil sat alone in the rocking chair in front of the fireplace rolling a cigarette.

Marie came to sit on the hearth in front of him, a glass of white wine in her hand. "I've seen you like this before," she said quietly. "You lost a friend today, didn't you?"

He looked up from the cigarette. "It's worse, actually."

"How so?"

"The Taliban captured one of our helicopter pilots yesterday." He licked the edge of the cigarette paper and smoothed it into place to make it look almost store-bought. "A Night Stalker. For the enemy that's a hell of a trophy. Almost as good as capturing a SEAL or a Green Beret would be."

"And you know him, I assume?"

"It's a *her*," he said quietly, poking the smoke between his lips and lighting it with a match. "She's twenty-nine. Pretty. It's gonna play like hell once the media gets hold of it."

Marie nodded, taking a sip of wine. "Another Jessie Lynch," she said sadly. "So when are you leaving?"

"They didn't call me for that."

"That's not what I asked you," she said.

He sat holding his temples with the same hand the cigarette was in. "They don't even know where she is yet, baby."

Marie set the wineglass aside with a sigh and rubbed her knees. "Gil, I'm sorry, but I don't have the patience for these little go-rounds no more. Are ya leavin' or not?"

He looked at her, his voice not much more than a whisper. "It's what I do, baby. I can't explain it, but I feel like the only other thing I was ever meant to do was love you. And how's a man's supposed to make peace with that?"

Her eyes filled with tears, and she wiped them away. "What about my peace?"

He looked down, unable to meet her gaze. She was the only person he had ever feared intellectually. "That's a fair question," he said. "If you ask me to wait for the call, I will. It might easily be another month . . . probably will be."

"Look at me," she said. "You're at the top of your game, aren't you?"

He considered that for a moment. "Yes, ma'am. I believe I am."

She lifted the glass, finished the wine, then reached for his cigarette, drawing deeply from it and giving it back. She exhaled and turned to stare into the flames of the fire. "That girl put herself on the line for this country, and now she's living a nightmare. I reckon she deserves the best this country's got in return." She turned to look at him. "But this time you *will* make me that promise. This time you *will* promise to come home alive. Otherwise, you do not have my blessing."

He puckered his lips to suppress his smile, knowing that she had him over the barrel. "I promise."

"You promise what?" she said, arching her brow.

"I promise to come home alive."

"And you *will* keep that promise," she said, pointing her finger. "Otherwise, when I eventually arrive in heaven, I *will* not speak to you. I will not speak to you for at least a thousand years, Gil Shannon. Do you understand me?"

"Jesus Christ," he muttered. "That long?"

"Do you understand me?"

"Yes, ma'am, I do . . . and I believe you mean it."

She stood up from the hearth, straightening the tails of her denim shirt. "You'd better. Now, I am going upstairs to have my bath. Will you still be awake when I'm finished?"

He looked up at her and smiled. "That depends. Do I get a kiss before you go up? A little something to prime the pump?"

She leaned over to kiss him affectionately on the mouth, then turned and left the room.

4

AFGHANISTAN,
Nuristan Province, Waigal Village

Sandra awoke the next morning to the sound of a very heated argument between two men in the next room. She couldn't understand a word of what was being said, but she knew that it must have something to do with her. She was no longer tied to the bed, but that hardly mattered. Given the inflamed condition of her leg, she was in no shape for escape or evasion, and she didn't even have socks to wear, much less a pair of shoes. The food she'd been given was coarse and unknown to her, but she suspected that it was a goat meat stew. What worried her was that the water tasted bad. She knew she wouldn't last long if she caught a gastrointestinal infection, but there was no other way for her to survive in the short term but to stay hydrated.

She wondered if her husband, John, had been told yet of her disappearance. She doubted it. John was her only family, stationed in the Philippines where he flew cargo planes for the Air Force, and Sandra knew that informing him of her abduction was less of an immediate priority than if he were a civilian. In other words, they'd tell him when they got around to it. Sandra was no fool. She knew she was photogenic, and she knew the State Department would already be scrambling in their attempts to get out in front of the story, possibly even scrambling to keep it under wraps. She was now a pawn in the big chess game, and she didn't give herself much of a chance, particularly since she had no extended family to apply pressure on her behalf. She also knew quite well that in the Hindu Kush even a Muslim woman was worth less than a good packhorse. And Sandra was a Catholic, quite possibly the next worst thing to being a Jew.

In her heart, she believed that her best chance of being brought out alive would lie with the men she flew for, men within the special forces community itself, men who would not easily stand for one of their own being left to languish for an indefinite period without a concerted effort to locate and bring her out before it was too late.

The door was suddenly kicked off its hinges and fell to the floor. In stalked a bearded man she had never seen before wearing a *pakol*, the ethnic headgear of the Afghan people. The man seemed violently angry as he stalked over to the bed and reached for the hem of her gown. She didn't resist him at first, believing that he only wanted to check the gunshot wound to her thigh, but he jerked the garment clear up past her waist, and another man came from behind him, pinning her shoulders to the bed.

She screamed and kicked, clawing for the bearded man's eyes, managing to gouge her thumb deep into the socket before the second man chopped her in the throat, temporarily collapsing her esophagus. The bearded man grabbed his eye, reeling away from the bed as more men came into the room shouting. They sat on her and tied her down. Then they ripped away her gown and left her naked, still gasping for air.

The men laughed while poking and prodding her. She closed her eyes and willed herself not to scream, knowing that would only excite them more.

The bearded man was not laughing. He shoved the others out of the way and stood over her glowering, his right eyeball bloody. He shouted into the other room, and a man with a video camera came in, ordering the others out. Then the bearded man dropped his trousers and climbed onto the bed with her, cursing her in a language she did not understand, and that's when she began to scream.

TEN MINUTES LATER, the man with the beard, whose name was Naeem, sat on a table in the next room trying to keep his head still as a young woman missing most of her nose examined his eye.

"You are lucky," she said quietly. "Any closer to the retina, and she might have blinded you."

Naeem pushed her away. "Don't tell me I'm lucky, Badira. Tell me what needs to be done for it."

"There are medicines to put in the eye," she explained, "but none that we have here. All you can do is wear a bandage over it while it heals."

"Fine. Cover your face," he ordered in disgust and got up from the table.

Badira backed away, obediently lifting the bottom of her *hijab* up over her mutilated nose so that only her eyes were showing. She was not forced to wear a *chadri* or a burqa around the village because she was a nurse and her husband was dead. Her husband was the one who had cut off her nose shortly after their marriage for refusing to wear a burqa. Mercifully, he had been killed by an airstrike near the Pakistani border a few years later. Their marriage had been an arranged affair, as were 75 percent of all Afghan marriages.

An older man stepped into the room from outside, and the other

Taliban men began to bristle, but Naeem settled them. "Never mind, old man. It's done."

The old man's name was Sabil Nuristani, and he was the titular head of the village. "Now you must take her far away from here." he insisted. "Otherwise, they will send men here to kill us all."

"No!" Naeem snapped. "We will show them the video, and then they will pay to get her back. They have paid before."

"You had better use your head," Sabil cautioned, stepping deeper into the room. "Kohistani hasn't given his approval for a ransom demand. He only said we were to—"

"Aasif Kohistani does not command here!" Naeem shouted. "Hezb-e Islami does not command here! I command here! We Taliban command! *We* captured the woman, so we will do with her as we please."

"You are a fool to risk crossing Kohistani. He is a powerful man."

Naeem stomped pugnaciously up to the older man. "What does Hezb-e Islami do for this village? Nothing! Kohistani did not even have men enough to send to the ambush. Why do you think he sent us instead of his own people—eh?"

Sabil shook his head in dismay. "So sad. Even now, you're too stupid to see that you were used. You Taliban mean nothing to the Hezbi."

"Shut up, old man. Get out!"

Nuristani left, and Naeem slammed the door after him, turning to his men. "He's lucky I don't have him beaten. Jafar, you will make five copies of the video. Tomorrow, you will take two of them to our people in Kabul. I will write down the instructions for them to follow. Soon the Americans will pay for the infidel woman, and we will have good things again. We will have medicine and more guns. You will see. Now get to work, all of you."

The room cleared, leaving Naeem alone with Badira.

"So will she live long enough?" Naeem wanted to know.

Badira shrugged. "Not if the leg becomes infected."

"Will she live a week?"

"Not if the leg is infected."

Naeem bridled with impatience. "Is the leg infected or not?"

"It must be," she said. "She hasn't been given any antibiotics."

"Then I will send for some," he said. "She is your responsibility. Do you understand?"

"Yes."

"Good."

He trudged out of the building, and Badira took her medical bag into the room, where Sandra was still lying tied to the bed, weeping with shame and revulsion.

Sandra had listened to all of the shouting, assuming they were fighting over whether or not to kill her. It was not until after she felt Badira sit gently down on the edge of the bed, pouring peroxide over the festering bullet wound, did she dare to open her eyes.

She tried to speak, but the words caught in her throat.

"I'm going to give you something to make you sleep," Badira said with a slight British accent. "You need your strength. Your leg is infected."

"Please untie me," Sandra managed to croak.

Badira shook her head. "I'm not allowed, but don't worry. You will be asleep."

"I don't want to sleep," Sandra pleaded. "I need to get out of here!"

Badira grew cross with her. "Listen to me. Your government will pay them, and then they will release you. You must be patient."

Sandra shook her head in desperation. "No, you don't understand! My government doesn't pay—especially not for soldiers! They'll let me die here!"

"We are not going to argue," Badira said peremptorily. "You are going to take some pills and go to sleep. I will try to keep you asleep as much as possible. He will leave you alone that way. In a week, your people will pay and you will leave."

Seeing the distinct lack of compassion in Badira's eyes, Sandra suddenly became angry (which was a much stronger emotion than terror), and she lost her willingness to beg. "What are you going to do about the infection?"

"Naeem has sent for antibiotics."

Sandra watched her tend to the wound, preparing a new dressing. "Where did you learn to speak English?"

"In Pakistan," Badira said. "I was enrolled in medical school in Islamabad until the Taliban took over the government here. After that, my father demanded that I return." What Badira did not go on to share was that she had been called home to marry the son of a man to whom her father owed a financial debt, a local leader who had supported the Taliban's rise to power. And those who found themselves owing money to Taliban officials were severely mistreated.

"Can I have something else to wear?" Sandra asked.

"I will cover you."

"And I need to be . . ." Sandra's voice cracked involuntarily. "I need to clean myself."

Badira understood. "I still cannot untie you, but I will clean you."

Sandra closed her eyes, forbidding herself to cry. "Thank you."

"You must not forget where you are," Badira admonished her as she began rooting through the medical bag. "You are not in New York City. You are in Afghanistan, and if you are going to survive here, you cannot be weak. You must be strong or you will die." She paused to look up. "Do you understand what I am telling you?"

Sandra nodded. "What's your name?"

"I am Badira."

"Thank you, Badira. I'll try."

Badira went back to rooting in the bag. "I am afraid you will have to do better than that, Sandra Brux."

5

AFGHANISTAN,
Jalalabad Air Base

As the hydraulic ramp was lowered on the C-130E military transport, Master Chief Halligan Steelyard stood by pensively chewing the end of an imported Cohiba Robusto cigar. His face grew taut as Master Chief Gil Shannon sauntered down the ramp with his SR-25 slung over his shoulder. The rest of Gil's gear, including the .338 Lapua McMillan sniper rifle and .308 Remington Modular sniper rifle, was stowed in the hold of the aircraft in eight different cruise boxes to be unloaded by the crew. The SR-25 was a semiauto, 7.62 mm, limited-range sniper rifle that could also be used for patrol work.

Gil didn't do much actual *patrol* work now that he was attached to SOG, but if the air base was attacked during his stay, he wanted the versatility and all-around knock-down power that a weapon such as the SR-25 might offer him over the standard M4 carbine which was chambered for the 5.56 mm NATO round.

The trouble with the M4 wasn't with the weapon itself, but rather with the modern ammunition. The 5.56 mm NATO wasn't the same as the 5.56 round that was used during the latter part of the Vietnam War. The current NATO round was designed to defeat the newest Russian body armor, before breaking up inside the body for the most devastating effect. Taliban and Al Qaeda fighters, however, wore no armor at all, so the round did not break up, or even tumble through the body in many cases, and this too often allowed the M4 rounds to pass straight through an enemy without putting him down. The bad guy might bleed out later on, but that wasn't much good if he ended up killing you in the meantime.

Gil shook hands with Steelyard. "What I miss, Chief?" They were of equal rank, but the sixty-five-year-old Steelyard had a great deal more time in grade, and Gil respected him more than anyone else he knew, so he was always *Chief.*

The graying, hard-eyed Steelyard didn't stand a millimeter taller than 5'6", and he didn't weigh an ounce over 150 pounds. A veteran of the Gulf War I, he was rock-hard muscle from his ears to his toes. "Gil, I hope you ate a light breakfast."

"Fuck breakfast," Gil said, the hair rising on the back of his neck. "How soon do we move?"

"Patience, grasshopper."

Steelyard led the way, setting a brisk pace across the tarmac. Aircraft came and went all around them—fixed and rotary wing alike. Black Hawks setting down and taking off, a number of the big Chinooks, a few of the battered old Russian Mi-17s operated by the Afghan National Police force. There was even a matte-black Iroquois Huey, without markings or tail numbers, sitting in front of a lone hangar on the far side of the airport.

"That's where we're headed," Steelyard remarked, gesturing with the wet end of the Cohiba.

They climbed into a waiting Humvee, and Steelyard drove them in a circuitous route to the far side of the tarmac where the black Iroquois sat before the hangar. Outside, they could see a pair of bored pilots lounging in the back with their feet up, playing some kind of handheld video game.

Immediately upon their approach to the hangar, Gil noted a pair of black MH-6 Killer Eggs—highly modified Cayuse attack helicopters—resting on wheeled dollies under armed guard inside the hangar. He had only seen the model up close one other time. A pair of black Black Hawk MH-60Ls sat near a pair of MH-60Ks on the far side of the hangar, hidden from general view, also under armed guard.

"I take it SOAR's here in force?"

"On unofficial extended engagement," Steelyard grumbled. "You'll understand soon enough."

They dismounted the Humvee and entered the hangar where Gil encountered half a dozen of his fellow DEVGRU members checking gear and cleaning weapons. There was an unmistakable tension in the air, and none of the crude jokes or insulting banter he would normally expect, only grim nods. He realized something had occurred since he'd boarded the C-130 late the night before in Oman. He couldn't pin it down because the tension he felt had an uncommonly hostile vibe to it.

Steelyard preceded him into a situation room on the far side of the hangar where Lt. Commander Perez stood talking with an investigator from NCIS. Gil had never gotten along very well with Perez, so he came to full attention, snapping a smart salute.

"As you were, Gil," Perez said, almost casually, before giving his attention back to the NCIS man.

That was all it took for Gil to know, unequivocally, that something, somewhere was very definitely fucked up. In the two years that he had been their intelligence officer, the lanky Perez had never called him by his first name. It was always Chief Shannon, and he was never casual. The fucking chip he carried around on his shoulder was too damn big for that.

The NCIS man was a personal friend of Steelyard's, and more than just an acquaintance of Gil's. He was a civilian named Raymond Chou, second-generation Chinese. He finished talking with Perez, then turned to shake hands with Gil.

"Sorry you had to cut your leave time short, buddy."

"I'm here by choice, Ray. What I miss?"

Chou sighed and looked at his watch. "These guys can get you up to speed. I'm already going to have trouble explaining where the hell I've been all morning." He returned his attention to Steelyard and Perez. "Listen, guys, I'm sorry I don't have any actionable intel for you—nobody does yet—but I thought you should at least see that damn thing."

Steelyard clapped him grimly on the back. "Indebted to you."

"Nonsense. But listen, I gotta get that chopper back before the wrong people start to wonder where it went. Just remember that I was never here, and you guys didn't get that damn thing from me, okay?"

"You got it," Perez assured him.

Now Gil was irritated. It always took some time to catch up and become "part of the group" again after returning from a leave, but Perez was not a "you got it" kind of guy, and he sure as hell wasn't the type of officer who conspired with enlisted personnel or noncommissioned officers. In fact, he normally bordered on being a sycophant to the higher brass.

So what the hell was going on?

Chou left the building and Gil stood staring at Perez. "Sir?"

Perez shook his head and looked at Steelyard. "Hal, I'll leave you guys to it." He nodded at Gil and left the room.

"Chief, what the fuck?"

"Come on."

Steelyard led him into the locker room where a laptop computer sat on a bench. He gestured for Gil to have a seat and thumbed the touch pad to bring the darkened screen back to life.

"I want to warn you, Gil. If watching the Towers come down shook you up . . . this'll be tough to take." He started out of the room, then paused and turned around. "And I suggest you leave the volume set where it's at."

He closed the door on his way out, and Gil prepped himself for the worst as he clicked the Play button on the screen.

The video started, and he sat watching as five men stood crowded around the same side of a bed, their backs to the cameraman who was obviously filming them through the doorway of an adjacent room. The men were laughing and struggling for position, almost as if they were competing for the opportunity to shake hands with whoever was lying on the bed. Then someone off camera shouted at them, and entered from stage right, shoving them out of the way. He turned toward the cameraman, revealing his bearded face and bloody eyeball. The cameraman waved the other five men out of the way with his free hand.

That's when Gil clearly saw the pale, naked form of Sandra Brux tied spread eagle to the bed, a vicious bullet wound to her leg, eyes clamped shut, nipples flame red from having just been twisted and pinched. The bearded man dropped his trousers and climbed onto the bed with her.

Gil clearly made out the Pashto word for *whore*, which was *dammay zo*. And then he made out, almost as clearly, *kuss di ughame*, which he knew was Pashto for "fuck your ass."

Sandra began screaming a few moments later, and the cameraman made sure to get the angle correct so the penetration would be clearly visible. Gil did not watch it directly, turning the volume down as low as it would go without muting it. The rape itself lasted nearly eight horrific minutes, and Sandra screamed the entire time. It was the most unholy thing he had ever witnessed, and the close-up of her face at the end, of her shattered humanity, brought tears to his eyes. He sat on the bench with his face in his hands for a long time after the video had finished, having never known such rage.

After a while, Steelyard returned and stood leaning against a locker with his arms folded.

Gil looked up, speaking in a calm voice, "When they made the video of Daniel Pearl's execution I could at least understand what they were trying to accomplish." He reached and closed the laptop. "But what can these fuckin' bastards hope to gain with this here . . . other than a violent death?"

Steelyard stood away from the locker, arms still crossed, toeing the floor with his boot. "They expect to gain twenty-five million dollars."

Gil's mouth fell open.

"They want twenty-five million dollars within seven days," Steelyard explained. "Otherwise, they promise to make an even more brutal video for Al Jazeera. All of this information is highly classified, so if word gets back to CID that we've seen this video, Ray's ass is grass. His opposite number with CID showed him in complete confidence, and the guy doesn't know Ray managed to burn a copy."

"We got any leads on where she is?"

"Nothing actionable, but the second there's a lead, I'm recommending you for the infiltration and identification—if you want the mission."

Gil was on his feet. "We're killin' these people, right? Every fuckin' one of 'em?"

Steelyard shrugged. "Nothing's come down from the Head Shed yet. I think maybe they're considering paying the ransom."

"That's no reason not to put DEVGRU on alert. Or are they going with Delta?"

"From what I've heard," Steelyard said, "nobody in SOG has been officially alerted yet."

"That doesn't make any damn sense."

"Well, I'm hearing through unofficial channels that Karzai's office has offered to function as the intermediary for a ransom exchange."

"Somebody needs to get rid of that son of a bitch," Gil said. "He's been playing footsie with these Hezbi cocksuckers for the last twelve months. Hell, he's the reason we've pulled out of almost every northern province."

Steelyard took the cigar from his mouth. "He's got a country to run, Gil. If he doesn't make deals with the local warlords, he gets deposed ten minutes after we pull out of this shit box. You know that."

"That cocksucker knows who has her, Chief!"

"I doubt that."

"Yeah? Then why the hell is he already offering to play the bagman?"

Steelyard put a boot up on the bench, bracing his elbow on his knee. "I understand you're pissed, Gilligan, but even if you're right, the situation remains the same. We're just pawns on the board like everybody else."

Gil kicked an empty trash can across the room. "Has SOAR seen that video?"

Steelyard gave him a wry look. "There's a pair of Killer Eggs and four MH-60s hidden out there in the hangar. What the fuck do you think?"

"Okay, so Chou musta paid them a visit even before he showed up here."

"Sandra's a Night Stalker, Gil, the first and only female pilot the 160th has ever recruited. They don't intend to leave her out there.

They've already decided that if we get actionable intel on this, they're going in after her—with orders or without. If they go in without, the question's going to be who's going in with them—DEVGRU or Delta?"

"Well, that's easy. We're already here. Delta's clear down in Kandahar."

"But you're okay if Delta sends a representative up to go along?"

An ironic smile spread across Gil's face. "I take it you've already had this discussion with your opposite number down in Kandahar?"

"It's the noncoms who run the fucking show, you know that."

Gil didn't need to think about who to ask for. "See if they'll cut that candy ass Crosswhite loose for a few days."

Steelyard stuck the cigar between his teeth. "That's exactly who we had in mind."

6

LANGLEY

Deputy Director of Operations for the CIA Cletus Webb strode into the Director's office and closed the door. "We've got a problem."

Director of Operations George Shroyer looked up from a file he'd been reviewing, his reading glasses perched on the bridge of his bony-looking nose. "How serious?"

Webb sat down in a leather chair in front of the desk, releasing an anxious sigh. "The Speaker of the House knows about Warrant Officer Brux."

"That she was kidnapped or that she's been raped on film?"

"Both."

Shroyer tossed the file onto his desk and removed his glasses. "How the fuck did that happen?"

Webb held up his hands. "What can I say? The bitch has more informants than a Russian political officer. One of them got word to her."

"Who?" Shroyer demanded. "And is he over there or over here?"

"Well, how the hell do I know, George? She sure as hell wasn't going to tell me."

Shroyer was on his feet and headed across the office to a large globe that doubled as a liquor cabinet. He opened the top and poured himself two fingers of Scotch. "What does she want?"

"She wants us to pay the ransom."

"After we just spent the morning talking the president *out* of paying."

"Well, don't lose your stack, George, but she knows Karzai's office has agreed to act as intermediary."

"How goddamnit, how?" Shroyer flared. "That information's only hours old!" His face was bright red. He hated the Speaker of the House, and it infuriated him that she was getting classified information almost as fast as he was.

"I don't know, but it's nobody low on the pole. That much we can be sure of."

"Well, damnit, somebody needs to be prosecuted—starting with her."

"She's chomping at the bit to take this story public," Webb assured him. "There's a ton of political points for her to score on this if she can make it look like the president is mishandling it."

Shroyer took a stiff belt of the Scotch and set the glass down. "Does she know what kind of precedent a payoff of that size would set—that we'd be putting a bounty on the head of every US soldier from Afghanistan to Korea?"

"I tried that reasoning already, and she's not buying it. She knows we've paid before, and she's even threatening to expose that. Though don't ask me how she thinks she can do it."

"We've never paid a ransom like what these sons of bitches are demanding." He stood mulling the dilemma over. "Okay. Tell her this . . . tell her we've directed Special Forces to make an evaluation of the—"

Webb was shaking his head. "Won't work. She knows about the lack of actionable intel."

Shroyer bit back the obscenity that came to his lips, forcing himself to calm down before asking quietly: "Has she seen the video, Cletus?"

Webb considered his answer. "She told me that it was described to her . . . but I'm sure she was lying. She's too fired up, too passionate not to have seen it."

"That does it!" Shroyer crossed the room again to retake his seat. "Ask for a meeting with Mike Ferrell over at NSA. Drive over there personally, in fact. He'll like that—us coming to him. Get him to find out who's leaking this information. Then I want whoever it is locked in a dungeon at the bottom of the Caspian Sea."

Webb crossed his legs, wrists dipped over the arms of the chair. "I don't think we want to get back into bed with NSA over this, I really don't. It took too long to get that camel's nose out from under our tent. Besides, I was just on the phone with Bob Pope over at SAD." Special Activities Division of the CIA, which oversaw SOG. "And from what he tells me, the rape story has spread through the special ops community like a brushfire—from DEVGRU to Delta. In other words, the informant could be anyone."

"Including the nutty Professor Pope," Shroyer muttered. "Okay, forget NSA."

Webb breathed a sigh of relief. "Whoever leaked this information, the message is very clear. The special ops community wants Sandra Brux out of there—now."

Shroyer squeezed the bridge of his nose. "If we pay, it'll be the shakedown of the century."

"Yes, it will, but we've got nothing to go on, and we're running out of time. You saw her condition, the way she's being treated."

Shroyer looked up, clearly troubled. "So what's happening with CID? General Couture told me there were Taliban bodies at the ambush site. We're supposed to be getting DNA evidence telling us what villages these murderers came from. The president can't make a military decision until he knows if this was the work of the Taliban or the goddamn HIK."

Webb straightened in the chair. "Because of the drawdown, the CID people in Jalalabad don't have access to micro-fluidic testing anymore, and even if they did, the indigenous DNA samples they would need for comparison are all kept in Kabul now. Long story short, it's going to be a few days before we get the results. And even when we do, there's no guarantee they'll lead us to any specific village, let alone the one holding Sandra Brux."

Shroyer frowned. "The president's not going to like hearing that. I think he's seen too many episodes of *CSI*."

"I hate to say this," Webb continued, "but it's probably better to pay the ransom before the damn video ends up in the hands of Al Jazeera. If that happens, the president's not going to have much time to sit around watching TV."

"Oh, I don't know about that," Shroyer said, rocking back in his fine leather chair, tapping an unsharpened pencil against the edge of the mahogany desk. "Isn't it possible such a video might put some fight back into the American people? We're losing in Afghanistan. This might be the catalyst we need to reignite the will to win."

Webb wasn't so sure about that. "Possibly, but—"

"But the president doesn't think like that, so it doesn't matter," Shroyer said, dismissing the idea. "I'm headed back over there after lunch. I'll tell him about the speaker's back-channel threats and see what he has to say. In light of this little development, I'm sure he'll choose to make payment. Christ, he hardly has a choice now. Can you imagine the backlash of that rape playing out on the internet? He'd be crucified in the liberal media."

Webb agreed that much was probably true.

"So, on to different business," Shroyer said. "The president green-lighted Operation Tiger Claw this morning. It's going into effect immediately. The Turkish government is supplying the aircraft and crew, and Agent Lerher and his staff are already in the ATO."

"Good to hear it," Webb replied. "It's bold, and it's original. The Iranians will never see it coming. It's going to Delta Force?"

Shroyer shook his head. "The Joint Chiefs want to give it to the Navy. It's going to be a black operation with a single player, which puts it in DEVGRU's court."

"A black operation? Is that necessary?"

"Well, we can't have the Iranians accusing us of an act of war in the event anything goes wrong now, can we?"

"No, of course not. Disavowing one of our own operators sounds like a much better plan."

Shroyer shuffled a stack of papers from one side of his desk to the other. "Well, they do volunteer for the privilege, after all."

Webb didn't like the sound of that. "I'm not exactly sure that's what they're volunteering for, George, though I guess I can see why some here in Washington may find it more convenient to see it that way."

Shroyer eyed him across the desk. "Cletus, I sometimes wonder if you understand what the military is actually for."

7

AFGHANISTAN,
Jalalabad Air Base

The briefer was obviously nervous. Gil had seen the fiftyish-looking man arrive in a British helo early that morning dressed in plain clothes and carrying a leather laptop bag. He now sat at a table near the wall in a folding metal chair, continuously checking his iPhone, making the occasional notation in a file, and he was careful to avoid eye contact. Though Gil initially believed him to be an advisor with British Special Forces, he was rapidly coming to suspect that circumstances were different from what he had assumed half an hour earlier, when he had unexpectedly—and somewhat urgently—been ordered to appear in this little building on the far side of the airport for an emergency mission brief.

His natural assumption was that DEVGRU had received actionable intelligence on Sandra Brux's whereabouts, but this brief was already starting to feel like something else.

He sat down in a chair near the center of the room. "Where is everybody?"

The Brit finally glanced up from his iPhone. "Oh, I should think they'll be along forthwith," he replied affably.

So they really did talk that way over there. "This doesn't have anything to do with Warrant Officer Brux, does it?"

The Brit looked confused. "I'm afraid I don't know that name."

This was all Gil needed to hear. He leaned back, an eager anxiety rising up in his gut as the adrenal glands began to secrete, bringing his internal combat systems online. He stared at the Brit until his suspicions were finally confirmed by a simple tell: a knee that began to jig up and down. Gil then realized he'd been selected for a mission that had nothing at all to do with Sandra, and this briefer—now very obviously an agent with MI6—was anxious as hell about it.

The door opened and three CIA men filed briskly into the room looking very official in their well-tailored suits and subdued neckties. Gil recognized the lead man immediately, an agent named Lerher whom he had worked with once before in Indonesia.

Lerher was an agent attached to JSOC, Joint Special Operations Command, and he was an ice-cold professional, long desensitized to the fact that he was moving live human beings around on the game board.

Gil stood up as Lerher crossed the room to offer his hand.

"Gil," Lerher said, his demeanor crisp and impersonal as always. "Good to see you again." He placed his briefcase on the table and watched in silence as the other two agents set up a digital photo projector on a desk at the back of the room.

Gil retook his chair to wait, pushing Sandra from his conscious thoughts. There would be no more room for her until mission complete.

"Lights," Lerher said.

The lights dimmed and the photo of a thirty-five-year-old Middle Eastern male appeared on the wall. He had a neatly trimmed beard and chiseled features. A white kufi covered his closely cropped black hair, and a battered 5.56 mm AK-74 with a folding stock hung from his shoulder.

"Okay," Lerher began, resting against the edge of the table. "This mission has been designated Operation Tiger Claw. The man you see before you is Yusef Aswad Al-Nazari—your primary target. He's a Saudi national, age thirty-five with no known relatives. He is also a Sunni. He studied physics at the University of Stuttgart, and he has managed to fly completely under our radar until last month when Mossad brought it to our attention that he is personally responsible for three different bombings in Tel Aviv and at least half a dozen here in Afghanistan over the past two years . . . killing at least one hundred twenty people."

During an intentional pause, Gil glanced at the Brit, now realizing he wasn't British at all, but an Israeli Mossad agent, very probably educated in London. His arrival in the British helo must have been a precaution against anyone knowing there was an Israeli operative roaming the base, a risky prospect in a Muslim country.

Lerher continued. "Recent electronic surveillance has revealed that Mr. Al-Nazari is presently working to construct a radiological weapon, strength unknown, for use against Israel. Next photo."

The photo of a woman with long black hair appeared on the wall.

"This is your secondary target. Her name is Noushin Sherkat. She's a native Iranian. Next—"

"Hold there a second." Gil sat forward on the chair, studying her face. She had fierce dark eyes and was no more than thirty years old. He had never been ordered to hit a woman before. "What's her story?"

Lerher's reply was noncommittal. "Her story is that she will soon be joining Mr. Al-Nazari in the afterlife."

Gil caught Lerher exchange a furtive glance with the Mossad agent before saying, "Next photo." There was a tentativeness about the JSOC man that hadn't been there the first time Gil had worked with him, and this told Gil the other shoe was yet to drop.

A satellite photograph appeared with a map overlay. Lerher took a laser pointer from his breast pocket. "You will make the hit here approximately ten miles southwest of the city of Zabol in the northern reaches of Sistan-Baluchistan Province."

Seeing the map, Gil felt a sudden surge of adrenaline.

He leaned forward, studying the overlay. The selected target area was twenty-five miles over the Afghan border into Iran, not much more than a couple of hundred miles north of where Operation Eagle Claw had ended in a humiliating failure during the hostage rescue operation back in November 1979, resulting in the loss of eight US Marines and Air Force personnel.

After pausing long enough for this reality to sink in, Lerher continued. "Al-Nazari has no idea that he's been compromised, no idea that we're listening to his telephone conversations. He doesn't even vary his schedule. It's not that he's careless as a general rule, rather, we believe he's simply grown complacent, living within the relative safety of Iran's borders."

Gil scrutinized the topography of the terrain, barren and largely deserted. He turned to Lerher in the dim. "So he's operating inside of Iran with or without Ahmadinejad's approval?"

Lerher seemed to vacillate for a moment. "Well, as you know, the right hand doesn't always know what the left hand is doing within the Iranian government. Our impression is that the Iranian president has been kept out of the loop on this one. We may safely assume, however, that someone with significant influence is supplying Al-Nazari with the necessary materials and logistical support. It is extremely important for this man to be eliminated before he constructs a radiation bomb or begins to pass his skills along. For the most part, he seems to be guarding his secrets at the moment, but we can't expect that to last.

"Gil, we've got this guy nailed down to a fairly specific and isolated location not very far over the border into Iran. We've had him under drone observation for the last three weeks. We know his routine. We know that he travels with minimal security. Now is the time."

"I obviously can't walk in there on my own. I assume you've made arrangements for transport at the Afghan border?"

This time Lerher's glance at the Mossad man was obvious. "No, we can't risk having your movement detected. Al-Nazari would vanish the second it looked as though anyone might be moving against him. You'll HAHO in, jumping from a Turkish commercial airliner during a scheduled flight from Kabul to Tehran. Next photo."

Another map appeared on the wall, this one showing in red the projected flight path from the city of Kabul to Tehran. A green *x* indicated the point at which Gil would exit the aircraft inside of Iranian airspace.

"We've got Turkey's cooperation on this?"

"We do," Lerher answered. "It's an audacious mission, Gil, no doubt about it. That's why it's going to succeed."

"What am I jumping out of?"

"A Boeing 727. It's out there on the tarmac. Our people are going over it now, making all the necessary modifications. It's in good shape. You'll be jumping during a black moon from thirty-five thousand feet, using GPS to guide you as close to the kill zone as possible before you touch down. You'll probably have to travel close to thirty miles under canopy because it would look suspicious for the pilot to veer off course. This is a black operation, so you won't be taking your usual gear. You'll use a Dragunov SRV for the hit."

Gil glanced again at the map, reaffirming that he would be jumping very deep into Indian country. "And my extraction?"

"After the hit, you'll lay low and evade until dark," Lerher said. "Once it's dark, you'll make your way south to the extraction point where the Night Stalkers will pick you up well inside the Iranian border. Now, we don't expect you to have any contact with Iranian troops. This province is a wasteland, and there's nothing there to protect. However, the area *is* rife with heroin smugglers sneaking back and forth across the border at all hours of the day and night. This is the reason we're so confident we can hit Al-Nazari inside of Iran without anyone suspecting US involvement. Allow me to illustrate."

He looked to the back of the room. "Next photo."

A map of Sistan-Baluchistan Province appeared on the wall, marked with multiple scattered dots of different colors.

"Sistan-Baluchistan is the hub for eighty-five percent of the world's heroin traffic. Each red dot that you see on this map indicates an assassination. Each blue dot indicates a bombing. And finally, yellow marks the spot of an abduction. *All* of these have taken place since 2008. As you can see, the region is basically a civil war zone—one of the best-kept secrets in the Middle East—so there won't be any reason for the Iranians to suspect outside involvement.

"Allow me to make one thing very clear, Gil . . . every reasonable attempt is to be made to prevent the Iranians from knowing you were ever there. If this operation works the way we're hoping it will, it can open the door for a multitude of future clandestine operations inside of Iran, and I don't need to tell you how valuable that's going to be."

"Are my comms Russian as well?" Gil never paid much heed to a briefer's admonitions about post-hit protocol. Once the hit was made, he was on his own time, and he would do whatever was required to get his ass back alive.

Lerher shook his head. "Your radio and GPS will be of Chinese manufacture. Your prep team from SOG will be in directly to brief you on the particulars." He paused again, glancing at the Mossad agent to see if there was anything to add. The man shook his head. "Well, then," Lerher said, "I guess that should about cover mission overview. Do you have any more questions before I call in the prep team?"

"Yeah," Gil said. "How soon do I leave?"

"You will board an Air Force cargo flight for Kabul in exactly"—Lerher checked his watch—"eleven hours, forty minutes. Shortly thereafter, you will board the 727 bound for Iran. Good luck."

8

AFGHANISTAN,
Nuristan Province, Waigal Village

Badira was eating her afternoon meal when Sabil Nuristani, the village headman, came into the hut asking where to find Naeem.

"I don't know," she said. "I've not seen him since this morning. I think he left for Kabul."

Sabil looked into the room where Sandra, dressed once again in a grubby gown, lay shackled to the bed by the ankle of her bad leg. She was sleeping. "How long will she live?"

"That depends," Badira said, tired of being asked that question.

"On what?"

"On how much more brutality she is forced to endure."

The old man stood brooding, deeply troubled on many levels. He was not Taliban, nor was he a Pashtun. He was Kalasha, and the Kalasha people were not like Naeem and his reckless band of

Wahhabi fanatics, an ultraconservative arm of Islam. Sabil's direct ancestors, those of the Nuristani line, had lived in the Hindu Kush for centuries. The province had even been named for them, in fact. The Kalasha people had their own traditions, their own customs, and they heavily resented the militant presence of both the Taliban and their new friends in the HIK.

Naeem was an upstart lieutenant from the Pashtun south, sent north to help bolster the Taliban presence in the face of the burgeoning Hezbi factions. He had chosen Waigal Village not only because it was isolated far up in the mountains, but also because most of the middle-aged men were dead from recent regional disputes over resources and land. This meant the rest of the villagers were easily scared into submission. The teenaged men of the village had no fathers to teach them tribal ways, no one to give them direction or to keep them on the straight and narrow. As a result, they had been highly impressed with Naeem's heroic tales of the jihad—most of which Sabil suspected to be lies—and they were beguiled by his promises of the afterlife and all of the women they would experience should they be killed fighting the infidel.

"I've sent word to Aasif Kohistani," Sabil confessed at length. "Once he learns that Naeem is trying to ransom the American wom—"

"But he's Hezbi!" Badira said, fearing the HIK even more than the Taliban. "You should not have done that. Naeem will kill you."

"It's done. The woman is a danger to us all. This village will be very hard to attack, so the Americans will not differentiate when they come. They will drop bombs on everything, shoot everyone." He stood gnawing his fingernails, convinced they were all in imminent peril.

"I wish you had waited," Badira lamented. "The ransom demand has already been delivered to Kabul."

Sabil waved his hand at her. "They will never pay. The amount

Naeem wants is insane. His Wahhabi ideas have addled his brain. I even heard him telling the boys around the fire that he once met the *Great Usama*. Can you believe it? As if Bin Laden would have bothered to even look at a fool such as him."

"Bin Laden was a fool," Badira said wearily. "His jihad has brought us nothing but trouble." She glanced into the room where Sandra was having a fitful dream. "You realize that Aasif Kohistani cares nothing for this village—or for you. He may come and take the American away, but he will not protect you from Naeem."

"As long he takes her out of here," Sabil said. "Then I will have done my duty to the village. Naeem is not long for this earth in any case. Fanatics such as him never are."

He left a short time later. Badira went into Sandra's room, waking her up. "You need to take your medicine and drink some water. You're dehydrating."

The antibiotics were keeping infection at bay, but Sandra's bullet wound was still fevered and painful. "You're sure you don't have anything stronger than aspirin?" she asked. "The pain . . . it's horrible. I can't take it anymore." She was in despair.

Badira sat looking at her. "I can give you opium. That's all I have."

"Heroin?"

"No, opium—from the poppy."

Sandra consented, whimpering, "Okay, anything."

Badira went to the door and told the teenage guard to go and bring her some opium and a pipe from one of the elders.

The boy got to his feet, an AK-47 hanging awkwardly from his shoulder. "For you?"

"For the American. Be quick. She's in great pain."

The boy looked at her skeptically. "The elders won't—"

"Tell them Naeem has given orders. Go!"

The boy eyed her balefully for a long moment, then turned and went away.

He returned about twenty minutes later with a small, handmade wooden box that he brought into the room where Badira was cleaning Sandra's wound.

"Fine," she said. "Please set it on the table."

The boy put the box on the table and stood looking down at Sandra with open disdain. "I thought they hated opium."

Sandra averted her eyes.

"She's in great pain," Badira explained. "Now please go back outside."

"Their pain is important enough for opium, but ours is not? She's a hypocrite—just as Naeem has said." He reached to pull the loose-fitting garment away from Sandra's neck, wanting a look at her breasts. Sandra grabbed the gown and batted his hand away.

He socked her clumsily in the side of her face and shouted, "Don't touch me, infidel whore!"

Badira jumped up from her chair, pushing him toward the door. "Get out! She is my responsibility when Naeem is not here. Now go!"

"Who does she think she is!" the boy demanded, throwing his hand in the air and shouting, "I am a soldier. She is our prisoner. She does as we say!"

"And you do as *I* say!" Badira hissed acidly, pulling the scarf from her face to expose her hideous disfigurement. "Now get out!"

The boy recoiled from her, frightened by the face that only moments before had appeared very pretty to him, two beautiful eyes peering over the top of a maroon *hijab*.

"I will tell Naeem!" he called over his shoulder as he fled the room.

"Sure you will!" she called after him. "You'll tell him you ran from a woman. If that I could live to see such a day!"

She jerked the curtain across the doorway and went to open the box on the table.

"What was he saying?" Sandra asked, the confrontation having taken her mind very briefly from the pain.

"They are young and stupid," Badira said, removing a pea-size pellet of dried opium latex, a small pipe, and a short candle stub from the box.

"I have to smoke it?" Sandra asked, painfully raising herself up onto one elbow.

"This is not a hospital," Badira reminded her.

The tiny ceramic pipe was no bigger than Sandra's thumb, made of fired white clay. Badira put the opium pellet into the bowl and gave it to her. Then she lit the candle and told Sandra to scoot closer to the table. "Get the pipe close to the flame," she told her. "Breath the flame into the blow and inhale the vapor."

Sandra did as she was told, sucking the vapor deep into her lungs, desperate to kill the pain in her leg. She inhaled twice and was rapidly transported to a separate reality. Every muscle in her body went limp, and her head suddenly seemed to weigh fifty pounds. Badira caught her and helped her to lie back on the bed, covering her with a blanket as she drifted off on the opium cloud.

Badira knew this was the beginning of Sandra's opium addiction, but if Aasif Kohistani arrived before Naeem returned to take her back to the Americans, addiction would be the least of her worries. For now, it was better to keep her doped up and out of pain. This way she would hardly realize what was happening, should Naeem choose to violate her again.

9

AFGHANISTAN,
Jalalabad Air Base

Gil stood in the tail section of the Boeing 727 looking down the short staircase extending from the rear of the aircraft to the tarmac six feet below. Chief Steelyard stood at the base of the stairs looking up at him with his hands on his hips, chewing pensively at the unlit Cohiba caught in the corner of his mouth.

"Now I know how D. B. Cooper musta felt," Gil remarked, recalling the story of the legendary D. B. Cooper who hijacked a 727 in November 1971, demanding a $200,000 ransom for the passengers. After the ransom money was delivered to the plane, along with four parachutes, Cooper ordered the jet back into the air, ostensibly en route to Mexico. But this was merely a ruse. Cooper bailed out the tail end of the 727—exactly as Gil was about to do—somewhere between Portland, Oregon, and Seattle, Washington, never to be seen again. The FBI had insisted ever since that Cooper could not have survived the jump. As far as Gil knew, no one had ever attempted such a jump before or since.

Steelyard snatched the cigar from his teeth, pointing at the fuselage over his head. "This shit right here comes real close to being beyond the call of duty. You've got three Pratt & Whitneys right over your goddamn head. If those pilots aren't flying this crate straight and level when you jump, the jet blast will tear you apart."

Gil trotted down the stairs. "They'll bring the airspeed down as close to two hundred knots as they can get it without stalling."

"I still don't like it."

"They never found Cooper's body, Chief. I believe he made it. I'll make it, too."

The older SEAL shook his head, adjusting his cap. "SOG really cooked one up this time. What about the passengers? Seems to me they might notice a sudden loss of cabin pressure."

"Lerher's techs already killed the feed to the emergency oxygen masks in the passenger compartment," Gil said. "The flight won't be full, only nineteen passengers. Three minutes before I jump, the pilot's gonna drop the cabin pressure to three psi and knock everybody out. My *stewardess* and I will already be on oxygen by then, hiding in the rear compartment. The passengers go unconscious within sixty seconds, and that gives us a minute to lower the stairs and for me to hit the silk. The cabin should be resealed and back under pressure inside of three minutes. A couple of minutes after that, everybody wakes up again—scared shitless but none the wiser."

Two CIA technicians rolled up in a maintenance truck and parked directly beneath the tail of the 727. They climbed into the back where a TIG welder rested against the cab. One of them switched on the welder, and the other opened a stepladder. The welder then donned a pair of thick leather gloves and dark goggles, climbing the ladder to place a couple of spot welds on the first of two pivoting metal airfoils, not much smaller than a ping-pong paddle, located on the fuselage on either side of the stairwell.

"What the hell are those things?" Steelyard asked.

"They're called Cooper vanes," answered the technician holding the ladder. "They're spring loaded. When the aircraft is in flight, the airflow rushes over the foils and turns them to lock the stairs in the up position. Once the plane slows down again, they automatically open back up. We're welding them open so the stairs can be lowered during flight."

Steelyard looked at Gil. "Learn something new every day." He lifted his chin. "Who's she?"

Gil turned to see a husky-looking woman stalking across the tarmac dressed in dark pants, a maroon turtleneck, and a purple head-scarf. She had a rough complexion and a hard look in her obsidian eyes. She was intercepted briefly by an Army sentry who reviewed her credentials and allowed her to pass.

"She's an operative with MIT," Gil said. Turkish Intelligence. "The stewardess I just mentioned."

"Jesus," Steelyard muttered. "I'm sorry to hear that, little buddy." *Little buddy* was a takeoff on Gil's nickname—Gilligan.

THE WOMAN APPROACHED, staring at Gil without as much as a glance at Steelyard. "Does the aircraft meet with your approval, Master Chief Shannon?" Her voice was deep, and her accent was thick, but her English was easily understood. She was obviously very proud to be working with DEVGRU on such an intrepid mission.

"It does, Melisa, thank you."

"We'll be taking off for Kandahar the moment the aircraft is ready," she said. "I understand you will be following a few hours behind."

"That's right," he replied. "I have to prep my gear for the jump."

"Very well," she said, offering her hand. "Until we meet in Kandahar."

Gil took her hand. "Until Kandahar," he said with a curt nod, resisting the ironic temptation to click his heels together, a gesture that he was sure she would not have found humorous.

They watched her go.

Steelyard took the cigar from his mouth and spit. "Too bad she's not jumping with you. She could probably take ten of the bastards with her bare hands."

Gil chuckled. "Let's go have a look at the gear Lerher brought me."

THE GEAR LERHER had supplied waited for him in the same hangar SOAR was using to keep their hi-tech helicopters out of sight. The kit itself was stowed in an aluminum case not much larger than one of Gil's own cruise boxes now stacked against the wall. There was no one else around as Gil and Steelyard unlocked the double padlocks at either end.

The first item Gil removed from the crate was a hard plastic gun case containing the Dragunov sniper rifle (SVD) with a Russian PSO-1 optical sight. He set the case down on a workbench and opened it up. The rifle's wooden stock was weathered, but it had recently been hand-rubbed with linseed oil and was in good condition. Gil disassembled the rifle at once without difficulty. The weapon was of high-quality Russian manufacture, not a Chinese or Iranian licensed production.

"At least it's an Izhmash," he said with a glance at Steelyard, naming the Russian manufacturer.

"I guess Lerher couldn't afford a synthetic stock," Steelyard muttered.

"Well," Gil said, knowing that Steelyard couldn't stand Agent Lerher, "if you think about it, how many *hajis* are running around inside of Iran with brand-new SVDs?" He stuck a curved plastic light into the breach of the weapon and looked down the muzzle to see the rifling was pristine. "The pipe is brand new. They put rounds through it to sight it in, but that's it."

"Goddamn better be." Steelyard looked around to see if anyone was nearby, then struck a wooden match from his pocket to light the cigar. "If I blow us up, don't worry. They'll know who to blame."

Gil smiled.

He found a pistol in the case and was pleased to see that it was an old government 1911 model .45 ACP, a weapon found all over the world. He was not pleased, however, to find that the recoil spring was weaker than it should have been. He tore the pistol completely down to its smallest parts and found that the firing pin was slightly worn as well. A quick check revealed that the barrel was brand new.

"Chief, my Kimber's in the number-two case over there," he said. "Would you mind getting it for me? I'm gonna switch out the spring and the firing pin. Might as well use my arched mainspring housing as well. I'm guessing Lerher's supplier must've thrown this thing in for free with the SVD."

Steelyard laughed, walking toward Gil's stack of cruise boxes.

"Uh-ten-*hut*—officer on deck!" suddenly echoed across the hangar.

Gil and Steelyard turned slowly around, both of them annoyed until they saw who it was. They smiled and shook their heads.

"What the fuck?" said Captain Daniel Crosswhite, United States Army Special Forces, as he came strutting across the hangar. "I thought a squid was supposed to snap to whenever he heard that."

Gil eyed him, an ironic grin coming to his face. "We're frogs, ya stupid shit."

"Well, fuckin' whatever." Crosswhite laughed, shaking their hands. He was an operator with Delta Force. "I understand you Navy pricks might need some help."

"Feel like jumping into Iran for me?" Gil asked offhandedly, knowing that Crosswhite was as solid as they came.

Crosswhite gaped at him. "No shit." He was a handsome fellow with dark hair and eyes, a light, muscular frame and an infectious devil-may-care smile.

"I'm jumping outta that fucker over there." Gil jutted his chin toward the 727 that was just beginning to taxi toward the runway.

Crosswhite let out a low whistle. "Those Pratt & Whitneys are liable to barbecue your ass, bro."

Gil looked at Steelyard. "See how fast these Green Beanies piss themselves over a little bit of prop blast?"

Crosswhite laughed. "You'll think prop blast when your fucking arms and legs go flying off. I'll bet you're jumping in the fucking dark, too."

"Is there any other time?"

Crosswhite became suddenly very serious. "Listen, you tuck and roll, Gilligan. I ain't shittin'. I mean you pull yourself tight as *fuck* when you hit that slipstream."

Gil nodded, equally serious. "I intend to. Believe me."

"Scary as it is, I am jealous. What about you, Chief?"

"When I was your age, yeah," Steelyard said. "Now? I'm a little too fucking old for that James Bond shit."

Gil jerked his thumb at Steelyard. "He's taking up finger painting next week."

Steelyard drew deeply from the Cohiba before exhaling a cloud of smoke. "I think what you mean is that I'll be finger fucking your sister next week."

Everyone laughed, and they set about helping Gil to check the rest of his gear.

"Fuck Lerher," Gil muttered a short time later. "I'm taking my oil-dampened compass. This Chinese piece of shit will freeze up there and break."

"What about this hunk of shit?" Crosswhite asked, holding up a Chinese military hand radio. "Is SOG for real?"

"Unfortunately, that goes along," Gil said with a frown.

"Well, this just won't do," Crosswhite said. "No frog friend of mine is jumping behind enemy lines with nothing but this Chinese piece of shit."

He got on his cellular.

"Joe, it's Crosswhite. Listen, I want you to do me a favor . . . Will you calm down! I haven't asked you yet." Crosswhite looked at the other two and rolled his eyes, whispering, "*He's G2*. Army Intelligence."

"I want you to loan one of the *things* to a frog friend of mine . . . You know what thing—the *thing* thing! He's gonna be down there in a few hours, and I want you to meet him on the tarmac . . . Yeah? Well, you still owe me for that little fuck-up in Dallas, dude—or did you forget?" Crosswhite spoke with Joe for another couple of minutes, then got off the phone.

"Okay, it's all set," he said to Gil. "Now, if that shitty radio goes eighty-six on your ass, we'll still be able to find you."

"But what is it?" Gil wanted to know, exchanging puzzled looks with Steelyard.

"A PDA prototype we've been working on," Crosswhite said. "Joe will explain it. Now, tell me what the hell's going on with Sandra. I've heard stories about some fucked-up video."

10

AFGHANISTAN,
Kabul, CID

Elicia Skelton was a US Army warrant officer attached to the Army Criminal Investigations Command. Twenty-seven years of age, she was half-Chinese and half-Caucasian with a youthful face and dark hair she wore in an army-style chignon. Wearing an army combat uniform with a CID patch on each arm, she marched up the hall and stopped in the doorway of her supervisor's office, knocking crisply on the doorjamb.

Brent Silverwood looked up from his computer, his mind elsewhere. "Yes, Elicia?" He was a senior civilian investigator with CID, fifty years of age, slender and handsome with brown hair graying at the temples.

"Mr. Silverwood, we've got the DNA results on the Taliban bodies from the Sandra Brux abduction."

Silverwood postured up in the chair, stretching his back and lending her his full attention. "Come in, Elicia. You don't have to stand there in the door like that."

She entered, offering him a thick manila file folder, noting the care lines in his face, the dark circles beneath his eyes. "Most of the DNA samples are too common to trace," she continued, "but we do have a probable match for one of the bodies, a Taliban teenager who was found a hundred yards from the ambush site where he bled out."

He set the file aside and rocked back in the squeaky chair. "Bring me up to speed."

She stood more or less at ease with her hands clasped behind her back as she spoke. "Well, it looks like we *may* have gotten lucky, sir."

He lifted his eyebrows slightly. "How so?"

"The young man's DNA is a definitive match with the Kalasha people living in the Hindu Kush. Certain markers in their DNA are unique to them because their gene pool has remained relatively small. Now, it's not a definite lead to Warrant Officer Brux's location, but we're certain this young man is at least related to the people living in the village of Waigal. There's no way of knowing whether he was operating out of there, but if he was, Sandra Brux just might be somewhere in the Waigal Valley."

Silverwood sat forward to reach for his phone. "Nice work, Elicia."

"Thank you, sir." She started to say something else but hesitated when he began to dial.

"Yes?" he said genially.

"Well, sir . . . may I . . . may I ask how your wife is doing, sir?"

He smiled lugubriously and set the phone back down. "She's still managing, but the pain is increasing almost daily now. I'm afraid I'll be going home soon to take care of her. She's decided to stop the chemotherapy."

Elicia lowered her gaze. "I'm very sorry for you both, sir."

"So am I. But thank you for asking, Elicia. Most everyone else around here prefers to pretend like I'm my usual self—not that I blame them. It's never easy to know what to say to someone in my situation."

"Yes, sir. You're welcome, sir." She gave him a tentative smile and left the room.

Silverwood lifted the phone and called Raymond Chou with NCIS. He sat flipping through the file as he waited for him to answer.

"Agent Chou."

"Ray, it's Brent. Hey, I think I may finally have something actionable for you on Sandra Brux."

"Excellent. What is it?"

"Before we get into that . . . did you make a copy of that video when I was out of the room?"

Chou was silent for a moment, then he said, "I sort of thought that was why you stepped out. I'm sorry if I misinterpreted, Brent."

"You didn't misinterpret. I just wanted to make sure you'd done it. Okay, so let's meet. I'm pretty sure I know where Sandra's being held and by whom, but it's complicated. I don't want to discuss it over the phone. How soon can you be in Kabul?"

"Couple hours."

"Let's meet at the usual place then."

"You got it. See you there."

Silverwood hung up the phone and then stood from his chair and went down the hall to find Warrant Officer Skelton sitting at her desk in her cramped little office. "May I come in?"

"Yes, sir," she said, rising to offer him the chair in front of her desk.

Silverwood sat down and grinned at her. "Why are you always so straightlaced with me?"

"Sir?"

He chuckled, perhaps for the first time in months. "You're more relaxed around the Army brass than you are around me? Why is that?"

She looked at him, very carefully considering her response. "Well, sir . . . I don't know. Maybe it's because I know what to expect from ranking officers."

"I see. Well, I'm flying home tonight, Elicia. You've given me the perfect excuse to leave you all in the lurch here, and I'm going to use it."

"Sir?"

"I came down here to tell you I'm breaking with protocol. I'm not going to forward those DNA results directly to State. First, I'm giving them to an NCIS contact of mine. I'm guessing he'll take them straight back to DEVGRU in Jalalabad. Have you kept up on what's been happening with the Hezb-e Islami movement since we began our drawdown of forces?"

"Yes, sir. The Hezbis are growing like a weed, both the Gulbuddin and Khalis factions. That's why the Army wanted to remove Aasif Kohistani. To keep him from—" Her eyebrows soared suddenly. "Wait a second! Kohistani has ties to the Waigal Valley—he was born there. But how could he have known we were preparing a raid?"

"Because the ISI guy we arrested yesterday has been feeding him information . . . and that's classified, so don't repeat it." ISI was Pakistani intelligence, short for Inter-Services Intelligence.

"Holy cow," she said. "The Hezb-e Islami parties have gained quite a few seats in the Afghan parliament. If they're the ones who took Sandra, that could end up putting Karzai in a real spot. It could force him to choose sides against the US."

"Very good," he said. "You're thinking. And that explains why his office was so quick with the offer to act as an intermediary for the ransom exchange."

"You think Karzai already knows who has her?"

"I'm convinced of it, as a matter of fact. That's why I'm back channeling this intel to DEVGRU. There's something fundamentally wrong with this ransom demand. Sandra's worth a lot more to these people than money. I refuse to believe that Kohistani's too stupid to see that."

Elicia felt her skin turn to gooseflesh. "You don't think DEVGRU will act without orders, do you?"

He checked his watch and got to his feet. "Whether they will or not, I'm giving them the option. It's very possible that DC already knows who has Sandra, and if that's the case, your brilliant DNA research will likely wind up swept under the rug by the State Department."

She stood up, a look of disillusionment in her eyes. "It seems all too possible now, doesn't it?"

"Whatever you do, Elicia. Do *not* let on that you've put any of this together. When you're asked, tell them you forwarded the results to me like you were supposed to."

"Okay, sir. But . . . but if DEVGRU does take action, won't State eventually figure out you were involved?"

"They might, but that will be my problem."

She nodded reluctantly, clearly uncomfortable with the idea of him getting into trouble.

"It's okay," he said with a smile. "We probably won't be seeing each other again, but I want you to know you're an excellent investigator, and it's been a pleasure working with you. You've a bright future with CID. Don't jeopardize it by trying to cover my tracks."

She smiled back, shaking his hand firmly. "We're going to miss you around here, sir."

11

LANGLEY

Deputy Director of Operations Cletus Webb was eating lunch in the CIA cafeteria with two of his assistants when he spotted Director Shroyer coming toward the table. He made eye contact, and the director stopped short, jerking his head back in the other direction as a signal for Webb to follow. Webb caught up to him at the elevator, and they stepped aboard, standing shoulder to shoulder as the doors closed.

"Breaking bread with the little people, are we?" Shroyer inquired dryly.

"They invited me," Webb replied. "I didn't have plans, and it felt rude not to accept."

Shroyer grunted, inspecting his freshly manicured fingers. "The president's ordered us to pay the ransom for Sandra Brux. Twenty-five million. I trust our people in Kabul have made the appropriate preparations?"

"Considering the players involved, this was anticipated, yes."

"Good. Be sure our people log the serial numbers so we can track the bills," Shroyer admonished. "We don't need to be accused of playing Fast and Furious with twenty-five million dollars."

Webb rolled his eyes. "It's being done."

Shroyer adjusted his trousers. "I've got Bob Pope waiting up in my office." The director of the Special Activities Division of the CIA. "Due to the rumors we're hearing, I want to make sure it's understood that SOG is not to make any unilateral decisions over there should the enemy fail to deliver after we've paid Sandra's ransom. It will be your job to keep SAD's people on a short leash in the coming days."

"And you expect me to accomplish this how exactly?" Webb wanted to know.

The elevator doors opened, and Shroyer turned to face him, his expression flat. "By making sure that Pope reminds his people *as often as necessary* exactly who the fuck they work for. Is that clear?"

"Oh, it's certainly clear," Webb replied. "I'm not so sure that SOG's forgetfulness is likely to be the problem, but it's certainly clear."

Shroyer started to say something but, thinking better of it, stepped from the elevator and made his way toward his office with Webb in tow. They strolled one behind the other past Shroyer's secretary and into the office where the SAD director sat waiting.

"Bob, you remember Cletus."

Pope stood from the chair, offering his hand. "Of course. How are you, Cletus?" He was tall and slender with a head of thick, gray hair. His blue eyes were very intelligent looking behind his glasses, and he had a disarming, boyish kind of smile. He was the sort of man who always seemed to be half thinking of something else, no matter who was speaking to him or what their title.

"I'm good, thanks." Webb took the chair beside Pope as Shroyer slipped in behind the desk.

"Sorry again for the delay, Bob," Shroyer said, smoothing his tie. "Cletus's secretary couldn't find him because he was downstairs in the cafeteria . . . eating with the help." All cellular calls were blocked within the building for security purposes.

Pope chuckled dutifully, and Webb smiled as benignly as he could.

"So," Shroyer continued, "just to make sure we're all on the same page here, Bob. The ransom for Sandra Brux is to be paid within the next twelve hours. Our people in Kabul are setting up the payment through an intermediary in President Karzai's office. As you know, we need to help Karzai maintain his alliances within his government, a number of which are extremely fragile. I'm sure you're aware of the recent parliamentary gains by both of the Hezb-e Islami factions in recent months."

"Yes, I am. As a matter of fact, I sent you a brief ten months ago forecasting the vast majority of those parliamentary gains."

Shroyer's face froze. "So you did," he said shortly, having forgotten about the brief entirely until just that moment. "In any event, Warrant Officer Brux's abduction seems to have completely eluded the media for the time being. So, all things being equal, I think we can count ourselves relatively lucky. Her husband is being flown to the ATO [Afghan Theater of Operations] as we speak, and if all goes according to plan, we should have her back in our care within the next twenty-four to thirty-six hours."

Pope sat nodding, an almost robotic smile plastered to his face as he absentmindedly scratched the back of his hand.

Shroyer sat watching him for a moment, finally realizing that Pope was someplace else. "Bob?"

Pope jerked his head. "Yes?"

"Your thoughts?"

"Oh, I was just wondering."

"Wondering? Wondering what?"

Pope crossed his legs, pushing his glasses up onto the bridge of his nose and laughing a dry, thoughtful laugh. "Well, George, I'm wondering how many of us in this room actually believe that's going to happen." He looked between the two other men, half raising his hand. "Show of hands?"

Webb dropped his gaze to the floor. He knew that Pope was borderline brilliant, so if he was seeing a flaw in the wiring somewhere, there was probably at least a 50 percent chance of a short circuit.

Shroyer, on the other hand, held no appreciation for Pope's intellect, so all he saw was a wiseguy. He steepled his fingers, lips tightly pursed. He appeared to be counting to ten before finally sucking his teeth and asking, "Is this your way of saying you know something we don't, Robert?"

Again the dry laugh. "Oh, well, I have all the same information as you do, George. Maybe I just have more time for interpretation."

"That is what you get paid for, is it not?"

"All of our latest intelligence indicates that we're dealing with some kind of a cursory alliance between the Taliban and Hezb-e Islami Khalis. These two groups were mortal enemies until six or seven months ago, as I'm sure you remember. And now they're working together to collect a ridiculous sum of money?" Pope shook his head. "Not likely."

"Why not likely?" Shroyer rapped. "Are you suggesting we not pay the ransom?"

"We don't even have proof of life, George."

"You've seen the damn video, Bob!"

"That's proof of rape, not life. What if they executed her immediately afterward?"

"An execution is precisely what we're acting to prevent."

"I appreciate that," Pope assured, Shroyer's aggravation touching him not at all. "And I understand we've paid ransoms before without real-time proof of life, but the size of this ransom is reckless. Something's wrong. I don't know what, but something. It feels like amateur night to me, and if it's amateurs, well . . ." He laughed. "There's no limit to how many different ways this could go wrong."

Shroyer stared across at Webb. "What do you have to add to this?"

Webb cleared his throat. "Well, the president has made a decision. I don't think he's going to change his mind a third time, and I certainly don't think it's a good idea to suggest that he does. The Speaker of the House is sitting up there on the Hill with her finger on the media button. All we can do now is follow the numbers and hope that Bob's intuition is wrong on this one. What do you think, Bob?"

Pope's mind had already begun to drift. "Oh, well I wasn't suggesting we could do anything differently by this point. I just don't want anyone being shocked if we end up giving away twenty-five million dollars for nothing . . . not that we don't do that anyway . . . but . . . well, you take my point."

Shroyer looked at Webb, a look of semi-exasperation plastered to his face. "Cletus, I understand you had something you wanted to bring up with Bob concerning SOG operations."

Webb chose his words tactfully. "In the event, Bob, that your concerns prove to be valid, and Sandra isn't returned, it will be extremely important for SAD to impress upon the SOG community—namely DEVGRU and SOAR—that no unilateral action is to be taken in an attempt to find her. We've heard the rumors, and we understand that emotions are running very high over there as a result of the treatment she's been forced to endure. So we need you to make sure our special ops people understand that we are doing everything we can to bring their sister soldier back home alive, and that we *require* not only their readiness to act, but their patience as well."

Pope reached out, briefly touching Webb on the arm. "You have my solemn word that no one within SOG will act before it is appropriate to do so."

Webb was about to ask for a clarification on that, but Shroyer cut him off.

"Very well then," the director said, rising from his chair. "Everyone's on the same page. Thank you for coming over, Bob. It's always a pleasure." He offered his hand and Pope stood up to shake it.

Webb sat in his chair watching Pope's face as the two men shook hands, awash in a sudden awareness that there was absolutely no guile in the man. Pope had given them his word that neither DEVGRU nor SOAR would take any action unless and until it was appropriate to do so, and Webb understood, unequivocally, that what Pope had truly meant was—just as sure as God made little green crocodiles— that DEVGRU would make the final decision as to when and what action would become *appropriate* in the event that the Taliban and their new best friends the Hezb-e Islami Khalis failed to honor their end of the bargain.

12

AFGHANISTAN,
Kabul

Silverwood met Chou in the same hotel lounge where they normally met, finding a secluded table at the back and ordering two coffees.

"Okay," Silverwood said, stirring a copious amount of sugar into his cup. "How familiar are you with the name Aasif Kohistani?"

"He's the guy the Army was rehearsing to snatch out of Nangarhar when Sandra was captured. He's supposed to be the leader of some Hezb-e Islamist group. That's about all I know."

"Okay, good." Silverwood said. "So how familiar are you with Waigal Village?"

"Not very," Chou said shaking his head. "I know its east of Shok Valley where ODA 3336 got pasted a few years back."

ODA 3336 was an Operational Detachment A-Team that had been sent into the Shok Valley to take out Gulbuddin Hekmatyar, the leader of the Hezb-e Islami Gulbuddin political party. The mission had been a disaster, and a number of Rangers had nearly bought it.

"Good," Silverwood said. "That's actually more than I expected you to know, being attached to the Navy."

"So educate me, Obi-Wan Kenobi."

Silverwood laughed. "Okay. ODA 3336 was sent into the Shok Valley to take out a guy named Gulbuddin Hekmatyar. Familiar with him?"

Chou shook his head.

"He's a sixty-five-year-old Islamic fundamentalist who founded the Hezb-e Islami Gulbuddin party back in 1977. We call it HIG for short. He wasn't too influential early on, but after the Soviets invaded, he became a big deal within the Mujahideen. There was a major problem with him, though. He killed damn near as many Afghans as he did Russians in his struggle to gain power. This made him pretty unpopular, so when the Taliban came along in the nineties, he got shoved aside. It wasn't until *we* invaded and kicked the hell out of the Taliban that he was able to regain his political stature." He saw the look on Chou's face, nodding in agreement. "Yeah, I know. We have a way of creating these monsters with our good intentions. Anyhow, he went right back to butchering anybody who stood in his way, and his power's been growing ever since. The failure of ODA 3336 to take him out back in '08 only made him stronger."

"Hold on a second," Chou said. "Isn't this the same nut responsible for the Badakhshan massacre?" He was referring to the massacre of ten foreign aid workers from the International Assistance Mission that had occurred in August 2010.

"Nobody knows for sure who ordered that attack," Silverwood said, "but if it wasn't the Gulbuddin faction, it was probably the Khalis faction—another Hezb-e Islami group that split off from HIG clear back in 1979—and it's the goddamn Khalis faction that brings us here today! Not only has Aasif Kohistani recently become the leader of the Hezb-e Islami Khalis party—we call them the HIK—but they're based out of Nangarhar Province where Sandra was taken."

Chou sat back, taking a drink from his coffee. He put the cup down on the table and immediately added more sugar. "I know there's more," he said with a smile, "so I'm going sit patiently waiting to hear."

Silverwood took a sip of his own. "Do you know how many parliamentary seats that the HIG and HIK parties hold between them as of this year?"

"First, tell me how many seats there are total, or the number isn't going to impress me."

Silverwood laughed. "They hold fifty out of two hundred and forty-six seats."

"Okay, that's impressive."

"So," Silverwood said, leaning into the table and lowering his voice, "suppose—just for the sake of conversation—that good President Karzai knows the HIK took Sandra. How likely is it that he'll go against them holding that damn many seats in parliament?"

"That would be a big risk," Chou agreed. "I'm sure he'd prefer to sit back and watch us work it out ourselves."

"Or to be on the safe side?"

Chou conceded the point. "Or to be on the safe side, he could offer to act as intermediary for the ransom exchange—which is exactly what the hell he's done. Okay, that much is clear, but there's a flaw in your theory."

Silverwood sat back again. "Which is?"

"I know there's already been a positive ident on one of the bodies at the scene of Sandra's abduction. She was taken by *Taliban* forces—we know that much for sure—and you just said the Taliban doesn't get along with the HIK."

"They didn't when they were strong," Silverwood said. "Now the HIK is a lot stronger than the Taliban, so teaming up with them is a good idea, considering their growing political power."

"You know this is still all circumstantial," Chou said, unconvinced there was a connection.

"It is, but only until you consider the fact that one of those dead Taliban fighters found at the scene of the abduction is an exact DNA match with the Kalasha people who live in the Waigal Valley . . . more specifically the highly inaccessible mountain redoubt village of Waigal. By the way, I haven't shared these DNA results with the State Department yet."

Chou pushed his coffee cup aside to rest his elbows on the table. "Is there a direct link to the HIK, or are you shooting in the dark on this?"

Silverwood allowed his imminent victory to show on his face. "Kohistani was *born* in the Waigal Valley, Ray. He's not Kalasha, but he speaks their language and has family ties through marriage. And in case you're still not convinced, we're ninety percent certain the ISI guy we arrested yesterday has been feeding intel to Kohistani and the HIK since he started working with us in Jalalabad three months ago."

"Say you've convinced me. What's the punch line?"

Silverwood shrugged. "You've got the same information I've got now. Follow the intel stream to its logical conclusion."

Chou took a moment to consider everything he'd just been told. "Oh, crap. You think State already knows the HIK has Sandra . . . maybe even where she's being held?"

"Well, if they don't already have *some* idea," Silverwood said with a smirk, "they're pretty fucking stupid, I'll give you that."

"But that doesn't make much sense," Chou said. "SOG hasn't even been put on alert. No one's even drawing up a contingency yet."

"Which must mean DC's decided to pay the ransom. Because

unless my entire theory here is bogus, I don't see any other explanation for the lack of military movement."

"Good then!" Chou said. "Problem solved. The woman's been through enough. Pay the fucking money and get her out of there. I'm all for it. Twenty-five million's a lot, but State spends a hell of a lot more on a hell of a lot less every day. It's not like they have to acknowledge the terms of her release."

"I agree," Silverwood said, "but doesn't the ransom demand itself concern you? It does me."

Chou sat looking at him. "Why should it? Afghanistan is full of kidnappers. Hell, it's their leading industry."

"Come on, Ray. If Kohistani and the HIK really do have Sandra, why would they give her up for something as trivial as money when she could so easily be used to drive a wedge between Karzai and the United States?"

"You mean by *forcing* him to choose sides?"

"Right."

"Well, that's an awfully big risk. Wouldn't Karzai have to choose the US?"

"I'm not so sure," Silverwood said. "Think about it. Not only does Karzai want us the hell out of his country, he wants us out before we jeopardize the alliances he's struck over the last twelve months. If we're leaving, he sure as hell can't afford to galvanize fifty parliamentary seats against him over the likes of an American woman. Throughout history, Afghanistan's been governed through alliances. It's never going to be any different, and Karzai knows this as well as anybody . . . better than most, in fact."

"So you think the ransom's a ruse," Chou said. "An attempt to steal twenty-five million without giving Sandra back. Or maybe an attempt to make Karzai look stupid?"

Silverwood shook his head. "I don't have any idea. I just know I don't trust the nature of the demand. That's why I want you to pass this information along to your friends in DEVGRU. If you'll agree to do that, then I can leave this godforsaken country tonight with a clear conscience."

Chou was startled. "You're leaving tonight. Has your wife taken a turn for the worse?"

"She's stopping the chemo." Silverwood gazed at his coffee cup. "She tells me the doctors say less than a month."

"I'm awfully sorry, Brent. I wish there was something more I could say."

Silverwood looked up again. "There's plenty you can say, Ray. Only say it to DEVGRU because I got a really bad feeling about this ransom deal. I'm telling you."

13

AFGHANISTAN,
Kandahar Airport

It was dark by the time Gil landed in Kandahar, and Crosswhite's friend Joe met him at the foot of the ramp of the C-130, not far from the 727 that sat waiting in the dark for Gil to load with his gear. Joe was a civilian contractor with Army Intelligence, over six feet tall with sandy blond hair and a hatchet face. He appeared edgy, looking all around and back over his shoulder, as though he was worried someone might be watching him from the shadows among the other military aircraft.

"You're Joe?" Gil said easily, trying to put the younger man at ease.

"Yeah, look," said Joe. "You never heard of me, okay?"

Gil smiled. "I'm not even here. How's that sound?"

Joe smiled back and pulled from his pocket what appeared to be nothing more than a common iPhone. "Okay, this is the smart phone prototype we've been working on. We're field-testing them with the Deltas right now, so there's only a dozen of them in existence. As far as anyone knows, this unit is malfunctioning and out of service until you bring it back—in one piece."

Gil chuckled. "Roger that."

Joe stood beside him so he could show him the display, working the apps with his thumb. "This damn thing is smarter than God, dude. Once we get the bugs worked out of it, all you special ops guys will be using them. It works just like all the others you use, but this fucker will do it *all*, dude—GPS, biometrics, encrypted text messaging, mortar ballistics—you name it. No more kit bags with PDAs for every different fucking device. See what I mean?"

Gil nodded enthusiastically, accepting the phone and running deftly through the different apps. Except for a few variations and all the extra options, it worked exactly like the other PDAs he had carried, only this unit seemed a bit more user friendly, and the GPS even featured an interface with the military version of Google Earth. Within fifty seconds he had triangulated his exact position on the tarmac to within three feet, and the screen was overlaid with a recent satellite image of where he was standing, allowing him to zoom in and out."

"Jesus Christ," he said, glancing at the taller man.

Joe's face split into a wide grin. "Pretty fucking badass, right?"

"And this covers, say . . . Iran, as well?"

Joe's eyebrows soared. "Assuming anyone was crazy enough to cross over the border? Yeah, they'd be good to go. And, dude, this ain't shit," he continued enthusiastically. "Within the year, you'll be able to use this fucker to tap into a live feed of the surrounding terrain—provided there's a satellite or a drone overhead—and zoom right in on your fucking enemy without having to expose yourself. No more fucking around with those little toy drones you guys are tossing into the air. This is the fucking future of combat tech, dude."

"Suppose it falls into enemy hands?" Gil needed to know. "Can it be traced back to us?"

Joe shook his head. "Dude, the parts are all made in China."

"Okay, suppose they try hacking into it?"

"No sweat. There's a couple different countermeasures. We can fry it from the command center right here in Kandahar—or you can set it up to do that automatically." Joe took a small black, shock-dampening nylon case from the canvas musette bag over his shoulder. "This is the case for it—it attaches to your molly gear. There's a chip inside it—like in a car key. You can set the phone to check in with the case however often you want it to—from up to a distance of a hundred feet. So let's say you set it to check in every three minutes, and then the phone falls out of the case while you're on the run. In three minutes, the phone will try to check in with the chip inside the case to be sure it's still with you. If it doesn't get the signal it's looking for, it checks again in three more minutes. If it still doesn't get the signal, it waits another three minutes, then fries itself. The second countermeasure is simple: after the enemy enters the wrong access code three times—"

"It fries itself."

"You got it," Joe said. "The access code for this unit is three-two-one-star. You don't want a complicated code in combat. After five minutes of nonuse, you have to reenter the code. Easy peasy."

"Can I fry it myself if I need to?"

Joe looked at him. "Dude, I just told you. Enter the wrong access code three times."

Gill chuckled. "Okay, *dude*. I got it . . . and you'll be here in the command center until when?"

Joe shrugged. "Until Crosswhite calls and tells me your mission is complete. I'm your overwatch, dude—*unofficially*."

Gil stuck the smart phone inside the case and zipped it closed. "What happened in Dallas?"

Joe shifted his weight uncomfortably. "Crosswhite kept me out of jail. That's all I'm gonna say."

"Can you track my location with this thing?"

Joe shook his head. "That app's still fucked up. It's one of the software integration problems."

Gil offered his hand. "Do me a solid and keep awake tonight, will ya?"

"Roger that." Joe took his hand. "Crosswhite said to remind you to tuck and roll—whatever the fuck that means."

"Wilco," Gil said.

GIL BOARDED THE 727 with all of his gear a short time later and sat down in the cramped rear compartment to wait for Melisa. Normally, the 727 did not have a rear compartment, but the CIA had customized the cabin to accommodate the parameters of the mission. The fabrication work was first rate and did not appear jerry-rigged in the slightest. In fact, Gil would never have guessed it wasn't an original feature to the aircraft.

Melisa came up the stairs a few minutes later dressed in the two-tone blue uniform of a Turkish Air flight attendant. She hit the button to raise the hydraulic stairs, and then sat down in the jump seat directly across from him, appearing slightly tense.

"You don't look at all nervous," she remarked.

Gil smiled. "Fear accompanies only the possibility of death. Calm ushers its certainty."

She couldn't help the tiny grin that came to her face. "In other words, you're very good at hiding it."

He laughed. "I'm jumping out the ass-end of a jet . . . in the dark . . . over Iran. Of course I'm hiding it."

She nodded, returning to business. "In five minutes, we will taxi to the concourse to take on passengers. I will help the other attendant to get everyone settled and then rejoin you back here."

"Is the other attendant with MIT as well?"

"The entire crew is MIT."

Gil had suspected as much, but during the rush to prep, that detail never came out. He had worked with foreign intelligence agencies before, but never with MIT. He had heard different reports about them, some good, some not so good.

"Who's vetting the passenger list?"

"We are," she said. "Is that okay? Mr. Lerher didn't have the resources in place."

"It's probably better that way," he said, not necessarily believing it, but what the hell, it hardly mattered now.

"Anyone suspicious," she went on, "or anyone matching a name on our list will be . . . *delayed* and forced to take the next flight."

The plane began to move a short time later, taxiing out onto the tarmac and over to the passenger terminal. The rear staircase would not be used to board any of the passengers.

Melisa got up from her seat. "I will go forward now to assist Kamile with the boarding of passengers."

"Okay." A quick glance into the passenger compartment and Gil could see that Kamile was a much more petite MIT agent than her counterpart. Then he spotted the bulge of what he suspected was a pistol in the rear waistband beneath Melisa's tight-fitting uniform. He doubted if any of the passengers would notice. Most of them would be too preoccupied with finding a seat and getting into the air.

Ten minutes after taking on passengers, they were airborne, bound for Iranian airspace.

"Well, I guess there's no turning back now," he said as Melisa retook her seat.

"No," she said. "This will be my first time in Iran."

"Worried?"

She smiled. "Fear accompanies only the possibility of death."

THE 727 WAS swiftly approaching Gil's high-altitude release point (HARP) some thirty miles north of his DZ. The plane couldn't deviate any farther south for fear of tipping off the Iranians to Turkish involvement, should they ever come to suspect the assassination of Al-Nazari to be the work of American forces, rather than the result of civil unrest.

Gil was rigged up and nearly ready to jump. He had the SVD slung barrel-down on his left side with the stock jutting up behind his left shoulder. The rest of his gear was stowed in a kit bag hanging in front of him, and the 106ci portable oxygen system was attached to his right side. Both his main and reserve parachutes were RAPS (Ram Air Parachute System), which would allow him to travel up to forty miles under canopy during his high-altitude, high-opening (HAHO) jump.

All that remained for him to do was don his Pro-tec helmet and oxygen mask.

The phone on the wall buzzed, and Melisa answered it, speaking briefly with the pilot and checking her watch. She hung up and looked at Gil. "We go on oxygen in two minutes. We lower the stairs in three."

"Roger that." Gil checked his own watch, then pulled on his helmet and buckled the oxygen mask into place. Two minutes later he and Melisa were both on oxygen, and the cabin pressure was beginning to drop. Kamile was in the cockpit with the pilots, all of them on oxygen as well. As luck would have it, most of the passengers were already asleep, and those who remained awake were unaware of a problem until moments before they were blacking out.

Melisa lowered the stairs, and the outside air rushed into the cabin in a great gust, forcing them to steady themselves against the bulkhead until the pressure equalized a few seconds later. Gil gave her a thumbs-up. He walked down the staircase and stepped off the bottom, tucking himself into as tight a ball as he could manage. The instant the turbulence struck him, he was reminded of the raging surf at Waikiki, only this was about ten times as bad. He was spun so furiously about that he felt like a rag doll. The oxygen mask was nearly ripped from his face, and for a moment it felt as though even his boots might be ripped off.

Then it was over, almost as quickly as it started. He was in free fall.

He waited for the automatic rip cord release to activate at thirty thousand feet. When it did, he felt the familiar tug at the harness, but something was wrong. He looked up to check his canopy. There was no moon, but he was still above the cloud layer, and the stars provided enough of a backlight for him to see that he was in deep trouble. The severe turbulence must have damaged either the RAPS or the automatic release system, because his reserve had deployed along with the main chute, and neither one could properly deploy. He was falling dangerously fast.

Finding his cutaway knife, he quickly began cutting away the cords of the main chute. The reserve was of the same ram air configuration and would still allow him to travel under canopy to the DZ, but only if he could cut away the main fast enough to leave him with sufficient air time. He cut the last cord, and the main slipped away into the night, allowing the reserve to deploy fully. Now he could dig out the Chinese GPS system and make corrections to his direction of travel. The fact that the unfamiliar unit was having trouble holding a satellite signal did not exactly surprise him. He put it away and dug out the Delta prototype, careful to keep the lanyard looped tightly around his wrist. He switched it on, and the satellite signal was instantly acquired. Within ninety seconds, he knew exactly where he was.

Taking hold of the steering toggles hanging at his waist, he corrected his course. Doing the math in his head, he was pretty sure that he could get himself to the intended DZ. According to the GPS system, he was traveling at nearly twenty miles an hour. If that kept up, he would be arriving in roughly an hour and forty minutes. For now, there was nothing to do but settle in for the ride. He checked his watch. It was 00:20 hours. There was plenty of time. He wouldn't be engaging his target until 11:30 hours the next day.

14

AFGHANISTAN,
Kabul, SOG Operations Center

Agent Lerher and his staff sat gathered in a conference room with Captain Glen Metcalf, USN. Metcalf was the senior DEVGRU officer inside the ATO. He had personally chosen Gil for the Al-Nazari hit the moment he learned of his arrival in theater. Now, everyone in the room was viewing Gil's descent via an infrared satellite feed visible on a wide-screen plasma television mounted to the wall.

Captain Metcalf watched with veiled apprehension as Gil's canopy descended into the cloud layer and disappeared from view.

"Well, that was anticlimactic as hell," announced a bored-sounding analyst from Lerher's team. He stood from his chair against the wall, taking a sip from a Styrofoam coffee cup as he attempted to appear widely experienced beyond his years. He was a Harvard grad, not a day over twenty-five, a child of the PlayStation generation who seemed to regard what they had just witnessed with the same emotional commitment of a teenager playing a game of *SOCOM: US Navy SEALs*.

Metcalf's heart had been in his throat during Gil's struggle to cut loose of the main canopy. No one else in the room had understood what was taking place beneath the flaring death shrouds until he explained to them what was going on. Now he resented not only the young analyst's presence, but his attitude as well. There was no reason for these kids with no understanding of combat—beyond the aspect of a video game—even to be in the room. True, they had done a fine job of gathering the intelligence required to put the op together, but they were well paid for their efforts, and so were not necessarily entitled to be *in on the kill*, as Lerher had put it. But the military existed to serve the civilian population, and Metcalf was an extension of that arm, so there wasn't much he could do but grit his teeth. However, he knew of no rule against a captain of the United States Navy asking a pointed question from time to time.

"What would you have preferred to see, son? A brave man plummet to his death?"

"Me?" said the analyst, startled to have been called on the carpet for his inane remark. He glanced at Lerher, who only stared back at him. "No, sir. I was just saying that . . . well, what I meant was that he handled that like a real professional."

"I'm sure that Master Chief Shannon would be glad of your approval," Lerher remarked, jerking his head toward the door in abrupt dismissal.

The analyst paled and exited the room, leaving his counterparts with their eyes lowered.

Feeling mollified, Metcalf allowed his gaze to fall charitably upon the rest. "So far, so good, ladies and gentlemen. Our man dodged a bullet tonight. Now, let's hope that cloud layer lifts soon so we can see what hell's going on down there. Any news from meteorology, Agent Lerher?"

Lerher shrugged. "It's not good, I'm afraid. We're hoping the ceiling will be high enough tomorrow for a predator to drop down and sneak a peek now and then, but it's going to be touch and go." He addressed his staff. "That's all for tonight, people. Try and get some sleep. We've got a big day tomorrow. Donaldson, I want you on duty in Operations with the Air Force people all night. If anything develops, anything at all, you wake my ass up. Understood?"

"Understood," replied a blonde woman who wore her hair pulled back in a tight ponytail.

The room cleared, leaving Lerher alone with Captain Metcalf.

"I'm sorry about the idiot," Lerher said. He didn't personally care about his analysts making stupid remarks. They were assets to him, nothing more, and their personal feelings were beneath his consideration. They were expected, however, to know when to keep their mouths shut, an expectation the analyst in question obviously hadn't understood, so he would be rotated stateside on the next available flight.

"It's a cultural symptom," Metcalf remarked, satisfied to leave it at that. "Does NSA have anything to report?"

Lerher shook his head. "Nazari made a call to his wife about an hour ago, the usual tripe . . . nothing new . . . no changes to the itinerary that we can detect. He should be right where he's supposed to be at eleven thirty a.m."

"Good," Metcalf said. "With some luck, this hit will go exactly by the numbers from here on out."

15

IRAN,
Sistan-Baluchistan Province,
twenty-five miles north of the Afghan border

Gil came gliding in over the rock quarry he had selected from above, knowing it would offer him minimal concealment while stripping his jump gear. Pulling hard on the toggles to spill the air from his canopy, he landed firmly with both feet together and turned to quickly collapse the chute. He hit the release catch on his kit bag and stripped his harness along with the SVD, shedding his helmet, mask, and insulated jumpsuit inside of a minute. Geared up and ready to move ninety seconds later, he balled the jump gear up in the chute and slung it over his shoulder, moving swiftly across the quarry to the base of the embankment, where he found a culvert with a concrete drainage pipe running parallel to the grade. He stuffed the chute into the pipe and used the SVD to shove it deep inside where no one would likely ever find it. With the changing climate, there had been no significant rain in this region for years, forcing many local inhabitants to migrate northward toward the border with Turkmenistan.

He slipped a pair of Russian army night-vision goggles over his head and surveyed the immediate area, noting the illuminated skyline a mile to the north where he had sailed over a small town only minutes before. The land was barren and relatively flat for as far as the eye could see, leaving him with the unnerving sensation of being stranded on Mars. The Afghan border and any relative safety lay no less than twenty-five miles to the south over deserted, desolate terrain, where his extraction team would already be awaiting his call in the event he declared an emergency. He realized the low-lying stratus clouds overhead would preclude any satellite or drone surveillance for the foreseeable future, but that didn't necessarily bother him. It wasn't as though he could call for a predator strike inside of Iran in any event. He was on his own in the belly of the beast.

He slipped the goggles off and let them hang from the D-ring on his combat harness. Prolonged use of NVGs reduced natural night vision and limited depth perception. He switched on the radio. Somewhere far above the cloud layer, cloaked in the latest stealth technology, a loitering communications drone would pick up his transmission and relay it to the command center in Kabul via satellite.

Depressing the button, he spoke quietly into the transmitter. "Typhoon main. Typhoon main. This is Typhoon actual. Radio check. Over."

The reply was almost immediate: "Roger, actual. This is main. We read you Lima Charlie. Over." *Lima Charlie* indicated they were reading him loud and clear.

"Roger, main. I am on the ground and proceeding to the target area approximately two clicks southeast of my position. My authentication is Whiskey Tango. Do you have traffic for me at this time? Over."

"Roger, actual. Be advised we do not have a visual on you at this time. Over."

"Roger, main." Gil checked his watch. It was nearly 02:00 hours. "My next transmission will be at 04:00 hours. Over."

"Roger, actual. Over."

"This is Typhoon actual. Out."

Gil switched off the radio and began to climb the quarry embankment. A pair of headlights appeared at the quarry entrance to the south and turned toward his position. He slid back into the ditch to take cover, believing he must have been spotted during his descent. He shouldered the rifle and sighted on the vehicle as it closed rapidly from a hundred yards away.

He was depressing the heavy trigger as the vehicle pulled up fifty feet abreast of his position and stopped. Seeing that it was neither a military nor police vehicle, he paused. The doors of the white Honda Civic opened, and loud hip-hop music spilled out into the night. He quickly slipped the NVGs over his head, counting six teenagers—three male, three female—and slipped them off again. The kids spoke loudly over the music as they climbed out, lighting up their cigarettes. Two of the girls sat on the hood between the blazing headlights, huddled together against the chill, giggling the way teenage girls do.

In and of themselves, these teens were not a threat—Gil could kill all six of them with his Ka-Bar before they ever knew what hit them—but there was no way to scale the embankment of the quarry and slip off into the night without the risk of being seen, so he was stuck where he was for the immediate future. Any delay, however minor, posed a potential threat to his schedule. He had two thousand meters to cover before he walked into the target area, and there was still work to be done preparing his hide for the hit. As yet, there was still time to spare, but the night was young, and there was never any telling how many delays you might encounter. Combat was a fluid, ever-changing dynamic, and Gil never took a single minute for granted behind enemy lines.

Over the next couple of minutes it became obvious the teens were smoking marijuana, and except for the fact that they were speaking Farsi, they were like any other group of teenagers partying in the dark, laughing and joking with one another, the girls squealing over God knew what. Tonight, however, these innocent young men and women had driven straight into the middle of a war, a war in which no prisoners could be taken.

Gil decided to give them all the time he could before attempting to scale the embankment unseen. If they were unlucky enough to spot him during his climb, he would have to turn back and deal with them . . . quickly and without gunfire.

After fifteen minutes of trying to think his way clear, Gil saw one of the males walking toward his position. The kid was talking back over his shoulder and unzipping his fly as he came. Gil drew the Ka-Bar fighting knife from the sheath strapped to his leg, adrenaline surging as he realized with great trepidation that he was going to have to kill them all. He could already hear the girls screaming for their lives as he ran them down, cutting their throats. His mind raced to develop a better solution, but there wasn't one. There could be no witnesses.

He remained motionless in the dark, flat against the bottom of the ditch, his face blackened, body camouflaged in the seven-colored multicam pattern. He did not breathe, he did not even blink. He would come off the ground like a striking anaconda, ramming the blade up through the bottom of the jaw to penetrate the brain, killing the kid instantly and lowering him gently to the ground where he would lay in wait for the others who would undoubtedly grow curious about their missing friend. An American commando lying in ambush would be last thing any one of them would expect to find.

The teenager stopped at the edge of the ditch and began to urinate directly onto Gil's boonie hat and shoulders, still talking loudly with his head partially turned, utterly oblivious to the fact that a trained killer lay but a few inches from his feet in the dark. He finished taking his leak and turned away as he zipped himself up.

Gil watched him go, the scent of the kid's urine lingering heavily in his nostrils. It was not entirely new to him. He had carried the bodily wastes of men on his uniform before, mixed with their blood and viscera. Killing a man hand-to-hand was a very personal thing, comparable with the most intimate of acts, comparable even with making love to a woman. As your enemy struggled impotently beneath your weight, you could feel his body writhing against your own in a desperate bid to save itself, his hot breath in your face as you penetrated him with your knife. As he died, he would shit himself, piss, and bleed all over you. This was war at its most fundamental level, and Gil was glad the boy had been so dangerously unaware of his environment. This lack of awareness alone had saved not only his life but the lives of his friends as well.

After another forty-five minutes of screwing around, the kids piled back into the car and sped out of the quarry trailing a cloud of dust, leaving Gil free to scramble up the embankment and make his way across the desert landscape. He skirted a dry lake bed, part of the sprawling Hamun Lake system, once a thriving commercial zone for many water-based businesses and activities, and now nothing but a wasteland, dotted with dilapidated buildings and boats left high and dry, appearing entirely alien in this increasingly arid wilderness.

A few hundred yards from the quarry, he realized that he was being dogged by a bony canine looking to mooch a meal. He hissed at the unfortunate wretch and tossed a stone, sending it skittering off into the night. Taking advantage of the brief stop, he donned the NVGs long enough for a quick 360-degree scan of the terrain, and then double-checked the GPS to be sure of his orientation. He found the road that Al-Nazari and his party would be driving the following morning and traveled parallel to it at 50 yards. He covered 1,800 meters before stopping again to survey the terrain through the NVGs.

He was looking for an ancient one-lane stone bridge over a dry creek bed cutting the road from east to west. Two hundred yards south of that bridge, he would find an even more ancient stone ruin, the perfect place for a sniper's nest. Three more clicks south of the ruin along the same road was a fenced-in group of rundown military buildings whose original purpose had been to house a garrison of Iranian border guards. According to intelligence reports, the buildings were now being used to house Al-Nazari's bomb-making activities. Satellite surveillance indicated that three or four different sentries provided round-the-clock security for the facility, driving government vehicles and wearing Iranian police uniforms.

These sentries were of no concern to Gil. He would bypass the facility the following night during his egress, moving south toward the Afghan border under cover of darkness to link up with his extraction team another thirty clicks beyond, far out into the wasteland where no one would hear the rotors of the Night Stalker helos as they flew in snake and nape across the Afghan border.

He spotted the bridge a hundred yards ahead and moved out. The sound of a helicopter to the southwest caused him a few minutes of concern, but the rotors faded and he was back on the move. The helo was likely flying a drug interdiction mission north of Zahedan. The capital city of Sistan-Baluchistan Province was only some twenty miles from the Afghan border. It stood as the preeminent staging area for international heroin smuggling. From Zahedan, the Afghan heroin made its way to Tehran. From Tehran into Turkey, and from there to the rest of the world. The smuggling didn't stop at drugs, either. Everything was smuggled from weapons to illegal Afghani immigrants. Iran had pretty much lost its war on drugs by the early twenty-first century, and its police forces were now so corrupt as to make even the Mexican police look like Boy Scouts.

Gil covered the distance to the ruin in good time, donning the NVGs and scanning carefully as he approached. This region was lightly scattered with different ancient ruins from the pre-Islamic period, some of them having once stood as temples or monuments to the god Zoroaster. He made sure the ruin was deserted and then went to stand looking at it from the road. Yes, even at a distance, the fallen stone walls appeared the perfect haven for a sniper.

That was why he crossed to the opposite side of the road, where he began to dig in with a Russian entrenching tool.

16

AFGHANISTAN,
Jalalabad Air Base

Agent Ray Chou was in the hangar talking with Steelyard and Lt. Commander Perez about the possibility of Sandra Brux being held in the village of Waigal. The Night Stalker crews were there, too, having arrived the hour before to begin prepping their aircraft for a possible rescue mission.

Captain Crosswhite pulled up in a Humvee and got out, stalking up to the three men with an almost casual salute to Commander Perez, whom he normally didn't care for. "So, are we on or what?" he wanted to know.

Steelyard shrugged. "We don't know yet. That's what we're discussing."

Crosswhite glanced around. "Where are your SEALs?"

"In the back breaking into their cruise boxes. Where's your gear?"

Crosswhite thumbed over his shoulder at the Humvee. "I packed light. Your people can hook me up with whatever else I need, right?"

Steelyard nodded. "Why don't you head back there?" Crosswhite walked off and the chief turned back to Perez. "Like I was telling you, Commander. I think it's better if this operation stays at the noncom level on the DEVGRU side. If word reaches the Head Shed about what we're up to, they'll yank the plug on us. I've assembled enough noncoms to pull this operation off, good men who aren't afraid of the consequences."

Perez was in a quandary because he was very much afraid of the consequences. At first, he'd been all for the idea of going in after Sandra Brux without orders, enjoying the heroic feel of the rhetoric around the hangar, but now that there was actionable intelligence to work with, he was getting cold feet.

Steelyard had expected this from Perez, knowing him for the rear echelon–type motherfucker that he was. So he had selected six seasoned noncoms and two enlisted men that he trusted implicitly for the rescue operation, knowing that Perez didn't possess enough spine to stand up to that many chevrons. Dan Crosswhite had already volunteered to lead the op, giving them the only officer they would need. What Steelyard was hoping for now was for Perez to go back to the Head Shed and keep his fat trap shut.

He took the cigar from his mouth. "Look, you know how solid these men are, Commander. If the mission goes bad, nobody's going to mention that you knew anything about it. There's no reason for you to risk being around here now."

Chou was watching Perez very carefully, knowing the man had the power to shut it all down with one call, and he could see that Perez was about to make that very decision. "Listen," he said casually, cutting Perez off before he could open his mouth. "It's not like you could have done anything to prevent SOAR showing up here with all those fucking helicopters. And it's not like you could have prevented the men from viewing the rape video."

Perez stared at him, understanding the implication of Chou's words. Perez had not only failed to prevent the men from watching the video, he had watched it with them, knowing very well that it was classified material. What Chou was saying, just as plain as day, was that if Perez backed out now, and the rest of them wound up with their tits in the wringer, Perez was going to wind up under the proverbial bus for not going to the Head Shed the second he realized classified information had been leaked to the rank and file.

Chou was a civilian with NCIS, and was therefore in no way subordinate to Perez. He didn't care if the guy liked him or not, and he sure as shit wasn't afraid of him. The potential consequences of the risks he had taken went far beyond any heat that Perez could bring.

Steelyard cleared his throat. "And we're going to need a man on the inside back at the Head Shed," he added, realizing they had Perez by the nuts. "Someone to run interference if anybody starts asking questions."

Perez knew he was had, and he was kicking himself for having gotten chummy with enlisted personnel, having certainly known better. There was nothing to do now but try and make sure the op was a success and hope they all became legend.

He looked at Steelyard, trying to appear more enthusiastic than he felt. "So what do you want to call the op, Chief?"

"Operation Bank Heist." Steelyard grinned and stuck the Cohiba back into his mouth, putting out his hand. "If it's any consolation, Commander, we probably couldn't pull this off without you."

Perez knew there was no *probably* about it, and that Steelyard and Chou had set him up for the op from the very beginning, knowing that an unauthorized mission of any real scale would need a man on the inside back at the Head Shed to run interference and keep the op from being discovered by the higher-ups. That was why Chou had invited him to view the video in the first place. Perez felt too stupid to speak, so he nodded and shook Chou's hand and left the hangar.

Steelyard and Chou smiled at each other.

"Warms my heart to see him stepping up to the plate like that," Steelyard said.

Chou chuckled. "Well, Chief, all we can do now is hope he doesn't suddenly grow himself a spine."

17

IRAN,
Sistan-Baluchistan Province

Gil lay prone beneath his hide fifty yards across the desert road from the ruins. The hide was a shallow trench, not much wider than his body, dug perpendicular into the back slope of a subtle defilade running east-west across the jagged, semirocky terrain. His firing aperture was six inches wide at two hundred yards, leaving him a visual arc of more than 90 degrees. This arc would allow him to sweep the target area for anyone attempting to flee on foot in any direction.

If Al-Nazari were traveling today as he normally did, there would be three SUVs in his caravan. He would ride in the middle vehicle with the woman, his driver, and his bodyguard. The lead and rear vehicles would carry three to four gunmen each. Gil would allow all three vehicles to cross the bridge, and then kill the lead driver, shifting immediately to the second, and then the third. There was no way to predict which way the vehicles would veer once their drivers were taken out, but firing at two hundred yards gave him plenty of time and room to adjust his fire.

The first three shots were key and would be the most difficult to place, firing at moving vehicles. The rough surface would keep their speed down, but a jouncing target was tough to hit at a distance. With this in mind, Gil had spent time during the night filling in some of the larger potholes in the road seventy yards out from the stone bridge. If one of the drivers dropped below his reticle as he squeezed the trigger, he would lose valuable seconds.

What the remaining security people would do after the drivers were dead was open to conjecture, but this wasn't a concern. They would be trapped inside a wide-open kill zone with nowhere to run and precious little cover save for the dry creek bed. The SVD's 7.62 mm, armor-piercing rounds would cut through any part of a vehicle except for the engine block, and with Gil's hide located at a slightly lower elevation than the kill zone, he should be able to fire beneath the vehicles well enough to hit anyone attempting to take cover behind the engine compartments.

He had been briefed to expect no more than twelve targets in total, but he considered this speculation. There was no accounting for luck in combat, and Murphy's Law held sway no matter the weather. He also had to count on the enemy possessing at least one sniper rifle, with optics at least as good as his Russian PSO-1 sight. This was the reason for not taking cover in the ruins across the road. Most of his targets would be carrying AK-47s, and the moment they realized they were under sniper fire, they would begin pouring rounds into the only visible cover they could see. A man with a sniper rifle, given time enough to find even lousy cover, might manage to get off a few rounds. The danger of an RPG, of course, spoke for itself.

Gil preferred to fight like the Comanche whenever possible, and the Comanche believed firmly in the safety of the earth. He sipped sparingly from his CamelBak, watching the road. "Typhoon main, this is Typhoon actual. Still no eyes on my location?"

"Negative, actual. Cloud cover is still too dense. Over."

"Roger, main."

Just then, the lead vehicle came into sight.

"Main, this is actual. Targets are inbound at this time. Over and out."

He pulled the stock of the Dragunov firmly into his shoulder and brought the lead truck into sight, a dusty black Nissan Armada. He knew all three vehicles would reduce their speed dramatically just before crossing the bridge because the road dipped severely on the downward approach, and Gil had dug away the natural taper of that approach to create an abrupt six-inch drop, not near enough to damage the suspension or to cause alarm, but more than enough to force the vehicles into slowing down as they crossed into the kill zone.

The lead driver wore dark glasses and some kind of ball cap, and Gil could see that he had not shaved that morning. As expected, the lead did not speed away from the bridge after crossing, but instead drove slowly, waiting for the others to cross, keeping the caravan intact.

After the third vehicle was across the bridge, Gil gave them time to put some distance between the caravan and the potential cover of the creek bed. When the bridge was fifty feet from the bumper of the rear vehicle, he drew a breath and squeezed the trigger.

The round struck the lead driver in the base of the throat, causing him to slump over into the passenger's lap.

Gil was already shifting his aim to the second vehicle, instantly spotting Al-Nazari in the backseat on the passenger side. He did not hesitate to squeeze the trigger. Al-Nazari's head exploded like a pumpkin on a fence post, and the forward momentum of the vehicle brought the profile of the driver's head into view as he turned to look into the backseat. Gil squeezed the trigger a third time and blew the driver's face away.

The driver of the third vehicle barely had time to jerk his shifter lever into reverse before Gil shot him through the sternum.

In less than four seconds, he had disabled all three vehicles and eliminated his primary target. Everything he did from this point on would be to ensure his own survival. He was reminded briefly of the motto he had learned to live by during his late teens as a choker setter for the Louisiana Pacific lumber company in the mountains of Montana: *In for your job—out for your life!* When the grizzled old foreman blew the horn, Gil and the other setters would rush in to set the cable chokers around four freshly felled trees. If they weren't clear again by the time the foreman blew the horn a second time, they'd be dragged off down the mountainside, crushed to death beneath a turn of trees.

Once, during his first week on the job, he'd been caught walking down the mountain alongside a turn being dragged downhill. The foreman had screamed at him, violently waving him away. As Gil jumped clear, the turn twisted, flinging a massive tree over the top to impact against the ground where he'd been walking.

"Never walk beside a turn," he muttered, squeezing the trigger a fifth time for a fifth kill. None of the vehicles had slewed off the road, but the rear vehicle continued in reverse until it hit the abutment of the stone bridge and came to an abrupt stop. Gil pumped the remaining five rounds from the magazine into the vehicle, killing the remaining three passengers and preventing their escaping into the cover of the ditch.

As he was loading a fresh magazine, he spotted the woman ducking from the driver's side of the second vehicle. He shot her through the passenger door, and she dropped to the ground. Shifting his aim, he prepared to engage the remaining four gunmen piling out on the passenger side of the two lead vehicles. They fired wildly at the ruins on the far side of the road, unable to determine Gil's actual position.

Bullets whined off the stone walls, kicking up small clouds of dust.

Gil had been firing for less than thirty seconds. Within another thirty, all of his targets would be down. He fired through the fender of the lead truck to send a man sprawling. Another reached out to grab the downed man's wrist to pull him to safety. Gil blew his arm off at the elbow. The remaining two men began a hasty retreat toward the bridge, keeping low as they scurried behind the vehicles. Gil shot one through the body of the second SUV, catching him in the head by pure luck. This frightened the last man into making a desperate break cross-country.

"Don't bother to run, partner. You'll die tired." Gil shot him dead center between the shoulder blades, severing the spine, and the man pitched forward onto his face.

There was no need to confirm that Al-Nazari was dead—Gil had seen his head explode—but there might be valuable intelligence inside the vehicles.

"Typhoon main, this is Typhoon actual. Do you copy my traffic?"

"Roger, actual."

"Main, be advised all targets are down. Repeat. All targets are down. Primary target is confirmed KIA. Over."

"Roger that, actual."

"Stand by, main. Moving into the target area to sweep for intelligence. Over."

"Roger, actual. Main standing by."

Gil emerged cautiously from the hide and moved forward with the Dragunov at his shoulder, ready to fire. He covered the two hundred yards at a trot, then pulled up short to move carefully around the front of the lead vehicle. The man with the missing arm was sitting up against the wheel hub, cradling the head of his dying compatriot in his lap. Both were slowly bleeding to death, their eyes closed in peaceful prayer.

Gil drew the .45, hating like hell the idea of shooting someone in the midst of a prayer, but he realized they would probably continue to pray until they finally blacked out from loss of blood. He shot them each in the head.

As the echo of the second shot faded, he heard a very disturbing sound from the far side of the vehicle—the beep of a cellular phone. He darted around the back end of the lead truck to find the woman was still alive behind the passenger door of the second, a bullet hole through her shoulder blade. Even with Al-Nazari's blood and brain matter spattered all over her, she was a very striking woman. She was obviously in tremendous pain and just as obviously very pregnant.

For a fleeting moment, Gil felt sick to his stomach. "How far along?" he asked, without even considering whether or not she would understand.

"Eight months," she gasped in good English. "There will be a place for you in hell if . . . if my baby dies."

"You might be right," he muttered, squatting to take the phone from her hand. "Who did you call?"

"My father. He and his men are coming for me. Your only chance is to leave me alive . . . run for your life and pray I can talk him out of chasing you."

Gil had only seconds to choose his course of action. As far as his orders went, they were very clear: shoot the woman, evade capture until nightfall, and get on the fucking helo. But he'd been suckered, and he knew it. Lerher had known the Sherkat woman was pregnant, known it would be a problem for Gil, and so had kept the detail to himself. This betrayal of confidence went well beyond the implicit *obsceneness* of assassinating a pregnant woman. Had she cleared the car door before Gil could shoot her, he would have seen her belly, and he would have hesitated to fire. He would have hesitated because he would have seen something in his scope that he wasn't expecting to see, and hesitation was every bit as deadly to a sniper as impatience or overeagerness. Lerher knew this, and it was his responsibility to provide his operators with *all relevant, available—pertinent* information concerning their targets.

Gil's hotheadedness made the call for him. He was on his own time now, so fuck Lerher. Let *him* shoot the woman if he had the balls.

He slipped his arms beneath her to pick her up. "You're coming with me."

"No!" She struggled out of his arms, and he rocked back on his haunches to look at her.

"Look, lady. Either I take you with me—*try* to take you with me—or I kill you. Because I can't leave a living witness to say I was here. Understand?"

She stared into his eyes, realizing it made sense to assume the Iranian government would not suspect America's involvement in this. Even she had believed they'd been attacked by bandits until Gil had stepped around the door, as did her father and his men who were barreling toward them at this very moment.

Gil's radio came to life. "Typhoon, be advised . . . electronic surveillance reports that a cellular call has been made by your female target. Repeat. Your female target is alive and in contact with enemy forces headed to your exact location. ETA—forty minutes. Do you copy? Over."

"Roger that, main. I copy. Target has been neutralized. Requesting immediate extraction. Over."

"Typhoon, are you declaring an emergency? Over?"

Gil knew that an emergency declaration was the only way to get clearance for the Night Stalkers to extract him during daylight. He had no right to endanger the flight crews just because he had decided to enter into a pissing contest with Agent Lerher.

"Typhoon, are you declaring an emergency? Over?"

Gil looked up at the gray sky, the ceiling still too low and thick for either satellite or drone observation. "Negative, main. Negative. I am not declaring an emergency at this time. Proceeding with mission as planned. Over."

"Roger, actual."

Under normal circumstances, a forty-minute head start would have been plenty of time to evade an enemy that had no idea who they were looking for. However, escaping and evading with a wounded, very pregnant woman was a horse of a much different color. There were no training ops for such a mission. He would have to improvise.

"Can you walk?"

"Not to the Afghan border!" she snapped. "You shot me, remember!"

He couldn't help chuckling. "And I'm fixin' to shoot ya again."

18

AFGHANISTAN,
Kabul

Two representatives from the US State Department, code-named
Tom and Jerry, had been ordered to deliver twenty-six million dollars' worth of Afghan currency, called afghanis, to the presidential
palace. There they would meet briefly with President Karzai's appointed intermediary, the appropriate agent tasked with delivering
the ransom payment to Sandra Brux's Taliban captors. The president himself was not in the palace that day. He was in Abbottabad,
Pakistan, ostensibly to discuss plans for a proposed trans-Afghan
natural gas pipeline that would extend all the way from Iran to
India.

Officially, Tom and Jerry were diplomats from the US Embassy
in Kabul, but in reality, they were two well-armed members of the
US Army's Delta Force, acting under the direction of SOG. They

were dressed in khaki pants and black leather boots, ball caps, and matching olive drab North Face jackets, under which they each carried an HK-MP7, a 4.6 mm submachine gun that fired 940 rounds per minute.

After delivering the money to the intermediary, they would wait for him outside, then covertly follow him and his two-man team to the delivery point. Their orders were clear: First, to ensure the cash was not hijacked en route. Second, if Warrant Officer Brux was at the exchange—which was not expected—they were to wait for her to be safely delivered into the hands of the intermediary, and then terminate—with extreme prejudice—all Taliban/HIK members at the scene before resecuring the twenty-six million dollars' worth of afghanis.

Tom sat behind the wheel of their beat-up white Nissan watching the palace from behind a pair of Oakley sunglasses. "I didn't trust that skeevy motherfucker, did you?"

Jerry held up a finger, listening to the real-time intelligence he was receiving in his earpiece via satellite from Creech Air Force Base back in Indian Springs, Nevada. Creech was home to the 432nd Wing, where the pilots of the UAVs (unmanned aerial vehicles) did the actual flying from the safety of their air-conditioned offices. The UAV loitering thirty thousand feet above them was watching the palace to be sure the intermediary didn't slip out undetected through a different exit point.

"Okay, they're coming," Jerry said. "Should be passing through the main gate any second."

They were parked down the street where they looked like any other white Nissan against the cluttered backdrop of the city. With the UAV on station, it wouldn't be necessary to maintain constant visual contact with the intermediary. CenCom would feed them directions if they got tied up in traffic. The trunk lid of their car had been painted flat black to make them stand out from above.

Tom shifted into drive. "Here we go." He allowed the black SUV to slip out of sight before pulling off.

They drove through the streets of Kabul for about twenty minutes, headed roughly southeast, until CenCom advised that the SUV was turning into an abandoned industrial center near the outskirts of town. Tom and Jerry pulled up and watched as the SUV drove straight across the complex and into a large warehouse half the size of a city block. Two casually dressed men with AK-47s over their shoulders pulled down the large overhead door right behind the SUV.

Tom shifted into park. "Those two pricks look like Taliban to you?"

Jerry shook his head. "CenCom, be advised two men in khakis with AK-47s were waiting here to meet Jackal." Jackal was the intermediary's code name.

They sat watching from across the street. As per the agreement, the location of the payoff had not been shared with the US Embassy. Kidnap for ransom was routine business in Kabul, and this was the standard procedure generally followed in order to secure the release of Afghan officials and wealthy citizens. With a few exceptions, the captive parties were always returned within twenty-four hours of payment, and for this reason, the US Embassy had advised State that it was probably best to stick with the system already in place if they wanted to facilitate the return of Sandra Brux as quickly and quietly as possible.

Tom and Jerry had been the only modification to that system, the ace up the sleeve of a US State Department very much wanting to send the message that the kidnap and rape of US servicewomen for profit was not a business that ambitious young terrorists around the world should aspire to. It was believed that leaving a bunch of dead bagmen at the scene of an exchange would help to send that message loud and clear, but this could occur only if Sandra was exchanged directly for the cash. There were a number of people within the CIA who believed very strongly that Sandra was likely to be there. Because why hold on to such a dangerous captive any longer than absolutely necessary—particularly if the ransom was paid and everyone was following the tried-and-true intermediary system?

"Think she's in there?" Jerry ventured, sitting back in his seat with his boot against the dash.

Tom shook his head. "Not a fucking chance. This whole thing stinks like shit. Where the fuck do those assholes think they're going with all that cash that we can't follow? They're not dealing with the Afghan government. They're dealing with the fucking CIA. How the fuck are they going to shake a UAV?"

"Well, we're talking about stupid mountain people," Jerry reminded him.

"Did those pricks with the AKs look like stupid mountain people to you? And even if they are, Jackal knows all about the eye in the sky. He didn't even ask if we'd be watching. All he did was smile, like he knew something we didn't. Fucker's up to something. I know he is."

"You think he's on the take?"

"All bagmen are on the take."

"But Karzai handpicked this guy."

"And where the fuck is *he*?" Tom said. "Conveniently out of the fucking country. I'm telling you, I don't like this. Advise CenCom we're moving in for a closer look."

"But we're—"

Tom checked his weapon. "Get ready to move your ass."

Jerry sat up in the seat. "CenCom, be advised . . . Tom wants a closer look. This doesn't look right." He listened a moment, then looked at Tom. "They're asking Langley for clearance."

"Fuck clearance," Tom said, getting out. "While Langley's busy scratching their balls, this thing's busy getting fucked up. Let's go."

Jerry got out of the car and started across the street after Tom. "CenCom, be advised we're heading in for a closer look."

"They can see us, numb nuts."

Jerry laughed. "Kiss my ass. I'm doing my job."

They kept an eye out as they trotted across the lot, watching for lookouts, but they saw no one at all.

"These people feel totally secure," Jerry said.

"Why wouldn't they?" Tom answered. "That's Karzai's guy in there, and if he's in bed with the fucking HIK, who's he got to be afraid of?"

They headed down the far side of the warehouse. There were no windows or cameras to worry about, so they moved fast, hands inside their jackets and ready to go guns-up at the first sign of trouble.

"Hey," Jerry said. "CenCom just got clearance from Langley."

"Good for CenCom." Tom stopped at the man door a few hundred feet down the wall, hoping they'd gone far enough down from the main entrance. "All right, get your ass wired up. We're going in."

He tried the knob, but it was locked. "Shit! Do your thing."

Jerry took a knee in front of the door and pulled a pick set from his pocket. Anyone who spotted them now would know something was up, so Tom took the MP7 from inside his jacket. Jerry had the door unlocked in a little over a minute, then stood back so Tom could precede him into the building. They slipped inside to find the building was lit by skylight. Light was shadowy along the walls where an overhead storage level ran the length of the building on both sides. Both levels were crowded with untold volumes of odds and ends junk, including pieces of cars and trucks, used earthmover tires, aircraft fuselages, various wooden crates, empty wooden spools, and stacks of empty pallets.

The two commandos moved in and out of the junk, keeping close to the wall as they negotiated their way back in the direction they had come, hearing hurried, bustling movement up ahead. They closed to within fifty feet to see five different vehicles of different models lined up, cars and vans, all of them nondescript. Jackal stood near a row of tables where close to twenty men had already divided the afghanis into five piles of equal amounts and were now stuffing the piles into five different army duffel bags, apparently to be loaded into the five waiting vehicles for transport to parts unknown.

"This look normal to you?" Tom said quietly.

"Hell if I know," Jerry said with a shrug. "What do you want to do?"

Tom was busy studying Jackal's posture and facial expressions. He was a man of medium build, late forties, with dark hair and thick dark eyebrows. He wasn't carrying himself like a guy playing the role of an intermediary; rather he looked a whole lot more like an overseer. What was more, he looked concerned, and he kept checking his watch.

"We're taking these guys," Tom decided, extending the buttstock of his MP7. "This isn't right."

Jerry followed suit, advising CenCom they were going into action.

Without waiting for a reply, they stepped from cover with their weapons shouldered.

"Freeze!" Tom screamed at the top of his voice, moving rapidly forward. "Hands in the fucking air! Hands in the fucking air, assholes!"

Most of the men nearly jumped out of their skins at the report of his rabid voice, and their hands shot skyward.

Jerry quickly swept the upper levels with his eyes, moving forward and to the left of Tom so they could fire into the men from the standard *L* formation without anyone escaping and without the danger of hitting each other.

Only Jackal, and the two men with AK-47s, remained composed, their hands at their sides.

"I said, hands in the fucking air!" Tom screamed. "And don't tell me you don't fucking understand!"

The AK men slowly obeyed, but Jackal only smiled.

"What are you doing here?" he asked calmly, his dark eyes steady. "Are you trying to get your pilot killed? We don't have time for this. You should not be here."

"What the fuck is going on?" Tom demanded.

"We are dividing the money for transport through the city," Jackal replied. "Do you expect us to transport it all in the same vehicle? That would be stupid."

"Jerry, advise CenCom what we've got."

Jerry began to describe their situation over the radio.

"May my men put their hands down now?" Jackal asked. "You've clearly scared them half to death."

Tom took a glance at their faces. They did not look scared to him; they looked desperate. "They can keep their fucking hands up. Now take away those two AK-47s and place them on the ground—slowly!"

Jackal sighed and did as he was told, speaking calmly to the men in Pashto as he did so.

"Shut the fuck up!" Tom screamed. "Speak English or not at all!"

Jackal sighed again. "All I did was tell them to keep their hands up. We are wasting valuable time with this."

Jerry was still talking quietly with CenCom, breaking the situation down for the boys back in Langley.

"How many of these men are Taliban or HIK?" Tom demanded.

"None of these men are Taliban or HIK," Jackal replied. "This is their job. They work for me—for us. They are professional intermediaries. You need to leave. You endanger your pilot every moment that you are here."

"Jerry?"

Jerry shrugged. "CenCom says Langley isn't worried about what we've got. We can clear."

"Are you satisfied now?" Jackal asked. "You should go. Let us do our jobs."

"No, I'm not fucking satisfied," Tom retorted. "Get your men lined up along the table with their hands behind their heads. We're going to search these vehicles. And if I even *think* you're trying to pull some shit in Pashto, you're a fucking dead man."

"Will you please talk to him?" Jackal said to Jerry. "He's crazy. You're going to get your pilot killed."

Jerry kept his weapon trained on the group of men. "Tom, Langley wants us to clear."

"Langley isn't fucking here, Jerry, and Langley isn't seeing what the fuck I'm seeing."

"What are you seeing?" Jackal demanded, sounding agitated for the first time. "Tell me what you think you see!"

"A bunch of nervous motherfuckers!" Tom shouted. "Now line 'em the fuck up. Get 'em down on their goddamn knees with their hands behind their fucking heads. Now!"

"Of course they're nervous," Jackal said with an incredulous laugh. "You're a crazy man with a gun!"

"Do it! Now!"

"Please!" Jackal said, almost pleading with Jerry. "Talk to your commanders. Get them to control this man. Your pilot is in grave danger because of this!"

Jerry could see it now, too. "He doesn't want us searching the vehicles."

"You bet your fucking ass he doesn't." Tom stepped toward Jackal and kicked him to the ground, aiming the gun down into his face and shrieking at the top of his voice, "I said line these fucking men up!"

"Okay!" Jackal shouted, his hands thrust up in front of him.

"Okay. But you are making a terrible mistake. You're in big trouble. I am an Afghan diplomat."

"You're a fucking bagman! Line 'em up!" He kicked Jackal in the ribs.

Jackal spoke quickly to the men, pointing, and they slowly began to form into a line.

Jerry was sweating bullets. If they ended up gunning these guys down, and it turned out to be nothing more than a misunderstanding, he and Tom would spend the rest of their lives in Leavenworth prison. "Tom, this isn't good, man."

"I know it," Tom said over his shoulder, his eyes boring into Jackal's. "But this fucking prick is lying." He backed away from Jackal and started kicking the men in the backs of their knees, dropping them one at a time until the rest got the picture and got down into the dirt with their hands behind their heads. "Tell 'em to cross their legs."

Jackal spoke to them from where he lay on his side in the dust, and they crossed their ankles.

At last satisfied the prisoners were sufficiently controlled, Tom stood back to cover them from behind, clearing Jerry to search the vehicles.

Jerry quickly searched the first two sedans and found nothing. He moved to the van and opened the side door, seeing at once a blood-soaked blanket wrapped around a lifeless form, a pair of female feet and ankles extending from the bottom. "Holy Jesus!" he said. "I got a body—a woman!"

"You don't understand!" Jackal said, leaping to his feet.

One of the other men took his hands away from his head and reached for a pistol concealed beneath the front of his shirt. Tom blew him away with a burst of automatic fire, catching the men on either side of him as well. The rest of the prisoners in line dove forward into the dirt and covered their heads as Jackal spun and ran for the SUV. Tom cut him down before he'd gone three steps.

Jerry was in a crouch near the van, his weapon trained on the men now lying facedown in the dust pissing their pants. "We clear?"

Tom switched out the magazine. "Clear!"

Jerry stood up and climbed into the van. He could see a matted mop of bloody brown hair protruding from the blanket. He pulled the cover away. "The cocksuckers beat her to death."

Tom marched forward and started kicking the men. "Who speaks fucking English here? Nobody, huh? Okay, motherfuckers, time to die!"

A hand shot up. "I English bad!"

"You English bad? On your fucking feet, Bad English."

The skinny young man got up trembling. The front of his pants were soaked with piss.

"Who killed her?"

The young man did not hesitate to point out two other men still lying facedown with their fingers laced over the backs of their heads.

Tom stalked over to see their knuckles were covered with fresh abrasions. He kicked them each in the rib cage with all the force he could muster. "This is just the fucking beginning."

Jerry closed the blanket and got out of the van. "CenCom, be advised, the principal is DOA. Repeat. Principal is DOA. Looks like it's been about twelve hours. Also, be advised that Jackal is KIA. We are requesting CID and enough security to deal with sixteen male prisoners." He listened patiently to the reply, smirking with disgust before making his response. "Roger, CenCom. All funds are secure."

19

IRAN,
Sistan-Baluchistan Province

Gil had some tough choices to make, tough choices to go along with the tough choice that had been forced upon him. Navy SEALs were not murderers, they were warriors, and they did not enter into combat with the intention of making war on women or children who did not make war on them. Collateral damage happened, and it was always unfortunate, but it was never a SEAL's intention to end the life of a noncombatant. Most did not allow it to bother them when it happened—at least not on the surface. They told themselves that it was war, that they were fighting for their country, and that God would sort it all out. How else could they live with the things they saw?

Gil could never entirely buy into that perspective, though at times he was left no other choice but to run with it. Regardless, he hadn't

joined DEVGRU to shoot pregnant women. He was not an automa-
tonic killer for men like Lerher to set loose in the wild backwaters of
the planet to do his dirty work. He would take the Sherkat woman
back with him, or he would die trying. He had a wife he wanted to
look in the face when he finally retired from this man's Navy, and
if he couldn't do that, then there wasn't much point in getting back
anyhow. Dishonor scared him a hell of a lot more than death.

Most of his DEVGRU counterparts, when faced with the same
repugnant decision of having to shoot a pregnant woman point-blank
in the road would have done so, regrettably, and then attempted to
shrug it off as part of the mission—much as Gil had shot the dying
gunmen in the midst of their prayers. And still there were others,
like Crosswhite and Steelyard, who probably would have shot her
and then raised holy hell about it when they got back. Gil wasn't
exactly sure why he couldn't be more like them. He wished he were.
Maybe he wasn't strong enough, or maybe he was just too much of
a goddamn idealist when it came to certain things. All he knew for
sure was that SEALs didn't treat women like those Taliban pricks
were treating Sandra Brux, and the only way he knew to lead was by
example. So this was the example he was going to set, come hell or
high water, and fuck anybody who didn't like it.

"Like I said," he muttered, "I'm on my own time." He put the
woman into the backseat where she would be more comfortable,
then went to find himself a good AK-47 and all the spare magazines
he could carry. During the hurried search, he found a worn-looking
grenade in the coat pocket of one of the dead men, an old Russian
RGD-5, packing four ounces of TNT. It wasn't likely to be of much
use to Gil, considering the open terrain and his close itinerary, but
there were other ways to employ a grenade besides throwing it at the
enemy. Leaving it behind for them to find often worked as well. He
pulled the pin and hid the grenade inside the man's jacket, resting
it on the safety lever. Any disturbance of the body, and the grenade

would roll over beneath the jacket, releasing the safety lever and igniting the internal fuse. Four seconds later . . . pop goes the weasel!

He found a first aid kit in one of the trucks and packed the woman's wounds with wadding front and back, strapping her arm to her chest to immobilize the broken clavicle.

"You should be running," she told him, sweat pouring from her face.

He checked his watch. "We ain't goin' all that far, lady. And unless you want your father shot, you'd better describe him for me."

"So you can shoot him first!"

He shrugged. "Have it your own way." He took hold of her hands to help her step out onto the road. "Now listen up. If you slow me down or pull any shit—*any shit at all*—I'll shoot you. Understand?"

She glared at him, nodding once with great reluctance.

With his shemagh wrapped around his head like a Bedouin and the AK-47 slung over his back, he set off overland leading her by the arm. They walked approximately a thousand meters out from the road where he made her sit down. Then he took the spade and began to dig.

"Your father's an opium smuggler, right?"

She gathered the coat he'd found for her about her shoulders and stared off back the way they'd come as if she hadn't heard him.

"Well, he has to be," Gil remarked, hacking at the hardened earth. "Otherwise, the guards from that radiation bomb factory would have been here by now. How many of his men is he bringing with him?"

She looked at him. "All of them."

He laughed. "You're never gonna warm up to me, are you?"

She looked away again. "You're a murderer."

"I suppose from a certain point of view that's true enough." He dug for a while, being careful to scatter the dirt to prevent there being any sign of a fresh dig should his enemy scan the terrain through a scope or a pair of binoculars.

"Do you remember Neda?" he asked a few minutes later, shaping the trench he was digging for her to take cover in. Neda Agha-Soltan was a twenty-six-year-old woman shot and killed during the Iranian freedom protests of 2009. Her graphic death was broadcast within minutes to the entire world via the internet.

She turned to look at him again, her dark eyes full of suspicion. "What do you know of Neda?"

"I know she was murdered by Pasdaran thugs in the streets of Tehran." He took a drink from his CamelBak. The Pasdaran were special Iranian police charged with protecting the nation's Islamic system of government. "I also know she was protesting for Iranian rights when it happened."

She shrugged him off. "No one knows who killed Neda."

"Yes, you do." He took up the spade again. "There are good people in your country, lady. You're not all drug smugglers and murderers."

She whipped her head around, hissing, "I am not a smuggler—and *you're* the murderer!"

He sat back on his haunches. "Your father's drugs kill more people in a month than I'll kill in my entire career. But that's okay, isn't it? Because they're just infidels."

She smirked and turned away again. "Dig your grave, American. Dig your grave and leave me alone."

He chuckled, muttering, "This grave here is yours." He dug a bit more before asking, "He was your husband, Al-Nazari?"

"He was more than that," she said proudly. "He was a hero. Now he is a martyr."

"But he was Sunni—you're a Shia."

She laughed at him. "Is that what they told you? My family is not Shia." She noted his wedding band. "What does your wife think of what you do?"

"She doesn't really know what I do. But if it makes you feel any better, I'll probably never get to see her again. Lookin' out for you is likely gonna cost me the ball game."

She turned to face him fully, her pride falling off suddenly. "I am in great pain."

"You're taking it like a champ, though." He admired her. "I'm afraid if I give you morphine, you won't be able to walk when the time comes." He stopped to rest against the spade, taking the shemagh away from his face. "On the other hand, all that pain could put you into labor, so I don't reckon I have much choice."

He dug into his personal first aid kit. Then he injected a small dose of morphine into her wounded shoulder. At once, the tension went out of her face, and he could see the relief, the slight drift of her eyes. He made her lie down in the trench, which was only a few inches deeper than she was.

"When the shootin' starts, you keep your head down unless you want it shot off. Now tell me what your father looks like, and I'll try to avoid shooting him."

The morphine had dropped her inhibitions enough to elicit some cooperation. "He wears glasses. A black mustache."

Gil finished his own trench and settled in with the Dragunov SVD pulled into his shoulder. He'd brought twenty 10-round magazines, which had been more than enough for the mission as planned, but in view of these new developments, two hundred rounds was starting to feel a little bit light. He had twenty-five 30-round magazines for the AK-47, but the AK put him on equal terms with the enemy. He would need to make every SVD round count.

Her father's men arrived a short time later in two trucks full of men, about twenty in all. A number of them spread into a defensive perimeter around the ambushed caravan while her father and his lieutenants walked the site. Gil studied the man's movements for a moment, and then scanned the rest of the men, looking for a sniper.

He found him standing near the tail of the second truck, studying the countryside through a large, powerful pair of binoculars. The shooter carried a Dragunov with a synthetic stock slung across his front, and the optics were far better than Gil's PSO sight. It was obvious from the way he carried himself that he was one confident son of a bitch. Probably, he'd been nailing rival drug smugglers at long range for quite some time, helping the Sherkat woman's father to become the local big shot.

Gil couldn't afford to let this character live, which meant he had to engage these people now. A sniper duel over open country was anybody's game, and Gil was not at all inclined to fighting fairly. He placed the *T* of the reticule on the sniper's heart and squeezed the trigger just as the grenade hidden in the dead man's jacket detonated.

The sniper jerked around toward the sound of the explosion, and Gil's round grazed his rib cage.

Shit! Someone had disturbed the body at exactly the worst possible instant.

He fired again, catching the sniper in the left shoulder to spin him back around. As he fired a third time, another man, running away from the explosion, slammed into the sniper and accidentally took the bullet for him, knocking him from his feet and out of sight behind the truck.

Gil knew he was in for some shit now. The sniper was not dead. He would be hurting like a bastard, but he was definitely still in the fight, and undoubtedly already moving to take up a firing position, looking to zero in on Gil's location. He checked his fire, ignoring the other gunmen who scrambled about as he scanned for the sniper.

The man had disappeared.

Inside of a minute, fifteen gunmen—including the Sherkat woman's father—were formed up in a wide skirmish line marching toward his location with their AK-47s shouldered and ready to fire. If Gil began to pick them off now, he probably wouldn't kill more than two or three of them before the enemy sniper spotted the dust kicked up by the Dragunov and burned him down.

"Looks like a bad day at Black Rock," he muttered, glad the

woman was doped up, otherwise she would certainly give away their position now, regardless of any danger to herself. The thought occurred to him briefly to use her as a shield, but that was the act of a coward, and even a cornered rat could do better. He could see the enemy had his general position worked out.

"Typhoon main, do you read? Over?"

"Roger, actual."

"Typhoon main, be advised . . ." He took a moment to choose his last words. "Typhoon main, be advised I am pinned down by ten-plus gunmen . . . up against a sniper of unknown talent. Will advise further if and when able to do so. Over."

The reply sounded vaguely anxious. "Actual, are you declaring an emergency? Over."

"Negative, main. This'll be over one way or another long before the cavalry shows up. Typhoon actual, out." He switched off the radio and studied the target area through the PSO. "Now where the fuck would I be if I were you, asshole?"

20

AFGHANISTAN,
Kabul, SOG Operations

Agent Lerher set down his cup of coffee with an anxious sigh, glancing irritably around the semicrowded op center. "What the hell does he keep signing off for? How are we supposed to gather real-time intelligence if he's not feeding us? He *knows* we can't see him. Somebody get me some eyes on the goddamn ground."

The Air Force liaison officer cleared her throat.

He turned toward her.

"Mr. Lerher, I've still got Creech on the line," she said patiently. "They advise there's a front coming in, but the ceiling is still under five thousand feet. The UAV will be visible if it drops down for a look."

Lerher was smoldering. Not being able to watch the operation he'd spent the past three weeks capering over was driving him nuts. He had already been denied seeing the Al-Nazari hit, and now he was about to miss what he guessed was going to be one hell of a shoot-out. He might as well have been back in his hotel room for all of the input he'd been able to offer thus far. He was tempted to order the UAV down from the clouds for a brief overview at the target area, but if it was spotted by any sort of Iranian government entity, that would be enough to put the bloody finger on the United States for Al-Nazari's assassination. Not that it mattered. Hell, it sounded like their operative was about to buy it anyhow.

"Captain Metcalf? Do you have any suggestions?"

Metcalf sat back stroking his chin. "You might consider letting my man do his job," he said easily. "We didn't send him in there to provide a play-by-play. We sent him in there to eliminate a target. He's done that. Now he's working to bring himself out. If he needs something from you, rest assured, he'll let you know."

Lerher smiled without humor, resenting the presence of top brass in his operations center. "Sounds like a plan, sir." Technically, Metcalf was there only as an interested observer, but if anything went wrong, or if Lerher made a bad call, the old man would make sure he was held responsible.

Metcalf gave him a wink.

To the Navy man, Lerher was just another CIA spook, standing over there with his shirtsleeves all rolled up like he was getting ready to do some actual work. Lerher was probably more reliable than most, but he was sneakier, too. He thought his reliability entitled him to special privileges. That was why Metcalf had chosen to remain in operations for every minute of the mission. It pleased him to watch the younger CIA man swilling coffee like he thought Juan Valdez was going to stop growing the beans. A simple Benzedrine capsule was all that was needed to keep a man sharp during the short haul, and it didn't keep you running to the damn head every ten minutes.

He watched Lerher duck out of the room, and chortled to himself, offering a wink to the black Air Force lieutenant.

She grinned and turned her head before any civilian in the room could notice.

21

IRAN,
Sistan-Baluchistan Province

Gil needed a break. The fifteen-man skirmish line was drawing to within five hundred yards and spread out roughly a hundred yards across his field of vision. If they closed to within a hundred yards before he started taking them out, he was a goner. Even being dug in as he was, the AK-47 was more than accurate enough for them to pick him off over open sights at that short range. He could see the woman's father marching boldly forward at the center of the phalanx, shouting orders left and right. He wanted his daughter back even at the risk of all their lives, and though Gil guessed the old man was counting on his sniper to get Gil before Gil got too many of them, it was obvious these people were fucking fearless.

What Gil would have given at that moment for his Remington modular sniper rifle with the suppressor and just twenty measly rounds of subsonic ammo. Instead, he was stuck with this Russian shoulder cannon that was going to kick up enough dust when he got rockin' and rollin' to reveal his location to everyone from Tehran to Abbottabad. The closer the phalanx drew, the farther he would have to sweep the rifle across his field of vision to pick the men off, and this would give them even more time to zero his position.

As if it were a gift sent straight from the God of War himself, a stiff gust of desert wind blew from behind, and Gil did not hesitate to take advantage of it, pivoting the Dragunov toward the gunman on the extreme left of the phalanx to find center mass and squeezing off the round. He pivoted immediately back to the extreme right to find center mass on a second gunman and squeezed off another shot, blowing the unfortunate skirmisher's guts out his back. The dust from both shots was blown downrange by the gust before it could ever form a cloud.

Gil took no return fire, and the remaining thirteen men in the phalanx slowed their pace, desperately scanning with their AK-47s. This was the sniper duel he had wanted to avoid. He had to find the enemy shooter now during this brief slowdown in the phalanx's advance.

Searching through the PSO, he broke the target area down into small quadrants, looking for the telltale silhouette of a man aiming a rifle. The phalanx would still be more of a hindrance to the enemy sniper's field of vision than his own. Combine that with the fact the shooter was severely wounded, his reflexes degraded, and Gil hoped he still had the upper hand.

Someone in the phalanx began to fire at what he must have thought was Gil's position fifty yards forward of his location and to the left, near a small depression near some rocks. Five others joined in with automatic fire. Gil took advantage of the loud cacophony by eliminating two more men from the far left of the line, wanting to spare the men in the center for as long as possible in the hopes they would continue to clutter the enemy sniper's field of vision. With the excessive enemy firing, Gil's dust cloud dissipated before they realized they had even taken fire. He was striking a very delicate balance here, learning on the job, exercising the patience that every sniper tried to master. If he panicked or lost his concentration for a fraction of a second, the game was up.

With only eleven men left in the skirmish line now at four hundred fifty yards, he was breathing a little easier. Thirty seconds passed and no one fired on him, but he was no closer to finding the enemy shooter.

The clouds parted somewhere behind him, and a wall of sunlight raced off across the landscape before him. He was backlit—out of time! The sniper's superior optics would differentiate the minor color differences between Gil's ACU and the terrain. A hot round tore a chunk of meat from his right shoulder, cutting a furrow down his back, penetrating the right cheek of his ass, and grazing the heel of his boot before impacting the ground. The next round would strike him in the head.

The wall of sunlight swept over the target area—a silvery glint from an unprotected sniper scope. Gil fired on pure reflex, seeing the enemy sniper perched on the running board of the lead truck, firing between the cab and the troop compartment with nothing to backlight him, no silhouette.

Gil's round went straight through the sniper's scope and blew out the back of his head.

AK-47 rounds from the phalanx rained down around him like micro-meteorites, but he was in the zone now. Pivoting the rifle right to left, he picked them off one at a time like ducks at a carnival. He did not care about the bullets striking around him any more than he cared when he shot the Sherkat woman's father straight through the heart. Even as the last man collapsed in the dust, he was on his feet, unslinging the AK-47 and bolting forward. He could not feel his wounds. He felt only the high-octane adrenaline surging through his body. A short burst from the Kalashnikov finished off one of the skirmishers who had survived a shot to the chest.

Before he knew it, Gil had reached the target area. He found the enemy sniper on his back behind the truck with the left side of his face blown apart. "So, you're a southpaw, huh?" He kicked him free of the rifle sling, jerking back the bolt on the fancy Dragunov to eject the round that would have killed him—the coveted "boar's tooth." Pocketing the round, he jumped into the lead SUV, hit the key, and tore off across the jagged landscape to retrieve the woman.

"Typhoon main, this is Typhoon actual. Be advised I am wounded and headed for the extraction zone. Repeat. I am wounded and headed for the extraction zone. ETA fifteen minutes. Over."

"Roger, Typhoon actual. Stand by."

Gil listened as Typhoon main passed the ball to the Night Stalker unit awaiting clearance for dust off: "Warlock, this is Typhoon main. Be advised, you are a go for emergency evac. Repeat. Go for emergency evac."

"Roger, main. We are winding up now. ETA ten minutes. Over."

"This is Typhoon actual," Gil called out. "I copy direct. Be advised I am driving a black Nissan SUV. Repeat. I am driving a black Nissan SUV. Over."

"Roger that, actual. We are inbound. Over."

"Copy that, Warlock. See you when you—"

Two green and white Iranian police Land Rovers were racing wildly over land to cut him off, both of them coming from the bomb maker's facility to the south. Gil slammed on the brakes and jumped from the truck, shouldering the AK-47 and running out to meet them. He fired an entire magazine into the lead Rover from fifty yards, killing both men and reloading on the run.

The second Rover skidded to a halt, and the military police jumped out, using the doors for cover as they fired their pistols in panic.

Gil dove forward onto his belly, putting a six-round burst through each door and killing them both. He leapt to his feet and ran to where the woman still lay in her trench, bleary eyed and limp.

"My father?" she asked as he lifted her out.

"I'm sorry," he said, grunting against the pain in his ass as he got to his feet. "He didn't make it."

She tried to slap his face, tried to struggle from his arms, but she was too weak.

"You will go to hell for this," she moaned.

"I'll save you a seat, darlin'." He put her into the back of the SUV and jumped in behind the wheel, dropping the lever into drive, tromping the accelerator, and throwing dirt. He drove the vehicle hard over the rugged terrain, traveling as fast as he dared, keeping an eye on the GPS device now Velcroed to his wrist. Within ten minutes, he could see the three inbound helicopters of the Night Stalker unit. Both top-cover helos were loaded with missile pods and bristling with machine guns, and no sight had ever been grander.

The Night Stalkers met him halfway, and he hit the brakes, jumping out to take the Sherkat woman from the backseat and trotting forward through the whirling dust storm as the evac was setting down.

The crew chief jumped out with an M16 rifle in his hands and ran forward to meet him.

"Who the hell is she, Master Chief?"

"She's pregnant!" Gil shouted over the whine of the turbines.

The young crew chief was shaking his head. "No can do! We don't have clearance for indigenous personnel. You'll have to leave her!"

Gil walked around him and placed her on the deck of the helo. "She's ready to pop!"

"Chief, I can't do it! We gotta go!"

Gil drew his .45 and offered it to the crew chief. Still shouting over the turbines: "Then you'll have to kill 'er, son! This is a black operation! No one can be left alive to say I was here!"

The crew chief glanced at the woman and then back at Gil. "I ain't shooting a woman!"

"Orders!"

"Goddamnit, Master Chief! You'd better be willing to take full responsibility!"

Gil holstered the pistol and jumped into the helo.

Ten seconds later, they were airborne and headed for Afghani airspace.

22

LANGLEY

Deputy Director Cletus Webb was sitting at his desk talking with Robert Pope when Director Shroyer came stalking into the office unannounced. The director was obviously somewhat surprised to see Pope sitting before Webb's desk, but that didn't deter him.

"What the hell happened at the ransom drop, Cletus? And why the hell am I having to come find you again? The old man just reamed my ass over the phone because I didn't have a goddamn answer. I looked like a fucking idiot! If Sandra Brux is dead, the president needs to get out in front of this."

Webb maintained a placid demeanor. Men like Shroyer and the president were not interested in the complicated logistics of collating reliable intelligence over thousands of miles and multiple time zones. They wanted the information instantaneously. He glanced at Pope. "Bob?"

Pope looked startled to have been passed the ball. "Oh, well . . . Sandra isn't dead, George. The body wasn't hers. That's what I came over to tell Cletus. The girl was the married daughter of the president of the Central Bank of Afghanistan." He turned in the chair to face Shroyer more directly, straightening his corduroy jacket and pushing his glasses up onto his nose. "From what we can put together so far, it looks like Jackal was the head of his own kidnapping ring. Turns out nobody in the Afghan government knew the poor girl was even missing because her father kept it quiet. Since he was slow to make the payment, Jackal followed through on his threat to have her beaten to death. Her general appearance, size, and hair color are all very similar to that of Sandra Brux, and with her face beaten to a pulp . . . well, it was the natural assumption for Tom and Jerry to make, given the circumstances. CID has interrogated the men taken into custody, and they all say the girl's body was to be dumped in downtown Kabul later in the day. All indications are that Jackal had every intention of delivering the ransom in exchange for Sandra—minus his cut."

With great effort, Shroyer held his temper. "And now that's not going to happen. So Tom and Jerry fucked up."

Pope shook his head. "No. No, they did everything by the numbers."

"I read the transcripts from Creech." Shroyer said. "Tom and Jerry were told to clear."

Pope shrugged. "Unimportant."

"Unimportant?!" Shroyer flared.

Pope sat scratching the back of his hand, speaking in an almost bored tone of voice. "The analysts here in Langley couldn't see what was happening in that warehouse. Tom and Jerry were sent in with orders to grab Sandra, eliminate her Taliban captors, and secure the money. Strictly speaking, they performed perfectly. They did, indeed, secure a kidnap victim, and every afghani dollar has since been accounted for by the Central Bank. They also broke up a major kidnapping ring that's been terrorizing the city." He glanced between the director and the DDO. "This is one of those times when a lab experiment yields an absolutely logical yet entirely unanticipated result."

Webb cleared his throat, wanting to draw Shroyer's ire away from Pope. "I wanted to get the details from Bob before I came to brief you. I apologize for not being quicker. I had no idea the president was going to be all over this so early in the morning. I thought we had an hour or so to work with. I accept complete responsibility for the lag."

Shroyer understood Webb's reasoning, but shit ran downhill, and the president had made it all too clear that he was not pleased by the lack of forthcoming information. "So that's it, then? No ransom, no pilot—no nothing."

Pope kept his face devoid of expression. "Jackal was the only known contact. All we can do is wait for another."

Shroyer jammed his hands into his pockets. "Which, sure as hell, will come in the form of another unholy rape video—this time all over Al Jazeera. The crazy bastards will probably double their demand as well. I'm going to advise the president that we should go public now. Can either of you think of a reason we should *not* do that?"

Webb looked at Pope.

Pope looked back at the two of them, disliking the need for political considerations. "Well, keep in mind . . . if *we* go public, the HIK has no reason to stay quiet, either. As things stand now, they still have the option of negotiating a financial resolution without the rest of the Muslim world knowing they're out to make a buck. But if we take the story public—turn it into a moral pissing contest—we leave them no choice but to forfeit profit in favor of propaganda. My recommendation is that we allow the situation to develop further. Allow them to make the next move. The ball is squarely in their court anyhow, and we risk making a mistake by attempting to preempt their next move. It's important we not forget Heisenberg's Uncertainty Principle."

Shroyer cut a glance at Webb, who stared back, a faint smile crossing his face.

"Which is?" Shroyer asked blandly.

"Simply stated," Pope replied, "we can never know anything for certain. For us to anticipate the HIK's next move could put Sandra in even more danger. The chances are good to excellent they're every bit as unsure of what to do next as we are. Let's not force their hand."

"You're saying it's the HIK now?" Shroyer said. "A second ago it was the Taliban. Exactly who the hell are we dealing with, Bob?"

Pope smiled. "It can get confusing. The entire history of Afghanistan reads the same way. Present intelligence indicates that the HIK has struck some sort of tentative alliance with the Taliban. What I believe is happening—more or less—is they're using the Taliban to do their flunky work."

Shroyer lowered his head in resignation, taking the other chair in front of Webb's desk. "Well, let's move on, then—since you're here, Bob. I'd like for you to explain what the hell happened with Operation Tiger Claw. As you know, the president gave clearance for a black operation inside of Iran. He did not, however, give his blessing for the abduction of an Iranian national—the potential political ramifications of which I'm sure need no explanation."

23

AFGHANISTAN,
Jalalabad Air Base

With the bullet wounds to his shoulder, back, and buttocks sutured, all of the appropriate injections administered and pills swallowed, Gil was finally cleared by the base surgeon to attend mission debrief.

Master Chief Steelyard came into the exam room grinning and tossed him a new pair of ACU trousers. "You ready to get the other half of your ass chewed?"

Gil chuckled as he got to his feet.

"What the hell were you thinking bringing that woman back here? Christ, didn't I teach you any better?"

Gil stepped carefully into the trousers and sat back down on the edge of the bed with just his left buttock. "Grab my boots, Chief?"

Steelyard took the boots from the chair and set them on the floor at Gil's feet.

"My orders were to kill her," Gil said, gingerly pulling on the right boot. "I couldn't see much of her at first, so I shot her through the door of the truck. I admit I was shocked when I walked up on her. Shit, she was pregnant as a pelican . . . layin' there with both arms wrapped around her belly, blood all over her face." He shook his head. "I wasn't ready for it—not at all. Could you have shot a pregnant woman point-blank?"

Steelyard frowned. "If she was a threat to the United States, yes—but it's not our job to make that determination in the field. You know that. That's what the intel people are for. Hell, if we all went into battle second-guessing the analysts, SOG would fall apart in a year. You're not special, Gil. And Lerher wants to barbecue your ass over this. He wants you busted down."

Gil pulled on the other boot. "I'm not worried about Lerher. It's Captain Metcalf I'm worried about—he picked me for the op. And I'm not worried about being busted down, either. I'm worried about being grounded and rotated stateside."

Steelyard was unsympathetic. "You'll probably get both. Regardless, you have to take your lumps in whatever form they're administered. You're the one who exceeded the mission parameters."

Gil looked up from lacing his boots. "I wasn't told she was pregnant, Chief."

Steelyard started to speak but paused. "Are you saying Lerher knew?"

"After he bragged up and down about how they've been listening to Al-Nazari's phone calls—what do you think the prick knew? The guy withheld pertinent information about a target that took me by surprise inside the kill zone. He knowingly sent me in there at a disadvantage."

"Okay," Steelyard conceded. "Maybe he did, but that doesn't mean you rewrite foreign policy out there in the field so you can make a personal point. Jesus, Gilligan, you abducted an Iranian national! You *know* how that could play internationally. Not to mention you brought a living witness to an assassination back with you."

"So let Lerher shoot her if he's got the balls," Gil said, getting pissed. "We'll bury her here on the fuckin' base with nobody the wiser. Hell, I'll dig the fuckin' hole for the prick!"

"It doesn't work that way, Gil, and you know it."

Gil got to his feet. "So how's it work, Chief? Tell me! It's okay to blow a pregnant woman away in the middle of fucking nowhere when nobody's lookin', but back here by the light of day it's against our moral code? Shit! You don't get to have it both ways. Pick one!"

"This is what we do," Steelyard rejoined. "Sometimes the job requires us to get our hands dirty. If you can't hack that, then I suggest you find another line of work, cowboy!"

Gil knew he'd made a mistake, but he knew equally there was no other way he could have played it. He would have sooner died than execute the Sherkat woman under those circumstances. It was a shit-packed submarine sandwich at both ends, and he'd been forced to take a bite. Only he took that bite from the middle this time, and now everybody was pissed.

"Point taken." He shrugged into his ACU and zipped it up. "Do they have photos of the target area yet?"

Steelyard drew a breath, forcing himself to decompress. "Yeah. So far, no Iranian forces have moved into the area. It would have been the perfect op with perfect execution if not for your lack of judgment. Head Shed's impressed with your body count and overall success. They're going to confirm all the KIAs to your official tally . . . for whatever that's worth to you."

Gil shrugged it off. "I'm not looking to win any contests. If the other shooter had proofed his scope against the sun, I'd be dead."

Steelyard wiped his nose and turned for the door. "No accounting for luck in combat. Now let's get you over to debrief before they send the MPs looking for us."

As they walked across the air base, Gil noticed a lot of activity inside the hangar on the far side of the tarmac. "What the hell's going on over there?"

Steelyard glanced briefly in that direction and continued walking. "Bank Heist is on for zero hundred hours. From what we hear, the ransom drop for Sandra was a goat fuck. But we've got a solid lead from NCIS that says she might be in Waigal, so we're moving against the village at first light. Crosswhite's in command."

"Waigal?" The hair on Gil's neck stood up. "That's deep in Indian country."

"Maybe so," Steelyard said, "but that won't be your problem. You're sitting this one out."

"It's sittin' that hurts, Chief. I can still run, jump, and swim as well as ever."

Steelyard paused to light up his Cohiba. "Your ass has nothing to do with it. You've got heat on you right now, and this mission doesn't need the extra attention . . . besides, I need to hold somebody in reserve who knows the parameters in case of a goat fuck in Waigal Valley. Hell, we might both end up busted down before this tour is over."

GIL ENTERED THE same room where he had received mission overview for Operation Tiger Claw, finding Agent Lerher and Captain Metcalf seated at a table waiting for him.

Lerher looked visibly wound up. "Have a seat, Master Chief."

Gil saluted Captain Metcalf and took a seat on the edge of the folding metal chair with his arm over the back of it, leaning slightly to the left to keep his balance.

"Do you need a cushion?" Lerher asked, trying to sound patient.

Gil looked at him. "Nope."

Lerher stole a glance at Metcalf, realizing by Gil's response that he wasn't about to apologize for bringing the Sherkat woman back with him. She was still in surgery having her clavicle repaired, but the report that Lerher had received on her condition minutes before entering the building had been favorable, and there didn't seem to be any immediate threat to the pregnancy.

He reached out to switch on the small video camera resting on a tripod near the edge of the table.

"Okay," he said, fishing a number of high-resolution photos from a file. The photos were no more than an hour old. "We'll start at the beginning. I need you to indicate on these photos exactly where you landed, where you stashed your jump gear, et cetera. As you know, Master Chief, it's important that you provide as much detail as possible."

"I thought you wanted me to start at the beginning," Gil said, glancing at the camera.

Lerher looked up from the photos. "Did something occur aboard the plane or during your descent that we need to know about?"

"I don't consider that the beginning either," Gil replied, his gaze set. From his demeanor, no one would have guessed that his commanding officer was seated only a few feet away.

Lerher sat back. "Okay. What do you consider to be the beginning?"

"The last time we were in this very room," Gil said. "When you withheld *pertinent* information from me about one of the people I was ordered to assassinate."

Lerher stiffened at the word *assassinate*, which was not generally used in this formal setting. He could see Gil was attempting to take control of the debrief by going immediately on the offensive. "Master Chief, nothing pertinent was withheld. You were given everything you needed to carry out the mission. Now, getting back to—"

"Staying on point—" Gil interrupted, his tone peremptory, "you sent me into Iran to assassinate a pregnant woman without informing me of her condition. It is your *responsibility* to do everything within your power to make sure that nothing appears in my scope that is not supposed to be there, nothing that could cause me to hesitate before squeezing the trigger or to question my purpose for being in country."

Lerher drew a breath, preparing to retort.

"Continuing!" Gil went on. "The unforeseeable is *my* responsibility, but you *willfully* withheld *pertinent* information, for reasons as to which I can only guess. Never mind trying to deny what you knew right now. Evidence as to what you did or did not know will be provided at my court-martial—which I will request rather than willingly accept any sort of demotion or disciplinary action. Have I made myself clear on this point, Agent Lerher? As you've asked me to provide you with as much detail on camera as possible, I am attempting to do precisely that."

Lerher straightened. "No one is seeking disciplinary action at this—"

"That's not what I hear." Gil's military bearing was firmly set. "At this time I am requesting representation from the Judge Advocate General's office." He turned his attention to Captain Metcalf. "Sir, under the Uniform Code of Military Justice I have the right to representation during any questioning that may lead to criminal prosecution. Given the parameters of the mission in question and the nature of my orders, which I carried out to the letter, I make that formal request at this time."

Captain Metcalf signaled for Lerher to turn off the camera, and Lerher wasted no time in doing so.

Metcalf laced his fingers on the tabletop. "Is that really how you want this to go, Gil?"

"In all honesty, sir?"

"Well, I don't want you lying to me, son."

"If I'm going down, sir, it's my intention to try and take this lying son of a bitch down with me. I may fail in the attempt, sir, but at least he'll be finished in SOG, and that just might save some other SEAL's life down the line . . . sir."

Lerher bristled, but he held his tongue, knowing that Metcalf's authority trumped his own in this matter. What he did not want was a JAG officer present during debrief, and Metcalf was the only hope of preventing that now.

Metcalf rocked back and crossed his arms. "Would you take that approach if it was I who ordered you be kept in the dark concerning the Sherkat woman's pregnancy?"

This took Gil completely by surprise. "Sir?"

"Would you still be requesting a JAG officer if you knew it was I who ordered you be kept in the dark?"

Lerher was hard-pressed to hide his satisfaction. More than that, he was shocked that Metcalf had come to his aid by accepting responsibility himself. Now the smartass Shannon was as good as gone.

Gil was briefly nonplussed. He felt betrayed from every angle, but he couldn't bring himself to go on the offensive against his captain. "No, sir," he heard himself say.

"Very well," Metcalf said rocking forward again. "Mr. Lerher, replace that memory card and give it to me. We'll start over."

Over the next few hours, the debrief went smoothly. Gil described the mission down to the very last detail, and Lerher was as magnanimous as he could be, even offering Gil praise on two separate occasions. Nothing more was said about the Sherkat woman in terms of his exceeding the mission parameters, but Gil knew that topic was not important to the debrief. The analysis would come later, and the disciplinary action soon afterward.

Fuck it, he told himself. He would retire. Let them fight their own wars from now on. Marie would finally get her wish.

"Thank you, Master Chief," Lerher said in conclusion. "That'll be all for now."

Gil got to his feet, saluted Captain Metcalf, then turned on his heel and left the room.

"Well, the question now," Lerher said, gathering up his materials, "is what to do about the Sherkat woman."

"I wouldn't worry about her," Metcalf remarked. "By the time she's shared her inside information with us concerning the drug trade over there, I'm sure she'll have proven herself a valuable asset. We might even manage to put her to work for our side."

Lerher had long thought of this, but he wasn't about to allow that to be used as pretext for Gil's exceeding mission parameters. He couldn't have word getting out that his operatives were flouting his hegemony. "That's a possibility. How do you prefer we handle the disciplinary action against Master Chief Shannon? Would you like to review my recommendations before I send them up the chain?"

Metcalf made a thoughtful face, then shook his head. "No, it wouldn't be productive for you write up anything negative ... particularly since I'll be recommending him for a Bronze Star."

Lerher darkened. "I'm afraid I don't understand, Captain."

"That's because you're a spook," Metcalf said, getting to his feet and straightening his desert ACU jacket. "Spooks don't understand the military. You people are too busy exploiting it for your own professional gain. Master Chief Shannon exceeded his mission parameters because you made a very basic mistake. I'm not talking about the aspect of pertinent information—an argument which may or may not fly, depending on the review board. I'm talking about an altogether different argument, an argument which *will* fly, particularly after any testimony that I provide at a court-martial. You see, there's an old rule in the American military that you're apparently unaware of."

Lerher sat staring up at him, his eyes half-lidded.

"A commanding officer is not to give an order that he knows will not be followed. If he gives such an order, and the order is not followed, the commanding officer is equally responsible. So my question to you, Agent Lerher, is this: Are you willing to accept equal responsibility for Master Chief Shannon's failure to assassinate a pregnant woman? If not, I suggest you keep your fucking mouth shut . . . otherwise I'll make it my mission to run you out of SOG myself. Now, I'm happy to write you a recommendation before you go, but I'd like you out of my theater within the next twelve hours."

24

AFGHANISTAN,
Jalalabad Air Base

Gil arrived in the hangar as it was growing dark, feeling more pissed off than he had in years. Not only was he out of Bank Heist, but before the end of the week he'd probably be back at Hampton Roads, where he'd be stuck cooling his heels until the end of his enlistment, and all because some spook in a suit thought he was Michael Corleone. He found Crosswhite chatting it up with another SEAL, both of them partially geared up, M4s over their shoulders.

"Gimme a fuckin' smoke," he said, putting out his hand.

Crosswhite took a crinkled pack of Camels from his ACU and shook one loose. "How'd it go?"

"Fuckin' shitty." He bummed Crosswhite's lighter and fired up the cigarette. "They're gonna ground me."

"You sure?"

"Writing's on the fuckin' wall." He took a long drag from the cigarette and stood fuming. "Sonofabitch!"

The other SEAL bummed a smoke as well. His name was Leskavonski, but his team members called him Alpha—short for Alphabet. He was young, only twenty-four with blond hair and blue eyes. "Is it because of the Sherkat woman, Chief?"

Gil nodded.

"Why'd you bring her back? She go into labor or something?"

"Because she'd seen my face."

Alpha's eyebrows soared. "They're pissed because you brought her back instead of wasting her ass?"

"You shoot an armed *haji* walking in the wrong direction, and it's off to fuckin' Leavenworth for twenty years," Gil bitched. "But refuse to shoot a pregnant woman, and you can kiss your fuckin' career good-bye. I'm fuckin' done."

Alpha exchanged looks with Crosswhite. "Fuck, I guess we know what's in store for us if Bank Heist doesn't come off."

Crosswhite grimaced. "Was it that fucker Lerher?"

"Who the fuck else?" Gil took another long drag.

"I never trusted that prick."

"Yeah, well, Metcalf had his fuckin' back." He spat in disgust. "I can't figure it out. He never struck me as a company man."

"Maybe he's looking to retire," Crosswhite ventured. "Get himself a job in the private sector with the big money. I hear Lerher's got real connections."

That made Gil's blood boil all the more. "I might just pay his ass a visit when we're both civilians again." Of course, he was only running his mouth. There was nothing to be done about the crooked machinery of government or the infinite supply of bastards looking to exploit it. Over the years, Gil had had his own opportunities to take advantage of it, and he'd let them all pass. So maybe he had only himself to blame, but he didn't want anything he hadn't earned for himself. And he sure as hell wasn't the kind of man to elevate himself on the corpse of a woman with a baby in her belly.

So let Lerher strut around like king shit—Metcalf, too, for that matter. At least the spook cocksucker hadn't gotten his way this time. This time he'd had to answer for himself, even if only in some small way, and by the time Crosswhite and Alpha got finished spreading the story, the sorry prick would be lucky to find anyone within SOG willing to work with him.

"So how the fuck are you guys set?" Gil flicked the cigarette away. "Ready to rock and roll those motherfuckers in the Waigal Valley?"

Crosswhite dropped his own smoke and stepped on it. "We got a six-hour hump just getting up to that fucking village. You seen the sat photos? Fucking place is built on a mountain ridge. Looks like a scene from Lord of the fucking Rings."

Gil had been over the entire op with Steelyard. The rescue team would dismount the helos at the bottom of the valley where the enemy couldn't hear the rotors—and even if they did, the helos would be far enough to the south not to cause suspicion; Army helicopters frequently passed through that region. If all went according to plan, the ten-man team would arrive at the village just before dawn, giving them time to reconnoiter the target area and make whatever tactical adjustments necessary.

The plan itself was relatively simple: silently neutralize any sentries, move into the village, kill any and all Taliban fighters stupid enough to show themselves, secure Sandra Brux, and call for evac. They expected a few dozen fighters max, because the village wasn't exactly large or easily accessed, but there was no way to be sure. They might well walk into the village entirely unopposed and find that Sandra had never been there. Then again, they might be going up against Fortress Waigal.

The greatest risk of all, of course, was that Sandra would be executed before they could reach her. If that happened, everyone involved would likely face a court-martial for acting without orders. Crosswhite and Steelyard had offered to take full responsibility if that happened, but none of the SEALs or Night Stalkers would likely allow it. They were determined to succeed together or stand trial together.

Gil knew they might well stand trial even if the mission was a resounding success. If the dead Taliban's DNA results had been sent through the proper channels, this mission wouldn't be getting the green light for at least another few days—if at all. The coneheads in the State Department had some kind of magic mathematical formula they used for weighing confidence against the potential for failure, and they got cranky whenever they weren't allowed to apply it.

Had Sandra been a politician or a civilian journalist, neither DEVGRU nor SOAR would have considered putting together an unauthorized rescue mission, but Sandra was one of their own, and she was a woman . . . and the Jessica Lynch story was evidence enough that captivity for a woman went above and beyond what any soldier should be forced to endure for his or her country. Every man involved in this mission was fully prepared to give his freedom and or his life in exchange for even the chance to bring her out.

One thing was certain: no matter what the result of Operation Bank Heist, everyone from the Head Shed on up would know and understand that the special ops community would not hesitate to take care of their own, and their attempt alone would be enough to send that message loud enough and clear enough to leave a lasting impression on future generations of State Department coneheads and politicians.

A Humvee pulled up in front of the hangar. Chief Steelyard got out on the driver's side. He came stalking in from the dark looking like he had a very definite purpose, the cherry of his cigar glowing bright red. "Alpha, get the men assembled in the briefing room."

Alpha said, "Aye, aye," and turned on his heel.

Steelyard turned on Gil. "I need you to run that Humvee back to Operations for me. Then find something to do for the next four hours while we get this mission off the ground."

Gil cocked an eyebrow, instantly pissed. He was not a valet, not even for Chief Steelyard, and especially not in that tone of voice.

Steelyard took the cigar from his mouth and stuck out his chest. "Don't make me pull rank on you, Master Chief." Even though they were the same grade, Steelyard had held that grade far longer than Gil, so technically he outranked him.

Crosswhite took a subtle step back, thinking the two might finally come to blows.

Gil held Steelyard's gaze for a long moment, thought better of a confrontation, and left the hangar angry enough to kill somebody. Word must have already come down that he was to be rotated back stateside, and it never took long for a body to become *persona non grata* in this man's Navy.

He walked out onto the tarmac and jerked open the door of the Humvee to see Captain Metcalf seated on the passenger side. For a moment, he didn't know what to do.

"Well, don't just stand there, Master Chief."

"Sir!" Gil mounted up, sitting painfully on his ass and shutting the door as Metcalf struck a match to light up one of Steelyard's fine Cuban cigars.

"You understand," Metcalf remarked casually, "that I am not here. Correct?"

"Yes, sir."

Metcalf motioned for Gil to pull out.

"You won't be disappointed to learn that Mr. Lerher has elected to leave the ATO," Metcalf went on. "Your mission into Iran will be listed as complete, and your kills will be credited to your tally.

Beyond that, there will be no more talk of what never took place. I'll recommend you for the Bronze Star to make it look good, but I don't expect it to be approved, nor should you."

"Thank you, sir, but I don't understand what—"

"I know you have questions, Gil, but you're going to have to live without the answers. I walk a very fine line sometimes, and how I choose to walk that line is my own damn business. Understood?"

"Yes, sir."

"Good. The bottom line in this instance is that only a fourteen-carat son of a bitch gives the order to assassinate a pregnant woman, and I won't have a man like that in my theater. Now, you can drop me off at Operations and then head back to your quarters for some sleep—that's an order. This jeep is mine, so you hang onto it until tomorrow. You'll be my aide de camp for the next couple of days while your ass heals up. Can you live with that?"

"Aye, sir."

"Good." Metcalf puffed at the Cohiba. "My aide is on his way to Kabul for some oral surgery, and I don't much feel like doing my own dog robbing while he's convalescing. He's having four wisdom teeth pulled at once. Can you imagine that? Jesus!"

Gil laughed. "My wife had it done that way, sir. It's a bitch, no two ways about it."

25

AFGHANISTAN,
Jalalabad Air Base

Gil parked the Humvee in front of his quarters and went inside. The bullet wound to his ass was throbbing like hell, and he was still smarting over the bullshit debrief with Lerher, but this was mostly due to a bruised ego now that Metcalf had fixed the problem. The incident with Steelyard was already forgotten. SEALs were harsh with one another from time to time, like wolves in a pack snarling over a fresh kill. It was rare that anyone was ever bitten, and hard feelings rarely endured. Steelyard had his reasons for the way he handled certain situations, same as Gil. They were warriors, not grade school teachers.

He found his satellite phone and sat down on the edge of a chair, debating whether to call Marie, debating because he didn't *want* to talk to her—he *needed* to, and he rarely felt that need while on deployment. Such a need bespoke of an emotional vulnerability, and a man couldn't afford emotional vulnerabilities in this environment. Still, a need was a need, and unfilled needs could fester into larger problems. He made the call, knowing it would be about nine o'clock in the morning back in Montana.

"Hello?"

"Hey, baby, it's me."

"How are you?" she asked, sensing at once a heaviness in his voice.

"It's been a rough day."

She knew better than to ask specific questions, but she didn't much care. "You didn't lose anyone, did you?"

"No, nothing like that," he said, his voice sounding thin to him.

"Well, I'm glad you called," she said, giving him time. "Oso just came into the kitchen. I think he can tell from my tone when I'm talking to you."

"I refused to carry out an immoral order."

"Well, good for you. I'm proud of you."

"I never thought I'd . . ." He gritted his teeth, hard put to conceal his emotions.

"It's nothin' to be ashamed of, baby."

He gripped his temples. "Listen, baby . . . you may hear somethin' on the radio tomorrow . . . or see somethin' in the paper . . . I dunno . . . but don't worry. I ain't involved in anything right now . . . not for at least the next forty-eight hours."

"I never listen to the news when you're gone. You know that."

"Well, in case some dumbass calls or somebody says somethin' at the store. Humor me a little, will ya?"

She laughed softly in his ear. "Aye, aye, sir."

He simmered down at the sound. "I just don't want you to worry."

"Well, that's an easy fix," she said helpfully. "Take an assignment at Hampton Roads until your enlistment's over."

He lowered his head, knowing he'd walked right into it. "I've got three more years until my twenty, baby. I'd lose my mind at Hampton Roads."

"All right," she said evenly, "then stop sayin' you don't want me to worry. A forty-eight-hour reprieve ain't nothin' to me, Gil. I don't take no comfort in it. If there's an emergency ten minutes from now, you'll be the first one on the damn helicopter, and you know it."

"Damn, woman. I called you 'cause I was feelin' down."

More of her gentle laughter. "How ya feelin' now?"

"Like paddlin' your backside."

"Then I guess it's a good thing you're callin' me from the moon," she said breezily.

He laughed. "I ain't *that* far."

"Well, you're far enough all the same. What time is it where you're at, anyway?"

"Nice try," he said.

She laughed again, enjoying teasing him. "I'm a trier, you know that. Mama says hi."

"Give 'er my love." He glanced up to see Steelyard through the window, coming toward the building with his cigar glowing. "Listen, baby, I gotta go. I love you."

"Got your boots back on the ground now?"

"Yes, ma'am."

"All right then. Love you, too."

He was off the phone a few moments later and opening the door for Steelyard. "They about ready to go over there?"

Steelyard grunted as he stepped into the room. "Nothing left to do but roll the birds onto the tarmac. You don't have any booze hidden around here anywhere, do you?"

"Ain't I in enough trouble?"

"Shit, Gilligan, you came out of this smelling like a rose."

Gil put his hands in his pockets. "Would you have shot 'er, Chief?"

Steelyard snatched the cigar from his teeth and looked him in the eyes. "I'd have blown her shit away."

Gil nodded and looked at the floor.

"And then I'd have spent the rest of my fucking life waking up to her face," the older man went on. "So what's that tell you? Anyhow, you made sure that's not going to happen to you. Listen, I support whatever keeps my SEALs alive and out of trouble. That's what I told Metcalf, and that's what I'm telling you. So let it go—it's over. I told Crosswhite what's up, and he understands why I jumped your shit. I didn't want him thinking you'd gone soft."

"Hell," Gil said. "He knows I'd never beat up on an old man."

"By the way," Steelyard said. "The Iranian broad went into labor half an hour after surgery . . . so congratulations. It's a boy. Damn kid will probably grow up to hunt your ass down in twenty years. That or drive a nuke into Times Square."

Gil smiled. "Ever heard the parable about the partisan and the horse?"

"Yeah, I've heard the damn thing." He stuck the cigar back into his teeth. "Don't play granddaddy with me, boy. What you know about life, I can fit under my foreskin."

26

AFGHANISTAN,
Nuristan Province, Waigal Valley

After fast-roping from two different Night Stalker helos to the valley floor six miles south of Waigal Village, Captain Crosswhite and eight SEALs from SEAL Team Six made their way two miles northward over rugged, forested terrain. Along for the ride was their Afghan interpreter, Forogh. He was as much a member of the team as any of them, equally armed and wearing the same multicam ACUs.

The column was stretched out over roughly eighty yards along the winding mountain trail, everyone wearing an IBH helmet with integrated radio headset and night-vision goggles. Their primary weapons were suppressed M4s. Most of them carried a variety of secondary weaponry as well, along with assorted types of explosives.

Alpha was walking point when the bleating of a goat caused him to stop short. He held up a fist and lowered himself into a crouch at the edge of the trail, then called Crosswhite forward over the radio. The rest of the team found cover among the rocks and trees.

Crosswhite arrived and took a knee beside Alpha. "What do we got?"

"Goats," Alpha said in a low voice—whispers carried in the dark. "Every fucking goat in Afghanistan, I think."

Crosswhite scanned the clearing ahead where a rock slide had shattered the forest centuries before. He saw what looked like hundreds of goats scattered among the rocks, most of them resting peacefully with their forelegs folded in front of them. A few kids wandered about. "What the fuck are they doing here?"

Alpha pointed out a pair of goat herders bedded down beneath a lone tree near the stream that ran through the rocks. Then he spotted two more herders fifty yards farther off, bedded down at the tree line where the forest began again. "Can we cut through these animals without waking those men up?"

Forogh arrived to take a knee between them, resting a hand on Crosswhite's shoulder. "No. The herd will spook and make a lot of noise if we try to cut through. They are very jumpy animals." His accent was thick, but he was easily understood. "I am afraid this is a problem. Do you see the goats sleeping uphill to both sides of the gorge? Going around them will take a lot of time. We'll have to go very far up the hill to avoid spooking them."

"Then fuck it," Alpha said. "Let's take out the herders from here and keep moving."

Crosswhite shook his head. "This is an unauthorized mission. We can't go murdering anybody. We'll have to think of another way. What if we just crawl slowly through them, Forogh?"

Forogh shook his head. "That is a bad risk. Wait a moment . . ." He rose up for a better look into the clearing. "Something is wrong here."

Aside from the odor of goat shit, the scene looked innocent enough to Crosswhite. "What is it?"

Forogh crouched back down. "They don't all look like goat herders to me."

Crosswhite strained his eyes, trying to discern in his greenish-black field of vision what Forogh was seeing that he was not. All four men wore herder's robes. There was an AK-47 leaning against the tree in the center of the clearing, but the land was hostile and this was to be expected. He checked his watch then double-checked the GPS he was using to keep track of their position. So far, they were keeping to the schedule, but they were beginning to lose time now, and the steepest part of their ascent still lie ahead of them. "How do you know they're not herders?"

"Because I was a goat herder," Forogh said. "These men are not goat herders . . . at least not all of them."

"Then why all the fucking goats?"

"Wait here." Forogh began to creep forward.

Crosswhite knew Forogh from around the base, but he had never worked with him in the field. "Does that *haji* know what the fuck he's doing?" he asked Alpha.

"If he says something's wrong," Alpha replied, "I believe him—we should let him do his thing."

Crosswhite crawled forward on his belly to stretch out with his M4 covering the man sleeping near the AK-47. Innocent goat herders or not, if one of them came awake and grabbed for that weapon, he'd have to go.

Forogh slipped up to a goat and crouched beside it, stroking its neck for more than a minute before finally coaxing it to its feet, holding it by the horn and guiding it along through the crowd. Using the goat as an escort, he was able to pass through the herd without spooking the rest of the animals. He crept to within ten feet of the tree where the herders slept and crouched behind a rock, letting the goat go and cradling his M4.

A moment later, Crosswhite heard him speaking softly over the radio net. "We can take these men. They're heroin smugglers—using the herd for cover. There will be more of them up the trail guarding their cargo. They're probably headed for Waigal the same as us."

"How do you know that?" Crosswhite said.

"I can't explain right now. You'll have to trust me."

Crosswhite slid back into cover to confer with Alpha. "What the fuck do you make of that?"

"If he says they're smugglers, I believe him."

"Well, that alone doesn't give us the right to kill them," Crosswhite said.

"You're in command," Alpha replied with a shrug.

By now, the rest of the team had closed ranks, and the column was stretched over no more than fifty feet. All of them keeping watch in every direction.

Crosswhite got back on the net. "Forogh, I have to know why you think they're smugglers before I can authorize taking them out."

After a slight pause, Forogh replied, "They *look* like smugglers."

Crosswhite looked at Alpha, feeling the devil beginning to bite at his ass. "What the fuck am I supposed to do with that?"

Alpha didn't need to think it over. "I trust him, Captain."

"You willing to risk prison on his advice?"

"I've risked my life on his advice more than once, and I'm still alive."

Crosswhite drew a breath and made his decision. "Forogh, how do you suggest we deal with these fucking goats?"

"Can you make your way over here the same as I did?" Forogh asked.

"Christ if I know. Stand by." He looked at Alpha. "Here goes nothing. Watch those *hajis* on the tree line."

Crosswhite crept out to a goat and crouched beside it the same as Forogh had done and began stroking its muzzle, making his way down the animal's neck. When he seemed to have the goat's confidence, he coaxed it to its feet and tried taking it by the horn. The animal immediately jerked its head away and butted him in the leg, its horn thudding against the suppressed HK Mark 23 pistol strapped to his thigh. He grabbed the horn again, this time much more firmly, and stood still, waiting to see what the animal would do. It bleated in protest, but this did not seem to rile the others nearby, so he set out along the same path as Forogh, leading the reluctant goat. They had another brief wrestling match along the way, but Crosswhite covered the distance to the rock and let the animal go, crouching beside Forogh.

"You did that very well," Forogh said.

"I felt like a fucking idiot," Crosswhite muttered. "So what's next? We can't bring the rest of the team through like that."

"Kill those two men," Forogh said, pointing around the rock.

Crosswhite looked at him. "How do you know they're not goat herders?"

"Kill them, and I will show you."

Crosswhite stared at him for a long moment, then scanned the high ridges along both sides of the canyon. Going around the herd to make their way back down into the trees would take a lot of time, and there was no guarantee they wouldn't spook the herd. Moreover, if Forogh was right about there being a band of smugglers farther up the trail, they could very easily end up in a damn firefight. Had this been a sanctioned mission with UAV overwatch, there would have been no problem. Infrared would tell them in two seconds whether or not the enemy was waiting up the trail. As it was, however, they were operating the old-fashioned way—on wit and instinct alone.

"Give me your piece," he said.

Forogh took the MK 23 pistol from his own holster and handed it over.

After informing the rest of the team as to his intentions, Crosswhite leaned his M4 against the rock and rose up. He drew his own pistol and checked briefly on the other two men still sleeping forty yards away at the edge of the tree line. He stepped carefully around the rock and crept toward the tree, gripping a pistol in each hand. Each MK 23 was chambered with a .45 caliber and fixed with a high-efficiency marine suppressor. Unlike the carbine's supersonic .223 caliber ammunition, the pistol ammo was subsonic, so there would be no sound at all when he fired, other than the cycling action of the pistols themselves. As an ambidextrous shooter, Crosswhite would—in effect—be able to kill both men with a single shot, thus further limiting the risk of alerting the other men or spooking the goats.

He crept to within four feet of the sleeping men, sighted on both their faces, and squeezed the triggers. Their heads exploded open like a pair of busted cantaloupes, and he dropped into a crouch, whipping around to cover the other two men. No one and nothing stirred. It was like nothing had happened.

Forogh was beside him with his M4 a few moments later, and they traded weapons again.

"Now show me how you know they're smugglers."

Forogh crouched beside the closest corpse and jerked open the dead man's robe to reveal the garb of an Afghan mountain warrior, complete with grenades and a bandolier of AK-47 magazines. "Do you see? They are using the herd as cover. I have seen this before."

Crosswhite breathed a sigh relief and turned to measure the distance between the other two men. "What about them?"

"We should take them alive," Forogh suggested. "They are the real herders. They will be happy to tell us how many men are waiting up the trail."

They reached the sleeping men a short time later to see that one of them was rather old, the other in his late twenties maybe. Crosswhite stepped hard on the younger man's throat and pressed the suppressor into his eye socket. Forogh clamped a hand over the old man's mouth, and put the pistol against his head, speaking harshly to both of them in hushed Pashto.

Both herders nodded their heads in fervent understanding, clearly petrified. They were rolled onto their bellies, and their hands were secured behind their backs with nylon zip ties.

Needing no prompting from Crosswhite, Forogh began to question the old man at once. "We can call the team forward," he said at length. "There are eleven smugglers with five burros bedded down fifty meters up the trail. The old man says *probably* no one is standing guard, but he doesn't know for sure. In the morning, they will continue up the trail to Waigal Village. Apparently, the village is expecting them sometime tomorrow."

Crosswhite was crouched across from Forogh, watching around warily. "Ask him where the fuck they came from. Why isn't there any goat shit back the way we came?"

Again, Forogh questioned the old man at length. "He says they travel an old goat trail down the eastern rim up that way." He thumbed north over his shoulder. "He says his people use . . . *have* used this clearing to rest and water their herds for centuries. He says the Taliban began to move opium through this area about six months ago, for a new market in Tajikistan. I believe he is telling the truth."

"Okay," Crosswhite said. "What will they do if we leave them alive?"

"Are you are asking me or them?"

"You."

"I think they will take the herd back the way they came, up the ridge to the east and down the other side into the next valley."

Crosswhite called the rest of the team forward, and the SEALs took up covering positions all around. By now, the goats were aware of their arrival and didn't seem to care one way or another. He broke out a map and gave orders for the old man's hands to be freed. He shined a red light on the map, and Forogh made sure the old man understood where they were.

"Ask him which direction they'll go," Crosswhite said.

The old man pointed out their route.

"Okay, Forogh, tell him this: They are to wait here until noon tomorrow before they leave. You tell him if they leave any sooner than that, they will be shot. Make sure he understands."

Forogh admonished the old man, and the old man nodded his head up and down, babbling away. "He says he understands. They will do as you order. He says they want no trouble. They love America."

Crosswhite nodded. "Yeah, everybody loves America. Just make sure they know they'd better stay their asses in this fucking clearing until high noon tomorrow."

"He promises to do as you order," Forogh says. "Also, he says you smell like cigarette smoke and asks if you will share some of your American cigarettes with him."

Crosswhite chuckled. Taking a pack of Camels from his arm pocket, he shook out half the pack and offered them to the old man. "Tell him not to blaze up before first light."

"Blaze up?"

"Not to light any cigarettes before morning."

Forogh translated and the old man shook his finger, babbling away. "He asks you not to worry. He says he fought against Russia with the Mujahideen and knows how to smoke safely in the night. Also, he would like to know if they may have the weapons of those two dead men by the tree."

Crosswhite nodded. "Tell him they are a gift to him, but he is not to touch them until morning."

Forogh made sure the old man understood. "He asks one more thing. He asks if you go up the valley to bring back the American woman."

Every hair on Crosswhite's body stood on end. "Ask him what he knows."

"He says you need to hurry. The HIK has moved into the village."

27

AFGHANISTAN,
Nuristan Province, Waigal Village

Sandra was deep in an opium haze when Naeem and Aasif Kohistani stepped into the room and stood over the bed. Naeem held out a kerosene lantern so they could get a good look at her, sweating with fever, her leg badly infected. She opened her bleary eyes just long enough to mumble "fuck you" before closing them again and drifting off.

"It is a good thing Brother Nuristani sent for me," Kohistani said. "Soon the leg will rot, and the poison will spread. She'll be dead soon . . . without proper care."

Naeem was still seething over the Americans' failure to pay the ransom as promised. He knew nothing of Jackal's death or of the arrests that had been made, only that the intermediary had not delivered the money to his contact in Kabul as planned. It was possible the intermediary had kept the money for himself, but he doubted it. The man in Karzai's office was reported as very reliable, and there would have been plenty of money to go around without the need for a double cross.

When Kohistani had arrived earlier in the day, Naeem had at first grown even more incensed, vowing to hang Sabil Nuristani over the fire by his heels, but after Badira reported that the woman would die long before another ransom attempt could be made, he had silently thanked Allah for his fortune. Perhaps he could work some kind of a deal with the Hezbi man to avert a total loss.

"Our nurse is not very good," he mumbled, disgusted with Badira's lack of medical skill.

"It is not the nurse, brother," Kohistani said gently. "It is the lack of medicine. And the raw opium she is smoking is suppressing her immune system."

Naeem scarcely understood how an immune system even functioned. "How much is she worth to you in this condition?" he asked gruffly.

Kohistani placed a friendly hand on his shoulder and smiled. "You should never have tried to ransom my prisoner."

"You left her with me," Naeem said. "I thought you'd finished with her after the interrogation. I was going to split the profits with you."

"I am not interested in profits," Kohistani said, glancing at his bodyguard Ramesh to make sure he was ready to kill Naeem if it became necessary. "I have much bigger plans for this woman than something as trivial as money."

"Money is not trivial," Naeem said, his gaze narrowing. "Perhaps if the Hezbi wasn't so secretive about its plans . . ."

"We are secretive for good reason," Kohistani said easily. "I will send you some rifles and medicine for your men."

"No," Naeem said, backing away. "That is not enough. She is

worth very much more to you than that. You have contacts with Al Jazeera. You will put her on the television and bring yourself much glory. I deserve a better reward for capturing her. So far you have given nothing."

Kohistani stepped forward again, putting his arm around the younger man's shoulder to guide him gently to the next room, where they sat down at the table in the light of the lantern. "We do not seek glory, you and I. We are servants of Allah. We are fighting a jihad . . . and anything we gain from this woman should be used for the glory of Allah alone." He watched Naeem's eyes, expecting an argument. "Do you wish to know why the ransom was not paid? I will tell you why—it was Allah's will that it not be paid. He, too, has greater plans for this woman." He paused again, long enough to accept the hot cup of tea one of his other men had just brought into the hut. "Now, my brother . . . I want you to turn her over to me in exchange for the rifles and the medicine that I offer—along with the video that you made."

Naeem saw his only chance for glory slipping quickly from his grasp. His uneducated mind raced for a solution to the problem. Defying Kohistani outright could definitely cause long-term problems, but he had to salvage something from the ransom debacle.

"Very well," he said decisively. "The woman is yours, for the rifles and the medicine—but the video is mine. It will take time, but I will sell it to Al Jazeera myself and use the money to help the village."

Kohistani smiled kindly, much preferring to kill Naeem, but the Taliban were still useful to the HIK, so it was worth treating them with patience. He realized that Naeem was an extremely ambitious young man, a Wahhabi fundamentalist with delusions of grandeur. If left to his own devices, he could all too easily become a de facto warlord in the region, and the last thing Kohistani needed was a powerful ignoramus operating inside his sphere of influence. Uneducated zealots were unpredictable, as much a danger to everyone else as to themselves. To make matters worse, Naeem was pride filled and greedy, a borderline psychotic. Kohistani believed he understood very well why this unruly fellow had been sent north by his Taliban mentors in the south—they had wanted to be rid of him and to make him the problem of the HIK.

"Very well, brother," he decided. "I will give you one of the big Canadian sniper rifles and fifty rounds of ammunition in exchange for the video . . . to be delivered with the other rifles and the medicine." Kohistani was talking about a captured .50 caliber McMillan Tac-50.

Naeem's eyes lit up. He would never get another chance to possess such a weapon. "I want one hundred rounds of ammunition."

Kohistani shrugged. "Fifty is all we have, brother, but the ammunition is far easier to come by than the weapon itself. You should accept the offer."

"Very well," Naeem grumbled, already feeling the weapon in his hands. With a rifle such as that, he would be equal to the Americans. He would make their bodies explode the way his cousin Muhammad's body exploded when he'd been shot two years earlier, delivered to his uncle's home in the back of a pickup truck, practically blown in half by a single shot. He ordered one of his men to go and fetch the video. "What will you do with it?"

"I will give it to men who know to use such a prize for the glory of Allah," Kohistani replied, relieved that the young fool sitting before him could be bought so easily with a toy. Now he had what he needed to draw the Americans into his kill zone. Soon, US citizens would be clamoring even louder for their troops to be called home where they belonged. "Now, brother, I must be leaving. We will take the American with us. I trust you don't mind us taking her nurse along to tend to her?"

Naeem shook his head. "They're both yours. The nurse is a widow. She belongs to no one. You will take the American east to Bazarak?"

Kohistani hesitated just a fraction of a second before answering. "No, north to Parun."

"I see," Naeem replied, thinking to himself, *So it's east to Bazarak like I expected.* He knew the HIK had already moved into the Panjshir Valley in force.

They spoke of the jihad as Kohistani patiently finished his tea, treating the young upstart with far more deference than he merited. Within the hour, Sandra was wrapped in blankets and strapped to a battered Russian army stretcher left over from the previous war. Badira was then shaken from a sound sleep in her hut and told she would be leaving with the HIK men who were taking the American pilot north to Parun. She was given time to dress and hurried out the door.

She walked down the narrow trail to the village gate, where she saw four men standing in the darkness bearing Sandra's stretcher.

Naeem exited a nearby hut, preceding Kohistani and holding a lantern head high. "Badira, you will go with them to keep the woman alive."

"There's nothing I can do for her," she said with contempt. "There's no more medicine to give her. Only the opium, and anyone can give her that."

"Then you will give her that whenever she needs it!" Naeem snapped. "Brother Kohistani's men can't be troubled with women's work. They're a war party! Now shut your mouth."

To Badira's immense relief, Sabil Nuristani came hurrying up the trail carrying a lantern of his own. "Wait, Naeem! You cannot send our only nurse away from the village in the middle of the night."

Kohistani stepped forward, speaking to Nuristani in Kalasha. "I will send her back very soon. Have no fear. You have done us a very great service keeping the woman alive. When Badira returns, I will send her with medicine for the village."

"Medicine that he will steal." Sabil stabbed a finger at Naeem.

"I will send enough for all," Kohistani assured him, willing to promise anything that might avert a confrontation between the two antagonists long enough for him and his men to get clear of the village.

"No," Sabil said. "We have sick people here! I am the head man, and I say our nurse does not go!"

Naeem grabbed a stick from one of his men and stepped forward, delivering a vicious strike to the side of Sabil's head. Sabil dropped like a stone, the lantern crashing to the ground next him.

"I should have done that days ago."

Badira ran forward and knelt beside Sabil. "He's dead!" she shouted. "You're a murderer!"

Naeem kicked her away from the body, striking her across the back with the stick. "Obey, woman! Go—and never come back! This is no longer your home!"

28

AFGHANISTAN,
Nuristan Province, Waigal Valley

Crosswhite made sure the team was set, then moved out up the trail with Forogh to recon the smugglers' position. They expected to make contact within fifty or sixty yards, but hadn't gone more than fifty feet before they heard a Pashtun voice speak to them from behind a large tree. Both men froze, bringing their weapons to bear but holding fire, scanning the forest through their NVGs to see the trees coming alive with men picking their way carefully through the darkness.

Forogh stepped forward, answering the Pashtun in a casual voice.

Crosswhite fell back a pace to give him room. The men moving through the trees couldn't see them, but they were obviously maneuvering to outflank the sounds of the voices. He could tell from the harsh tone that the man behind the tree was giving Forogh a hard time, demanding to know who they were and what was going on back at the clearing, keeping his voice loud enough for his men to hone in on his position.

Crouching low, Crosswhite keyed his radio three times without speaking, waited three seconds, and then keyed the radio three times more. This was the signal for Alpha to bring the rest of the team forward expecting a fight. He could see from Forogh's posture that he was prepared to engage the man behind the tree, but the interpreter's voice remained casual. He would have heard the radio signal as well and would know it was his job to buy time for the SEALs to get into position.

Of course, the man behind the tree was doing the same thing for his own people, stalling for as much time as possible. Crosswhite doubted the fellow realized there were any Americans in the area. More likely, he suspected they were tribal bandits looking to steal his cargo. The tree was too big for Crosswhite to get an angle on him, so he would have to trust Forogh to handle the fellow on his own. He quickly sized up the ten men working their way blindly among the rocks and the trees, divided evenly on either side of the trail, assessing that he and Forogh would be surrounded in less than a minute's time.

Alpha and his SEALs drew within visual range, and Crosswhite listened as Alpha assigned them targets from left to right.

The talking between Forogh and the Pashtun stopped abruptly, and the forest was thrown into an eerie silence, both men having run out of bullshit.

Alpha quietly gave the command: "Fire."

The SEALs' suppressed M4s hissed in the darkness, and Crosswhite saw eight Pashtun fighters drop dead across his field of vision. A pair of AK-47s let loose down the slope to his extreme right, but the gunners were taken out an instant later.

A grenade popped on the other side of the tree, and Crosswhite heard it clatter among the rocks behind him as the man took off. Forogh dove behind a rock and Crosswhite threw himself flat against the earth, instinctively aware that he was well within the grenade's kill zone. The force of the explosion lifted him from the ground and threw him against a boulder, knocking the wind from his lungs. He could hear nothing but a high-pitched whine as he struggled to move and then blacked out.

He came to with a white light being shined into his eyes.

"Captain, can you hear me?"

His thoughts were slow to clear. When he could move again, the first thing he did was grab for his groin.

"It's all there, Captain. You're fine. You got your shit rattled—that's all."

"Get me on my feet." He groped clumsily in the dark.

The corpsman kept a firm hand against his chest, holding him down. "No, your brains are scrambled. Keep still."

"What about the guy behind the tree?"

"He's down," Alpha said.

"Forogh?"

"He's fine, Captain. We're intact and the perimeter's secure. Just keep still until you got your shit together."

Alpha stood up and took Forogh aside. "Did that guy say whether there's anyone else nearby—anyone who might have heard the grenade blast?"

"I got the impression they were surprised to find anyone else in the area," Forogh said. "That *should* mean we're okay, but you never know . . . we're in the Hindu Kush."

One of the two SEALs who had been sent forward to locate the pack animals came over the radio: "Alpha, its Trigg. We've got five donkeys about seventy-five yards up the trail. There's nobody else here, but we've got something you should see."

Crosswhite was on his feet again within a few minutes, but he was still fogged, so Alpha retained temporary command. They had to assume they were exposed now, so the mission took on a sense of urgency as they moved out to link up with Trigg and the other SEAL. When they found them, Trigg was standing beside a quintet of hobbled donkeys. The opium cargo was bundled and stacked off to the side of the trail.

"Whattaya got?" Alpha said.

Trigg motioned for him to follow. "I almost walked right into it," he said quietly. He stopped Alpha about forty feet up the trail where it began to narrow and used a handheld laser trip-wire illuminator to illuminate a series of monofilament lines zigzagging across the trail at knee height. The wires showed up white in their night-vision goggles. "Ever seen that before?"

Alpha shook his head in the darkness. "No. Is this how they were covering their approach or what? What's this lead to?"

Trigg turned to face back the way they'd come. "Those two claymores set in the trees there."

Alpha turned to see a pair of M18A1 claymore antipersonnel mines mounted head-high in the trees, one to either side of the trail. It was immediately obvious that anyone who came marching down that trail in the middle of night would have gotten himself and anyone following within fifty feet blown away.

"Drugs are a dirty business," Alpha muttered. "We have to be extra careful now . . . and we're behind schedule."

They disarmed the booby trap, packing the claymores away for safekeeping. The donkeys were set free, and the team formed up to move out with Trigg on point, using the trip-wire illuminator whenever he felt unsure of the trail.

Crosswhite recovered within the hour to resume command. They were racing the sun now, so he kept them moving almost at the double, never stopping to rest, checking the GPS on the move as they ascended ever higher into the mountains. It was a grueling climb, and they sucked their CamelBaks dry. Anyone who fell out to take a piss had to run extra hard to catch up. There would be very little time now to reconnoiter the village and get set up before first light.

Three hours into their ascent, the lead element rounded a bend in the trail and ran head-on into a Pashtun patrol of seven men working their way down the mountain to link up with the opium smugglers.

The Pashtun men had their AK-47s slung over their shoulders, and they were talking casually among themselves when five American commandos came barreling around the bend. Trigg and Crosswhite ran smack into the two lead men of the Pashtun patrol, and all four of them went sprawling, their feet and weapons tangled together in a jumbled mess.

There was a lot of shouting and yelling from the startled Pashtun as they tried to sort out what the hell was going on. Forogh added his own haranguing voice to the fracas, trying to sow extra confusion among the Afghanis, but someone snapped on a flashlight, and the situation went immediately critical. The rest of the American column rounded the bend, and the Pashtun AK-47s were unslung. Within half a second shit was flying everywhere. Men were fighting hand-to-hand with rifle butts and knives, kicking and shoving as everyone fought for space.

Crosswhite bit down hard on the hand of the fellow he had collided with, tasting blood as he fought to straddle the flailing man who beat at his face with his free hand. He finally managed to drive his thumbs deep into the Pashtun's eye sockets and jumped to his feet, only to be knocked over again as Forogh was knocked off balance by a SEAL just joining the fight. The SEAL went flying past them to deliver a vicious butt-stroke to a Pashtun blindly firing his AK-47 in a sweeping horizontal arch. Miraculously, the SEAL was able to cave in the Pashtun's face before he could complete the sweep, saving at least two American lives besides his own. Had Trigg and

Crosswhite been on their feet during the first half of that sweep, both of them would have been cut down.

The last four SEALs to round the bend had a very clear picture of the battle. They could see the last three men in the Pashtun column gripping their AK-47s in terror. Without night vision, they were unable to see what the hell was going on, and therefore had no idea which of the shadowy forms slugging it out on the trail before them were the enemy. The Pashtun broke and ran, and were cut down before they had gone more than a few yards.

The melee ended a few moments later, and Crosswhite grabbed up his M4 calling for everyone to sound off. Everyone was alive, but two SEALs had broken their night-vision goggles in the fight, and another named Fischer had a bullet hole through his left shoulder blade.

"I can make it," Fischer insisted a short time later as the corpsman strapped his upper arm to his side. "Just leave my forearm free so I can reload."

Crosswhite was still spitting Pashtun blood. His face was covered with lacerations, and the bridge of his nose was gashed open and bleeding. "You left-handed, son?"

Fischer shook his head. "No, Captain."

"Small mercies," Crosswhite muttered, selecting three SEALs at random and ordering each of them to trade Fischer all but one of their pistol mags for his M4 ammo. "Okay, listen up," he announced in a low but peremptory voice. "This mission is fast becoming a goat fuck, and there's no telling how many motherfuckers up the trail know we're coming now. So we're gonna take a vote on whether or not to continue. There's ten of us, but if anyone wants to call *no joy*, we'll call the game now without anyone giving you any shit. I'll take full responsibility for the mission and lie my ass off when I get back about who really knew what."

"Nobody votes to go back because of me!" Fischer blurted. "I can make it."

No one else immediately spoke up.

Finally, Alpha cleared his throat, and Crosswhite turned to look at him through his night-vision goggles. "What's on your mind?"

"Is that how they do things over at Delta, Captain? Turn back at the first sign of trouble?"

Crosswhite chuckled. "Let's move it out. We're behind schedule."

29

AFGHANISTAN,
Nuristan Province, Waigal Valley

Halting their descent through the mountain darkness, Sandra and her Hezbi captors listened to the Pashtun AK-47s chattering on the far side of the valley. When the firing subsided after a couple of minutes, a pair of scouts was dispatched to investigate. The column settled in to wait, and Kohistani drew his fighting men close, briefing them to expect an American attack from any quarter. He did not believe in coincidence, and he was not naïve about American UAV capabilities. If the Yankee murderers knew or even suspected that the woman pilot was being held in Waigal Village, one of their drones could be scanning the valley with its infrared cameras at that very moment.

Sandra was coherent enough to discern the change of mood in her captors. Before the rattling of the AK-47s, they were moving smartly down the mountain with a minimum of apparent caution. Now they were stopped and pulled into a tight defensive perimeter encircling her stretcher, whispering back and forth like a pit of agitated vipers, ready to strike in any direction. With only Badira paying her any attention, Sandra began to work at the knotted ropes securing her to the stretcher, readying herself to move if an American rescue team were to appear suddenly. She promised herself that she would summon the strength to get up and run when the time came, despite the opium doping her reflexes and the pain ravaging her leg.

The time dragged on, however, and as the minutes stretched into an hour, her faint adrenaline surge faded to nothing and her determination flagged. Her mind fogged, and the pain began to take over once again. After an hour and a half, she squeezed Badira's arm in the darkness, signaling that she needed another hit from the opium pipe.

Badira ignored her request, knowing that Kohistani would not allow her to strike a match under the circumstances.

As the pain increased, Sandra began to think more clearly. She summoned all of her strength and drew a deep breath: "I'm here!" she screamed in desperation. "I'm here! Come and—!"

A fist slammed into the side of her head, knocking her senseless. Another fighter jumped up and knelt heavily on her diaphragm to prevent her from drawing enough air for another scream in the event she came to.

The scouts returned ten minutes later, reporting to Kohistani that they had found seven dead Pashtun on the trail across the valley. One of the scouts dropped a fistful of spent 5.56 mm shell casings into his hand.

"The Americans killed them all and kept moving up the mountain toward the village," the scout said. "They won't arrive before first light. By the time they discover she's no longer there, we'll have reached the truck."

Kohistani smiled in the darkness. "Allah be praised," he said with great satisfaction, having believed until that moment that the woman's screams had doomed them all. "It is no accident that we are at this place in time, brothers. Allah does not deal in coincidence."

He stepped over to the stretcher, using his own flashlight to check on their prisoner whose left eye was now swollen almost shut from the blow that had silenced her screams. He shined the light in Badira's eyes, telling her, "You should have thought to hold a hand over her mouth."

"Perhaps you should have thought to tell me," Badira retorted.

He rapped her in the face with the butt of the flashlight, splitting her upper lip. "Do not mistake me for a simple village head man," he said, his voice almost friendly. "Now gag the American, and make sure she remains gagged until we reach the truck. If she calls out again, *you* will be held responsible."

30

AFGHANISTAN,
Waigal Village

Shortly before first light, Crosswhite and the SEALs from SEAL Team Six arrived on the southern perimeter of Waigal Village. They were exhausted and out of water, but they were only twenty minutes behind schedule. Crosswhite ordered the corpsman to dole out two time-released Benzedrine capsules to each of the men, then gave orders for Trigg and Alpha to recon the east and west perimeters of the village. The northern periphery of the village was built into the mountain itself, which extended upward another thousand feet.

From their vantage point below the village, Waigal resembled a giant house built from playing cards, each hut looking as though it was built upon the other. Though in reality, each dwelling was built into the steep, rocky slope of the mountain. The village was above the tree line, so tree cover was very sparse. The SEALs would need to move into the village as soon as possible in order to take advantage of their night vision.

Crosswhite crouched behind a boulder, looking up at the village through his NVGs. "That's an imposing sight," he said to Forogh.

"It is," Forogh agreed. "They speak mostly Kalasha here. I don't speak Kalasha."

Crosswhite turned to look at him. "You might have mentioned that before we left the fucking house!"

Forogh shrugged. "It wouldn't have mattered. No one speaks Kalasha except these people." He patted Crosswhite on the shoulder. "Don't worry. Many of them will speak Pashto as well. I doubt very much the Taliban who are holding your pilot are of the Kalasha tribe. It's not their way. You should mention that to your men."

Crosswhite grunted. "We won't kill anyone we don't have to."

He got on the radio: "Bank Heist Two, this is Bank Heist One. Do you read? Over."

The Night Stalkers were quick to respond: "We read you five-by-five, Bank Heist. Over."

"Bank Heist, be advised we are in position and preparing to move on the target."

"Bank Heist Two standing by . . ."

Crosswhite glanced over at Fischer, who crouched behind another boulder gripping a suppressed MK 23 pistol in his free hand. "Good to go?"

Fischer nodded.

Alpha was the first to call in: "Captain, I can't see into the village from over here. The mountain's too steep. All I can see are the fronts of the huts. I've got no movement whatsoever."

"All right," Crosswhite answered. "Work your way back here. Trigg, what do you got?"

"Still maneuvering," Trigg replied. "But so far nothing at all."

"Okay, get back here."

When the team was reassembled, Crosswhite gave them his assessment. "This shit hole is too big to search it hut by hut. We're going to have to take over one of those lone huts near the bottom of the village and get somebody inside to talk. Anybody got a better idea? The clock is running."

Trigg pointed up the mountain. "I vote we take that lone hut just below the village on the ridge. It's isolated enough from the others that we should be able to interrogate the family without disturbing the other huts."

The hut was about half the size of a small one-car garage.

Crosswhite took a last look around and gave the order to move out, leading the way toward the lone hut some ninety yards up the slope. They covered the distance with the night wind blowing cold against them, picking their way over the rough and jagged terrain to arrive outside the hut in less than five minutes. Crosswhite signaled that he would enter first, followed by Alpha and then Forogh. The other seven SEALs would cover the village with their suppressed M4s.

The battered wooden door was not locked. Crosswhite lifted the wooden catch and slipped inside quiet as a ghost, followed closely by Alpha and Forogh. In the greenish-black field of vision, it was immediately obvious there was only one room to the hut. A lone inhabitant lay sleeping on a bunk against the wall on the far side, wrapped in multiple blankets. The room smelt faintly of what Crosswhite could only think to describe as *old people* . . . and an odor similar to rot.

"Shit, I think this one's dead," he muttered.

"I don't think so," Forogh said warily.

Alpha prodded the figure, and Forogh said "wake up" in stern Pashto. The person stirred and coughed beneath the blankets.

"Wake up!" Forogh repeated.

The figure stirred again, making a wet, phlegmy hacking sound beneath the blankets as it began to sit up.

Crosswhite reached out with his gloved hand to pull the blanket away from the face, revealing the severely distorted visage of an old woman, a face that seemed to be caving in on itself. She opened her eyes, and they rolled immediately white with no visible retinas or pupils. She mumbled something in sleepy confusion, her words unintelligible even to Forogh, and wiped at her face with a grotesquely deformed hand, nothing but worn stubs where her thumb and fingers had once been.

Crosswhite looked at Forogh and covered his face with his shemagh. "Is that what I think it is?"

"Jesus Christ!" Alpha blurted in panic, jumping away and falling backward over a chair. "Holy fuck—she's a fucking leper!"

Crosswhite whipped around. "Calm the fuck down!"

"We gotta get the fuck outta here!" Alpha kicked the chair and scrambled away on his hands and knees.

"Relax!" Forogh said, holding his own shemagh over his face. "Ninety-five percent of people are naturally immune."

"The *fuck* you say!" Alpha leapt to his feet and dashed for the door. He stood just outside the hut looking in. "Shit, we've already breathed her fucking air—motherfucker! Look at her fucking face!"

Crosswhite went to the door, hissing under his breath: "You'd better shut the fuck up, boy."

"She's a fucking leper, and we breathed her fucking air!"

Trigg grabbed Alpha from behind, clamping him in a rear naked choke, shutting off the blood to his brain and hauling him off around the other side of the hut into the shadow of an overhanging boulder. Alpha blacked out a few seconds later, and Trigg laid him down on the ground, assigning a SEAL named Speed to keep an eye on him.

Back inside the hut, Forogh began to question the blind woman in Pashto, telling her exactly who they were and not to be afraid. The old woman's responses came in a mixture of Pashto and Kalasha. Her words were slurred and difficult for Forogh to understand.

"I can't tell exactly what she means," Forogh finally said to Crosswhite. "Her verb tenses are confusing. She's either saying the American woman *is* being held in the hut overlooking the rest of the village or she *was* being held there."

"Get her to clarify it," Crosswhite ordered, still rattled by Alpha's unexpected loss of cool.

Forogh shook his head in frustration. "I've tried to five or six times already. She doesn't know the correct word in Pashto, so she keeps telling me in Kalasha."

"Christ Almighty," Crosswhite said. "Are the languages really that different? Fuck, it all sounds exactly the same to me."

Forogh shrugged. "We can move on the building overlooking the rest of the village, or we can take over another hut."

"Shit," Crosswhite said. "Is she going to cause trouble after we leave?"

"I doubt it," Forogh said. "She keeps saying how tired she is. I think all she wants to do is go back to sleep. She probably thinks this is a dream."

Crosswhite looked out the door to see the sky was growing light in the east. The villagers would be waking up soon. "We don't have time. We're moving on the hut overlooking the village. You're sure about that part, right?"

"She seems very clear about what building, yes."

"I guess that's something," Crosswhite said. "Let's go."

When they stepped from the hut, Alpha was back on his feet and looking at the ground. He was very obviously agitated and embarrassed over what had taken place. He stood between Trigg and Speed, each of whom had a hand resting on one of his shoulders.

Crosswhite stepped directly into Alpha's face, their noses almost touching, talking in a low growl. "Do you think you can carry out the rest of this mission, sailor?"

"Aye, sir."

"You jeopardize these men or this mission again, and I'll drop you where you stand. Is that understood?"

Alpha met his gaze. "Aye, sir."

Crosswhite turned to Speed. "This man is your baggage."

Speed nodded. "He'll be fine, Captain. I guarantee it."

"He better be!"

Forogh then briefed them on their objective. The hut overlooking the rest of the village was perched another one hundred fifty yards up the mountain, and they would have to move through the center of the village to reach it, climbing a 9 percent grade and weaving in and out of the conjoined buildings most of the way.

"Forget any flanking maneuvers or splitting up," Crosswhite said. "We don't have the time or the necessary intel for that shit. We're going in strong through the front door, hitting the vault, and fighting our way back out any way we can—just like a fucking bank heist. You see anyone with a weapon, you drop their ass. Now let's move, people. Sandra's up there waiting for us."

They worked their way past the first few huts without seeing anyone, moving upward through a narrow alley toward the second tier of buildings. It was growing light now, and they no longer needed their night vision to see where they were going. A door opened and a man froze in the doorway, eyes wide with fear. Forogh ordered him back inside and the man obeyed without hesitation, gently closing the door and bolting it.

There seemed to be five tiers of huts, more or less, but the mountain's surface was uneven, so it was difficult to discern exactly where they were within the village. All they could do was keep climbing and shifting course toward the northwest. They mounted the third tier and rounded a corner to see a pair of teenage boys standing outside of a hut with AK-47s over their shoulders. Crosswhite sprayed them with automatic fire from his suppressed M4, and they flew backward off of their feet to land with their heads thudding against the wall of the hut.

The column of ten SEALs shuffled past the bodies with the wounded Fischer covering their ass.

A man opened the door to the hut to see what the commotion was about, and Fischer quickly clouted him over the head with his MK 23, knocking him cold and stepping into the hut to see who else might be inside. A woman stood near a table with two small children clinging to her. She looked as though she was about to scream when Fischer aimed the pistol at her face and held a finger to his lips. When he was sure she wasn't going to scream, he dragged her husband inside by the arm and hurried back outside to catch up with the column.

When they finally came to a dead end, they grabbed a man stepping out for water, and Forogh told him where they needed him to take them. The man immediately told them that Sandra was already gone, that she had been taken away during the night. This of course did not go over well with Crosswhite, who all but jammed the suppressor of his pistol down the man's throat, demanding the truth.

The man began to cry, swearing that he was telling the truth.

"Make him take us to the fucking hut!" Crosswhite ordered.

Forogh called the man down, saying, "The Americans need to see for themselves. Take us to the hut so they can do their jobs and leave."

The man led them through an empty hut and out the back door, which opened onto a kind of terrace. Across the terrace was a lone hut with two sleeping teens sitting on the stoop, their heads tilted back against the door, AK-47s propped between their knees.

"Take 'em out," Crosswhite said to Alpha, wanting to find out if the SEAL was back in the game.

Alpha stood in the doorway and shouldered his M4, preparing to fire.

The village guide began to protest.

Crosswhite whipped around and coldcocked him. "Fucking liar! Who posts guards on an empty building?"

Alpha fired a round through each of the teen's foreheads, and they toppled off the stoop with their brains splattered on the door.

The team poured out of the hut and onto the terrace, taking up positions to cover every possible avenue of approach. Crosswhite and Trigg approached the hut and stood listening through the door. The only sound was that of a heavily snoring man. Trigg opened the latch and pushed the door inward, stepping inside with Crosswhite following.

There was a table and chairs in the main room and a curtain that hung down in the doorway to an adjoining room. The SEALs drew their pistols and advanced on the curtain. They pulled it aside and saw a bearded man sleeping in a bed.

Crosswhite was sure he'd seen that room before. He stalked across the room and aimed the suppressor of the MK 23 down into the sleeping man's face. "Wake up, cocksucker!"

Naeem's eyes opened and grew instantly wide with shock.

"Get the photo," Crosswhite said to Trigg, ready to put a round between Naeem's eyes if he so much as twitched.

Trigg produced a blown-up photo made from the rape video. The scar near his left eye was unmistakable. "Well, what the fuck do you know!" he said, flipping his pistol around to grip it by the barrel and using the butt to bash Naeem in the testicles.

Naeem let out with a deep groan and doubled up on the bed.

"Get Forogh in here," Crosswhite ordered.

Trigg left the hut and sent Forogh inside.

"Ask him where they took Sandra."

Forogh looked at Naeem and instantly recognized him from the video. "Where did they take the American woman?" he demanded in Pashto.

"Fuck you!" Naeem snarled in passable English.

Crosswhite bashed in his front teeth with the butt of his M4, and Naeem grabbed his face, howling in pain. "Ask him again!"

"Where's the American woman!"

Naeem shouted something that sounded like, "Pfuck you!"

Trigg came back inside. "Captain, we gotta make a decision. It looks like we got about thirty gunmen working their way up through the village. We lost sight of them as soon as they mounted the second terrace, but they were moving fast. Are we calling for air support?"

"Flex cuff this cocksucker!" Crosswhite ordered. "He's coming with us."

He got immediately on the radio to the Night Stalkers: "Bank Heist Two, this is Bank Heist One. Do you read? Over?"

"Roger that, Bank Heist. Reading you five-by-five. Over."

"Bank Heist, be advised we are in the vault, but the money has been transferred. Repeat. The money is no longer here! However, be advised that we have taken Romeo into custody. Repeat. Romeo is in custody! Over."

"Roger that, Bank Heist. Rotors are turning. We'll be wheels up and headed toward your location in sixty seconds. ETA fifteen minutes. Over."

"Be sure to hold at the outer marker, Bank Heist. We're going to have to shoot our way out of here, and we don't need you taking RPG fire. Will advise when it's safe to enter Waigal airspace. Over."

"Roger. Wilco—will hold at the outer marker until you advise."

31

AFGHANISTAN,
Waigal Village

Crosswhite grabbed their shaken tour guide and looked at Forogh. "Tell this son of a bitch he's leading us out of this fucking rat maze."

Forogh translated, and the guide became frightened, talking very rapidly. When he finished, the fellow dropped to his knees and began to pray.

Forogh looked at Crosswhite and shook his head. "He won't do it. If he helps us escape, the Taliban will kill him and his entire family. If he refuses to help us, you may kill him, but his wife and children will survive."

"Shit, I'm not going to kill him," Crosswhite said. "Tell him to get up. I want him to tell us the route out of this shit hole so we can leave."

The guide got to his feet gratefully, showing obvious relief as he spoke directly to Forogh, using his hands to indicate a number of sharp turns that seemed to zigzag their way down through the village.

"Jesus," Crosswhite muttered. "Haven't these people ever heard of a straight line? Tell him to come to fucking New York—we'll show 'em how to lay out a fucking town!"

Forogh ignored him, trying to concentrate on the guide's directions. When he felt he understood as well as he was going to, he thanked the man and apologized for Crosswhite punching him in the face. "Okay," he said to the others. "Let's go before I forget."

Crosswhite turned to Naeem, who stood grinning nearby, his hands flex-cuffed behind his back. He drew his Ka-Bar and pressed the blade up beneath the Taliban leader's chin. "You tell this cocksucker that if he pulls any shit on the way out of here—*any shit at all*—I'll cut his eyes out and leave him behind."

Forogh translated, and Naeem's grin abruptly disappeared. The idea of being killed didn't bother him much, but the idea of having to live the rest of his life as a blind invalid scared him, particularly since such a disfigurement could well end up following him into the afterlife should Allah find him wanting upon his death.

"Not so goddamn funny anymore, is it?" Crosswhite said, looking him in the eyes. "Speed, this prick is your responsibility. Alpha, back on point. Forogh, you're right behind me. Let's move!"

The team moved out down the alleyway behind a row of huts in the direction the guide had indicated. By now, word of their presence had long spread throughout the village, so no one was visible, but there was a lot of excited talking inside many of the dwellings they passed.

"Some of the villagers are panicked," Forogh said. "They're afraid of an air assault."

Crosswhite stopped and wheeled around. "Good—use that. Tell them we've called in an airstrike. Get them to evacuate the fucking village! We'll use the confusion to cover our egress."

Forogh looked at him, hesitating in his response.

"What is it? Spit it out."

"There are too many old and sick people here, Captain. The Kalasha don't want trouble from anyone. Don't make me do that to them."

Crosswhite bit back an obscenity, knowing Forogh was right. He ordered Alpha back on the move.

Alpha reached the end of the alley and stole a quick peek around the corner, seeing a mob of Taliban fighters charging toward them. He jumped back and tore a grenade from his harness, biffing it around the corner. None of the SEALs had to be told to hit the ground. The explosion blew away the corner of the hut and body parts flew through the air. Men and women screamed from inside the shattered dwelling. An infant began to shriek.

"Move!" Crosswhite shouted, jumping to his feet and charging around the corner. Half a dozen blasted bodies littered the alleyway between a stone wall and a row of huts. Bleeding civilians scurried for cover inside the shattered dwellings as the SEALs dashed by. There was nothing to be done for them. They would have to fend for themselves as best they could. This was the ugliest part of war.

At the end of the alley they came to a stone staircase, very steep, very narrow, perhaps fifty feet in length. Crosswhite hated the idea, but there was no other avenue of escape. Halfway down, a Taliban gunman opened up on them with a semiautomatic SKS from behind a pile of firewood. Two of the SEALs were hit. Crosswhite and Alpha poured fire onto the sniper's location and took him out, but another pair of Taliban fighters appeared behind them at the top of the stairs and opened fire.

Fischer was hit again in the same shoulder and thrown off balance. He fell backward down the stairs, firing his pistol one-handed. He hit one of the Taliban in the neck and drove the second one back long enough for Speed to recover from the shock of being hit. Bleeding from a bullet wound in his lower back, Speed charged back up the stairs, firing the instant the Taliban's face came back into view and blowing away his forehead. He took a knee atop the staircase and called down for the rest of the team to continue on to the bottom.

"I'm right behind you!" he shouted, making brief eye contact with Crosswhite before turning to fire a burst back in the direction they had come, driving three Taliban back around the shattered corner of the hut. He swiped at the wound to his back and brought up a handful of blood.

"Fuck me," he muttered. "This isn't too good." He found the remaining Benzedrine capsule in his arm pocket and swallowed it dry, feeling it stick in his throat halfway down. He swiped at his wound again and managed to suck enough blood from his glove to choke the capsule down.

"How bad is it?" Fischer said from behind.

Speed jerked his head around. "What the fuck are you doing here?"

"I ain't leaving your ass."

They waited until the rest of the column reached the bottom of the stairs, then Speed yanked a grenade from Fischer's harness and hurled it down the alley toward the corner. They were a quarter of the way down when it detonated four seconds later. At the bottom, they found the rest of the team formed up around the corner in a defensive half circle where they waited for the corpsman to treat a severely wounded SEAL named Blane.

Naeem was belly-down in the dirt beneath the knee of a SEAL everyone called the Conman. Conman was the smallest guy on the team, not much over 5'6" at 145 pounds. He was a true gunfighter, a gambler with a killer's disposition. He had the barrel of his MK 23 screwed tightly into Naeem's ear, at the same time gripping his M4 in the opposite hand, ready to throw down again at any second. He gave Speed a shrug, as if to say, "Just another day at the office."

Forogh got his bearings, pointing toward a hut with a rusted blue rain barrel in front. "There's the rain barrel," he said, remembering the guide's directions. "When Doc's finished, we need to move east through that hut over there."

"Christ, no matter which way we go, it's gonna be ambush fucking central." Crosswhite looked on as the Latino corpsman treated the wounded Blane. He was bleeding profusely from the thigh, the femoral artery severed.

"How's he doing, Doc?"

Doc shook his head, hurriedly ripping the plastic wrapper from a scalpel. "I gotta cut down to the artery and clamp it off before he bleeds out." He ordered a SEAL named Jackson to sit on Blane's chest. "This is gonna hurt like a motherfucker, Blane, but this ain't fuckin' Mogadishu—you *ain't* fuckin' dyin' on me!"

As Doc began to cut down through Blane's thigh muscle, more firing broke out from the huts across the clearing. The SEALs poured fire into the huts and the firing stopped.

Blane growled and gnashed his teeth like a rabid animal, squeezing Jackson's hands in his own and biting down on the folded leather glove that Doc had jammed between his teeth. He bit down so hard that he thought his teeth were going to crack.

"Fuck!" Jackson said, feeling Blane's grip beginning to overpower his own. "You gotta do that raw, Doc? Give this motherfucker some morphine."

Doc desperately wiped the sweat from his eyes with the back of his sleeve. "How the fuck's he gonna fight all doped up? Keep your leg still, Blane!"

More firing broke out from the far end of the alley to the west of where they were formed up. Crosswhite fired an HE round from his M203 and blew the hut apart. He ejected the spent casing and briefly met Trigg's gaze.

Trigg was bleeding from a neck wound, but it wasn't too serious. "We can't absorb much more of this, Captain. You ready to call in Bank Heist Two?"

Crosswhite kept his eyes on the hut he had just blown to smithereens, shaking his head. "There's nowhere for them to land in here. The helos would have to hover overhead and lower the lines. Any jackass with an RPG could blow them out of the sky, so we have to make it to the EZ—there's no other choice."

"Yes, there is. The helos could—"

"I'm not wiping out a village," Crosswhite said. "If we'd found Sandra, that would be one thing, but we didn't, so we have to tough this out."

"Found it!" Doc exclaimed. "Fuckin' A!" He took the artery clamp from his lapel and clamped off the artery deep in Blane's thigh. Then he took a compress and pressed it down hard against the wound, wrapping it tightly around with green duct tape so that Blane would be able to walk, and hopefully fight, without shaking the clamp loose.

Jackson got off of Blane's chest, and Blane sat up sweating, his face pale, eyes glassing over. Doc took a stainless steel flask from his medical bag and put it to Blane's lips.

"Chug it down!" Doc said, tilting the flask up to pour it into the back of Blane's throat. "We gotta stop the shock from setting in, or you'll be too fucked to fight."

Blane choked down the burning liquid and jerked his head away, coughing and shaking his head. "What the fuck is that—Tequila?"

"It slows down the shock," Doc said, quickly jamming his gear back into the bag. "You stick close by me all the way out of here, *vato*. You're in bad shape." He looked at Crosswhite. "Ready to go when you are, Capt—" He noticed for the first time a SEAL named

McAllister applying a bandage to the lower right of Speed's back. "How bad are you?"

Speed shrugged. "Bad enough there ain't shit you can do. If we don't make the EZ pretty soon, I'm fucked."

Crosswhite made a quick assessment. Counting the bullet hole in his own leg, five of them were carrying wounds, two of them critical. Even Fischer had been hit again in the same damn shoulder, though he didn't seem to be complaining.

Doc and Jackson helped Blane to his feet. Blane winced badly when he put weight on the leg, but he assured them all that he could continue the mission.

Alpha got back on point, and they made toward the hut with the blue rain barrel.

Once inside, Crosswhite took one of the claymore mines from Trigg's pack. "Alpha, keep the column moving down through the village. I'll catch up. Those cocksuckers at the top of the stairs are going to try and dog us all the way to the EZ."

The rest of the team rousted the cowering Kalasha family from their hiding places and took them along out the back door, finding the narrow passage the tour guide had told Forogh about.

Crosswhite unfolded the scissor legs on the bottom of the claymore and stuck them into the dirt floor at the back of the hut, facing the door. Then he got up and fired a burst out the window at the small squad of Taliban fighters who were just emerging from cover at the top of the stone staircase. He didn't hit anyone, but he managed to drive them briefly back under cover. As he returned to work setting the claymore, a hail of AK-47 fire rained through the hut, forcing him down onto his belly. He quickly ran the trigger wire from the mine to the door, securing it around a rusty nail protruding from the wood near the floor. A bullet struck his helmet a glancing blow and embedded itself in his back between his shoulder blades near his spine. Now more than ever he was regretting the decision to leave their body armor behind, but this was a moot point. Wearing armor, they would never have completed a forced march up the mountain.

As the Taliban gunners paused to reload, he leapt to his feet and dashed out the back door, running down the passageway to catch up with the team. A door opened and he plowed right into a pair of Taliban fighters in the midst of displacing to outflank the hut with the blue rain barrel.

All three men went sprawling, and a furious free-for-all ensued as they scrambled back to their feet. Crosswhite knew better than to try and recover the M4, or to even bother with the pistol. He simply drew his Ka-Bar and went to work, jamming it up under the rib cage of the much bigger Taliban fighter, pivoting to keep the dying man between himself and the other man in the narrow passage. The younger fighter who couldn't directly engage just sort of stood there as his skewered compatriot screamed in agony, trying desperately to gouge out Crosswhite's eyes.

Crosswhite gave the man a shove and jumped for space, leaving the knife embedded in his torso. He jerked out his pistol and shot both men down.

At this same moment, the Taliban squad from the staircase arrived outside the hut with the blue rain barrel. The leader jerked open the door and detonated the M18A1 claymore mine. Seven hundred ⅛-inch steel balls blasted outward in an arc of 60 degrees, at a velocity of 3,900 feet per second. The front of the hut disintegrated, and all nine Taliban fighters more or less disintegrated right along with it.

Crosswhite retrieved his weapons, pausing to make sure their pursuers were dead before dashing back down the passageway. He called out over the radio: "Alpha, the claymore did its job. I'm moving to catch up."

"Roger that," Alpha replied. "Take a left at the end of the passageway, then another right. We're about fifty yards from your position, behind a stone wall. Be advised we are taking fire!"

Crosswhite could hear the rotors of the Black Hawk helicopters arriving high overhead now, well inside of the outer marker. He got them on the radio next.

"Bank Heist Two, be advised we're in a running fight down here! There's no way for you to extract us safely at this time. Pull back to the outer marker. Over!"

"Bank Heist One, be advised we are maintaining an altitude of thirty-five hundred feet. If you will activate your infrared strobes, we'll try and put a little bit of heat on those bad guys for you. Over."

Crosswhite kept moving, realizing the helos were maintaining an altitude of 3,500 feet because an enemy RPG-7 self-detonated at a distance of roughly 3,000 feet. He doubted, however, that an RPG would fly that high if fired straight up into the air. "Negative, negative, Bank Heist! The bad guys are all mixed in with the civilians down here."

He could hear small arms chattering elsewhere in the village now and realized the helos had already begun taking fire. He switched on the infrared strobe attached to his combat harness and ordered the rest of the team to do the same so the helo gunners could tell friend from foe. He heard a loud explosion high over the village and realized that some wing nut had just tried to shoot down one of the helos with an RPG.

"Bank Heist Two, did you take any damage from that RPG? Over."

"Negative, Bank Heist." The pilot's voice sounded almost bored. "Listen, we've got a pretty good visual on both you and the enemy now. They seem to have anticipated your march route out. They're assembled and waiting for you in the rocks just below the village. Why don't you clear us to fire and let us expedite your exfiltration? Over."

Crosswhite realized that by now either the NSA or the CIA—or both—would be intercepting all of this excessive radio traffic and that pretty soon their unauthorized mission would be hitting prime time. "Bank Heist, you advise they're clear of the village? Over."

"Roger that, Bank Heist. But we'd better fire soon, because they're moving back toward the village now. Over."

"Take 'em, Bank Heist."

"Roger that. Get your heads down, gentlemen."

Crosswhite managed to reestablish contact with the rest of the team just as the Night Stalker gunners began to engage the Taliban fighters outside the village with a pair of M134, 20 mm Gatling guns that fired up to 6,000 rounds per minute. From their position behind the stone wall, they watched as the Taliban broke from the cover of the rocks, running for their lives in every direction. The hot 20 mm tracers sought them out like red laser beams, exploding their bodies with hundred-round bursts of fire, raking the mountainside with great, sweeping arcs of fire. Within a few seconds, twenty-five Taliban fighters were obliterated.

Crosswhite ordered the team out from behind the wall. They made their way five hundred yards down the mountain to a relatively flat piece of real estate they had preselected as their extraction zone and waited for the first Black Hawk to set down. The second helo remained on station high overhead, providing top-cover.

The crew chief jumped out and saluted Crosswhite. "The word's out, Captain. We've just received orders to return to base immediately. We haven't acknowledged the transmission, but they know we're listening. We should have F-15s buzzing the area any time now."

Crosswhite signaled for Naeem to be brought front and center. "Sergeant Major . . . this is Romeo."

The crew chief raised the visor on his flight helmet and grinned in the Taliban leader's face. "Congratulations, Mr. Taliban. At this particular moment in time, you have the distinction of being the unluckiest man on the entire planet."

32

LANGLEY

Robert Pope stood in a dark room before a bank of high-resolution video monitors used for viewing the live feed from a CIA spy satellite locked in a geosynchronous orbit some two hundred miles above the earth's surface. He allowed his mind to drift as he watched the Black Hawk helicopter lift into the air. The battle of Waigal Village was apparently over, but it did not appear that the rescue team had located Sandra Brux, and the identity of their male prisoner remained to be seen. The call sign Romeo meant nothing to him. He patted a lone pair of technicians on their shoulders and turned for the door.

"Nice work, ladies. Make sure that video card disappears into the proper black hole, will you, please?"

"Yes, sir."

He gave them a wink and slipped into the hallway. Pope wasn't remotely worried that anyone would ever find out he had watched the unauthorized mission—from start to finish—without reporting it to the director of the CIA. He was at the very tip-top of the intelligence food chain. No one knew more about the systems than he did, and no one oversaw his work. The buck stopped with him in his private little corner of the world. Many of the computer programs he used these days were programs that he had custom written for his own personal use, secret programs running parallel to the authorized programs he was supposed to be using for the intelligence-gathering tasks he was charged with carrying out on behalf of the United States Government. As a result, if anyone ever did attempt to backtrack his activities, they would find nothing more than series after series of very boring, very legitimate, and routinely mundane intelligence exercises . . . all of them accurately dated, reviewed, and evaluated.

Pope's philosophy was very simple: Why stop at having one brilliant, exceedingly loyal young woman for a protégée when you could have two? This not only doubled the amount of work they could get done on his behalf; it doubled the amount time he could spend ignoring what he was supposed to be doing while researching the things that truly interested him. For instance, what was the Russian navy up to in the Sea of Okhotsk—and why had he been ordered to ignore it? Why were American oil prospectors poking around in regions of the African continent where there wasn't supposed to be any oil? And why was the Israeli Mossad suddenly so interested in spying on the Mexican government?

The answers to these sorts of questions might all end up being very benign by the time he puzzled them out, but Pope found the questions themselves much too intriguing to ignore. Similarly, once he had realized that elements of the American Special Forces community were preparing to go off the reservation in an attempt to rescue Sandra Brux—rather than sit idly by while Washington considered the political angles—he had been far too fascinated by their audacity even to think about blowing the whistle. Still, he had warned the director of the possibility, even if only subtly.

He sat down at his desk and passed the time musing as he awaited the inevitable text message from the DDO. The NSA had certainly intercepted the clandestine mission's radio traffic, and by now an emergency action message would have been sent directly to the CIA station chief in Kabul, who would have then gotten into immediate contact with the chief of the Middle East bureau, who would have in turn made a direct call to the deputy director of Operations for the CIA—Cletus Webb.

Almost to the exact minute of Pope's estimated time, the iPhone resting on his desk began to buzz with the anticipated text message: CONTACT ME AT HOME IMMEDIATELY!

He picked up the landline and pressed the auto dial for Webb's house. He was often in his office until the wee hours of the morning, so there was no reason to worry about this raising any real suspicion. And he was well aware that most everyone regarded him as something of an eccentric anyhow—a perception he never hesitated to take advantage of.

Webb answered on the first ring. "Bob?"

"Yeah. What is it, Cletus? Is something wrong?"

"I was hoping you could tell me," Webb said. "You haven't heard any chatter coming out of Afghanistan tonight?"

"I haven't been listening for any," Pope said, yawning audibly. "Electronic eavesdropping isn't exactly in my job description."

"Well, that's never stopped you before," Webb muttered. "Listen, Bob, it sounds like elements of both DEVGRU and SOAR may have just carried out some kind of a joint rescue mission in the Waigal Valley. I'm calling to find out what you might know before I call Shroyer at home. I'll need to brief him so he can call the president before the president hears about it from someone else."

"Someone else, as in the NSA?"

"As in anybody, Bob. What can you tell me?"

"Well, Waigal is in the Nuristan Province," Pope said. "North of Jalalabad. The people there tend to speak mostly Kalasha. I also seem to remember that—"

"Bob, are you telling me you know *nothing* about this operation— that your people are capable of pulling off an unauthorized rescue mission without anyone knowing anything about it until it's over?"

In that moment, Pope noticed that he'd forgotten to tear the page from his desk blotter after the change of the month. He began to clear the desk so he could tear the page away without knocking anything over.

"Bob!"

"Yes? Oh—well, sure, it's possible, Cletus. These people are in operation thousands of miles away. We can't monitor every single move they make. They are highly trained adults, after all. At some point, we have to trust them to look after themselves ... and I did warn you about the Uncertainty Principle. Who contacted you, by the way, the Mideast section chief?"

"No, Bob, it was the chairman of the Joint Chiefs of Staff," Webb said. "General Couture called him directly from the ATO." General Couture was the Supreme Commander of all US forces in Afghanistan. "He was apparently in the middle of his breakfast when he was informed that a clandestine operation had taken place within his theater of operations during the night and without anyone having had the common decency to mention it to him. He's hopping mad."

Pope chuckled. "Well, knowing Couture, I can imagine. I'll look into this, Cletus, and get back to you. How's that?"

Webb let out a dissatisfied sigh. "That'll be fine, Bob. Call me the minute you have something you're willing to share with the rest of us."

"You bet." Pope hung up the phone.

Having forgotten about the desk blotter, he stretched and yawned and rocked back in the leather chair, remembering himself as a young man, as a very green operative skylarking with Air America, a covert airlift operation run by SAD for the CIA from 1950 to 1976. It was during the final days of the Vietnam War that Pope had stumbled across his first big chip in the poker game of American intelligence gathering.

He and his CIA copilot were flying a battered C-130 full of top-secret files out of the US Airbase at Bien Hoa bound for the Philippines. They were over the jungle when the aircraft suffered a catastrophic engine failure. To this day, Pope still suspected sabotage, but there would never be any way to know for sure. They went down in the jungle, and the plane was torn to pieces. The copilot was killed, and Pope was left with a broken leg. The plane caught fire, and he barely managed to drag himself clear before it exploded.

There had been no time for a Mayday, and the plane had no transponder, so Pope believed he would either eventually die of exposure there in the jungle or be found and murdered by the Viet Cong operating in that area. When the sun came up the following day, he made himself a crutch from a dead tree limb and hobbled around the burned-out fuselage in a halfhearted attempt to find anything that might be useful to his survival.

All he found was a single diplomatic pouch full of classified documents that had flown from the cargo bay as the fuselage was torn apart. Having nothing better to do, he sat down against a tree and went through the pouch. Within the documents were the names of dozens of American CIA operatives and officers, both in Vietnam and back in the States, who had spent the Vietnam War growing rich off of Air America's illicit drug trafficking operations.

An A-Team of American Green Berets found him the next day, but they were ambushed by the Viet Cong en route to the extraction zone. When the firefight was over, only Pope and a single Green

Beret noncom remained alive. The Green Beret's name was Master Sergeant Guy Shannon. He carried Pope on his back the last click to the extraction zone, where they were finally lifted from the ground by an Iroquois Huey in a cloud of purple smoke.

Over the next few years, Pope had used the information contained in those classified files to encourage loyal patrons among the CIA's upper echelon, and over time, these patrons helped him collect the names of vulnerable people working in branches of government outside the CIA as well. By the time his hair finally began to turn gray, almost no one in DC had the courage to refuse him a favor, their natural assumption being that if he was asking them for something, he must have information on them as well.

Pope understood better than anyone that information—not money or guns—was the true source of power in the emerging world, and that information was to be guarded at all costs and never shared . . . except with a trusted and worthy few.

33

AFGHANISTAN,
Jalalabad Air Base

Steelyard stalked into a room at the back of the hangar where Gil, Trigg, Forogh, and Lt. Commander Perez stood in a semicircle around Naeem, who now sat strapped to a steel armchair with a black bag over his head. The chief dropped his smoldering cigar onto the concrete and stepped on it with the heel of his boot.

"We have to do this fast," he announced. "The second the Head Shed realizes who this prick is, they'll send the MPs to take him away from us. Trigg, get me a box of garbage bags and fistful of nylon zip ties. Commander, you probably shouldn't be here for this."

Perez took a self-conscious glance at Gil before straightening his posture and putting out his chest. "It's all right, Chief. I'll stay."

"You're sure, sir? What I'm about to do is against the Geneva

Conventions. Getting caught taking part in this type of interrogation could end your career."

The very faintest of smiles crossed Perez's face. "I know how much that would break all of your hearts, Chief . . . but I'll stay."

"Very well." Steelyard gave Gil a nod, signaling for him to remove the black bag from Naeem's head.

Naeem sat looking up at them, a defiant sneer on his bruised face. "Fuck you!" he said, still lisping because of the missing teeth.

Steelyard looked at Forogh. "Ask him where they took Sandra."

Speaking in Pashto, Forogh asked Naeem where the American pilot had been taken.

Naeem smirked. "Fuck you."

Long having recognized Naeem's particular brand of contempt, Forogh said to him, "You're Wahhabi, yes?"

Naeem stared back, his eyes glassing over with loathing.

Forogh looked at the others and shook his head. "He's not going to tell us. He's a Wahhabi fundamentalist. This is his chance to prove himself to Allah."

"Does he speak English?" Perez asked.

Forogh shook his head again. "Only enough to say, 'fuck you.'"

Steelyard snatched one of the black garbage bags from Trigg, saying, "That's all I needed to hear." He slipped the bag over Naeem's head, smoothed the plastic over his face to remove the excess air, and looped a zip tie around the prisoner's neck, jerking it tight. "Tell him he'd better start talking pretty fast."

Forogh told Naeem that if he didn't reveal where Sandra had been taken, the Americans would let him suffocate.

"Fuck you!" Naeem gasped, already beginning to struggle for air. Each time he tried to draw a breath, the plastic would suck into his mouth and he would blow it back out in a panicked gasp. He shook his head around in a furious attempt to locate a pocket of air within the bag, but to no avail. Within a few seconds, he began to panic, screaming and jerking wildly at the restraints in an impotent attempt to free himself.

Gil gripped the back of the chair so Naeem could not rock it over onto the floor and attempt to tear the bag against the concrete.

"Tell them where the woman is." Forogh urged him. "Tell them now, or you're going to die!"

A few moments later, Naeem lapsed into complete panic, like a man drowning in a pool, jerking madly around within his restricted scope of movement, arms and legs immobilized, repeatedly sucking the plastic in and out of his mouth, over and over again with increasing desperation. He began to grind his teeth against the plastic in a frantic, last-ditch effort to put a hole in it, but Steelyard boxed his ears between the rock-hard palms of his hands, dazing the shit out of him. Naeem swooned deliriously around in the chair. At last, his head lolled off to the side, and his body convulsed for a few horrible moments before growing still.

Steelyard tore a hole in the bag and jerked it down over Naeem's head so the unconscious, blue-complexioned man could begin to breathe again.

Perez looked a little green around the gills himself. "How many times does this usually take?" he asked nervously.

Steelyard met Gil's gaze. "This tough fucker might be able to fight for longer than we've got."

Forogh stood watching them uncomfortably. This was his first such interrogation, and he was beginning to have misgivings.

"Can we move him someplace else?" Gil said.

"No," Perez said. "No place else is secure."

Naeem was beginning to come around.

Gil turned to Trigg. "Run and find Doc! Get him to give you a bottle of albumin and a hundred-cc syringe."

Trigg gave the box of trash bags to Perez and ducked out of the room.

"Any chance we can reason with the MPs when they get here?" Gil ventured.

Steelyard took another garbage bag from the box in Perez's hand. "Nope. Hardcore MPs don't break the rules for Special Forces people. They're too busy resenting the shit out of us."

Gil took smelling salts from his pocket and cracked it under Naeem's nose. "Wake up, fucker."

The Taliban came to almost instantly, jerking his head away from the burning aroma of the smelling salts.

"Where is the American woman?" Forogh quickly demanded.

"Fuck you!" Naeem swore, spitting on Forogh's tunic.

Gil viciously boxed Naeem's ears from behind, causing him to cry out with pain as Steelyard slipped the second bag over his head, repeating the same process as before, only this time jerking the zip tie around his neck even tighter, cutting off the blood flow to the brain and causing intense physical discomfort.

Naeem flailed around in the chair even more hysterically than before, gasping horribly as he began to strangle. He blacked out in half the time, and Steelyard used a pair of diagonal cutters to snip the nylon tie-down from his neck, restoring the blood flow to his brain and pulling the plastic bag from his head.

Naeem's face was distorted into a puffy, purple effigy of itself.

"Bring his ass back around fast," Steelyard said. "We'll have another go."

Naeem came awake to the smelling salts once more and began struggling to get free even before the bag was placed back over his head.

"Tell them where the woman is!" Forogh pleaded. "Tell them now and this will stop!"

Naeem gnashed his teeth, calling them the filthiest names he could think of, wailing that they were all going to hell. "Allah will punish you all!" he shrieked, nearly berserk with rage and shame. "He will punish you all for this!"

Forogh looked uneasily at Steelyard. "He's beginning to crack."

A Humvee squealed to a halt on the far side of the hangar. Trigg came through the door in that same second. "It's the fucking MPs!"

Gil grabbed the syringe and the bottle of albumin, looking at Perez. "Commander, you have to stall them—two minutes."

Perez began to protest.

"Damnit, sir, will you just act like a SEAL for once in your goddamn life!"

Perez glared at him and fled the room.

"That wasn't cool," Trigg muttered, worried that Perez might tell the MPs to arrest them all.

Gil spoke to Forogh as he held up the bottle of blood expander and stuck the needle into it to fill the big plastic syringe. "Tell him this is swine serum—made from pig blood. Medics use it as a blood expander to keep wounded men from bleeding to death."

Forogh hesitated, started to stammer.

"Translate what I said, goddamnit!"

Forogh did as he was ordered, and Naeem's eyes filled with genuine fear for the first time.

Steelyard slipped the bag back over his head, and Gil grabbed his arm, jamming the needle into a bulging vein.

Naeem jerked his head wildly around, screaming in vain for Forogh to help him.

"Tell him his ass is going straight to hell," Gil ordered. "No Muslim could ever get into heaven with swine blood in his veins."

Forogh was a Muslim himself, and the notion of what Gil was about to do shook him on a very fundamental level. "Gil, you can't . . . it's not—"

"Fucking tell him!" Gil shouted. "Tell him now!"

"Brother!" Forogh said in a panic. "Please! Tell this crazy infidel where the woman is. He's going to make you filthy in the eyes of Allah—you'll spend eternity in hell!"

"Stop him!" Naeem shrieked. "For the love of Allah, I will tell him!" He was shaking with genuine terror now, sure that he could already feel the foul swine serum burning in his veins. "I will tell him—I will tell him! Just make him stop!"

"Where is she?" Gil bellowed. "I'm injecting now."

"Brother, he's pressing the plunger!"

"Bazarak—she's in Bazarak in the Valley of Panjshir! You have to stop him!"

Forogh translated, spitting out the words as rapidly as he could.

"Is he telling the truth?" Steelyard demanded. "Do you believe him?"

Forogh stood adamantly nodding his head. "Yes! Yes, I believe him. He's terrified—he's only seconds away from meeting the devil!"

Steelyard gave Gil a wink just as the door flew open and six towering Army MPs came barging into the room.

"We have orders from General Couture to take this prisoner into custody," announced a hulking first sergeant who looked as though he'd been carved from black oak.

Gil depressed the plunger, and Naeem let out an unholy shriek of terror. "He's all yours, First Sergeant."

The MPs shouldered their way past and unbuckled the straps securing Naeem to the chair. Naeem went limp in their arms, blubbering and refusing to bear his own weight as he began to babble away with despondent prayers for forgiveness.

The first sergeant looked at Steelyard and shook his head in disappointment. "I really wish you hadn't put me in this position, Master Chief. I gotta report this."

Steelyard took a Cohiba from his pocket and stuck it between his

teeth. "This piece of shit sodomized one of our female Night Stalkers, and we were trying to find out where they're holding her . . . but
you do what you have to, First Sergeant."

A crease formed in the first sergeant's brow. "You're telling me
they've got one of our female GIs out there somewhere?"

Steelyard took a moment to strike a match. "That's still classified
at the moment." He paused long enough to light the cigar. "But yes,
First Sergeant, that's what I'm telling you."

The first sergeant told his men to put Naeem in the Humvee. He
watched them carry him out the door, then stood thinking things
over. "I'll leave the chair and the needle out of my report," he decided.
"But don't ever put me in this situation again." With that, he turned
and left.

Perez came back in right after.

Gil and Steelyard stood glaring at him.

"Don't look at me like that," he said with indignation. "I had
them convinced they were at the wrong hangar until you assholes
started screaming back here."

Forogh shoved Trigg out of the way and made for the door.

Gil grabbed his jacket. "What's your fuckin' problem?"

Forogh wheeled him, eyes full of fire. "You're a liar! You said you
wouldn't inject him if he told you where she was. You lied to me—
and now his soul goes to torment unnecessarily. You're a bastard liar,
and I won't work with you anymore."

Gil let go of the jacket and exchanged smiles with Steelyard.
"You wanna tell him, Chief, or should I?"

Forogh stood looking back and forth between them. "Tell me
what?"

Steelyard took the cigar from his teeth. "Son, the only thing
in that bottle was saline solution. There's no such thing as albumin
made from swine blood. But we needed *you* to believe that's what
it was so that rapist son of a bitch would believe it, too. Otherwise,

it might not have worked. Desperate moments sometimes require desperate measures."

Forogh went slack in the jaw. "It was a trick?"

Gil chuckled. "And don't be mad at me. I voted to shove a pork chop up the fucker's ass, but the chief here, he didn't think that would have the same effect."

34

AFGHANISTAN,
Jalalabad Air Base

Crosswhite and the four wounded SEALs were all rushed into surgery moments after the returning Black Hawks had set down on the tarmac. No one from the top brass had been there waiting to ask them any questions, and as far as anyone else on the airbase still knew, Bank Heist had been a sanctioned operation.

By now, night had fallen, and still no one from the SOG brass had arrived to arrest Crosswhite or even to debrief him. He sat propped up in his hospital bed still feeling loopy from the anesthetic and the pain medication he'd been given. The bullet wound to his leg wasn't particularly serious, but an Air Force spinal surgeon had been called in to remove the bullet from his back near his spine. After the hour-long procedure, the surgeon had gravely informed him that he'd come a mere five millimeters from being paralyzed.

He looked over at Gil and Steelyard, who'd come to sit with him after having first visited their wounded shipmates. "Know what?" he said. "I'm going to recommend Doc for the DSC. He saved Blane's life. If our medics in Somalia had been trained to do a cut-down like that in the field, Jamie Smith probably would have survived that fucking battle." Corporal Jamie Smith was the US Army Ranger who had bled to death on October 3 back in 1993 during the infamous Black Hawk Down mission to capture Mohammed Aidid in the city of Mogadishu. Smith had been shot too high in the upper thigh for either a tourniquet or direct pressure to stop the bleeding from his severed femoral artery.

Gil rolled his eyes. "That'll go over like a fart in church."

"Fuck 'em."

Steelyard waited for Crosswhite's nurse to finish taking his vitals. When she was gone, he said, "We'll be lucky to avoid landing in the brig after this fucked-up mission, you idiot. And you want to start making recommendations for the Distinguished fucking Service Cross?"

Crosswhite winked at Gil. "Would you remind your mentor there that he's addressing a superior officer?"

"I'm pretty sure he knows," Gil said grimly, the bullet wound to his ass still very sore.

"What'd Captain Metcalf have to say about that rapist prick we brought back?" Crosswhite suddenly wanted to know. "He hasn't even dropped by to see how I'm doing."

Steelyard grimaced, signaling for Gil to push the door closed. "Captain Metcalf knew *nothing* about the mission—that was the agreement. The onus was on us to pull it off . . . and we failed."

Crosswhite sat almost straight up in the bed, his many IV lines pulling against the steel post where his IV bags were hung, threatening to topple it over. "Hey, Chief . . . we didn't fail at a goddamn thing. She wasn't fucking there!"

Gil sat forward to put his hand on Crosswhite's leg. "Dan, that's not what he meant. Relax."

"That's the morphine talking," Steelyard muttered, crossing his arms. "Listen, Dan, you're right. I misspoke. We took our shot, and the fuckers moved the target. That's just how the cookie crumbled this time. The silver lining is that you brought that rapist son of a bitch back with you—that and none of our people got killed. This way we may at least stand a chance of avoiding the brig."

The door suddenly opened and in strolled General William J. Couture, wearing a starched ACU with four black stars down the front. He was flanked by Captain Metcalf of the United States Navy and his aide-de-camp, a tall, hard-nosed looking army major with a Ranger tab and a .45 caliber Glock pistol suspended beneath each arm.

Gil and Steelyard got quickly on their feet, snapping to attention. Gil had heard one or two tall tales about General Couture being somewhat Pattonesque, but the sight of his aide-de-camp's *non*-government issue pistols gave him pause to believe the tales might not have been so tall after all.

Ignoring the wounded Crosswhite, General Couture trained his attention on Gil and Steelyard. He was over six feet in height and wore his graying hair cropped close to his head. He had merciless, piercing gray eyes and a wicked scar that ran up the left side of his face. Everyone in the theater knew the scar was the result of an RPG attack on his Humvee during the early days of the Second Iraq War, back when he was still just a major general with two stars.

"Shannon," he said in a deep, contemplative voice. "I seem to remember hearing that name recently. Been to Iran lately?"

Gil remained at attention. "My apologies, sir, but I'm not at liberty either to confirm or deny such a thing."

Couture grunted. To Steelyard he said, "Master Chief, how much of this mess was your doing?"

"All of it, sir. I accept full responsibility."

Crosswhite sat back up in the bed. "General, with respect, sir, the master chief is a liar. The entire mission was my idea. I ordered him and his men to assist me in a mission to—"

Steelyard cleared his throat, cutting him off. "Sir, I'm afraid that Captain Crosswhite doesn't know what he's saying at the moment . . . it's the morphine, sir."

"The hell I don't!" Crosswhite said.

A faint light began to show behind the general's eyes. "Should I take it, then, that when the time comes both of you two hardheads are willing to fall on your swords for the good of everyone else who participated in this misbegotten *bank heist* of yours?"

"Yes, sir!" both men said in unison.

"Excellent," Couture said, somewhat dryly. "That makes my job a hell of a lot easier than I expected it was going to be." He turned to Captain Metcalf. "Captain, it looks like we have a head from both Army *and* Navy to offer up to the president. I think that should probably cover it, don't you?"

Metcalf stole the very briefest of glances with Steelyard. The two men shared a lot of history. "Yes, sir. I think that should probably cover it."

"Very well, then," Couture said. "As you were, gentlemen." He paused before leaving the room to meet eyes with Gil. "Well done over there, Master Chief."

"Thank you, sir," Gil muttered, dropping his gaze.

The general's aide pulled the door closed after them, and the three warriors sat in the gathering silence until Crosswhite finally sat back with a sigh. "Fuck 'em," he said again, smoothing his blankets. "Now I'm definitely going to recommend Doc for the DSC."

Gil leaned over to rest his head against the wall. "I got a better idea. Why don't you do Doc a favor and leave him out of it?"

35

WASHINGTON, DC,
The White House

The President of the United States did not appear even remotely amused as he sat looking across his desk at Director Shroyer in the Oval Office. "Ultimately, George, both SAD and SOG are your responsibility, are they not?"

Shroyer felt his anus start to pucker. "Yes, Mr. President."

The president nodded, looking across the room at a painting of George Washington, lost in thought. He was a graying man in his midfifties, very presidential looking with expressive blue eyes and a Florida tan. Having been a businessman during civilian life, he knew very little about the military and was therefore very dependent upon his advisors when it came to dealing with the Armed Forces community. "Well, okay," he said finally. "Suppose you tell me what you've been able to find out . . . if anything."

Shroyer felt his face flush, never having been so on the spot in his entire life. "Well, Mr. President, it appears that two elements of the Special Operations Group—specifically SEAL Team Six and the 160th Special Operations Aviation Regiment—"

"Wait a second, what about DEVGRU?"

Shroyer smiled somewhat lamely. "I'm sorry, sir. DEVGRU and SEAL Team Six are the same the thing. I'm sorry to confuse you."

The president cast an annoyed glance at his chief military advisor, Tim Hagen, a bony little man who stood off to the side wearing wire-rimmed glasses. "Why am I only now hearing this?"

Inwardly, Hagen rolled his eyes, but outwardly he put on his most compassionate smile. "Mr. President, we went over this yesterday, but as I've mentioned, it takes time to get these military acronyms straight."

"He's right," Shroyer said helpfully. "You can't be expected to remember them all, Mr. President. That's our job."

The president settled into his chair, allowing himself to be mollified. "Go on."

"Apparently," Shroyer continued, "the enlisted men taking part in the mission had no idea the operation hadn't been sanctioned. From what I understand, the plan was hatched by an Army captain and a Navy master chief, both of them working in unison to act on a piece of DNA intelligence that—we *think*—was passed on to them by a senior CID investigator in Kabul."

"You *think*," the president echoed.

"Yes, sir. I say that because the Army warrant officer who ran the DNA tests reports that she forwarded the results to her supervisor shortly before Operation Bank Heist took place. Her supervisor left Afghanistan the same day to return home to Iowa, where his wife is dying of cancer. He's not answering the phone, and we haven't yet had time to send anyone to the house."

"What was significant about the DNA results?"

"The DNA of a Taliban fighter killed during the Sandra Brux abduction led straight to the village of Waigal in the Hindu Kush. Our most recent intelligence indicates that Sandra *was* being held there, but our SEALs arrived a number of hours after she had been moved. We now believe she's being held in the town of Bazarak, which happens to be an HIK stronghold at the moment. We're already tasking satellites to—"

The president held up his hand to stop him. "We'll get back to Bazarak in a minute. What you're telling me is that Operation Bank Heist came very close to making this office look like it didn't know what the hell it was doing? Is that about right?"

Shroyer shifted uncomfortably in the chair. "I suppose in a manner of speaking, Mr. President, but—"

"And I take it this business about Bazarak is recent intel coming from the Taliban prisoner they captured in Waigal?"

"Yes, sir. His name is Naeem Wardak. We don't know much about his history yet, but he seems to have been a midlevel Taliban enforcer." Shroyer paused briefly, preparing to kick what he hoped would be a game-saving field goal for his side. "The most significant fact about him is that he's the man seen to be raping Sandra in the ransom video."

The president sat back in his chair, exchanging startled glances with Hagen. This was the first either of them were hearing about the Taliban prisoner being Sandra's rapist. Suddenly, here was a ray of sunlight in the middle of the thunderstorm. Already having the rapist in custody would go a long, long way toward making them *all* look pretty damned efficient if that god-cursed video showed up on the internet in the near future.

Even if the president was keeping these thoughts to himself, Shroyer could see the relief in his eyes. *Thank God for that scatter-brained Pope!* He had gotten the call from Pope on his way to the

White House only half an hour before, just in time for this meeting with the president.

The president sat forward to rest his elbows on the desk, lacing his fingers. "What's being done about the Army captain and the Navy chief who planned the operation?"

"From what I understand," Shroyer said carefully, "General Couture has spoken with them, and they've taken full responsibility. The captain was seriously wounded during the mission along with a few of the SEALs, but the SAD director, Robert Pope, informs me they're all expected to make a full recovery."

"What's your opinion of that guy?" the president asked suspiciously.

"Of Pope, sir?" Shroyer realized this was his golden opportunity to ask for Pope's head on a lance. "Well, to be honest with you, Mr. President, the man frustrates the hell out of me . . . but I think that's mostly because I don't understand him."

"I ask," the president said, "because the Joint Chiefs aren't happy with him. They want him out. They think he's too independent."

Shroyer had only seconds to make a decision: Save Pope or leave him to his fate? He wished that Webb were there to advise him, but he decided quickly that Webb would probably advise against cutting Pope loose at this time, and he knew that Webb was smarter than he was, so . . .

"In and of itself," he replied, "it's not really a bad thing that the Joint Chiefs don't like him. When anyone inside the CIA thinks further outside of the box than they do, they always tend to get a little frustrated. I think Pope probably helps to strike a balance."

"I can see why you might feel that way," the president said thoughtfully. "So, getting back to the captain and the chief for a moment . . . exactly whose authority are they under: SAD's or the Joint Chiefs'?"

Shroyer smiled, seeing the president's gambit. "Technically, sir, they still belong to the military, but you're the Commander in Chief. They can fall under any authority you decide to designate."

"Very good," the president said, satisfied that he'd found a stop-gap solution to his immediate problem. He looked across at Tim Hagen. "Call Bob Pope over at the Special Activities Division. Tell him that in light of this new information about the Taliban prisoner, this office is inclined to leave the disciplinary actions concerning those two renegades in his court . . . for the time being. Be sure he understands, however, that this office reserves the option to *reinvolve* itself at any time. . . . should it become necessary to do so."

"Yes, sir." Hagen slipped out of the room.

Shroyer breathed a small sigh, satisfied that he had gained Pope a temporary reprieve, a suspended sentence that would hang over his head and those of his two *renegade* operatives until the Sandra Brux dilemma had been resolved to the president's satisfaction—one way or another.

36

AFGHANISTAN,
Jalalabad Air Base

Steelyard was still asleep in his quarters when he heard a knock at
the door. He sat up in bed, glancing at the clock to see that it was
only six o'clock in the morning. Expecting it to be the MPs coming
to arrest him, he took his time about getting up and getting dressed
before answering the door. If they wanted to kick it in, that was up to
them. A couple of minutes later he opened the door to find Captain
Metcalf standing on the steel staircase with a slightly disconcerted
look.

"I can't remember the last time anybody kept me waiting that
fucking long to answer a goddamn door."

Steelyard stepped back to let him inside. "That's because everybody's been kissing your ass for the last ten goddamn years." He shut
the door after his old friend and turned to shake his hand. "It was

nice of them to send you instead of the MPs. How soon will I be stateside?"

Metcalf sat down in a government-issued folding chair near the window. "You're not going anywhere," he said, motioning Steelyard into the other chair. "At least not yet. They're playing politics back in DC. Believe it or not, Bob Pope's in charge of your disciplinary action."

Steelyard bridled. "Pope's a fucking civilian. On top of that, he's a fucking nut!"

Metcalf sat looking at him. "You've never even met the son of a bitch."

"I don't need to."

Metcalf blew him off with a wave of his hand. "Your bitching isn't going to change anything. This is the president's way of keeping you and Crosswhite on ice until Sandra is recovered one way or another. If all goes well, you can expect the White House to take credit for Bank Heist."

"Of course they'll take credit for Bank Heist," Steelyard remarked. "Hell, they'll probably put the entire team on David Letterman. Expose the op the same way they did after the Bin Laden hit. Turn us all into fucking celebrities."

Metcalf cocked an eyebrow. "It wasn't quite that bad, Hal. What'll be more likely to happen in that event is that you and Crosswhite will be swept under the rug—which is exactly what you'd better hope for, because if Sandra ends up dead, you're both gonna get the cross."

"That's already been decided?"

Metcalf rocked back in the chair, letting out a sigh. "That's right. You've been sleeping. You haven't heard yet."

Steelyard cocked an eyebrow. "Heard what?"

"Sandra's rape is all over the fucking internet. It's fast becoming a political nightmare for the president."

Steelyard shook his head. "Well, we knew it would."

"To make matters worse," Metcalf went on, "she's not in the hands of the Taliban anymore. The HIK has her now, and they aren't making any stupid ransom demands. They know her value as a propaganda tool, and it looks like that's how they plan to use her. *America can't protect its women. Look how weak they are.* All that shit."

Steelyard stood and went to the refrigerator. "It's true, though, isn't it? We can't protect her." He took a bottle of milk from the fridge and sat back down. "Is she still in Bazarak?"

"We think so, but it's an HIK stronghold. We can't move against the village without them killing her."

"Have they made that specific threat yet?"

"They don't need to," Metcalf said. "It's common sense. This is the Iran hostage crisis in miniature. The HIK's going to make Bazarak famous over the coming months. They've been moving men into the Panjshir Valley since we stopped patrolling it six months ago. Nothing's been done about it because President Karzai doesn't want trouble with the Hezb-e Islami factions. They're too strong in the parliament now."

Steelyard drank from the bottle of milk and offered it to Metcalf, who leaned forward to take it. "Those kill-crazy bastards will never give that woman back alive," he said. "They'll use her to humiliate the country for as long as they can, and when it looks like we're finally going to attack, they'll dump her headless body on some fucking street in Kabul."

Metcalf wiped his mouth with the back of his hand. "Regardless, this is going to be handled at the diplomatic level. It's been decided."

"Does the president understand these sons of bitches don't know the first fucking thing about diplomacy? That they aren't looking for a fucking bargain? All they *want* is chaos."

"What the president understands is that he's only eleven months away from the election," Metcalf said. "He also understands that a crisis like this could easily extend as many months if it's not handled properly."

"Well, he'd better count on it extending at *least* that long unless we go in there and bring that woman out. They'll use her to make him look like a chump—just like the Iranians did to Carter. And then, a week before the election, they'll dump her body in the street."

"Hal, we don't know that."

"No, not yet," Steelyard conceded. "But you can bet your last dollar the HIK's going to be thinking long and hard about who *they* want for president between now and November."

"Well, whatever we think we know doesn't matter," Metcalf said. "I just came over here to get you dialed in on what Pope expects from you."

"Which is?"

Metcalf couldn't help the grin that came to his face. "He said for me to tell you and Crosswhite to try and stay out of trouble."

"That's it?" Steelyard asked, suddenly wary. "'Try and stay out of trouble'?"

"Word has it that the Joint Chiefs want him out of SOG," Metcalf went on. "My conversation with General Couture was too short for me to get any details—and there was no way for me to ask without creating suspicion—but I think they suspect that Pope knew about Bank Heist and kept it to himself."

"Did he?"

Metcalf smiled crookedly. "How the hell would I know? I just work here."

37

AFGHANISTAN,
Village of Bazarak

Aasif Kohistani stepped into Sandra's new quarters at the edge of
Bazarak Village and took a seat in the corner to watch as the village doctor treated her leg wound, which was now badly infected.
Gangrene had set in, and she was in grave danger of losing the leg
entirely. Badira sat in a chair beside the doctor with a clay bowl of
maggots, which the doctor was placing into the wound one by one
with a pair of elongated forceps.

"Why the maggots?" Kohistani asked, feeling repulsed by the
sight of the insect larvae squirming about in the gangrenous flesh.

The doctor's name was Khan. He was not much older than
Badira, and he resented the HIK presence in the village, though he
knew there was nothing to be done about it. "This is the only way for
me to remove the rotted tissue," he said. "They will eat the dead flesh,

and leave the living flesh alone. She is fortunate that you arrived here when you did."

"So she will survive?"

"I believe she has a chance," Khan said, "but you should send for stronger antibiotics. All we have here is simple penicillin, which may not be strong enough. This infection is bad. She has a fever and there is the serious danger of her catching pneumonia. If that happens, she will probably die because she is too weak to fight that kind of infection."

"I will try and send for better medicines," Kohistani said, "but you should plan on making do with what you have. Soon this village will come under a great deal of American attention, and that may make it difficult to get supplies."

The doctor became even more unsettled, and some of his contempt began to show. "You're saying they already know she is here?"

Kohistani was amused by the courage of Khan's open contempt. From time immemorial, doctors had gotten away with disrespecting authority at times when regular people simply could not. "They will soon if they do not already," he said easily. "Do not be concerned. We Hezbis are very strong here, and the Americans will know they can't mount a rescue mission without forcing us to kill her. We have them by the testicles this time, and we'll be rubbing their noses in dung for many weeks to come."

"They will cut off all supplies to the village," the doctor warned, turning his attention back to his work.

"And then we will cut off her fingers," Kohistani said matter-of-factly. "And then her toes . . . her hands and feet. So you see . . . they will have no other choice but to leave the village in peace . . . so long as you can keep her alive."

Khan dipped a strip of muslin into a greenish liquid, squeezing out the excess before laying it over the wound to keep the maggots in place. "May I suggest then," he asked, "that you use some of that influence to get some stronger antibiotics . . . and not just for her?"

"Make a list," Kohistani said with a smile. "I will see what can be done." He got to his feet and left the room.

Khan looked at Badira, the shape of the veil over her face telling him that she was missing most of her nose. Her eyes were beautiful, however, and he could not help smiling at her, though it was a sad kind of smile. "Whose idea was it to turn her into an opium addict?"

"Mine," Badira said. "There was nothing else to give her."

Khan smiled knowingly. "She's probably going to die, you know that."

She nodded.

"But we will do what we can for her," he said.

They noticed that Sandra was awake now and watching them talk. Her eyes were glassy and sunken slightly in her bruised and sweating face.

"Ask her about the pain."

"Are you in pain?" Badira asked.

Sandra nodded and closed her eyes. Badira had told her of the American assault on Waigal Village, thinking it might boost her spirits to know that her people had not forgotten about her, but the news of the near rescue had had the opposite effect, and Badira was regretting having told her, for it was clear the American woman was on the verge of giving up hope.

"I will tell the women to brew her a special tea," Khan said. "See that she drinks it. Keep her hydrated and feed her three times a day. I will tell the women what foods to prepare." He was about to rise, then paused. "And lie to her, Badira. Tell her that negotiations are taking place to facilitate her release. Otherwise, she won't fight to stay alive."

"Perhaps it's better that she dies," Badira ventured. "Her suffering has been terrible, and it's likely to go on and on . . . and the Americans *will* come, despite what Kohistani believes . . . eventually, they will come. They always do, and when they do, many villagers will die."

"Yes," Khan said, getting up from the chair. "They will come, but not until they have exhausted every other option, and by then Kohistani will have achieved his goal. His plan is intelligent for his purposes. He will make the Americans play his game—make them believe there is a chance to win her release without violence. Not until after many weeks of being made into fools will they realize he has no intention of ever returning her alive. He has but one purpose: to make the Americans look weak. That will strengthen the Hezbi image all around Afghanistan and bring more fighters to their cause."

"He shared this with you?"

Khan shook his head. "Kohistani shares his thoughts with no one. This is what I believe will happen."

Badira was not accustomed to the company of a man who confided in her as an equal. "Where did you go to school?"

"I went to medical school in Pakistan," he said. "I was born here in Bazarak. I returned home to care for my parents in their old age. They were both very sick at the time. After they died I thought to return to Pakistan, but in the end, I decided to stay. This was a peaceful village before the Hezbi took it over. Perhaps it will be again . . . if it is the will of Allah."

"Perhaps," she echoed, willing herself to ignore the strange feeling of warmth in her loins which she had never known before.

"And you?" he asked. "Where did you go to school?"

"I was also educated in Pakistan."

Khan retook his chair. "May I ask about your nose?" he said gently. "Did you displease your husband?"

She nodded, fighting the tears that suddenly began to build behind her eyes.

"He's dead now?"

"Yes," she murmured, her eyes filling with tears.

"Allah be praised," he said with a smile.

38

WASHINGTON, DC,
Starbucks Coffee Shop

Two weeks after the brutal rape of Sandra Brux had become world news, Cletus Webb walked into the coffee shop where he found Tim Hagen, the president's military advisor, drinking a double latte and reading the *Washington Post*. Hagen set the paper aside and stood up to shake Webb's hand. The two of them then found an empty corner at the back of the shop and sat down at a table.

"Since both our bosses are stuck in this mess up to their necks," Hagen said, "I thought it might be a good idea for the two of us to meet in private."

Webb had never met the thirty-year-old Hagen in person, but he knew the skinny little man by reputation. He had a photographic memory and had earned himself both an MBA and a PhD from MIT by the age of twenty-four. The MBA was from the Leaders for

Global Operations Program. The PhD was in Aerospace Computational Engineering. Why he had chosen to work for the president was anybody's guess, but most assumed he was drawn to the power of the office.

Webb wasn't terribly confident there was anything to be accomplished by their meeting. "What's on your mind?"

"As you know," Hagen said, "the president ordered that a cordon be thrown up around the Panjshir Valley last week in an attempt to halt the flow of supplies and insurgents into Bazarak."

"Yes, he did that against our recommendation," Webb said, wondering if Hagen was the reason or if it was because of the Joint Chiefs. "He's trying to be tough with them, and that's not going to work."

"Well, it appears you were correct," Hagen said. He removed a small laptop computer from its case and opened it, plugged in a small set of earphones, and offered them to Webb. "NSA intercepted this video six hours ago via the internet. They've been reading all of Al Jazeera's email for the better part of a year now—that's classified, by the way—and we expect Al Jazeera to go public with it very soon."

Webb wasn't entirely surprised to hear it about the NSA. They had worked their way into practically every electronic nook and cranny on the planet, with China being the sole exception due to their strict controls over the internet. He put the phones into his ears and moved around to Hagen's side of the table so no one else in the coffee shop would be able to see the screen.

"I warn you, this is graphic as hell." Hagen pressed Play.

The first thing to appear on the screen was the terrified visage of Warrant Officer Sandra Brux. The shot pulled back to reveal that she was once again tied completely naked to a bed.

"Please don't do this," she said, begging someone off camera.

The shot panned around to show a smiling Aasif Kohistani sitting in a chair. "Greetings," he said in English, "and may the blessings of Allah be upon you. American military forces have surrounded the Panjshir Valley, cutting us off from the outside world in an attempt to starve our women and children. This will not be tolerated." He signaled the cameraman to train the camera on Sandra.

Kohistani spoke to her off camera. "Sandra, tell your president what you want him to do."

Sandra was sobbing with fear and shame, unable to look at the lens as she spoke. "I want him to pull our troops back."

"Why?"

"Because if he doesn't, you're—" She began to weep.

"Tell him!" Kohistani snapped.

"Because you're going to cut off my fingers and toes."

"And then what?"

"My feet and hands," she said, sobbing even harder.

Kohistani said something in Pashto, and Ramesh stepped into the shot holding what looked like a pair of aviation snips. He took hold of Sandra's left wrist.

"No!" Sandra screamed, fighting in vain against the leather straps they had used to secure her to the wooden frame of the bed. She balled her hand into a tight fist, but Ramesh easily pried her ring finger free and cut it off with the sheet-metal cutters. She shrieked in pain and horror as the blood began to gush from the stump of the knuckle.

Ramesh cut her hand loose from the strap and held it up to the camera so that it was plain to see the amputation had been not faked. He held up the severed finger in his other hand.

Sandra jerked her hand from his grasp and put the knuckle into her mouth, attempting to stanch the blood. A moment later, she turned to lean over the edge of the bed and began to vomit. The camera swung back around to Kohistani. He was no longer smiling.

"*You* did this, Mr. President, you and no one else! Pull your troops back, or every day this village remains surrounded, your woman will lose a finger. Do not attempt a rescue, or she will be killed instantly. You will wait patiently for our demands—or she will die!"

The shot then swung back around to show Sandra lying on the bed sobbing with her fist balled up tight against her breast, blood covering her chest and belly. The video came to an end and froze.

Hagen closed the laptop.

Webb plucked the earphones from his ears and moved back around to his side of the table, visibly shaken. "Has the president seen this?"

"Yes," Hagen said. "He's called a meeting for this afternoon with your boss and the Joint Chiefs."

"He's looking for advice?"

Hagen shook his head. "He's already ordered our troops pulled completely away from the Panjshir Valley. The meeting is to ensure that no one inside of SOG acts without orders this time. He doesn't want *anyone* to do *anything* to put Warrant Officer Brux into any greater danger than she's already in."

"Okay," Webb said. "So what do you want from me? Shroyer isn't going to have any trouble going along with that program."

"I realize that," Hagen said. "What I was hoping was that the two of us might be able to continue looking at the bigger picture."

A shadow crossed Webb's brow. "What bigger picture?"

"Well, it's obvious what the HIK is looking to achieve here," Hagen said. "They're using Sandra to make the US look weak—and it's going to work."

"Of course they are," Webb said, hunching his shoulders and letting them fall. "Have you told the president that?"

"Certainly, I've told him," Hagen replied, "but . . . well . . . this *has* to stay between the two of us."

"Okay."

"The president's having a very human reaction to this crisis. You might even say it's traumatized him . . . he's afraid it's going to cost him the presidency."

Webb sat back in the chair. "You call that a *human* reaction?"

Hagen seemed not to have heard him. "He's been okay the past couple of weeks. The uproar over the rape video was pretty rough on him, but after he went on television to report that we'd captured the Taliban rapist, things began to settle down. This video, however, is going to have an even deeper impact than the first, and there's virtually no way for us to get out in front of it. The president ordered that valley surrounded, and Sandra has been mutilated as a direct result of that order . . . at least that's how the people are going to see it."

"I'm sorry," Webb said, now thinking Hagen must be some kind of a cold-blooded reptile, "but I don't see how any of this involves you and me in any sort of private manner. This crisis is going to be handled at a higher pay grade than yours or mine."

"I agree," Hagen said, taking a drink from his latte. "But the president needs to change his thinking, and I can only influence him so far. If you can influence Shroyer to offer him the same advice that I'm offering him, we might be able to change his mind. I'm not kidding myself about our chances, but it's worth a try."

Webb was hard-pressed to hide his irritation. "What advice?"

"Full-scale assault into the Panjshir Valley. This is the perfect opportunity for us to annihilate hundreds of HIK fighters. They've made a grave tactical error in their reach for a strategic advantage here."

"Yeah, well, Sandra's presence in that valley fairly well trumps the error."

"Only if we allow it to," Hagen said, pressing hard now. "You have to think about this *mathematically*, Cletus. Sandra's dead anyway. You know it, I know it—hell, even *she* knows it! Why let it be a total loss? If she has to die, why not let it be during a rescue attempt? And why not use that rescue attempt as an excuse to wipe out as many of the enemy as we possibly can? These are the crazy lunatics who are likely to take over Afghanistan after we leave. We can't allow our humanity to cause us to lose sight of the bigger picture here."

"What the hell is this bigger picture you keep talking about?"

"It's very simple," Hagen said. "If we smash that valley flat—along with everyone and everything in it—this will be the *last* time we ever have to worry about these crazy people using one of our women to humiliate the United States."

39

AFGHANISTAN,
Jalalabad Air Base

The mood around the base was pretty somber. News of Sandra's finger amputation and the subsequent troop pullout from the Panjshir Valley had been a double whammy to most everyone's moral. At least with Bazarak surrounded they had felt like *something* was being done for Sandra. Now, though, the overwhelming feeling was that she had been left behind, and that didn't sit well with any of the American forces based in the Afghan Theater of Operations, much less her fellow Night Stalker pilots, the Army Rangers, and Navy SEALs—a number of whom had risked lengthy prison terms in the unauthorized rescue attempt.

There was little or no talk about another unauthorized mission. What little talk there was was nothing more than blowing off steam, and none of it took place in front of the officer corps. The president himself had made it very clear through General Couture that *any* un-authorized action of *any* kind would be punished to the full extent of the Uniform Code of Military Justice, and no one wanted to risk being charged with entering into the planning stages of such a mission.

Opinions of the president's decision to pull out of the valley were equally divided. Half the troops in the ATO at least sympathized with the president for wanting to spare Sandra any additional tor-ture. The other half, however, were busy putting themselves in San-dra's shoes, boasting that it would be better to die on American terms than it would be to die at the whim of a lunatic Muslim cleric. They wanted to attack right now with every available fighting man and wipe the village of Bazarak clean off the map.

Newly released from the hospital, Captain Crosswhite limped into the ready room in the hangar where Gil, Steelyard, and a number of other SEALs—many of whom had taken part in Bank Heist—were sitting around smoking cigarettes and nipping from a pair of illegal whiskey flasks.

Gil flicked the butt of his cigarette into a dented steel trash can and grinned. "I expected you to be on a plane back to Kandahar by now."

"Shit," Crosswhite said, reaching to take a cigarette away from a very junior SEAL sitting near the wall. "They don't want me back down there." He took a long drag from the smoke and gave it back. "I'm *persona non grata*. Soon to be dishonorably discharged—or worse." He winked at Steelyard. "Like my buddy over there."

Steelyard chuckled. "If I was ten years younger, I'd be humping the Panjshir Valley as we speak. As I am, I wouldn't do anybody any good. Sucks getting old, boys—remember I told you that."

There were a number of dutiful chuckles.

Crosswhite took a seat and reached for the flask.

"That a good idea for you right now?" Gil asked.

"Hell, no." Crosswhite tipped the flask. "Thanks, I needed that. I just got cornered outside the hospital by John Brux. He said he flew in here to thank me for trying to rescue his wife. I told him he didn't have to thank me for a fuckin' thing. I asked him if he wanted to walk over here with me to thank the rest of you Bank Heist boys, but he asked me to do it for him. He's pretty down at the moment. I guess nobody gave him the news about Sandra's finger until a few hours ago. He says nobody wanted to be the one to tell him."

"Jesus, can you blame them?" Alpha said.

Crosswhite's face lit up, noticing Alpha for the first time. "Hey, Leper! Your pecker drop off yet?"

The room broke up in laughter and Alpha jumped up, turning in a circle to give them all the finger with both hands. "Right here, motherfuckers!" He grabbed his package. "None of you fucking pussies would have acted any different."

Even Gil was having trouble suppressing a smile. He caught a glimpse of Forogh signaling to him from outside the ready room and slipped quietly out into the hangar as the jokes about Alpha's Bank Heist meltdown began to fly.

"What's up?" Gil asked guardedly, expecting Forogh to level more complaints about the interrogation.

"I need to talk to you," the interpreter said. "Alone."

"Look, Forogh, if it's about the interrogation—"

"No, it's not about that," Forogh said in a hushed voice.

"All right, come on." Gil led him out behind the hangar, where the two of them climbed up into the back of a deuce-and-a-half truck.

"Okay, what's eating you?"

Forogh stared at him, as if taking a final moment to make sure of himself. "I have family in Bazarak."

Gil felt his skin turn to gooseflesh. "How much family—a lot?"

Forogh shrugged. "Many uncles, cousins. They fought with Massoud against the Russians."

"Do you think you can get in there with the place being under HIK control?"

Forogh nodded. "My uncles will vouch for me. No one in my family knows that I work for American Special Forces."

In his mind, Gil was suddenly halfway to Bazarak. "Do you think you could get in there and find out where Sandra's being held? Would you be willing to try?"

"Yes," Forogh said. "I'm worried, though. I don't trust the CIA."

"Don't worry," Gil said. "We're not telling SOG. We're keeping this a nice tight little unit. But first I gotta get permission."

This confused Forogh. "Permission? But you just said to forget about SOG."

"SOG's not in authority now." Gil bumped him on the shoulder. "I'm talking about getting permission from a higher source. Give me two hours, then meet me back in the hangar."

Gil went to his quarters and dug out the iPhone he'd gotten from Joe the night of Operation Tiger Claw. He'd spoken with Joe since and talked him into letting him borrow the hi-tech PDA indefinitely.

He typed out a detailed message and sent it off to Langley, Virginia. Then he lay on his bunk to take a nap. An hour later, he received a lengthy answer to his message and jumped up to go find Major John Brux.

40

AFGHANISTAN,
Jalalabad Air Base

Major John Brux was sitting in the mess hall by himself, picking at a compressed beef patty, when a man he didn't remember ever seeing before sat down across the table from him.

"John Brux, right?" the man said.

Brux looked at him, not really appreciating the intrusion. "Who's asking?"

"My name's Gil Shannon. I'm a good friend of Dan Crosswhite. I also know your wife."

Brux was a big man with dark eyes and broad shoulders, but his shoulders were uncharacteristically drooped beneath the weight of the burden he was carrying these days. He noticed the trident on Gil's uniform. "Were you on the Bank Heist mission with Crosswhite?"

"Unfortunately, no," Gil said, sitting back with a sigh. "I was stuck back here nursing a bullet wound to my ass. I'd like to talk to you about something off the record."

Brux took a look around. The closest people were a pair of civilian intelligence analysts sitting five tables away. "I'm listening."

Gil lowered his voice and sat forward, keeping his face casual. "If I can get an indigenous operative into Bazarak to mark the exact building where Sandra is being held, do I have your permission to go in there and try to bring her out?"

Brux stole another startled look at the analysts who stared back at him for a curious moment before continuing with their meal. "What are you talking about?"

"Yes or no?"

"No," Brux said. "Ten men nearly died already. Two of them are facing court-martial. She wouldn't want anyone else taking that kind of a risk. Besides, what could one man do?"

Gil shrugged. "That depends on the man and how big his balls are. More important, it depends on whether or not there's a Spectre gunship watching over him."

Brux shook his head, thinking Gil must be some kind of a hero type. "No. I appreciate your willingness to try, but no. Sandra's best chance now is for the State Department to negotiate her release."

"John, no offense, but that's dog shit, and you know it. The HIK has her, and those people are fixing to take over this country after we leave. Weakness and mercy are not the paths to power."

Brux stared at him, his face clouding over with a mixture of fear and anger. "You think I need to hear shit like that right now?"

Gil went on, keeping is voice low. "I've got a plan to bring your wife out. You in or not?"

Brux watched the analysts getting up to leave, and then lowered his voice. "What the fuck's so special about you, huh? Why should I trust Sandra's life to some renegade adrenaline junkie with a death wish?"

Gil's eyes twinkled. "Because to me . . . this mission will be just another one . . . way . . . trip."

Brux sat back in the chair. Very few people on earth knew about Operation One Way Trip, the mission during which he had been the pilot of the MC-130H Combat Talon II aircraft that had extracted Master Chief Gil Shannon from the Chinese coast via the Skyhook Surface-To-Air Recovery (STAR) system first employed by the CIA during the Vietnam War. Brux had never been told Gil's name nor been allowed to see his face for security reasons.

"So that was you," he said quietly.

"If half a billion screamin' Chinese couldn't kill me, how the fuck are a hundred *hajis* gonna manage it?"

"The HIK has close to a thousand fighting men in the mountains around the Panjshir Valley."

Gil shrugged. "That's in the mountains around the village. There won't be more than a few hundred in Bazarak."

"How did you know it was me in the cockpit?" Brux wanted to know. "We were never supposed to know each other's identities."

"Sandra and I had a talk one night," Gil said. "We all landed back here after a snatch-and-grab just across the border into Pakistan. She and I had a few laughs . . . she mentioned her husband flew rubber dog shit of out Manila once in a while . . . one question led to another . . . you know how it goes."

Brux failed to stop the grin that spread across his face. "Damn girl never could keep her mouth shut. Did you know about her and Captain What's His Name?"

"Sean Bordeaux?"

Brux lowered his eyes and nodded.

"Not until just now."

Brux looked up. "What's that mean?"

"Well, they were tight," Gil said. "I could see that, but I never thought anything was going on between them. You're telling me you don't have a special friend back in Manila? Nobody to take the edge off?"

Brux shrugged his shoulders. "Do you really think you can get her out of there?"

"I think *we* can get her out of there."

"Suppose I agree. What do you need me to do?"

"You got any friends in the 24th STS? I mean, friends with balls?" This was the 24th Special Tactics Squadron, the SMU under the auspices of the United States Air Force.

Brux grinned. "Is a frog's asshole watertight?"

Gil reached back to grab his ass. "It was the last time I checked."

"How many men do we need?"

"Enough to help you fly the Spectre . . . run the guns . . . and operate the STAR system."

"STAR system?" Brux said in surprise. "On a Spectre? There aren't any C-130s matching that configuration. Never have been, as far as I know. Hell, the Skyhook I flew to pull *you* out was special-rigged for that mission and disassembled that same night."

"What if I told you there's a CIA Spectre down in Diego Garcia with a custom STAR rig?"

Brux felt chills. "I'd ask how the hell you could know something like that."

"I didn't know until about ten minutes ago," Gil said. "I sent a message to a friend of mine asking for ideas, and he came up with the Spectre. I'm going to trust you with something that only two people know about, John, and only because Sandra's life is riding on it. I'm connected back in Langley, very deep, to a guy I've never actually met. If we go through with this, it might well end up costing him everything, but he's willing to roll the dice ... *if* you're willing to put it on the line for your wife and fly the fucking plane."

"From Diego Garcia?"

Gil shook his head. "If you tell me you can find us a crew within twenty-four hours, that fucking plane is going to magically appear out there on the tarmac at zero dark thirty tonight."

A smile broke out across Brux's his face. "Now I know why you're the one they sent into China. So you're actually a spook."

"No," Gil said. "But my old man saved a spook's life once in Vietnam."

"Okay," Brux said, pushing all his chips forward. "I'll have a crew here in twelve hours, but listen, tough guy ... every one of them's going to be AWOL, so we'll need a good place to hide them."

"Shit, John, this is the Sandbox. There's holes to hide in all over this motherfucker."

AN HOUR LATER Gil sat down on his bunk and called his wife using a borrowed satellite phone. "Hey, beautiful. It's me. Sorry to wake you."

"I wasn't sleepin'," Marie said. "I was layin' here waitin' for you to call."

"What are you talkin' about? I didn't decide to call you till half an hour ago."

"Well," she said, letting out a girlish yawn, "I woke up half an hour ago feelin' like you were gonna call me. So I've been waitin'."

Gil wasn't sure he liked the sound of that. He didn't believe in premonitions, good or bad, but it was an odd coincidence. "Everybody okay—mom, Oso, the horses?"

"Yep. Everybody's good. What's happening?"

"I'm going off the reservation, baby. I may end up getting in some real trouble for it, too."

She said, "Which means you're goin' after Sandra. What's 'off the reservation' mean—that you don't have nobody's permission?"

He felt a sudden lump in his throat, unable to help putting himself in John Brux's boots. "I have her husband's permission."

"Then that's plenty. As far as I'm concerned, you don't need nobody else's."

"But I do," he croaked. "I need yours."

"You have it," she said softly. "Of course you have it. You're going in against the odds this time, aren't you?"

"Very much."

"Then the real reason you're callin' me is to give me the chance to say good-bye. Is that right?"

He lowered his head. "Maybe," he whispered, his voice suddenly raw.

"I'm grateful to you for that. I know how difficult it is . . . and it's the sweetest thing you've ever done."

His guilt was too great. He couldn't speak.

"Gil, listen to me," she said. "I ain't never loved nobody on this earth the way I love you . . . but I've always known this day was comin'. I've known it because I know you. I've been preparin' for it. And the idea of not gettin' to say good-bye was always what scared me most. You need to know you're the finest man there is," she said to him. "The best this country's got to offer that woman . . . and I'll tell you somethin' else, my husband. It makes me proud knowin' you're goin' in to get her back without the damn Navy's say-so . . ."

41

AFGHANISTAN,
Jalalabad Air Base

Late that night Gil opened the door to his quarters and snapped on the light to find Master Chief Steelyard sitting there waiting for him. "What the fuck are you doin' in here?"

Steelyard struck a match to light a cigar. "Looking to find out what the fuck you're up to."

"That's none of your business. Get outta my quarters. I'm tired."

There was a quick knock at the door, and Crosswhite slipped inside. "Whatever the fuck you're up to, Gilligan, I want in on it."

"Jesus Christ!" Gil said. "Has Forogh been running his mouth?"

"I wish. I did everything but threaten to waterboard his ass. He's not talking."

"Good. Because there's nothing to talk about."

"We're not blind," Steelyard said. "You two have been creeping around the base all day like a couple of cockroaches. Now, are you cutting us in, or am I ratting you off to the Head Shed?"

Gil smirked. "What do you want in this for, Chief? Ain't you two pricks in enough trouble already?"

Crosswhite tapped Steelyard on the shoulder. "Hey, Chief, how about giving me one of those cigars, buddy?"

Steelyard turned his head to look up at him, arching his eyebrow. "How about washing my balls . . . *buddy*?" He got up from the chair and stepped toward Gil. "You owe me for Indonesia, Gilligan. Now what the fuck is going on?"

"Oh? You sure you want to call that one in, Chief? That's a pretty big chip to risk at the roulette wheel."

"I'm a risky motherfucker!"

Gil sat down on the edge of his bed. "Forogh has family in Bazarak. I didn't know it before, but his family's a warrior clan—or they used to be. Anyhow, I'm gonna hide up in the mountains outside the village while he goes in and fingers the building where they're holding Sandra. Then I'm going in to bring her out."

"You and the *haji*," Crosswhite said, slightly incredulous. "Alone."

"Well, not exactly," Gil said. "Anyhow, I need to get in there by tomorrow night . . . ahead of Operation Fell Swoop . . . so we're leaving in the morning. I know an SAS helo pilot who's gonna drop us off south of the valley."

Steelyard exchanged harsh glances with Crosswhite. "What the fuck is *Fell Swoop*, and how the hell is Forogh gonna finger fuck the building?"

Gil put a hand into the cargo pocket of his ACUs, bringing out an MS-2000 Firefly, an infrared strobe light that would be visible for miles, though only through the lens of an infrared night-vision device. "He'll toss this onto the roof, and the enemy will never even know it's there. Simple as it gets."

Steelyard stepped over, lifting his boot to rest it on the footboard of the bed. He braced his elbow against his knee and pointed at Gil with the wet end of the cigar. "It's not that simple, and you know it. The HIK's been occupying that valley for months. You're gonna need tac-air to get out of there alive, amigo."

"I've already taken care of that."

"You're telling me you found somebody else stupid enough to put their ass on the line with you?"

"Look outside."

Steelyard went to the window with Crosswhite. On the far side of the tarmac sat what appeared to be an AC-130J Spectre gunship, bristling with a 25 mm Equalizer rotary cannon, a 40 mm Bofors auto-cannon, and a 105 mm howitzer . . . though something wasn't quite right about the plane's configuration.

Steelyard turned around. "You're telling me that's here for you?"

"Officially?" Gil shook his head. "Officially, it landed an hour ago with avionics trouble. From what I understand, it could take a few days to get the right parts in to make the necessary repairs."

"Bullshit," Steelyard said. "How'd you manage that?"

Gil got to his feet. "Wanna see it up close?"

"I want to know how you managed to pull it out of your ass."

Gil put out his chest and got in Steelyard's face. "I've got friends at the Vatican. You wanna see the fuckin' thing or not?"

FIVE MINUTES LATER, they stood on the tarmac beside the Spectre. The three guns protruding from the left side of the fuselage were covered with canvas covers to protect them from the elements. Attached to the nose of the aircraft were two incongruous steel booms, both approximately twenty feet long and folded back from the nose, locked into place along either side of the fuselage.

"I've never seen a Spectre like this," Crosswhite said. "What are those arms for?"

Steelyard took the cigar from his teeth and spit. "It's some kind of a modified Skyhook." He looked at Gil. "This is a CIA bird. Probably isn't even on the goddamn books."

Gil pointed at the "USAF" emblem on the fuselage. "No, it's an Air Force bird, Chief. Says so right there on the—"

"You can stencil a swastika on the fucking thing," Steelyard grumbled. "That don't make it no Nazi plane. The Air Force discontinued the STAR system clear back in '98, so this plane's not even supposed to exist. Now, I'll ask you again—who did you get in the CIA to loan it to you?"

"Sorry, Chief. I gave you all the clues I'm givin' ya."

Steelyard stood staring at him for a long moment, the gears slow to mesh. Then he recalled Gil's crack about the Vatican. "Pope!"

Gil's face split into a grin.

"Christ Almighty. How long have you been in bed with that crazy bastard?"

"I got a handwritten note from him about five years ago—right after the last president appointed him to run SAD. He said he'd been following my career, said he owed my father his life, and if there was ever anything he could do for me, to let him know. So earlier today I sent him an email telling him what I had in mind. I asked him if he had any suggestions." Gil pointed at the plane. "This is what he suggested."

Crosswhite whistled tonelessly. "They say he's protected by the devil himself."

"He *is* the devil himself," Steelyard said bitterly. "So where's the crew?"

"They caught the next thing smoking back to Diego Garcia."

"Then who's going to fly the fucking—Brux! You got Brux mixed up in this?"

"See there?" Gil said. "I knew you Gulf War One frogs were sharp."

"Brux is a wreck," Crosswhite said in disbelief.

Gil stood pulling on his chin. "To be honest, Dan, I didn't think a rescue was possible until you told me he was on the base. It wasn't easy getting his permission to make the attempt, but once I got it, I had everything I needed. He's the only pilot I know who's ever flown Skyhook."

Steelyard jerked his head toward Gil, pointing at him with a stubby finger. "You lying son of a bitch. *That's* how you got out of China. I knew that submarine story was bullshit."

"Like you said, Chief . . . Skyhook was officially discontinued *clear back in '98.*" He shook his jaw as he spoke, imitating Steelyard's jowly way of talking, but it came out more like a bad Nixon impression, and Crosswhite laughed out loud.

"Fuck you!" Steelyard said to Crosswhite, turning to Gil. "You could've told me the truth, you prick. I share everything with you."

"Everything, Chief?" Gil stepped up, reaching into Steelyard's jacket to take a pair of cigars from the inside pocket, passing one off to Crosswhite. "So who was the girl in Manila, Halligan—the doxy you keep in your wallet?"

"Eat me, Shannon! She's no doxy." Steelyard took a step back, self-consciously hitching up his trousers. "And you're the only fucker who's ever even seen her picture."

"Hey," said Crosswhite. "You still haven't told us about Fell Swoop. What the hell is that, and how'd you find out about it?"

"The second answer is obvious," Steelyard said. "Pope told him about it when he agreed to supply the plane. So what is it, Gilligan? Does General Couture finally have clearance to attack the Panjshir?"

Gil bummed a match to light the cigar. "Hasn't your buddy Metcalf said anything?"

"I told you already," Steelyard said. "Metcalf only sticks his neck out so far. He didn't make captain by taking stupid risks. That's something you should keep in mind, by the way . . . if you ever expect to make Command Master Chief."

The three of them exchanged looks before laughing out loud at the very absurdity of such a remark.

"Come on back to my place," Gil said. "Brux's crew will be here soon. They're all going AWOL to get here, so we'll have to figure out a secure place to hide them until kickoff."

42

AFGHANISTAN,
Kabul, Central Command

General Couture stood before a large map of the Panjshir Valley hanging on the wall. The map was festooned with large red arrows indicating the directions of the planned American troop movements into the valley. Captain Metcalf and a number of other officers sat in rows of chairs watching on as Couture prepared to share the particulars of Operation Fell Swoop.

"We'll start with some background on the Panjshir Valley for those unfamiliar with this infamous piece of real estate," he began. "It's one hundred kilometers in length with the Panjshir River running right through the middle of it. It is of significant strategic military importance, and for this reason remained a Mujahideen stronghold throughout the Russian war—back when our old ally Ahmad Shah Massoud was still their leader. The Soviets launched six different offensives against the Panjshir, and got throttled all six times. The valley remains littered with knocked-out Soviet armor to this day. The reason for the Panjshir's strategic importance is that Panjshir Highway leads directly to both the Khawak and Anjoman mountain passes. These passes are absolutely essential to any army wanting to move large numbers of men and materiel over the Hindu Kush. Even Alexander the Great passed through the Panjshir.

"As you know, Al Qaeda assassinated Massoud with a camera bomb back in 2001, but the valley has not been greatly contested since our arrival in Afghanistan—not until now. As a result of the scheduled drawdown of our forces here in the ATO, the Panjshir has not been occupied or even patrolled by US forces for the past six months. At the moment, the valley holds no real strategic value to us, but we don't particularly want it in HIK hands, either. As you know, these Hezbis have occupied the valley for the past four months now, and all of my requests for permission to drive them out have been refused. Karzai doesn't want them making a concerted effort to force him from office, so he's been making certain concessions. Allowing them the Panjshir was one such concession, and our president has seen fit to keep us out of it . . . until now.

"For those of you who have not heard, the HIK is holding Warrant Office Sandra Brux in the village in Bazarak, using her as a kind of human shield to further curb any attempt at our reoccupation of the valley. UAV reconnaissance indicates they are dug deep into the mountains surrounding the valley. They have filled every position with RPGs and heavy machine guns. Despite the fact they possesses limited artillery, they've taken a page right out of the old Mujahideen-Massoud playbook, employing the same tactics that were used to thrash the Soviets. It's become more and more obvious to me over the passing weeks that the HIK's overarching, long-term objective is to draw our forces into that valley in the hope of killing off hundreds of our troops, knocking out our armor, and forcing us to wrap up our involvement here in Afghanistan in the face of a final humiliating defeat—much like the Soviets were forced to do.

"We are not, obviously, going to fall into that trap, but the mathematical truth of the matter is undeniable: if we wait much longer to move in there and take Warrant Officer Brux away from these people, it's going to end up costing us a lot of men and materiel. The truth is that none of our intelligence people believes there is a realistic chance that this Hezbi cleric—Aasif Kohistani—is ever going to release Sandra alive, so it's been decided we're going in there to get her."

At this point, Metcalf realized that Sandra was being used as a pretext to go against Karzai's wishes and rid the Panjshir Valley of the HIK once and for all.

"The name of the operation is Fell Swoop," Couture continued. "It is tailor-made for the Rangers of the First Air Cavalry Division, and the Joint Chiefs believe it's the best way of both securing Warrant Officer Brux and eliminating large numbers of the HIK at the same time. The mission will begin with shock and awe. Air Force will pummel their mountain strongpoints ringing the valley in order to reduce the RPG threat to our Black Hawks and Apaches. Directly thereafter—before the smoke has cleared—the helos of the First Air Cav will swoop in and deploy two full companies of Rangers at either end of Bazarak Village.

"The Rangers to the south will establish blocking positions to prevent the enemy's escape. Rangers to the north will sweep down through the village, clearing each building along the way in search of Warrant Officer Brux. All of our people will be wearing infrared strobes, of course, so the Apaches flying top cover will be able to differentiate friend from foe. Meanwhile, Air Force will continue to hammer the mountain strongpoints to prevent the mountain fighters from reinforcing the village. Our troops on the ground will be outnumbered, but our superior air power will neutralize the enemy's numerical advantage."

Couture took a look around the room. "Don't worry," he said with a smile. "Up against our night vision, our superior weapons, and our training, the enemy's resistance within the village itself should quickly degrade into pockets of panicked gunmen just hoping to survive the night. We've mapped every inch of the village into the global positioning system, so our people on the ground will be able to call for tactical Apache strikes against any pockets of resistance they cannot quickly reduce themselves. The name of the game here is speed. After Sandra is secured, our troops will be pulled out of the valley, and Air Force will finish the job. We do not intend to reoccupy the valley, only to eliminate great numbers of the HIK."

Couture paused again to look around the room. "Any questions?"

Captain Metcalf cleared his throat. "I have one question, General."

"By all means, Captain."

"Well, sir, I'm wondering if we're giving enough consideration to securing Warrant Officer Brux. SOG remains ready and eager to participate in this operation."

Couture nodded gravely. "I share your concern, Captain, and I understand that our people in Special Forces remain ready. However, it's been decided that conventional shock and awe is our best means of bringing Warrant Officer Brux out of there alive, especially since we still have no idea which building she's being held in. The size and shape of the village itself is very problematic. Bazarak is too big and too heavily occupied at present for a special ops team to go in there alone with any chance of survival, and it's just too damned small for a joint operation. We can't have Rangers and SEALs running around in there at the same time. The simple truth is that they oper-ate differently, and the heads back in DC have decided to keep this a conventional fight."

Metcalf appreciated the elaborate explanation, but he recognized it as so much bullshit. It was obvious to him that the Special Forces community was being punished for Bank Heist. Even in these modern times, there existed elements within the United States Army that hated Special Forces—even their own Green Berets—elements who would seize any opportunity to make Special Forces look unnecessary or overhyped in order to brush them aside and keep them out of the fight. There were many egos to feed, and too few operations to satisfy their voracious appetites for glory, recognition, and ever-important funding.

Warrant Officer Elicia Skelton with CID, seated in the back row, put up her hand.

Couture wondered briefly what she was doing there, then remembered that CID would be needed to begin an immediate investigation in the event Sandra Brux was found dead in Bazarak. He recalled that Elicia's immediate supervisor, Brent Silverwood, was the man suspected of leaking the DNA evidence that had led to the execution of Bank Heist. "What is it, Skelton?"

If Elicia felt self-conscious with all of the brass turning to look at her, it didn't show. "Sir, I'm curious how much consideration has been given to the fact that the vast majority of people living in the Panjshir aren't Pashtun. They're mostly Tajik and therefore largely sympathetic to the West. I believe it's possible we may end up killing a large number of our allies, sir."

Couture's brow went up, but he immediately regained his composure. "This is presently a hostile village, Skelton. While it may be predominantly Tajik under normal circumstances, you may rest assured there are hundreds of Pashtuns living there now." He took his eyes from her and addressed the entire room. "Remember, people, this is first and foremost a rescue operation. Our primary goal is to recover Warrant Officer Brux, but this is also an excellent opportunity for us to eliminate a large number of HIK fighters . . . all in one fell swoop."

43

AFGHANISTAN,

in the mountains above the Panjshir Valley

Gil and Forogh were dropped off well south of the Panjshir Valley by a British Special Air Service helicopter shortly before dawn,
both of them wearing the robes of Tajik goat herders. The significant difference between them, of course, was that Gil wore a combat
harness loaded with ammo, grenades, and incidentals beneath his
disguise. He carried a .308 Remington Modular Sniper Rifle with
a folding stock and Schmidt & Bender optics, rail-mounted behind
a PS-22 Night Vision Scope with infrared illuminator. The rest of
his loadout consisted of an M4 carbine, a Kimber Desert Warrior
model 1911 pistol, and his father's Ka-Bar fighting knife. He carried
ten magazines of ammo for each weapon: 100 rounds for the sniper
rifle, 300 for the carbine, and 80 for the pistol. Both the Remington
and Kimber were fixed with suppressors. Gil wore no armor other

than an integrated ballistic helmet (IBH) fitted with attachments for his night-vision monocular and infrared strobe light. All of this was concealed beneath the heavy, bulky brown robe.

They both carried AK-47s over their shoulders to make sure they looked the part, and though Forogh wore the traditional *pakol* on his head, Gil wore a shemagh to hide the fact that he was Caucasian. Anyone observing them at a distance would assume they were Tajik or Pashtun. Anyone who encountered them closely enough to identify Gil as a white man would likely catch a round from a silenced 1911.

They hiked all morning to reach the foot of the mountains ringing the Panjshir Valley to the south.

"I feel like a Tusken Raider in this getup," Gil remarked, sucking water from his CamelBak.

"What's that?" Forogh said.

Gil chuckled. "The Sand People from *Star Wars*. Ever seen the movie?"

"Yes," Forogh answered glumly. "On a DVD in Pakistan a long time ago."

"In a galaxy far, far away?"

Forogh didn't even come close to catching the joke. He stopped to lean against the walking stick he had picked up during their hike to reach the mountains. "Is that how you see us? As ugly, wild creatures who live in caves?"

"No," Gil said, realizing why Forogh might take exception with the comparison to Sand People. "I was talking about myself. You gotta remember, man, Americans lead sheltered lives. We don't mean nothin' by it when we say stupid shit like that."

"It's not the stupid things you say," Forogh said, starting off up the mountain. "It's the lack of thought before you say them."

Gil chuckled as he fell in behind. "I don't reckon I can argue with that."

The climb up the back side of the mountain took an hour, and they stopped just shy of the summit. Gil took out the map, orienting it with a compass and using the GPS in the hi-tech iPhone he'd gotten from Joe to pinpoint their exact coordinates. He had marked on the map the precise locations of all the enemy's mountain gun emplacements, intelligence that Pope had been able to supply him with over a secure internet connection with encrypted software.

"Okay, we're right at the eastern opening to the valley," Gil said, folding the map away. "The closest enemy emplacement is a full five hundred meters to the west of us. Once we crest this ridge, we should have an unfettered view of the valley without having to worry about anybody spotting us."

Forogh's thin lips drew into a tight smile. "You could have just asked me where we were."

Gil busted him on the shoulder. "You're sure you can get into that village without those HIK pricks giving you any shit?"

Forogh gestured with the sack of extra AK-47 magazines he carried over his shoulder. "This gift should be enough to convince them I don't like Americans. Beyond that, my uncles will vouch for me."

"And you're sure they'll help with the extraction?"

"They fought beside Massoud against the Russians in this very valley." Forogh beamed with pride. He pointed eastward. "My uncle Orzu was wounded right over in that pass. They were Mujahideen then, but they fought in the Northern Alliance against the Taliban with your CIA. Then Al Qaeda murdered Massoud. My uncle Orzu and Massoud were friends. I told you before, there's no chance they will not help. But they won't be able to help you inside the village. There aren't enough of them now. But they will secure the extraction zone and help us escape into the mountains once the woman is safe."

"Where's the trail they'll use to leave the village?"

"I will show you."

They crawled to the crest and lay on their bellies looking out over the valley floor.

"It cuts up the side of the mountain there above the village to the north." Forogh indicated with the knife edge of his hand. "My uncles harvest timber for a living now. The HIK isn't interfering with the villagers' lives. They can come and go as they please." He then pointed down into the valley where the village men were playing buzkashi on horseback. "See? The Taliban outlawed buzkashi, but the HIK like to play with us." Buzkashi was a game similar to polo, only it was played with the headless carcass of a goat, and there were virtually no rules. "The HIK doesn't like the Taliban. They take advantage of them."

Gil watched the riders playing buzkashi through the sniper scope, a patch of nylon stocking stretched tightly over the lens, held in place by a rubber band, to prevent the sun glinting off the lens. He watched the horses carefully, seeing that they were strong, most of them just fine for what he had in mind. He noted the strange padded helmets many of the riders had on their heads and took his eye from the scope. "Are those Russian tanker helmets their wearing?"

"They are."

"Where'd they get 'em?"

Forogh gestured at the rusted hull of a Russian T-34/85 tank at the bottom of the mountain. There were many such hulks dotting the valley floor, though not all of them as dated as the T-34. "From the Russians."

Gil put his eye back to the scope. "Stupid question, I guess."

Forogh put his hand on Gil's shoulder. "I should leave you now. We're too close to the village to risk being spotted together."

They crawled back from the crest, out of sight.

"Got the marker?" Gil asked.

Forogh knocked on the hollowed-out stock of his very beat-up AK-47 where he had hidden the infrared strobe against the pos-

sibility that he would be searched for a satellite phone on his way
into the village. The rifle's fore-grip was split and held together with
a very sticky, sap-coated twine wrapped many times around. He had
selected the battered rifle to make sure that no one from the HIK
would attempt to trade weapons with him.

They shook hands. "Good luck down there."

"Good luck to you," Forogh replied. "You're going to need it
much more than I will." He got to his feet, dusted off the front of his
robe, and walked up over the crest of the mountain.

Gil waited awhile, then crawled back to the crest and lay watching as Forogh slowly worked his way down the rocky slope. There
was a white pickup truck down on the road with four heavily armed
HIK sentries. Two of them sat in the back of the truck napping. The
other two lolled against the fender talking. They were watching the
road coming into the valley, and so far hadn't spotted Forogh trudg-
ing down the mountain above them.

When they finally noticed him, they didn't get particularly excited. They woke up the two men in the bed of the truck, and all
four of them waited patiently as Forogh completed his descent to
the road.

"Peace be with you," Forogh said in Pashto, giving a casual wave.

"And with you," one of the guards replied affably. "Where do you
come from?"

"From Charikar," Forogh said. He unshouldered the bag of magazines and offered it to one of the junior guards. "These are a gift. I've
come to visit my uncles in the Karimov clan."

The young guard rifled the sack and then dropped it into the
back of the pickup and put out his hand for Forogh's AK.

Forogh tightened his grip on the shoulder strap. "I'm keeping
this."

The younger guard looked at the sentry in charge.

"We need to search you," the leader said. "To be sure you're not smuggling anything into the village."

Forogh gave up the rifle, consenting to the search. "What would I be smuggling?"

"The Americans know we're holding one of their people here," the sentry explained. "They might try to send a spy with a radio. Why didn't you follow the road up from Charikar? Why come up over the mountain?"

Forogh smiled dryly. "Because the Americans have blocked the road into the Panjshir . . . which I'm sure you know."

The guard accepted that. "What business do you have with the Karimovs?"

"I told you . . . they're family."

"Do you come to herd goats with them?"

Again Forogh's dry smile. "They do not herd goats. They cut timber in the mountains to the north."

The guard grinned crookedly. "Give him his rifle."

Two of the sentries remained at the pass while the leader and his partner drove Forogh into the village. They stopped in front of the home of Orzu Karimov, the oldest of Forogh's uncles, the family patriarch. Forogh jumped out of the back and called into the house.

Orzu and two of his sons came outside.

Forogh noted the surprise in his uncle's eyes, but it was brief enough that the sentry would not have picked up on it.

"This man claims to be your nephew," the sentry said from the passenger seat.

Orzu Karimov was sixty-five. His face was lined and weathered, but his eyes were keen, teeth strong. "He's the son of my oldest sister. Welcome, nephew. It's been a year. Are you finally ready to work?"

Forogh shrugged. "Is there any?"

His uncle laughed and looked at the guard. "He's been lazy his entire life. He prefers following after goats to working for a living!"

The sentry laughed back and slapped the driver on the shoulder with the back of his hand, signaling for him to pull off.

Orzu signaled Forogh to precede him into the house, giving his sons a menial errand to run. Once inside, he barred the door and turned around. "I've received word you're working for the Americans." It sounded almost like an accusation. "Is this true?"

"Who else knows?" Forogh was very surprised. "Who told you?"

Orzu leveled his gaze. "I have friends everywhere. You should know that by now. You're here because of the American woman."

Forogh took a knife from inside his robe and used the tip of the blade to remove the screws from the buttplate of the AK-47. The infrared strobe slid out onto the table. "This flashes a light that only the Americans will be able to see. I will use it to mark the building where she's being held."

Orzu's eyes were steady and unblinking. "They pay you well, the Americans?"

"Well enough, but that's not—"

"Well enough to endanger your clan?" his uncle asked harshly. He pointed at the strobe. "That's enough to see every one of us shot."

Forogh was surprised by his uncle's anger. "I promised them you would help, Uncle."

"That was a naïve promise to make." Orzu dropped into a chair. "Why would I ever agree to such a thing? The Americans are leaving this country, and the Hezbi grows stronger every day. Making friends with the US now would be suicide."

Forogh sat across from him. "I told them you would help because Massoud was your friend, and Massoud would not have tolerated the Hezbi taking over the Panjshir."

Orzu remained obdurate. "Massoud is dead, and the Hezbi is a devil we must learn to live with. Once the Americans have gone, they will leave the Panjshir because there's nothing here for them."

"Aren't they taking a portion of your profits from the timber?"

"If they are, that's no reason to take twenty men up against six hundred. They leave us alone to live our lives, and that's how I intend to keep it."

Forogh understood his uncle's reasoning. "In truth, I knew I was lying when I told them why you would help."

A shadow crossed his uncle's face. "Lying?"

"The real reason you will help, Uncle, will be to save the village from total destruction."

Orzu sat forward, making a fist on the tabletop. "The Americans aren't that stupid. If they attack, the woman dies—instantly."

Forogh slipped the strobe back into its hiding place. "There is a man hiding in the mountains above the village. You will help me find a way to mark the woman's building with this light." He began to screw the screws back into place with the knife. "After the building is marked, we will ride out of the village with your men, up into the mountains as if we're leaving to cut timber. Then we will circle back to the junction with the Khawak Pass to set up a defensive perimeter for the Americans' extraction zone. While we are doing this, the American will sneak into the village and take the woman. He will then ride north with her to meet us. After the woman is lifted from the ground, we will all disappear into the mountains to begin cutting timber." Forogh chuckled. "Well, you and my cousins will begin cutting timber. The American and I will make our way back to friendly territory on horseback . . . and the Hezbi will never be wise to your helping. Even if we have to fire on them to protect the extraction zone, they won't know who's shooting at them, and they'll never be able to give chase in the mountains without horses."

Orzu gaped at him. "The Hezbi aren't stupid, either! And even if they were, this American of yours will fail."

"If he does," Forogh said with a shrug, "then I will be stuck working with you in the mountains until you decide to return to the village."

Orzu stood up from the table. "No, Nephew, I will not help you mark the building, and I will not put my men in danger to help the American."

"Yes, you will, Uncle. Because if you do not, tomorrow night the village will be attacked with bombs and helicopters and soldiers. The Hezbi will fight to the last man, and many Tajik will die in the crossfire . . . and so will their horses—so will *your* horses."

"I could warn them," Orzu threatened. "Tell them to get the woman out of here before the attack begins."

"That would change nothing," Forogh replied. "They would keep the woman here, and Americans would still attack. But that's unimportant because you would never warn the Hezbi."

"Why are you so sure, Nephew?"

"Because of Massoud, Uncle. Massoud would never do such a thing, and I know that he is *still* the only man you have ever admired."

44

AFGHANISTAN,
Bazarak

Khan sat listening to the rattle in Sandra's lungs, then plucked the stethoscope from his ears and turned to Kohistani. "I warned you this would happen. She's been in this bed fighting infection for ten days and now she has pneumonia. She'll be dead in a week."

Kohistani stood looking at the withering American woman who lay sleeping, her eyes beginning to sink in her face. "You're certain?"

"That she has pneumonia or that she'll be dead?"

"Of both."

"Yes," Khan said. "Penicillin isn't enough. I told you."

Kohistani bridled at the continued impudence of the village doctor. "You had better learn to curb your tongue with me, Doctor, or I will have you beaten before the entire village as an example."

Khan's mouth remained a thin line, his gaze not quite defiant.

"Are you going to ask the Americans for medicine for her? They could drop it from a plane."

Kohistani shook his head. "If they suspect she's dying, they'll attempt to rescue her—there would be nothing for them to lose at that point. Is the leg wound healing?"

"Yes, finally, but that's the least of her worries now."

"I see." Kohistani stood stroking his beard. He didn't want the American to die yet, but her death was inevitable, and she had already served the greater part of her purpose. The last two of weeks of preparation had been critical to the valley's defenses. If it was the will of Allah for her to live, she would live whether she was given a different medicine or not. Doctors put too much faith in medicine and too little in Allah.

He turned to the teenage guard sitting in the corner sharpening a knife. The boy was his dead brother's only son. "They could come for her any night now, Nephew," he said in Arabic so that neither Khan nor Badira could understand. "When the village falls under attack . . . as it must . . . you are to cut the American's throat first . . . then that of this pig doctor as well."

"It will be done, Uncle."

"Very good." Kohistani left the building.

The moment he was gone, Sandra's bloodshot eyes opened and she looked at Badira. "So what's going on?"

Badira averted her gaze. "Kohistani has sent for the medicine."

Sandra coughed, and a sardonic chuckle slipped out. "Like hell, he did. He's going to let me die. He's worried my people will do something desperate if they find out I'm sick . . . right?"

Badira looked at Khan, started to say something, then stopped and nodded her head. "Is he correct? Will they attack if they think you are dying?"

Sandra drew the blankets up close to her chin, shivering with fever. "I don't know what the hell they'll do anymore. Can you give me some opium . . . please?"

"No. Khan says it will weaken your lungs."

"Oh, for Christ's sake, Badira, I'm dying. What the fuck does it matter? Just let me have the goddamn shit."

Khan heard the crossness in her tone. "What is she upset about?"

"She wants opium."

He reached for his bag on the table. "I can give her pills for the pain."

"It's not only her leg she wants it for. She seeks oblivion."

Khan shook his head and got up from the chair. "In that case, no. Opium smoke will speed the deterioration of her lungs. If she dies sooner than expected, Kohistani will hold me responsible."

"Perhaps you could inject it," Badira suggested. "We have heroin."

Again, Khan refused. "Give her pills for the leg pain and keep her warm. Also, water and hot tea . . . lots of water and hot tea. And get her on her feet at least once every hour when she is awake, and keep her sitting up as much as possible."

Badira let out a sigh. "We might as well put her on a horse and send her out to play buzkashi with the Karimov clan."

Khan smiled his gentle smile, remembering their tender love-making the night before, Badira agreeing to remove the veil only after the candle had been put out. "I know you have become friends. But if you want her to live, you must be firm with her."

"What's he saying?" Sandra wanted to know, aggravated by all of the unintelligible talking going on around her. "He's saying I can't have the opium, right?"

"Yes," Badira said. "He's also saying that you need to get up and walk more."

"Sure," Sandra said, even more agitated. "Why not send me out to play a game of football while I'm at it?"

Badira's eyes twinkled above the veil. "I told him the same thing . . . but you're going to have to try. Also, you have to drink more of the tea."

"It tastes like goat shit. Khan can drink the tea his damn self."

Khan was watching Sandra with curious eyes, unaccustomed to seeing a woman so outspoken. "What's she saying now?"

"That she doesn't like the tea."

He snorted. "You didn't tell her what's in it, did you?"

"Do you think I'm stupid? Her guesses are close enough."

"So what's in the tea?" asked the teenager in the corner.

"A fermented fungus," Khan said offhandedly, knowing it was the boy's job to kill Sandra at the first sign of American treachery and detesting him for it.

Sandra inched up against the wall, drawing the blanket back to her chin. "So, have you two done it yet?" she asked out of the blue. "Fill me in here before I'm dead. Have you two lovebirds hooked up yet, or what?"

Badira's eyes grew wide above the veil.

Khan saw this. "What did she say?"

Sandra recognized his inquisitive tone, snickering as she made the gesture for sexual intercourse with her thumb and forefingers. "Sex, Khan. Have you two had sex yet?"

Khan recognized both the gesture and the word *sex*. He looked at Badira and laughed, his face flushing slightly. "Americans," he said, shaking his head. "Irreverent to the last."

45

AFGHANISTAN,
Panjshir Valley, Bazarak

Gil watched the young sentry search Forogh at the foot of the mountain, relieved they had decided against an attempt to smuggle any sort of communications device into the village. The sentry's search was thorough; nothing the size of even a small cellular phone would have escaped him. Gil lost sight of the pickup truck almost at once when they drove into the village, but he took it as a good sign when the truck returned to the roadblock without delay and the sentries resumed their lackadaisical watch.

He then spent the next six hours resting his body and his mind. This was done without napping or closing his eyes, utilizing a technique he had developed over the years, consciously resting his body while remaining alert to his environment. Breathing deeply from the diaphragm to fill his lungs completely allowed him to stretch the muscles of the chest and shoulders where the tension could tighten the tissues and endanger his accuracy. This type of exercise also helped to regulate the heart rate and keep the muscles well oxygenated and ready to move. The stresses of combat were not always caused by bullets and blood. For a sniper they were often caused by extended periods of motionless anticipation. During these dangerous periods, the sniper had to be careful to occupy his mind in a way that did not lull him into a lethargic state. Both the mind and the body needed to remain alert and elastic, ready to spring into action the instant the shit unexpectedly hit the fan.

With the coming of twilight, he shook off the calm and got mentally attuned to the mission ahead. Forogh had been in the village for a little over six hours now, and though there was still no sign of the infrared strobe, he told himself it was too soon to worry. He continued to study the various sentries around the village for any hint of where Sandra might be. Some of them held static positions while others roved freely about. Fortunately, these rovers did not wander randomly. Their routes were not set, but it was apparent each group of sentries had a particular zone they were responsible for. Also, there were three shooters with Dragunovs posted on a few of the higher rooftops.

The valley floor south of the village was sectioned off into more than forty farm plots, each varying in size and shape, none larger than a quarter acre in size, and each of them enclosed by a waist-high stone wall. There were a number of trees between the farm plots and the buildings, and Gil judged that from ground level the snipers would probably not have a clear view of his approach. This would allow him to creep within two hundred yards of their positions—the effective range of the subsonic rifle ammunition he would use to silently remove them from the game board.

There were various stables and mangers located south of the village as well, and Gil had already made a mental note of the route he would take to reach the horses. Luckily, the goats and sheep were not allowed to roam free, and he hadn't seen or heard a single dog all day. With luck, this meant that canines were few and far between. A dog could see ten times better than a human in the dark, and there was something about a shadowy figure in a combat crouch that put your average dog in the mood to bark its ass off. Gil thought of Oso and smiled. He was in no mood to shoot a dog tonight.

As the light continued to fade, his attention was drawn abruptly to a building located on a small rise in the center of the village. He lifted the Remington and watched through the night-vision scope as six armed men gathered on the roof. At least four more took up positions on the ground below, and electric lights came on inside and out. A pair of pickup trucks appeared out of nowhere and began to unload half a dozen men each.

"Shit," Gil muttered, watching as the building quickly took on the appearance of a well-defended command post. "He got himself caught!"

He continued to watch, and a few minutes later, a band of twenty men appeared, making their way down the alley toward the stables where the horses were kept. Each man led a horse from the stable into a square paddock where they began to saddle them up.

Swearing like the sailor he was, Gil made ready for a quick departure. Even from this range and elevation, he wouldn't stand a chance against the HIK with just three hundred rounds between the Remington and the M4. All they would have to do would be to use their trucks and cavalry to outflank him, and then, once he was good and surrounded, they could zero his position with a mortar and burn him down. There was no way of knowing whether Forogh had been made to talk yet, but there was no point in waiting around. Everybody talked sooner or later, and Gil didn't figure on

Forogh giving up too many fingers before he told them what they wanted to know.

FOROGH TIGHTENED THE horse's girth strap and pulled himself up into the saddle.

His uncle Orzu mounted up next to him. "Can you still ride, Nephew?"

"It hasn't been that long, Uncle." Forogh switched on the infrared strobe hanging from his neck by a lanyard. He couldn't see the light that it emitted even in the dark.

"Good!" his uncle said with gusto, reining the horse around. "Before this night is over, you may have to ride to save your fruit!"

Forogh's uncles and cousins laughed.

"You're sure no one can see that thing but the American?" one of Forogh's other uncles asked.

Forogh held up the strobe. "It's working now. Can any of you see anything?"

Satisfied that the instrument could be trusted, Orzu tapped his heels against the horse's flanks to set it walking. "Remember, don't place it before the shouting starts."

"I won't, Uncle."

The column rode out of the paddock, each man with an AK-47 across his back, their extra magazines hidden beneath their cold-weather clothing. They rode two abreast up a slight incline toward the river, then turned north up a dirt lane, passing before a row of concrete houses on the left toward an intersection shaped like a *T* turned over on its left side. The top of the *T* ran north to south, and the bottom ran east to west through the center of town past the well-lighted command post.

As Forogh and the others started to cross the *T*, Orzu led them within a few yards of a deserted-looking, ramshackle building where the east-west lane came to a dead end.

Four gunmen came pouring out of an open doorway and began shouting for them to get away from the building, aiming their AK-47s at the column and kicking at the horses. General pandemonium ensued as Forogh's uncles and cousins all began shouting back at them, intentionally creating chaos.

Orzu sat defiantly in the saddle haranguing the HIK men to stop kicking their horses, threatening to trample them if they didn't get out of the way.

"This is not your village!" he shouted down at them. "We go where we please here!"

More HIK came running down the lane from the command post a hundred yards away.

A door opened on the far corner of the lane, and Aasif Kohistani hurried outside followed closely by Ramesh, the brute who had cut off Sandra's finger.

During all of this confusion, Forogh pretended to lose control of his horse and sidled backward up against the building, tossing the strobe up onto the flat-top roof.

"What is going on out here?" Kohistani demanded. "Why are all of you mounted and armed? Where are you going?"

Having seen Forogh place the marker, Orzu raised his hand as a signal for his men to settle their horses and end the tumult. "We're riding north to timber country. There's work to be done."

"Now?" Kohistani said in dismay. "It's dark!"

"Of course it's dark!" Orzu said with a hearty laugh. "Do you expect us to cut illegal timber by the light of day?" This brought a guffaw of laughter from his nephews and brothers.

Orzu knew that Kohistani knew almost nothing about the timber-smuggling industry that was so rapidly deforesting the Afghan landscape, and thus would likely believe about anything he was told, within reason.

"But . . . but what about your tools?" Kohistani said.

"You think we carry all those tools back and forth with us, Kohistani? Why don't you come with us? It will do you good to try working for a living!" Again came the haranguing laughter from his cohorts.

Kohistani was immediately angry to be insulted in front of his men. "I see then, Orzu Karimov!" he shouted over the laughter. "I see! Then since you are cutting illegal timber, you will obviously need to pay a higher tax. Otherwise word could get back to Kabul of your illegal activities!"

Orzu feigned indignant anger. "Since when does the Hezbi collect taxes for the Karzai government in Kabul, Aasif Kohistani?"

"Why, the Hezbi does no such thing," Kohistani replied with a smile, believing he'd gotten the last laugh. "I merely state that a higher *local* tax will be required to prevent Karzai from learning of your illegal exploits . . . Now go if you're going! Get your men and these stupid animals away from here. You know very well this area is out of bounds."

Hating the Hezbi cleric, Orzu was tempted to say more, tempted even to trample the man to death, but it would not serve their purposes to delay further. The building was marked, and there was no sense to risk an open confrontation that might result in bloodshed. He turned in the saddle, calling for his brothers and nephews to follow him out of the village.

Kohistani stood in the road watching them go.

"We should move the woman now, Aasif," Ramesh said. "If the Americans are watching from above, they may have seen enough to know the command post is a decoy."

"You're right," Kohistani said, his ego bruised over Orzu's insult. "But we can't move her tonight without them seeing where we take her. We'll need to devise a plan first." Then he added: "Select a man, someone who knows horses well enough to ride at night. I want him to follow that foul-mannered Karimov to make sure of what they're up to. He was a friend of Massoud, and I think the time has come to remove him. Our people in the north can see to it that he and his clan do not return. Also, announce to the rest of the villagers in the morning that they're restricted to the village. We don't need them evacuating before the American attack comes. The more dead Tajiks when the battle is over, the better. They deserve it anyhow."

"It will be done, Aasif."

GIL WANTED NO part of fighting a running battle on foot against mounted cavalry in this territory. There were simply too many ridges for the enemy to pop up from behind and shoot. His only chance was to reach the bottom of the mountain and put as much real estate between himself and Panjshir Valley as possible before having to dig in. Before retreating down the back side of the mountain, he took a last look at the valley through the monocular in infrared, looking for the marker. Seeing nothing, he turned away.

But wait a second.

He had another look and saw that one of the horsemen was blinking.

"Son of a bitch," he muttered, taking a knee. "Is that you, Forogh?" He flipped up the monocular and raised the sniper rifle for a closer look at the rider. Sure as hell, it was Forogh. Gil slid back into his nook between the rocks. "You were supposed to mark the building, not yourself, son. What the hell are you up to?"

He watched through the scope as the column rode down from the stable and turned north up the lane. When he saw the four gunmen come pouring out of the deserted-looking old building, the hairs stood up on the back of his neck. He studied the altercation closely, keeping his focus on Forogh. If he had blinked, he would have missed Forogh toss the strobe onto the roof.

"I'll be damned. The command post's a decoy. It ain't like you fuckers to be so creative."

He spotted Kohistani and Ramesh coming from the building to the right of the intersection on the north side of the lane. "So it's you doing the thinking, eh? Well, okay, Mr. Kohistani, I guess I'll have to priority your ass, too . . . along with that ugly cocksucker behind you who owes me a fuckin' finger."

46

AFGHANISTAN,
Panjshir Valley, Bazarak

From his hide dug into the slope overlooking the village, Gil had a good view of the target area eight hundred meters below. It was just after midnight as he lay watching through his night vision. He could see by their movements that the sentries posted around the village were still max attentive to their environment, but he knew their vigilance would flag significantly toward the coming of dawn. He could see Sandra's building clearly from where he was, the infrared strobe on the roof still flashing away. It was nestled into a small cluster of crumbling structures one hundred meters from the river, nondescript and unobtrusive. Through the nightscope of the sniper rifle he saw clearly the guards lurking inside the darkened doorway beside hers, and he idly wondered whether they realized the darkness afforded them no real concealment in the twenty-first century.

He saw, too, the decoy building that was intended to foil any rescue mission the US might attempt to execute. Positioned in the center of the village, the structure was well lighted with power from a diesel generator. Six men still stood guard on the roof, and there were more posted on the ground outside the main entrance. The building showed every indication that its inhabitants were ready for a fight, and still more men were billeted in other lighted buildings nearby.

A decoy building was a smart ploy. Without Forogh's involvement, Gil would never have guessed Sandra was being held in the ramshackle cluster of buildings on the slope above the river where she was fairly well isolated from the rest of the village. To keep her near the center of town, surrounded by guards in a well-lighted concrete structure would have been a sensible defense against a modern enemy who generally attacked from above in the dead of night, coming in through the windows and doors in overwhelming numbers when you least expected it.

The first thing Gil would have to do in order to execute the extraction was clear a path to the building on the western side of the village. He would have to do this in complete silence, with zero room for error. If a roving sentry—or even one of the villagers—spotted him or one of his kills, it could easily bring the entire place down on his head.

He spent the next three and a half hours studying the sentries' movements, focusing primarily on those to the west near the river. He counted twenty-nine of them, nearly half of whom were roving. The three rooftop snipers were a separate issue to be dealt with at a greater distance. It was obvious there were few if any radios among the guards, but Gil was confident there would be at least one radio among Sandra's personal guards. He was equally confident the men in the decoy building one hundred yards up the lane would be listening for the slightest hint of trouble, ready to respond at a moment's notice. The main road through the village ran directly past the decoy building down the slope to the dead end where Sandra was being kept.

This setup was obviously intentional, meant to allow for immediate support in the event Sandra's guards needed assistance.

At 03:30 hours, Gil sent a text message to Sandra's husband: KICKOFF. This was the signal telling Brux the rescue was about to begin and that it was time to get the Spectre airborne. The gunship had enough fuel to loiter over the target area for an extended period, but once it was in the air, Gil would be up against the clock, working against any number of variables that might serve to blow the timing for the delivery of tactical air support and, ultimately, their extraction from what was almost definitely going to be one hot EZ.

Cradling the Remington MSR, he slipped from the hide with his M4 and rucksack slung across his back. It was time to begin culling the herd.

He made his way down the mountain to the river and crossed to the other side using a path made of large stones he had seen the villagers using earlier in the day. The farm plots were fallow with the coming of winter and would provide no concealment other than the walls, so he kept close to the river, using the sound of the rushing water to cover the sound of his running as he made for cover. A slim crescent moon hung low near the horizon, providing good ambient light for his night optics, but not enough for anyone to detect his movement with the naked eye beyond fifty yards.

He crept along the river to within one hundred yards of the first two sentries he would have to eliminate before penetrating the southern perimeter of Bazarak. He crouched behind a stone wall, unfolding the stock of the MSR and pulling it into his shoulder. The two men stood close together on the far side of the farm plot smoking beneath a coppice of trees, standing out as plain as day in the night vision.

Judging that he could take both targets out with one shot by shifting his angle a few degrees, he hurried to take up a new position halfway down the wall, centering the reticle on the lower back of the man closest to him, and squeezed the trigger. The gun recoiled with a whisper as the subsonic round left the barrel. Both men went down in a heap, their guts blown apart by the hydrostatic shock. He put a second round into each of them to make sure they were dead. It wouldn't be necessary to hide their bodies because they had chosen such a well-secluded spot to smoke.

Now it was time to engage the rooftop snipers. The first and closest of the three would be the easiest to eliminate. He was perched on a lower building than the other two and out of their immediate line of sight. The second two would be tricky because they could see each other and were only about a hundred yards apart from east to west. Gil judged he could hit the first from where he was, but sniper work could sometimes be like a game of pool. A player wanted to sink each of his shots in such a way as to leave the cue ball in good position for the next. From his present position, he would have to displace rapidly after taking the first sniper, leaving a time lag before placing his shots on the second two, which he preferred to avoid for the sake of efficiency and safety.

He hopped the wall and skirted around the farm plot to the east side on a northerly heading, moving away from the river to stop near the rusted-out hull of the T-34/85, a hundred fifty yards south of the farthest snipers out to his left and right. The closest shooter was only half that distance away, perched at the acute angle of an inverted isosceles triangle. Placing the reticle on the shooter's sternum, he squeezed the trigger and the rifle did its whisper kick.

The target flew backward as if he'd been mule kicked in the chest and landed flat on his back. Gil saw his Dragunov go flying off the edge of the roof and out of sight, and he knelt behind the tank waiting for the telltale shouting that would signal he'd just screwed the pooch. After a minute of silence, he raised up to check on the other two sentries. Neither of them seemed aware anything untoward had taken place, so he took a few moments to practice moving the rifle within the confines of the arc between them. It was a fairly large sweep at almost 45 degrees.

The plan was to hit one of them when the other wasn't looking, then sweep across the arc to tag the second one before he realized his counterpart had just been blown out of his socks from a hundred yards across the village. The sniper on the right seemed to be the less vigilant of the two, so, technically speaking, it would be best to start with the sniper on the left, but Gil preferred to sweep right to left, rather than left to right whenever sweeping more than 20 degrees. The movement was more natural to the body, and he would be slightly faster on the bolt.

He waited until the sniper to the left wasn't looking in the other's direction, then swept to the right, shot his target in the center of the back over the heart, and swept back to the left again, working the bolt without taking his eye from the scope and finding that the third sniper had disappeared from the rooftop just that fast. Gil held his position, visualizing the posture of the sniper's body as he'd swept the scope off to the right. Had the shooter been pivoting to turn, already moving down the staircase before Gil squeezed the trigger on his buddy? It was possible, and if so, the alarm might not be about to sound. The sniper may simply have gone below to grab a cup of hot Joe or take a dump.

Five long minutes passed in utter silence before the sniper re-emerged with a plate of food, his Dragunov slung over his shoulder. The fact that his counterpart was facedown on the rooftop a hundred yards away did not even register with him.

"Apparently, it's amateur night here in Bazarak," Gil muttered, half criticizing himself. He shot the sniper through the side of the head and moved out. There was no telling how soon the bodies would be detected, and there was no time to lose.

He skirted back toward the river to the west, moving up the grade into the village through a patch of trees, spotting a pair of roving sentries making their way toward him down the worn and rocky path at forty yards. Going immediately to ground, he pulled the rifle into his shoulder. The men were only sauntering along, talking quietly with each other with their AK-47s slung. Gil waited for one of them to lag a step or two behind the other, but they continued to stay abreast, coming toward his position. If he shot one of them now, the other might realize what had happened quickly enough to shout a warning before Gil could cycle the bolt and fire the second round.

He set the rifle down and drew the 1911 pistol, waiting for them to draw within fifty feet. Concentrating on the illuminated front sight, he squeezed off the first round, blowing the target's brains out the back of his skull. His partner had just enough time to gasp and turn his head before Gil put 230 grains of lead through his right ear.

Even before the second fellow was twitching in the dirt, Gil was up and moving, slinging the rifle around his back as he ran to grab him by the ankle, dragging him from the trail into the shadowy dark. Seconds later, with both bodies off the trail, he was crouched beside a thick Chilgoza pine, scanning the darkness through the helmet-mounted monocular. On missions like this he always went with the monocular mount to keep his left eye adjusted to the darkness.

He moved up the trail to a clearing and took a knee near yet another stone wall, this one stacked chest-high with firewood. He was about to move across the open expanse toward a manger where a small flock of sheep were held, when raw instinct gave him a moment's pause. Someone coughed in the night, and he turned his head to spot a lone sentry perched atop a stone building with his back against the chimney. A Dragunov SRV stood upright between his knees, and he was almost invisible, even in the night vision, the rumpled shape of his winter clothing blending perfectly with the large stones used to construct the chimney.

From a hundred feet, Gil shot him in the center of the face. The only sound was that of the body and the Dragunov hitting the ground, but this was enough to bring someone from inside the house to investigate. Gil got him in his sights and fingered the trigger, realizing the villager was probably a Tajik, and therefore, in all likelihood, an ally of the West. He felt a cold sweat break out across his chest as he prepared to kill the first innocent human being of his career. In these final instants before it became necessary to make his decision, Gil recalled the stories that his Green Beret father had told him of the Vietnam War, of the dozens of innocent villagers— men, women, and children alike—he had been forced to kill during his countless LRRP (Long Range Reconnaissance Patrol) missions north of the DMZ. In the end, his father had not been able to live with his conscience and drank himself to death.

Just go back inside, Gil said to himself.

The man crouched down to check the body and recoiled the instant he realized the sentry had no face, shrinking against the wall and retreating quickly back into the house. Gil waited three full minutes to see if he would reemerge to sound the alarm. There was only one way to make certain the villager stayed quiet, so he moved to the end of the stone wall, then crossed to the building, where he knocked lightly on the door, knowing the incredible risk he was taking.

The door opened a crack, and he pulled it all the way open, grabbing the villager by his clothing to yank him outside and using hand signals to order him to drag the body into the house. The villager hurried to comply, and Gil picked up the enemy rifle and followed him inside, where a dim oil lamp burned on a table in the center of the room. He stared hard at the villager, weighing the man's mettle. His eyes were steady and guileless, and he didn't stink of fear the way the deceitful so often did. This was no guarantee, but it was good enough for Gil. He put a finger to his lips, and the Tajik nodded once, indicating that he understood.

A mountain cloak hung from a nail beside the door. Gil pointed to it and then back at himself, asking with his eyes if he could have it. The man nodded and gestured for him to take it. Gil let the MSR dangle from its sling and shrugged into the heavy cloak. The villager showed him how to shape the hood so it would cover his IBH helmet, leaving only the monocular showing, and then reached for the Dragunov Gil had placed against the wall, offering it with both hands.

Gil tucked the Remington inside the cloak and slung the Dragunov. He didn't like having to lug the bulky hunk of junk, but the villager was right about it helping him to blend in.

The Tajik stood back to look him over, making a "good enough" expression and cracking a smile.

Knowing the Afghan people considered it rude to shake hands with gloves on, Gil pulled off his Oakley tactical glove and offered his right hand. The Tajik's grip was firm and confident. Gil nodded his thanks and slipped carefully out of the house.

47

AFGHANISTAN,
Kabul, Central Command

General Couture stood up from the table in the darkened command center to extend his hand as Captain Metcalf entered the room looking half asleep. "Thanks for coming over, Glen. Sorry to wake you up."

Metcalf shook his head. "Don't be silly, General. What've we got?"

Couture turned to indicate the large plasma screen on the wall. He and his staff were watching the UAV feed from over Bazarak in real time. "What do you make of that strobe on the rooftop there?"

Metcalf stepped forward, staring at the black-and-white infrared video of the Panjshir Valley. The steady flash of the infrared strobe that Forogh had tossed onto the roof of Sandra's building was clearly visible in the center of the screen. "Can you zoom in?"

Couture turned to the Air Force lieutenant. "Cynthia, advise Creech you're taking control of the aircraft, will you please?"

"Yes, sir." A few seconds later, they were looking at a tight enough shot of the strobe light to see that it was an MS/2000 Firefly, the same model used by American forces.

Metcalf turned around. "Somebody's sure as hell up to something, aren't they? Has there been any indication the enemy knows it's there?"

Couture shook his head, jutting his chin toward the soundproof office at the back of the room. "Talk to you a minute?"

"Certainly, sir."

Metcalf followed Couture into the office and pulled the door closed after him. They could still see everything that was taking place on the screen, but here in the glass room they could speak freely.

Couture sat down on the corner of the desk. "I hate to ask you this, Glen, but do you have any idea what the fuck is going on? Over the past ten days, we've spent a few million dollars' worth of taxpayer money in preparation for Fell Swoop, and now it looks like we may have to scrub the entire goddamn operation."

Though the general was maintaining a military bearing, Metcalf could see that he was on the boil. It was no secret that Operation Fell Swoop was to be his first large-scale offensive since taking command of the ATO the year before. With the scheduled drawdown of troops, it was unlikely he would get another opportunity. "No, sir. I have no idea what's going on."

"But you knew about Bank Heist, correct? Don't lie to me, Glen. I'm not looking to—"

"I had an inkling about Bank Heist, General, yes. But I have absolutely no idea what's taking place on the ground in the Panjshir Valley tonight. In fact, I know even less than you do because I just got here."

"Okay, I believe you." Couture put his hands on his hips, chewing the inside of his scarred cheek. "But goddamnit, this has SOG written all over it. If this is another unauthorized rescue attempt, the president's going to fire everybody from here to Diego Garcia. It'll make Stalin's purge look like a night at the fucking Oscars."

At this point Metcalf realized Couture feared for his career. The president must have handed down some pretty serious threats in private after Bank Heist. There was only one consolation that Metcalf could think to offer the general. "Well, sir, if this is another unauthorized rescue attempt—and I repeat that I have no intelligence to that effect—it may well be in our interest to provide whatever help we can to see that it succeeds."

"And suppose it does. Then what?"

Metcalf smiled. "Well, General, it's obvious you'll have to take credit for it—as will the president once it gets kicked up to him."

Couture blew out a gust of air. "And if it fails?"

Metcalf shrugged and sadly shook his head. "I can only speak for myself, General, but I'll be too busy mourning Sandra's death to feel sorry for myself. I've had a good career."

"Goddamnit," Couture muttered. "I'd like to hang these bastards over a fire by their bootlaces—whoever they are."

There was a rap at the window. The general's aide was pointing at the screen where the white infrared image of a soldier was running parallel to the Panjshir River.

Both men slipped out of the office to find a couple of chairs just as Gil was setting up to take out the two men on the far side of the farm plot. The trees mostly obscured what they were up to, but it was easy enough to see that Gil took them both out with a single shot.

"Now, damnit, that's one of our people!" Couture insisted, getting back to his feet. "Cynthia, give me a tight in-shot, as tight as you can get."

The Air Force lieutenant zoomed in on Gil as he hopped the wall and bolted for the trees west of the farm plot.

The UAV was not directly above the target, but the angle was too acute for a positive ident. Still, it was good enough for Captain Metcalf to be confident he was witnessing one of his SEALs in action. He looked over at the general's aide-de-camp with the dual Glock pistols.

"Major, would you please call the MPs at Jalalabad Air Base and tell them to locate Master Chiefs Shannon and Steelyard?"

The major looked to General Couture for permission to carry out the request.

"Do it," the general said. "And tell them to add Captain Cross-white to that list."

The major left the room. Couture said to Metcalf, "The MPs aren't going to find any of them, are they?"

Metcalf shook his head. "I honestly don't know, sir . . . but it's a hunch."

"Sirs!" An intelligence officer with the CIA pointed to the screen. Gil had just taken out the first sniper from seventy-five yards.

They turned and watched as he eliminated the other two. When Gil shot the third sniper in the side of the head, his plate of food went flying.

A short time later they watched as he took out a pair of roving sentries at fifty feet with a model 1911 .45 from the prone position.

Metcalf drew a breath and let it back out. "That's Master Chief Shannon. I'm sorry, General. It is one of mine."

Couture looked at Metcalf, then back at the screen and then back at Metcalf. "The SEAL who jumped into Iran? How do you know?"

"Because he's too stubborn to give up his 1911 for a higher-capacity forty-five."

Couture smirked and held his hand out to the screen. "The way he shoots . . . it doesn't look like he needs one."

"That's exactly what he said to me," Metcalf muttered.

They continued to watch as Gil popped the sniper on the roof, and then held their collective breath when the door opened and the vil-lager emerged to investigate the commotion . . . everyone except Gen-eral Couture, who griped, "Now you've done it, Shannon!"

But the villager went back inside.

"He'll wait to see," Metcalf said. "Then he'll go in after him."

It happened as Metcalf predicted, and they all waited again, breath bated, while Gil was inside with the Tajik. At last, he reemerged dressed in the heavy mountain garb.

"Who the hell is that?" the General asked. "Is Shannon dead?"

The Air Force lieutenant tightened the shot so they could see Gil's monocular sticking out from beneath the hood.

Couture looked at Metcalf, pointing at the screen. "That son of a bitch is going to give me a heart attack."

Metcalf couldn't help the sardonic grin that crossed his face. "Perhaps you shouldn't watch, General."

"T-yeah, right," the General smirked. "Everyone listen up! For the duration of this exercise, everything—and I mean *everything*—you people see and hear is to be considered beyond top secret. Is that clear?"

The room was filled with "Yes, sirs."

"We will now treat this as if it were a sanctioned rescue operation," he went on. "That means I want a pair of Predators in the air and loaded with warshot. Cynthia, get on the horn to Creech and make that happen."

"Yes, sir."

Couture glanced at Metcalf. "The nautical term was for you there, Captain."

Metcalf gave him a wink. "I thought as much, sir."

"Major Miller!"

"Yes, General."

"Get the president on the horn. If this is going to be our last hurrah, by God, we're doing it by the numbers."

Within three minutes, the President of the United States was on the line.

"Mr. President, this is General Couture. I'm sorry to disturb you, sir."

"What is it?" the president said, his voice anxious.

"Mr. President, at this time we're looking at a live infrared UAV feed from over the Panjshir Valley. Though it remains unconfirmed at this time, sir, we are witnessing what *appears* to be an unauthorized mission to liberate Warrant Officer Brux from the enemy."

"Are you fucking kidding me!" the president snarled.

Couture's reply was crisp. "No, sir."

"Exactly what the hell are you seeing?" the president demanded.

Couture described what they had witnessed so far and that the unidentified shooter had just shot another sentry dead from beneath a donkey cart.

"Who the hell is it?" the president wanted to know.

General Couture watched as Gil hefted the body from the road onto his shoulder, dumping it into the donkey cart and covering it with a tarp. "Though his identity remains unconfirmed, Mr. President, we believe it may the same operative who carried out Operation Tiger Claw."

There was an extended silence at the president's end, so Couture continued. "Sir, I've ordered a pair of Predators armed and into the air in case we end up having to assist him in bringing Warrant Off—"

"You just said you don't even know who know who the hell it *is*!" the president hissed.

It was at this moment Couture realized the president wasn't assessing the situation from a rational point of view. "Mr. President, allow me to be clear, sir . . . confidence is quite high that this operative is a member of DEVGRU."

"General, here's what you're going to do," the president said, his aggravation clear and evident. "First, you're going to keep those drones on the ground where they belong. Second, you're going to continue to monitor this situation and keep me apprised. You are to take no direct action of any kind. Is that understood?"

"Yes, Mr. President."

"If this *hero* manages to bring that woman out of there alive, we'll have no trouble playing the success of the mission to our advantage. If he fails, then he's disavowed, simple as that. That was the deal in Iran, was it not? These SEALs seem to be comfortable with that arrangement, so let this hero's fate be a lesson to the rest of them. Understood?"

Couture eyed the screen as Gil ducked into a long building with a dozen horses standing beside it in a stone corral. "Mr. President, with respect . . . this operative is very good—possibly the best we have. With our help, he stands a legitimate chance of success."

"Do you even know what his plans are, General?"

"No, sir, not specifically."

"Well, suppose we *do* get involved and that poor woman dies anyhow?"

Couture didn't immediately respond.

"I asked you a question, General."

Couture glanced at Metcalf and shook his head in resignation. "I see your point, Mr. President."

"I thought you might," the president said. "This isn't your doing, General, and it sure as hell isn't mine. I see no reason either of us should swing for it. Now, I'll ask you this: are you in a position to stop him without wiping out that village in the process?"

"Not at this time, sir, no."

"Then we're not responsible for his actions, are we?"

"Not in a manner of speaking, sir, no."

"Very good," the president said. "Keep me apprised through the normal channels."

The line went dead. Couture hung up the phone. "Shit."

"What's the bottom line?" Metcalf asked quietly.

Couture dry-wiped his mouth, glancing at the screen where Gil was yet to reemerge from the stable. "Master Chief Shannon—if that's who we're watching—has been disavowed."

48

AFGHANISTAN,
Panjshir Valley, Bazarak

Inside the stable, Gil felt comforted by the familiar smell of horses and manure. He found the sorrel-colored mount he was looking for near the back, a few hands higher than the other animals and with stronger flanks. He needed the strongest horse he could get for what he had in mind, and after watching this particular horse carry its rider through the grueling paces of an entire buzkashi match during the day, he believed it had more than enough endurance. The trouble would be getting the animal to Sandra undetected. He sure as hell couldn't bring Sandra to the horse, carrying her over his shoulder, fighting a running gun battle all the way.

He slipped a coarse wool blanket over the animal's back and pulled one of the buzkashi saddles from a pile in the corner. It had metal stirrups, and both pommel and cantle were higher than those of a Western cowboy saddle, creating a deeper seat designed to help keep a buzkashi rider from falling off.

"It's not exactly a Hamley Formfitter," he muttered to himself, cinching up the single girth strap, "but it'll have to do."

The door opened at the other end, and Gil instantly faded into the corner, drawing the Ka-Bar from the sheath strapped to his thigh. He watched the man through infrared, noting the AK-47 barrel slung up over his left shoulder. The horses began to fidget in their stalls, tamping at the floor and snorting. Gil realized they were smelling his sudden adrenaline dump.

"Achmed?" said the interloper. "Achmed!"

Gil guessed that Achmed must be the dead guy outside in the donkey cart, so he grunted a response and began coughing as though he were trying to hack something up from deep in the back of his throat.

The interloper came straight toward him in the darkness, unable to see Gil except for the faint silhouette of the mountain cloak. "Achmed," he said, followed by a bunch of harsh-sounding gibberish that Gil didn't understand.

When the unlucky fellow came within arm's reach, Gil grabbed him by the shoulder of his coat and rammed the Ka-Bar up through the bottom of his jaw to penetrate so deeply into the brain that the tip of the blade scraped against the top of the skull. The Pashtun was dead on his feet, though his body hadn't quite gotten the message, twitching spasmodically as Gil lowered him to the dung-covered dirt floor. He cleaned the knife on his victim's jacket and jammed it back into the sheath.

He got up and stood on the body to peer out the gap between the roof and the top of the mud wall. Seeing the strobe flashing in his infrared viewfinder farther up the hill, beyond another cluster of buildings, he estimated the distance to Sandra's quarters at ninety yards. This was too far to walk the horse without better knowledge of the layout. Besides, he wanted to make a careful reconnoiter of Sandra's quarters before moving in to take it over. At least, he had to consider the possibility that Forogh had been caught and forced into helping the enemy to set up a trap.

The God of War is a fickle son of a bitch, his father had always been fond of saying. *Don't ever trust his ass.*

Gil folded the body into a corner and piled it over with saddles before slipping back outside. He backtracked his route for a short distance south, then turned west for the river. Having memorized the sentries' sectors during his long vigil from on high, he felt confident that he'd cleared the southwestern corner of the village. There were no guarantees, of course, but his instincts told him that he was safe for the moment. After moving north along the river for fifty yards, he turned east again toward the back side of the building where he had dumped the sentry into the donkey cart. As the infrared strobe continued to illuminate the night sky with its intermittent flashes, Gil found it eerie to flip up the infrared monocular and see only darkness over the rooftop where he knew there was light. He glanced farther up at the stars, wondering if the strobe had been picked up by an Air Force UAV yet, guessing that somebody somewhere was probably having themselves a shit hemorrhage by now. He also wondered idly whether the MPs had been sent to his quarters to look for him.

He stood on a rain barrel and crawled onto the roof of the building, setting the .45 beside him. If any innocent Tajiks came snooping around this close to Sandra's quarters, he'd have to shoot them dead without a thought. From this height, he could just see the windows and doorways to Sandra's cluster of buildings over the rooftops between there and where he was. He brought up the sniper rifle and sighted on the open doorway next to Sandra's. Four men with blankets over their shoulders sat at a table playing *teka*—an Afghan card game—by candlelight. Either they had only recently lit the candle, or the light of the flame had been too dim for his optics to detect from high on the slope.

The door to Sandra's place suddenly swung open, and Ramesh stepped out. Gil immediately recognized him as the brute who had cut off her finger. In the moments before the door closed again, Gil saw her, and a sense of urgency swept through his veins. She was lying on the bed, doubled up beneath heavy blankets with a man and a woman sitting beside her in the warm glow of an oil lamp. They seemed to be caring for her.

Gil held Ramesh in his sights as he walked eastward toward the decoy building. Forty yards up the slope, he stopped and knocked at a door on the north side of the lane. The door opened and Aasif Kohistani stepped out, pulling his winter coat closed as he led Ramesh at a brisk pace back toward Sandra's quarters.

Kohistani and Ramesh went into the building. They were inside for perhaps five minutes before coming back out. Ramesh turned west and stepped inside where the sentries were playing cards. Kohistani went east back to his house. As Gil shimmied carefully back from the edge of the roof, he wondered if the Hezbi cleric could feel the shadow of death moving with him up the lane.

The God of War is a fickle son of a bitch, Mr. Kohistani.

49

AFGHANISTAN,
Kabul, Central Command

General Couture stood staring at the screen with his arms crossed over his chest, watching intently as Gil shimmied slowly back from the edge of the roof. Captain Metcalf was beside him. The unexpected sighting of Aasif Kohistani minutes before had caused a stir in the room, leaving everyone convinced that Sandra Brux was definitely being held inside the building marked by the strobe.

Couture leaned closer to Metcalf. "If you have someone you can call in to assist your man," he muttered, "now would be the time to do that."

Metcalf looked at him in confusion. The president had just ordered them to stand down.

"You're telling me you don't have anyone you can call?" the general asked.

Metcalf scratched his head. "Well, the truth is, General, we've already sent for them . . . and the MPs can't seem to find them."

Couture gave a curt nod, glancing at the screen. "What about back in Langley . . . inside of SOG?"

"General, what about the president's—?"

"Look, Glen. I'd like to kick Shannon's ass for pulling this fucking stunt, but Sandra's in that goddamn building. So if you've got some kind of SOG voodoo you can work here, nobody in this room is going to say anything."

The Navy captain drew a breath, pausing before making his reply. "General, if I may speak frankly . . . ?"

Couture made a "come on" gesture with his hand.

"Master Chief Shannon doesn't think he's a ninja, sir. He knows he's not infiltrating that village and stealing Sandra away from those people without help. It's my guess that whatever *voodoo* he's going to need has already been laid on."

"Which, I presume, is why the MPs can't find Steelyard and Crosswhite."

"I don't know, sir, but whatever those two lunatics are up to . . . you can bet they're not hiding under the bed someplace waiting for the all-clear."

"Fine," Couture said. "Then neither are we." He snapped his fingers to get the attention of his communications officer. "Lieutenant, get Colonel Morrow on the horn."

"Yes, sir."

Metcalf and Couture stared at the screen as Gil made his way north along the river.

"Where the hell is he going now?" Couture wondered aloud.

Metcalf sucked his teeth. "I believe he may have it in his head to kill Kohistani."

"Just grab the girl and go," Couture quietly urged. "She's right there, for Christ's sake!"

"We can't see everything that he sees, sir. He may be seeing something we can't."

Couture gave him a glance. "You're worse than my wife, Captain. Let me watch the damn game, will ya?"

Metcalf chuckled. "Yes, sir."

"Cynthia, widen the angle a bit, please."

Gil began to shrink as the shot pulled back, revealing a section of the village about as long and wide as a soccer field.

"Shit, who the hell are those guys?" Couture pointed to the top of the screen. "Cynthia, tighten it up."

The shot zoomed directly in on half a dozen armed men marching along the river toward the village from the north. They were all heavily armed with RPGs and belt-fed Russian PK light machine guns. Only one of them marched with his weapon at the ready, but they were on a direct collision course with Gil.

"Those are mountain fighters," Metcalf said, rubbing the back of his neck where he was beginning to tense up. "They're coming down from the Hindu Kush to answer Kohistani's call for jihad. Probably marched all night to get there."

Gil froze when the mountain men closed to within seventy-five yards, going immediately to ground with the Remington extending out in front of him.

"Shoot!" Couture muttered. "Shoot!"

Breathe, Metcalf thought to himself. *Breathe.*

A few seconds later, the fighter marching with his PK at the ready, jerked as if he'd been stung by a wasp. Less than a second later, the man beside him dropped dead to the earth.

With the sudden realization that they were taking fire, the other four gunners raced to unsling their machine guns. The next man in line dropped dead, and then another. There were three left alive. The first fighter hit was down on his knee, hammering at the receiver of his machine gun with the heel of his fist.

"Shannon shot his weapon in the receiver," Metcalf said.

By the time Metcalf had completed his remark, the man with the disabled weapon was the only one left alive. He flung the broken machine gun aside and jumped up to run but didn't travel a full step before his head exploded and he went down.

"My god!" someone said. "How long did that take?"

"I'd say just over ten seconds," Couture remarked, turning to Metcalf. "This is what you missed not being able to watch the Iran mission."

Metcalf nodded, lips puckered, deeply concerned for his man on the ground. Couture was a good general, highly educated, a solid tactician. As a major general, he had even been shot in the face with an RPG, surviving a terrible wound to go on and earn himself another couple of stars . . . but he had never killed anyone. As a combat veteran with seven Cold War kills under his belt, Metcalf had a great deal of appreciation for what he was seeing on the screen, but he still did not consider it a spectator sport. He sneaked a look at the chronograph on his watch. Gil Shannon had killed six heavily armed men in nine seconds with a bolt-action rifle at a distance of seventy-five yards, and judging from the lack of HIK activity within the village, he had done so without allowing his enemy to get off a single shot.

"General, I've got Colonel Morrow on the line." Colonel Mack Morrow was with the Air Force 24th Special Tactics Squadron, another Special Mission Unit under the auspices of the CIA's Special Operations Group/Joint Special Operations Command.

Couture went to the back of the room and took the phone. "Mack, sorry to wake you. Listen, I want a pair of Black Hawks loaded and ready on the tarmac for an emergency extraction, ASAP. I may or may not end up needing them, but if I do, it's going to be soon. They'll be going into the Panjshir, Mack, so keep this as low-profile as possible. You'd better ready a pair of Cobras as well."

He returned to the front of the room, where Captain Metcalf stood watching him.

"All set, General?"

"Yeah," Couture said. "I've got it set up so you and I both will be in the unemployment line by the end of the week."

"You have to admit, General, Fell Swoop was a death sentence for Sandra."

Couture grunted. "Well, for what it's worth, I did try talking the president into going with DEVGRU . . . not real hard, but I did try."

50

AFGHANISTAN,
Panjshir Valley, Bazarak

Gil was up and moving the second the last gunman was down, sprinting the seventy-five yards to where they lay. One of them was still breathing, choking blood with an exit wound the size of a coconut in the right side of his back. Gil knifed him. Ditching the Dragunov for good, he gathered up all six of the RPGs the gunners had been carrying and trotted back toward the village with them. He didn't have an immediate use for six rockets, but he didn't want them lying around for the enemy to pick up and fire at him on his way out of Dodge. His intended EZ was three full clicks to the north, and he didn't need any extra hurdles to jump along the way.

He stashed the RPGs behind the rusted bed of a pickup someone had leaned against the back wall of a lone outbuilding, then made his way toward the rear of Kohistani's house. A roving sentry was coming down the hill, crossing through a beam of light that shined from the back window of a house farther up the lane. The man held up his hand to wave. Gil waved back and stopped, waiting for him to approach, feeling almost as though he could walk among these people with impunity now. The sentry drew within ten feet, and Gil shot him through the eye with the .45. He dragged the body into a gap between Kohistani's house and the one next door, then slipped beneath an awning to peek in through Kohistani's window. A candle burned on a table beside a bed where the cleric lay sleeping, an open Koran on his chest.

Gil slipped in through the back door and crept around the corner into Kohistani's room, taking a seat on the chair beside the bed. He pressed his finger into the candle to snuff out the flame and sat looking at Sandra's tormentor in infrared. He set the Koran aside on a table and placed a gentle hand on the cleric's shoulder.

Kohistani came instantly awake, sitting up in the dark.

"What's wrong?" he asked in Pashto. Without night vision, Gil would have appeared very much like the Grim Reaper sitting there beside him in the heavy mountain cloak. He reached for the matches to relight the candle. "You're supposed to knock before you come in here."

Gil didn't understand a word. He realized the cleric spoke decent English, but he couldn't risk him calling for help, and there wasn't much to be said anyhow. He produced a garrote from a pouch on his harness and gripped the wooden toggles in his fists. A garrote wasn't exactly a combat weapon, but it was a weapon of stealth. A weapon of assassination. And Gil believed that Kohistani had earned himself the right to be assassinated.

Kohistani struck the match, and with catlike speed, Gil looped the strand of piano wire around his throat, giving it a stiff jerk to choke off all air and blood flow to the brain instantly. Kohistani grabbed for the wire, and the match went out. He clawed desperately but it was no use. The wire was slicing through his flesh like a cheese cutter. Gil knelt with a knee on the edge of the bed, applying steady pressure but stopping shy of killing him.

As the cleric slowly died in agonizing, strangled silence, Gil whispered into his ear: "Sandra's husband sent me here to kill you. I want you to know that before you die."

In the violent throes of death, Kohistani thrashed wildly about, his legs kicking with fury beneath the heavy wool blankets. Gil gave the toggles a vicious jerk in opposite directions, and the piano wire sliced clean through to the spine. The cleric's bowels let go, and the room filled with the acrid stench of raw shit.

Gil let go and Kohistani flopped over, falling half out of the bed with blood gushing from his severed neck. This was the most intimate kill of his career, and even as he was slipping from the house like a wraith in the night, he was aware that something within him had just shifted. His heart filled with a violent hatred unlike any he had ever known, and he suddenly found himself wanting to destroy the entire village and everyone in it. He thought of the RPGs and went to retrieve them.

He pulled the bed of the truck away from the wall and began to remove the individual rockets from their launchers, checking them over to make sure they were serviceable. He would only need one launcher. The rockets he could carry over his shoulder in a sling he would fashion from the cloak. He would leave this place a smoking effigy of the village it once had been. No one could stop him when he was on the attack—he knew that now, felt it in his veins. These backward jackasses weren't soldiers. They were clumsy imposters stumbling their way through a modern war, the full scope of which they couldn't even begin to conceive. How could they possibly touch him if he decided they were going to die? He was death from within, walking among them without so much as an if you please, come to kill them in midstride as punishment for their sins against humanity.

Was this what war really was? Was this sudden and violent urge to kill indiscriminately the same as what his father had experienced all those years ago in Vietnam, north of the DMZ, where life had blurred into one long and bloody nightmare of death and destruction? *Kill 'em all and let God sort 'em out!* Was this the frame of mind that had enabled an otherwise kind and gentle man to become a mindless butcher of women and children?

If so, Gil understood it now, understood it on a level more visceral than he had ever thought possible, and it was the most powerful feeling he had ever known—*bloodlust*! He shrugged out of the cloak and was about to use the Ka-Bar to cut it up the back when he thought of Marie, his wife. Suddenly, there she was before him, lying in their bed sleeping, the faint smile still on her face after making love. His eyes flooded with tears and his mind began to clear. The hatred dissipated, leaving the faint residue of shame in its place as the mission slid back into focus.

"Jesus," he muttered to himself, shoving the rockets back behind the truck bed and getting to his feet. There was plenty of killing yet to be done before this mission concluded.

51

AFGHANISTAN,
Kabul, Central Command

Everyone in the operations center breathed a collective sigh when Gil slipped out the back of Kohistani's house and headed toward the river.

"I think it's safe to assume that Mr. Kohistani won't be joining us for the duration," General Couture remarked, almost casually. "Christ, this guy's bold. To watch him move, you'd think he owned that goddamn village."

"At the moment, he does," Metcalf muttered, taking his chair. He had suffered a spinal injury years earlier during a parachute jump, and his lower back was killing him. "Forgive me for sitting, General. It's the old bones . . ."

"Warrior's bones," Couture replied. "Put your feet up on the table if you need to."

Metcalf shook his head. "This will do, sir. Thank you."

They watched Gil return to the outbuilding.

"What's he doing with the damn rockets now?" Couture wanted to know. "Jesus, this guy's killing me! Grab the woman and go, son!"

Metcalf stared at the screen, a shadow creasing his brow. "Looks like he's got something in mind, sir." This was the first worrisome thing that Gil had done so far. He was wasting time now. There was nothing he could accomplish with those rockets that wouldn't bring every Pashtun hiding in the mountains down into the village. Could that be his plan? It hardly made sense.

They watched on as he paused and seemed to reconsider his decision. In the end, he shoved the rockets back out of sight and pulled the bulky cloak back on over his multicam ACUs.

"Thought better of it," Couture mumbled, "whatever it was . . . thank God."

Gil trotted back down the river to the south, turning east at the end of the row of houses and sneaking back into the building near the stone corral. A couple of minutes later he came back out leading a saddled horse.

Metcalf rocked back in the chair, gaping at the screen.

"Oh, you've got to be shitting me," Couture said, turning to look at Metcalf. "Is he kidding? Is he kidding me?"

"He certainly isn't," Metcalf replied, scratching his head. "I guess now we know his plan for extraction."

"Shit," Couture said, putting his hands on his hips. "I wish he'd gone with the RPGs. At least then he'd have taken some of the bastards with him."

Gil led the horse north up the lane toward Sandra's quarters, crossing in front of the row of houses this time, rather than behind.

"I wish we knew what the hell he can see that we can't." Couture griped. "Anybody in here got a cigarette?"

No one did.

"Goddamnit."

As Gil was passing the last house on the lane, a villager came from inside and walked out to intercept him, his hands spread out before him in a gesture of confusion.

"Must be the owner," someone remarked.

Gil put the suppressor of the .45 right up against his forehead and started walking him backward into the house. It seemed an eternity before he finally reemerged.

"That does it!" Couture hissed. "Sergeant Becker! Go find me a pack of cigarettes. I don't care what brand or who you have to mug to get them."

"Yes, sir!" The Air Force sergeant jumped up and hurried from the room, obviously wanting to get back before he missed anything.

Gil was leading the horse straight across the road now toward Sandra's quarters, bold as a shiny brass tack.

"Look at the balls on this guy." Couture stole a glance across the room where the black Air Force lieutenant sat behind the console, piloting the UAV. "You didn't hear that, Cynthia."

"Hear what, sir?" she replied without looking up from her monitor.

The sergeant returned with a pack of Pall Malls.

"Throw them here, Sergeant."

"Sir." The sergeant pitched the smokes over the console, and the general caught them with two hands, finding a green pack of MRE matches tucked inside the cellophane.

"You're a good man, Sergeant. I take back all of the foul and disgusting things I've said about you."

"Sir!"

Moments later Couture stood puffing away, obscured in a cloud of smoke. "Christ, I'd forgotten how good these damn things are under stress. Thanks to this son of a bitch," he said, gesturing at the screen, "I'll probably be smoking for the rest of my life now."

Metcalf chuckled in spite of himself. He couldn't help it. There was too much tension in the air.

52

AFGHANISTAN,
Panjshir Valley, Bazarak

Luckily, the owner of the horse had spoken some broken English; otherwise, Gil would have had to kill him. He'd lied to the man instead, saving his life by telling him, "CIA! Danger outside! Stay here. I bring horse back."

The villager was angry about the horse, but he believed Gil when he said there was CIA in the village and that they would kill him if he made trouble. It hadn't been all that hard to convince him, really. The CIA was usually pretty good at following through on their threats to kill someone, especially the operatives who were crazy enough to infiltrate a village so heavily occupied by enemy forces.

He walked the horse to the end of the lane and out into the open, approaching Sandra's cluster of buildings. He could see the guards through the open door of their shack, still playing cards by candlelight. Ramesh appeared in the doorway and stood leaning with his forearm against the doorjamb, watching him. Gil didn't like the way the guy's bulk was blocking the doorway, so he stopped and pointed back in the direction he had come, waving for the man to come and see. Ramesh said something over his shoulder to the others and then stepped out to follow Gil.

Seeing the other guards were too involved in their card game to be interested, Gil turned to lead the horse back the way he had come, wanting to lure Ramesh out of view. He turned the corner and walked the horse beneath a tree, quickly tying it to a hitching rail and shrugging out of the robe. He hung the robe by the hood from a limb and hid behind the tree.

The brute came around the corner with his AK-47 in both hands. He was alert but not overly circumspect as he strolled up to the horse and said something to the robe in Pashto. In the same instant he realized he was talking to an empty coat, Gil stepped out behind him and jammed the Ka-Bar through the side of his neck, instantly severing the trachea to stifle any sound. In the same movement, he grabbed his prey by the hair with his left hand and kicked him behind the load-bearing knee to bring him down, ripping the knife out the front of the throat to sever both carotid arteries and the jugular in one swipe. Blood gushed in a fountain. Gil kicked him forward onto his face.

"You can keep the finger, motherfucker." He shrugged back into the robe and turned around. "Now," he muttered, flipping up the hood, "if the mountain won't come to Mohammed . . . Mohammed must come to the mountain."

He took the stallion by the bridle and led him back toward the corner, where he set out on a direct course for the guard shack. The men were now arguing over the game. It looked like one of them was pissed over having lost. But who the fuck could tell, the way they were carrying on? He covered the thirty feet to the shack without them paying him much attention until he stepped into the doorway and brought up the 1911.

They all grabbed for their weapons with a shout, but it was far too late. Gil shot each of them once, center mass, inside of two seconds. Then he shot them each in the head. Barely four seconds had passed by the time the slide on the 1911 locked back and the last empty shell casing tinked across the table. He pressed the magazine release with his thumb, and the empty mag clattered against the stone floor. He slipped a fresh one into the pistol and pressed the slide release, loading a round into the battery. Then he brought the horse into the guard shack to keep it out of sight.

A quick glance up the lane toward the lighted command post gave no indication that anyone had heard the brief tumult. In truth, the argument over the game would not have sounded very different from the shouts of panic. The stallion recoiled at the pungent smell of blood and shit that now filled the guard shack, but Gil stroked his neck and calmed him. He stripped the shepherd's robe and stepped out, pulling the door closed and going next door.

Without knocking, he opened the door and stepped inside, pointing the 1911 at Khan and Badira sitting beside the bed. The instant he saw the rag stuffed into Sandra's mouth, her fevered eyes blazing with fear, he knew he'd fucked up—he'd forgotten to clear the corner. He hadn't so much forgotten as deemed it unnecessary . . . which was a mistake.

He felt the cold burn of the blade pierce his rib cage from behind and whipped around to grab the wrist of his teenage assailant, viciously twisting the arm to force the young man toward the floor, snap-kicking him in the throat with the toe of his boot. The teen went unconscious, and Gil stomped his neck, separating the brainstem.

Khan got quickly up from his chair, more to get out of Gil's way than anything else, but Gil alerted to the swiftness of movement and spun to deliver the doctor a powerful Muay Thai kick to the liver.

Khan went down in a heap, crumpling against the wall and covering his head.

"Don't kill him!" Badira shouted. "He wasn't going to hurt you. He's a doctor!"

Gil holstered the pistol and shoved her aside, taking the rag from Sandra's mouth and jerking back her blankets to find her wrists hastily bound with a boot lace.

"Oh, thank God!" Sandra gasped. "I can't believe you're real!"

"I'm Master Chief Gil Shannon. I don't know if you remember me."

Tears spilled from her sunken eyes. "You're from Montana. Your wife raises horses."

He brushed the hair from her eyes and took the radio from his harness, pointing up at the sky. "John's up there in a Spectre. He's waiting to hear from you. Remember your authentication code?"

She nodded, choking back the tears with no little effort. She was still a soldier, and it was time to ruck up.

"This mission is unauthorized," Gil said, giving her the radio. "In all likelihood, I've been disavowed by now, so they may not respond to a distress call from me. You have to do this like I'm not here—like you're a downed pilot in enemy territory. Understand?"

She nodded. "Help me sit up."

He helped her sit up against the wall, then went to check the street.

She drew a breath and depressed the button on the radio: "Mayday! Mayday! This is Track Star broadcasting on the emergency band. Repeat! This is Track Star broadcasting on the emergency band. Authentication: Alpha-One-Bravo-Lima-Charlie-Five. Repeat! Alpha-One-Bravo-Lima-Charlie-Five. Does anyone copy? Over!"

The response was immediate. "Roger that, Track Star. This is Big

Ten reading you five-by-five on the emergency band. What is your location? Over."

She looked to Gil for the information as he came back in from the street.

"They already know," he said, "but we need to make it sound good. Tell them you're in Bazarak Village . . . directly beneath the infrared strobe."

Sandra repeated what he said, looking somewhat dubious. "Will that be enough for them to—?"

"It's been scripted. Don't worry, they already know their part."

Big Ten came back with their response: "Track Star, be advised we are in your vicinity and able to respond. What is your condition? Over."

"Tell them you're being aided by indigenous forces. They're moving you to a suitable extraction zone. Ask them to stand by."

She depressed the button. "Big Ten, be advised . . . indigenous forces are moving me to a suitable extraction zone. Will advise further. Please stand by!"

There was a longer pause this time, then a different voice came over the radio: "Track Star, be advised . . . Big Ten will remain on station as long as it takes."

Sandra recognized the tone and timbre of her husband's voice immediately. She covered her mouth, and her face contorted with raw emotion.

Gil kicked the leg of the bed. "Soldier up and answer him."

She fought to regain her composure but couldn't. She shook her head and tried to give him the radio.

He kicked the bed again, harder this time. "I said soldier up, Brux."

She swallowed hard, depressing the button to reply in a choking voice: "Roger that, Big Ten . . . Will advise."

"Good job." Gil disappeared from the room and returned with

the heavy cloak, throwing it at Badira. "You speak English, right? Get her bundled up and ready to ride a goddamn horse."

"Gil, I can't—"

"Relax," he said, digging into a pouch on his harness. "I'm driving. All you gotta do is hold on to me." He produced a bottle of clear liquid and a syringe. "First, we're going to inject that wound of yours with enough Novocain that you can use the leg if you have to."

She sat up with her legs over the edge of the bed a minute later, wincing as he administered the first injection.

Khan inched forward across the floor, saying something to Badira.

Gil looked at Badira. "What the fuck does he want?"

Badira's eyes were fearless above the veil. "He says you should let him do that. He knows where the nerves are. It will be more effective that way."

Gil looked at Sandra. "You trust this *haji* doc?"

She gave Khan a weary smile. "He's the only reason I'm still alive."

Gil gave the Novocain and the syringe to Khan, then went to check the street again. "It'll be getting light in an hour. We need to roll."

Sandra saw for the first time that he had a knife sticking from his back. "My god. There's a knife in your back!"

"I've noticed," he said grimly, still watching up the lane through a crack in the door. "It'll have to stay where it is for now. If I pull it out, the lung cavity's gonna fill up with blood, and I'll strangle."

"Doesn't it hurt?"

He looked at her. "Fuck yeah, it hurts!"

She snorted a laugh and covered her mouth with the three remaining fingers on her left hand. "I'm sorry," she said, speaking through the gap where the ring finger was supposed to be. Then she laughed again, feeling lightheaded, almost giddy with relief at the total absence of pain in her leg now.

Badira was busy talking back and forth with Khan.

"What the fuck are they jabbering about?" Gil grated. "Christ, tell 'em to shut the fuck up."

Badira looked over from where she sat beside Sandra on the edge of the bed. "Khan says he can remove the knife . . . that he can make a breathing . . . a breathing valve if you need one. Is that the right word . . . *valve*?"

"Yeah." Gil took a moment to think the offer over. It was a risk, but he decided the check valve would be better than riding into a possible firefight with a blade in his lung. "Okay, yeah. Let's do it."

Khan finished with the injections, and Badira started to get Sandra bundled into the robe.

"Are you really here by yourself?" Sandra said, still only half believing he was real.

"Not exactly." He sat down backward on a chair, and Khan tore open his jacket to get a look at the knife wound. "I've got a horse in the next room."

Sandra was feeling dizzy, her vision blurring. "You're crazy for coming here. Your wife is going to . . ." She started to cry again, shaking her head. "You shouldn't have taken such a risk for a . . . for a fucking adulteress."

He was worried about her, able to see that she was in terrible shape, probably dying of pneumonia. No way could she walk even with her wounded leg numbed. He was only barely masking his own pain, keeping shock at bay through sheer force of will alone.

"I'll tell you a secret," he said to her.

She stared at him as Badira helped her put her arms into the cloak, her eyes glassing over. "What?"

"He didn't say so, but I'm pretty sure John had a girlfriend in Manila . . . if that makes you feel any better."

"If that makes me feel any better?" she said, suddenly lucid. "I can't believe you'd tell me that in my condition!" She jammed her arms into the sleeves and almost fell over on the bed for lack of strength and balance. "You wait till I see that son of a bitch!"

Gil was glad to see his statement had the desired effect. "If all goes according to plan, you'll be seeing him a hell of a lot sooner than you think."

Khan took a firm grip on the handle of the knife and spoke to Badira, telling the American through her to breathe deep and hold it.

Gil did as he was told, and Khan slowly pulled out the knife, immediately covering the wound with the palm of his hand to prevent any air from sucking back into the chest.

Khan spoke again to Badira.

"He says you're lucky. He doesn't think any air got into the cavity."

"Good," Gil said. "Now slap a patch on that fucker and let's get this show on the road."

Suddenly there was a great deal of shouting from outside across the intersection toward the Kohistani house.

Badira and Khan looked at each other, their eyes wide with fear.

"What the fuck's goin' on out there?" Gil said, unable to get up from the chair because the palm of Khan's hand was the only thing keeping his chest cavity from sucking air when he breathed. If too much air got into the pleural cavity, the lung would collapse and twist the trachea, creating a tension pneumothorax and suffocating him.

Badira's eyes were still full of fright. "Did you . . . did you kill Kohistani?"

"Shit, they found him already?"

Sandra sat up on the bed, her eyes dancing. "You killed the fucking bastard?"

"Why did you do that?" Badira demanded. "He's like a god to these fanatics!"

Gil looked at her and shrugged. "He needed killin' . . . and it seemed like a good idea at the time."

53

AFGHANISTAN,
Kabul, Central Command

As far as General Couture was concerned, the moment that Sandra Brux's Mayday call went out over the emergency band, the entire game changed. He didn't require the president's permission to commence rescue operations for a downed pilot of either sex.

"Chief Shannon's one clever son of a bitch, Captain. He's left us no choice but to help him." He turned his back to the screen. "Okay, listen up! I want two alert F-16s scrambled out of Bagram, right now—with whatever they're carrying—and find out exactly where our airborne B-52s are. I want to keep those bastards in the mountains at bay until we can get a napalm strike in there! Get those Air Force helos inbound for the extraction, and tell them they're flying into a hot LZ. Also, I want SOAR prepped and standing by to back them up in case this goes to shit. Lastly, somebody find out who the hell *Big Ten* is and what the hell kind of support he's providing."

"Sir, I've already got Big Ten here on the flight roster!"

"Feed me, Sergeant."

The sergeant poked his head out from behind his computer screen. "It looks like he might be a CIA Spectre gunship, sir, but it's . . . well, it's confusing. I've cross-referenced the tail number, and this aircraft was supposed to have been taken out service back in '98. Which doesn't make any sense because on the next page it says it's presently based out of Diego Garcia. So I don't know what the hell to make of it, sir. I *think* we're safe to assume that it landed in Jalalabad early yesterday for unspecified electrical repairs . . . but I can't guarantee it, sir."

"Where's it supposed to be now, Sergeant?"

"Says here, sir, that it departed Jalalabad forty-five minutes ago, bound for Kabul."

Couture turned toward Metcalf, hands on his hips. "For unspecified electrical repairs," he echoed. "And since nobody in Jalalabad would ever *dream* of poking around in CIA business . . ."

Metcalf lifted his eyebrows and looked toward the console. "Sergeant, what's the airplane's configuration? Are we talking about a run-of-the-mill Spectre?"

The sergeant ran his hands over the keyboard. "It doesn't look like it, Captain. This aircraft keeps changing its designation. It's been listed as damn near everything at one point . . . a Combat Talon I, Combat Talon II, Dragon Spear, Spectre . . . a Combat Shadow, a Commando II—the list goes on, sir. I have no idea how it's configured now. I'm sorry, but it could be damn near anything."

Metcalf caught and held the general's gaze, asking over his shoulder: "Was it ever STAR-equipped, Sergeant?"

The sergeant paged down. "Yes, sir. It's been STAR-equipped twice—according to what it says here—but it's not now."

Metcalf grinned at General Couture. "Are you taking bets to-night, General?"

Couture shook his head. "I suddenly smell Bob Pope back in Langley . . . and I'd never take a bet where that cagey son of a bitch was involved."

"I'd say that's probably smart money, sir."

The general shook one of the filterless cigarettes from the pack of Pall Malls, offering it to Metcalf, who shook his head. He pulled the smoke from the pack with his teeth and struck a match. "The funny thing," he said, shaking out the match and tossing it onto the table. "The president himself ordered Steelyard and Crosswhite into that crazy bastard's custody. Word around the Hill is that he's got files on everybody . . . or at least everybody seems to be afraid he does."

Metcalf watched the screen, wondering what the hell was taking Gil so long to get Sandra out of the building. "This is taking longer than it should, General. I think something's wrong this time."

They stared at the screen as a man entered Kohistani's house. A few seconds later, he came running back out and up the lane. A few seconds after that, men with guns starting pouring out of the command post and heading down the lane toward Sandra's quarters.

Couture drew pensively from the cigarette, his eyes fixed on the screen. "Looks to me like the proverbial shit just hit the fucking fan." He looked to the back of the room. "How much longer on those F-16s?"

"Taxiing for takeoff now, General. ETA ten minutes."

"Where are my B-52s?"

"Twenty minutes south, sir. They're going to have to refuel before they can make the strike."

Couture spit a fleck of tobacco from his lower lip. "Might as well be twenty days."

54

AFGHANISTAN,
Panjshir Valley, Bazarak

Khan slathered an overly generous amount of petroleum jelly over the compress Gil took from his harness and used that to seal the knife wound to his back. There would be no time for sutures.

Gil jumped up and grabbed his M4. "Sandra, call down a one-oh-five strike." He went to the door and checked up the street to see a mob of men running down the lane toward the house, closing fast at fifty yards. "Make it danger close!"

Sandra, sitting up on the edge of the bed again, keyed the radio. "Big Ten! Big Ten! This is Track Star. Be advised, I am still beneath the strobe. Need one-oh-fives on my position—danger close!"

"Roger that, Track Star. We have them in sight. Take cover."

"Get down!" Gil shouted at Badira and Khan, grabbing Sandra from the bed and rolling into the corner to shield her with his body.

Seconds later the first 105 mm artillery shell fired from the AC-130J Spectre's M102 howitzer slammed into the earth so close that it blew a hole in the wall, shattering the oil lamp and killing the lead element of the attacking force just as they were arriving outside the building. Six seconds later another shell struck fifty feet away, blowing seven more men to oblivion. The remainder of the charging column stopped in its tracks, unable to hear the Spectre performing a tight pylon turn 10,000 feet over their heads, firing the howitzer at its maximum rate. Every six seconds a round exploded against the earth as the onboard digital fire-control system walked an unceasing barrage straight up the lane, effectively annihilating the entire attacking force, then going on to pulverize the command post.

Gil activated the infrared strobe he'd attached to the top of his helmet and dashed from the building with Sandra over his shoulder. "Big Ten! This is Track Star Two," he called out over the emergency band. "Be advised were are mobile. Heading north on horseback for the EZ. Follow my strobe!"

"Roger that, Track Star, we have you in sight. Be advised they're coming out of their holes. We've got multiple heat signatures. You're totally surrounded except for the gap to the north. We'll do what we can to keep it open for you. Over."

"Roger that."

Khan and Badira dashed from the house and hurried off into the darkness.

"Vayan con Dios," Gil said after them, kicking open the door to the guard shack and hefting Sandra into the saddle facing backward. He mounted up with her in front of him and told her to wrap her arms around him. "Keep a hand against that bandage for me. Duck your head now. We're going out the door."

The stallion was good and spooked because of the artillery barrage, and it started to rear up the second they left the safety of the building, but Gil dug in his heels and reined him hard around.

"Hyah!" he shouted. "Move your ass!" The horse bolted north toward the gap in the mountains three thousand meters away.

Gil could see the bursts of orange tracer fire streaking down farther up the valley to the north, the Spectre's 25 mm Equalizer cannon clearing the way for their escape as HIK fighters flooded in to block the pass. The human body splashed apart like a water balloon when hit by even a short burst of fire from the obscenely accurate weapon that flew so high above the battlefield that you couldn't even hear it firing at you. To behold such an awesome display of firepower made it easy to feel like they were home free, but Gil realized that the Spectre's forward-looking infrared eyeball could not see into the many caves surrounding the valley. His only hope was that the Spectre could keep the HIK fighters pinned down in their holes long enough for him and Sandra to slip through the mountain pass to the north, where Forogh and his uncles would be waiting to provide them a defensive perimeter.

In order to perform the complicated extraction maneuver, the Spectre would have to break off its attack and fly a very precise south-north heading. The maneuver would take several minutes to complete and severely limit the aircraft's ability to provide them covering fire.

The stallion was strong and fast, and he bore their weight easily as Gil forced him on, faster and faster, keeping one eye to the night-vision monocular, watching out for any holes or rocks that might trip the animal up. He thought of his own horse, Tico, back in her stable in Montana. No way would Tico ever be forced to charge headlong into the dark like this at top speed. As he thought of this, a strange feeling overtook him, like a ghost finally catching up to him from behind. He felt suddenly as though he weren't going to make it back this time, that he had pushed the envelope too far and that the God of War was about to turn his back.

"Doesn't matter," he said to the night. "I never trusted you much."

"Me?" Sandra said into his ear, clinging tightly against him with both of her hands pressed against the occlusive bandage covering his wound, her face nestled into the crook of his neck.

"No, I was talking to myself."

"I had a really bad feeling the second before you said that."

He laughed. "Well, that's not good, 'cause I had it, too."

"Just don't let 'em take me back, Gil."

"Don't worry." He wrapped an arm around her waist to hold her tight in the saddle. "John promised to bring those one-oh-fives right down on our heads before he'd let that happen."

55

WASHINGTON, DC,
The White House

It was shortly past dinnertime, and the president was in the corridor talking with the secretary of commerce when Tim Hagen walked up, casually clearing his throat and using his eyes to say, "We've got a problem."

"Excuse me a minute, will you, Mike?"

"Certainly, sir," said the commerce secretary.

The president led Hagen into the Oval Office and closed the door. "You know I don't like it when you do that," he admonished. "You can say, 'Excuse me, Mr. President,' like everybody else."

"I'm sorry, sir," Hagen said, "but Sandra Brux is broadcasting from the Panjshir Valley on the emergency band. General Couture is mobilizing elements of the 24th Special Tactics Squadron, the 160th Special Operations Aviation Regiment, a pair of B-52s from the 40th Expeditionary Bomb Squadron, and the entire 391st Expeditionary Fighter Squadron. This is an all-out effort to effect her extraction, Mr. President. She claims to be receiving assistance from indigenous personnel on the ground, and from what I understand, sir, a CIA Spectre gunship is already in the act of providing fire support."

The president darkened. "That's odd. I gave orders half an hour ago that no one was to take any action at all. Now it's World War Three over there!"

"Yes, sir, but . . . well, sir, there's no way Couture could possibly ignore a mayday call from a downed pilot anywhere inside the ATO. He'd be court-martialed, Mr. President."

"Fine! So is it that renegade SEAL or not?"

"Nobody knows for sure yet, sir. There aren't many details because the situation is so fluid . . . but I don't know how else Brux could've gotten her hands on a prick one-twelve."

The president made a face. "On a *what*?"

"Sorry, sir. The PRC-112 handheld radio—it's used by downed pilots. That's just what they call it, sir."

The president cut him a hard look, crossing the room to the desk, where he sat down and took his pipe from the center drawer. He stuck it between his teeth without lighting it and sat chewing the stem. "Okay, correct me if I'm wrong." He took the pipe from his teeth. "But I'm thinking this is the point where we have to start praying for that hero over there to succeed."

"I'm afraid it's worse than that, Mr. President. This is the age of Wikileaks. You need to get behind this operation yourself. Otherwise, word could leak out that you were initially against it."

The president's temper flared. "It's an unauthorized operation, Tim! I'm *supposed* to be against it!"

Hagen held his ground. "With all due respect, Mr. President, that doesn't matter now . . . not in the eyes of the public. This situation has turned into a full-scale military operation to rescue a female pilot—a photogenic female pilot!—who was raped and tortured by the enemy *on camera*. If this mission succeeds, and word leaks out that you didn't back it up—*or worse*—if it *fails*, and word leaks out that you didn't back it up—"

"Okay, I got it!" The president sat knocking the dried tobacco from the pipe into the crystal ashtray on the corner of his desk. "Most powerful man on earth, my ass," he muttered in disgust. "Here I am at the mercy of a single lunatic running around over there against my direct orders, and if he succeeds, I have to treat him like a damn hero! But if he fails, *I'm* the one who ends up looking like the dumbass."

"That's why they say the buck stops here, Mr. President."

"I never said that," the president snapped. "*That* idiot remark belongs to Truman!" He tossed his pipe back into the drawer and slammed it closed, grabbing the telephone. "Get me the White House Chief of Staff," he ordered. "Tell him I want to see him—now! And tell him I want to see the Joint Chiefs as well."

He hung up the phone and rocked back in the chair, pointing his finger at Hagen. "Now, what *you're* going to do, my young friend, is figure out a way for me to burn this fucking SEAL to the ground—no matter *what* happens. Is that clear?"

Hagen hesitated.

"What, Tim?"

"Well, sir, if the mission fails, burning him probably won't even be an issue. He'll likely be dead—he may be dead already. But if it succeeds, sir . . . well, sir, a photo of you putting the Medal of Honor around the neck of the hero who saved America's new sweetheart will look fantastic in all the papers."

The president's gaze turned flinty. "That's not burning him."

"Begging your pardon, sir, but that's *exactly* what it is. The entire modern world will know his face, and within a week, they'll know everything else there is to know about him. For an operational US

Navy SEAL, Mr. President, particularly one as gung-ho and private as this one . . . there's nothing worse."

A slow grin took shape on the president's face. "That's perfect. Hell, it's perfect all the way around. Remind me so I never forget to send you a Christmas card, Tim. You're a ruthless bastard. Now what about Pope? Wasn't he supposed to be keeping these SOG people under control?"

Hagen stood tugging on his lower lip, taking the time to give his response some very serious consideration before finally saying, "Well, sir, to be frank, Pope's a horse of a different color. He's . . . well, we don't want to mess with Pope. Nobody really knows what he's capable of. My recommendation is to think of him in these terms: in four years—provided we win the election—he's somebody else's problem."

"What happened to *the buck stops here*?"

"Well, like you said, sir . . . that's an idiot remark."

56

AFGHANISTAN,
Panjshir Valley, Bazarak

Gil reined back on the stallion to slow him. The terrain had grown too rugged for a full gallop, and there were too many trees for someone with a rifle to hide behind. He knew the Spectre was watching from above, but there were ways for an infantryman to evade infrared temporarily, and Afghan mountain fighters knew them as well as anyone. He trotted the horse down into a dry arroyo and aimed for a gap in the trees.

"You're going to have to keep yourself in the saddle," he said to Sandra, letting go of her and switching the reins to his left hand to draw the 1911. He felt her arms tighten around him as he urged the stallion to pick up the pace where the ground began to smooth out across a natural paving of trap rock. He unscrewed the suppressor from the pistol and stuck it into his pocket. The hair on his neck had begun to stand up, and he didn't need the extra eleven ounces of steel hanging off the front of the weapon if it came time to throw down.

There were plenty of HIK fighters in the mountains to the east, west, and south, many of them moving in their direction, but the gunners up in the Spectre were saving their ammunition for any targets that might pose an immediate threat.

"Key the radio for me," he said.

Sandra lifted the PRC-112 that hung from a lanyard around his neck and keyed the mike.

"Big Ten, this is Track Star, do you have a visual on our friendlies to the north? Over?"

"Roger that, Track Star. Twelve hundred meters due north of your position. We count twenty-plus individuals arranged in a phalanx south of your designated EZ. We also count twenty-plus horses in the trees. Over."

"Roger that, Big Ten."

Farther on Gil rode the stallion up out of the arroyo into an almond orchard. The earth was dry and hard-beaten by the goats and sheep that trampled it day after day. The low limbs made it hard to ride, but it would be quicker than skirting the orchard. As they made their way through the trees, the air pressure seemed to increase suddenly around them. A pair of sonic booms clapped overhead, and the sky was filled with the brain-scrambling roar of two Pratt & Whitney afterburning turbofan jet engines. The horse reared up, and Gil nearly fell from the saddle as he fought the animal under control.

"Son of a bitch!" he hissed. "I guess that's the goddamn cavalry."

"Crazy flyboys," Sandra said into his neck.

They could hear the distant explosions of ordinance being dropped on the mountain to the west, but they couldn't see exactly where because of the trees.

"That should drive them back into their holes for a minute or two," Gil said.

They cleared the orchard as the F-16 Vipers were completing their bomb run and turning back toward the south for Bagram Air Base. With just over a thousand yards to go before they linked up with Forogh's people, a pair of spider holes opened up in the ground right in front of them, and out popped two young Hezbi fighters hoping to catch a glimpse of the jet fighters before they were gone. At first, they seemed every bit as surprised to see Gil as he was to see them. He reined the horse left to give himself a better shot with his right hand and popped off two quick shots, killing them both.

Four more spider holes instantly opened up, and this time the men inside them came out firing. Gil shot two and killed them outright, digging his heels into the horse to send it bolting toward the gap in the mountains. The two remaining gunners continued to fire wildly at them from behind. The horse was hit multiple times and whirled around, groaning in pain and terror. Gil fought to get him under control as the gunners stopped to reload. Sandra held onto him for dear life, but the centrifugal force of the horse whirling around broke her grip, and she flew from the saddle.

This is it, Gil thought, fighting to keep the horse from trampling her. *This is how I go out—fuck.*

A 105 mm howitzer shell impacted between the gunners and blew them both to atoms. A shell fragment struck the horse in the brain and killed it instantly, sending it toppling from its feet toward where Sandra lay on the ground. Instead of jumping clear, Gil stayed tight in the saddle trying to steer the animal away, not realizing that it was dead on its feet. It crashed down on its right side, pinning Gil's leg beneath it.

He pulled with all of his force, trying to free the leg, but it wouldn't budge an inch. "Sandra!" he said, grabbing her wrist.

She lifted her head and dragged herself up against him. "I'm okay."

He jerked the M4 from his back and put it into her hands. "Keep under cover here behind the horse." He unclipped the Remington from his harness and rested the bipod on the horse's rib cage, putting his eye to the scope and searching the surrounding terrain. The enemy was moving toward them now from both the east and the west.

"Here they come," he said. "It's time to get you the fuck outta here."

"What about you?"

He keyed the radio. "Big Ten! Big Ten! This is Typhoon! You're gonna have to make the drop on my present position! I'm pinned under the horse and cannot make the EZ! No time for cover fire! You have to line up for your drop run now! I will keep the enemy at bay! Over!"

"Roger that, Typhoon. Lining up for the run. Give us three minutes. Over."

"I don't understand." Sandra was saying. "What drop run?"

"Surface-to-air recovery," he said, switching out the subsonic ammo in the Remington for a ten-round magazine of .308 Lapua Naturalis hunting ammunition. The Naturalis round had a special valve in the nose of the bullet to not only guarantee its expansion upon entering the body, but to control that expansion so the round did not break apart, not even upon striking bone. He put his eye to the scope, placed the reticle on the closest bad guy five hundred yards out, and squeezed the trigger. The bad guy grabbed the base of his throat, flipping over backward as if he'd been clotheslined.

Gil took his eye from the scope and touched Sandra's face. "You're going out of here on a Skyhook, honey."

"No," she said, shaking her head and starting to cry. "I can't leave you down here. We don't leave our people behind!"

"The Northern Alliance will come for me," he said. "Well, they're not exactly the Northern Alliance anymore, but they used to be, so don't worry."

"Where are they?" she demanded, swiveling her head around. "Why aren't they here? They don't even know the horse is dead!"

"There aren't enough of them for a fight this close to the village, but they'll see the drop. They'll see the drop and they'll come. Don't worry about it. Your mission is to get—hey, what the fuck is this?" He grabbed at her belly where the bloody gown was showing through the open cloak. "You're fucking bleeding, Sandy!"

"I didn't want to you worry," she said lamely. "I got hit just before the horse went down."

He grabbed up the radio. "Big Ten! Expedite! Expedite! Track Star is hit! Repeat! Track Star is hit! Belly wound! Repeat! Belly wound!"

57

AC-130J SPECTRE GUNSHIP,
in the sky over the Panjshir Valley

John Brux unbuckled his harness and climbed out of the pilot's seat. "Jesus, Dave, she's been hit in the fucking belly!"

"Where the fuck are you going?" the copilot called over his shoulder. "I've never done this before, John!"

"I'll be right back! Just get us lined up!"

Brux found Master Chief Steelyard and Captain Daniel Crosswhite in the cargo hold, where they stood on the open ramp helping the load master ready the drop kit for the STAR system. The wind was howling, and he had to shout to be heard over the roar of the aircraft's four T56 turboprop jet engines. "She's been hit!"

"Sandra?" Steelyard shouted back. "How bad?"

"In the belly. Shannon's pinned under the fucking horse. I think he plans on sending her up alone, but if Sandy's bleeding—"

"If she's bleeding, we can't loiter up here long enough to cover Gil until the cavalry gets here!"

"That's right!" Brux shouted. "CenCom's sending everything they've got, but they're twenty minutes out. Those Northern Alliance guys can't see Gil from where they are, and all he's got down there is a rifle!"

Steelyard turned to grab an emergency aircrew parachute from the bulkhead, throwing it at Crosswhite. "Put that on, asshole, we're going in!"

Crosswhite grinned and began stepping into the harness. Steelyard grabbed a chute for himself.

"What the fuck do you mean, you're going in?" Brux shouted in disbelief. "Jesus Christ, Chief! We're dropping the kit from three hundred feet!"

"It's a called an *E*-LALO!" Steelyard said with a laugh. "*Extremely* low!"

Brux adamantly shook his head. "You can't do it! That's just an old C-9! Those chutes aren't made for LALO-ing. They take too long to open. You'll hit too fucking hard!"

Crosswhite's mind raced to form a solution to their dilemma. He considered briefly deploying the chutes inside the bay. This would allow the wind to drag them off the ramp behind the kit, but the idea was just too damn dangerous, and they might not land anywhere near the kit that way. "I got it!" He turned to the load master. "Get us some five-fifty cord—we'll rig a pair of static lines!"

Steelyard took Brux by the arm, shouting into his ear. "Better get back up front, John. If Gil's pinned under the horse, he won't be able to set up the STAR system anyhow. We *have* to go in!"

By the time they were lined up for the drop, Crosswhite and Steelyard were armed and ready to jump with the kit. They had each attached a thirty-foot-long, double line of parachute cord to the chute carriers on their C-9 parachutes and secured the opposite ends of the lines to the deck of the ramp on either side. These static lines would rip the chute carries open the second they stepped off the end of the ramp and deploy each of their parachutes more or less instantly.

Crosswhite stood on the ramp beside Steelyard waiting for the load master's signal to step forward. "You ever jump this low with one of these pieces of shit?"

Steelyard grinned at him. "What do you think? I used to be six feet tall!"

They broke up laughing, and the load master held up his thumb. "Thirty seconds to drop!"

They stepped off to either side of the kit, and Steelyard stuck an unlit cigar between his teeth. "I hope they got a couple a wheelchairs down there. 'Cause we're gonna fuckin' need 'em!"

58

AFGHANISTAN,
Panjshir Valley, Bazarak

Gil was having a hell of a time drawing a bead on his targets with one leg pinned beneath the horse. The only good thing about having the animal between him and the enemy was the fact that the incoming AK-47 and SKS rounds wouldn't penetrate its body. With effort, he could raise up well enough to hit whatever target he needed to, but he couldn't maintain a sight picture while working the bolt. After each shot, he had to fall onto his back again to eject the spent round and jack a new one into the battery before rising back up to shoot. It was costing him valuable time, allowing the enemy to encroach much closer on his position than they would have otherwise been able to. He was engaging targets at only a hundred yards now, and they should strictly not have been able to get that close.

"Goddamn you!" he swore at the man he caught belly crawling

through the scrub at fifty yards, blowing the top of his head off. "Last time I saw that fucker he was clear over there!"

"Let me help you!" Sandra said for the third time, curled up in a ball beside him.

"You keep watching our six. The plane's gonna be overhead any minute now." He took off his helmet and gave it to her. "Use the infrared scope to spot the strobe when they drop the kit. You're gonna run out and drag it over here so I can help you assemble it."

"Gil, I'm not sure I can even walk."

"Yeah, well, you're gonna run if it comes to that." In his mind, he was wondering how in the bloody hell he was going to assemble the extraction kit and keep the enemy off their backs at the same time. He was hoping the Spectre would be able to beat the bastards back far enough one last time before breaking off to circle out again for the extraction run, but even sixty seconds was too far in the future for him to worry about. He rose up over the horse with the Remington and instantly spotted three desperados charging their position at a dead run.

"Fuck did they come from?" he swore, grabbing the saddle with his left hand to keep himself upright and taking the M4 away from Sandra. Keeping a grip on the saddle, he waited for the desperados to draw within fifty yards so he could see them well enough without the night-vision scope, using his left eye. He fired once, twice, three times, moving right to left across his field of vision, hitting each of them once in the belly . . . and every damn one of them kept right on coming.

"You mother*fuckers!*" he hissed, jerking the 1911 from his harness. "Come the fuck on then!" He gripped the pistol in both hands, using his already strained back muscles to keep himself upright.

Concentrating on the front sight, he squeezed off three more rounds . . . one . . . two . . . three. The last desperado toppled over less than twenty feet from their position, pitching a grenade at them on his way down. It hit the belly of the horse and bounced off.

"Grenade!" Gil shouted, pulling Sandra close to him.

The grenade exploded several feet away, disintegrating a large portion of the horse carcass and bathing them both in guts, blood, piss, and manure.

"You hit?" he asked, wiping the gore from her face.

"I don't think so, no."

He jerked his leg from beneath what was left of the horse and found that his ankle was either badly bruised or broken. "That's about par for the fuckin' course," he said, casting a look around for his rifles. The M4 had disappeared, but he found the Remington ten feet away, the optics destroyed by the blast. He tore out the bolt and stuck it into his pocket with the pistol suppressor, then limped over to take the AK-47 from the desperado who had thrown the grenade. The fellow was still alive and moaning in agony.

"Life's a cock in the mouth, ain't it?" Gil stepped on his neck as he jerked the rifle from beneath him. He gathered the magazines from the other two and limped back to where Sandra was still hiding behind the horse carcass.

"I think I'm going to pass out," she said. "Thanks for coming to get me."

He took the helmet from her head and scanned the terrain through the infrared, seeing multiple targets moving their way.

"The only easy day was yesterday," he muttered, reciting the SEAL motto for perhaps the five hundredth time in his career. He crouched down to touch Sandra's gore-matted hair. "You ain't got nothin' to thank me for yet. You just sit tight. The plane's comin' in now."

He took a knee and began firing on the enemy when they rose up from their positions to fire at the belly of the Spectre as it came roaring in over the valley floor, three hundred feet off the deck. Both the 25 mm Equalizer and 40 mm Bofors auto-cannon raked the enemy positions off the port side as it passed over the valley.

Gil fired into a group of men who were shooting at the Spectre's defenseless starboard side. They couldn't hear anything over the roar of the engines, and by the time they realized they were being fired upon, Gil had killed eleven of them at two hundred yards from the standing position over open sights.

The Spectre roared overhead, and three parachutes appeared in Gil's night vision, all three of them twirling around as they descended quickly toward the earth. The aircraft was already climbing to circle back out and over the valley.

Gil fired the rest of the magazine at the enemy before turning to watch the kit come down, wondering why there were three parachutes instead of one. He got his answer when the kit hit the ground, followed by two parajumpers, both of them hitting the ground with bone-breaking force.

He ran forward, recognizing them immediately. "What the fuck are you assholes doin' here?"

Steelyard sat up, shrugging the harness off his shoulders. "Saving your ass, Gilligan. Now help me the fuck up! I broke my fucking fibula."

Gil gave him a hand up, glancing over to see Crosswhite limping toward them holding his hip. "How do know you it's broken, Chief?"

"Because it's sticking out of my fucking calf, *Chief*!" Steelyard looked at Crosswhite. "How about you, you Delta pussy? Break anything?"

Crosswhite nodded. "My ass, I think. You two faggots set up the kit. I got some goddamn killing to do." He trotted crookedly over to where Sandra was still hiding behind the horse. He knelt to squeeze her arm for moment and then began taking shots at the enemy.

Gil and Steelyard broke open the aluminum trunk containing the ground elements of the Fulton Skyhook Surface-to-Air Recovery system. Inside were a harness, a steel cylinder full of helium, a camouflaged, deflated barrage-type balloon, and 500 feet of high-strength, braided nylon cord. Gil screwed the coupling onto the balloon valve, and Steelyard cranked open the tank. The balloon began to inflate instantly. There were a pair of infrared strobes attached to it to make it visible to the pilots without drawing too much attention from the enemy.

Crosswhite fired on full auto to drive back a group of ten, spotting them encroaching through the rocks to the east. He dropped the magazine and quickly switched it out. "They're loading into trucks over by the village," he said to Sandra. "Find out if Big Ten has an angle on those pricks to the east, honey."

"Big Ten," Sandra called over the radio, struggling against unconsciousness. "Can you see the trucks to the east? Over?"

"Roger, Track Star. We don't have the angle. We're lining up for the final run. Sit tight."

As the balloon raced toward the sky, Gil gimped over to pick Sandra up. She passed out in his arms, and the PRC-112 fell to the ground. "You got the radio, Dan. We gotta hook her up."

"Roger that." Crosswhite continued to fire on the enemy. "Here come those fucking trucks, Gil!"

Gil glanced over his shoulder through the monocular to see three pickups full of men rolling out of the village 1,500 meters to the south. He set Sandra down, and with Steelyard's help they got her quickly buckled into the harness.

"Thank Christ there's no wind," Steelyard said, looking up at the balloon now swaying gently at the end of its tether five hundred feet off the deck. "Brux has to get this on the first run, or she's had it."

"Sit with her, Chief." Gil grabbed up the AK-47. "I'm going to help Dan."

"Be right behind you the second she's off the ground, Gilligan."

Gil could see the Spectre dropping to the deck on the far side of the valley, racing toward the village. He nearly swallowed his tongue when he saw a pair of RPGs go streaking up into the sky. One of the rockets struck the outboard starboard engine. It started to burn immediately.

The AC-130J slewed off course to the right and began to lose altitude.

"Holy Jesus," Crosswhite said. "We're fucked."

59

AC-130J SPECTRE GUNSHIP,
in the sky over the Panjshir Valley

Brux and the copilot hauled back on the yoke with all their strength to level the aircraft at two hundred feet. Brux cut the fuel to the outboard engine and feathered the prop, hitting the fire suppression system.

"We gotta go around again!" the copilot said, fighting the yoke to help bring the plane back on course.

"No!" Brux said. "We can't risk that!"

"We don't have enough altitude, John! We came in too low!"

"Just get us back on fucking course! There's still time to bank into the fucking line!"

"Christ!" Dave shouted, seeing the balloon looming above them as they raced toward the line. "There won't be enough line below us. She's gonna smack into the bottom of the fucking plane, John!"

Brux chopped the throttles, and together they hauled back on the yoke to gain another fifty feet of altitude.

"We're gonna miss it!" Dave shouted.

"No, we're not!" Brux kicked the rudder to swing the tail of the aircraft around just enough so that the far left edge of the *V*-shaped pickup yoke, extending from the front of the Spectre, caught the line less than a foot inside of the left turnbuckle. The line rode the yoke down into the eye and locked into the Skyhook at the bottom of the *V*, snapping against the windscreen and slapping back over the top of the fuselage, tearing away from the balloon as it was designed to do.

The unconscious Sandra was snatched up into the sky with little more force than that of an opening parachute and disappeared into the night. As the AC-130J leveled off, the line extending from her harness ascended to a parallel position with the bottom of the aircraft. She trailed seventy-five feet behind the plane, twisting slowly in the wind as the load master reached down from the end of the ramp with a retrieving hook attached to a long pole to grab the line. After the line was hooked, he and one of the gunners ran the line through a pulley anchored over the ramp and fed it back into a winch that reeled Sandra up into the plane.

Within three minutes of being snatched from the ground, she was lying on the deck with an Air Force medic starting an IV of O-negative blood.

John Brux appeared a minute later and knelt beside her to take her hand, both seeing and smelling that his wife was covered in filth. When he looked into her face, he thought she was dead. "Is she going to make it?" he asked, shattered by what he saw.

The medic nodded. "Her vitals are weak, but not that weak. She should make it if we haul ass for home. No way can we afford to stick around and help."

Brux nodded, shaken to his core by the feel of Sandra's missing ring finger. "Roger. I gotta get back up front." He felt Sandra's grip tighten and looked down to see her looking up at him in the red glow of the cargo hold.

"Baby, I'm so sorry for everything!"

His face contorted, and he leaned down to kiss her filth-covered face, fighting the deluge of emotions threatening to break him down. "I love you! I gotta go fly the plane now."

"Okay," she said. "Love you."

He went forward and strapped himself back into his seat, taking the yoke and wiping his eyes on his upper arms.

"She okay?" Dave asked.

"For now," Brux choked, checking the starboard outboard engine to make sure the fire was still out. "Jesus Christ, Dave, she's a god-damn mess. I don't even fucking recognize her."

Dave reached across and grabbed his shoulder. "Hey, you did it, man. You got her the fuck out of there. Everything else from here on is fucking gravy."

"Yeah?" Brux said. "What about them back there?" He thumbed over his shoulder. "We have to leave them, and help is still ten min-utes out."

Dave shook his head. "We can't worry about them. They volun-teered for this same as you and me . . . same as everybody on this plane. They're down there for Sandra. Now get on the fucking radio."

Brux keyed the radio. "Big Ten to Typhoon. Big Ten to Typhoon. Do you copy? Over."

"Roger, Big Ten. Is she up there with you now? Over."

"Roger that, Typhoon. Be advised . . . be advised we have to bug out on you. She's lost too much blood. Over."

"Roger that, Big Ten. We knew that already. Godspeed!"

Brux choked up and Dave took over the radio.

"Typhoon, be advised that Big Ten is very grateful for all your help. Over."

"We're grateful for yours, Big Ten! Gotta get back to the fight now. Typhoon out."

60

AFGHANISTAN,
Kabul, Central Command

By now, Couture and the others in Central Command were watching the battle via satellite in addition to the UAV feed, providing them a more expansive view of the valley. People came and went from the room like bees working a hive, delivering communiqués from DC, Langley, and various other locations from inside the ATO.

Couture stared at the screen where Gil and his compatriots were taking cover behind a pickup truck that Crosswhite had disabled with a grenade. It was easy to see from the way all three men moved about that they were carrying wounds, slowly being picked apart. Their situation was perilous, to say the least, and degrading rapidly. A large HIK force numbering close to eighty had gathered west of their position on the far side of the river, and it was readily apparent that Gil and the others had no idea they were about to be caught in a lethal crossfire. They were too heavily engaged by the hundred or so men fanned out ninety yards in front of them to the southeast. What kept the enemy from overrunning their position from both directions was anyone's guess at this point, but Couture assumed it must have something to do with their not having any idea how large a force they were up against.

"It's a damn good thing these people have no command structure to speak of," he said to no one in particular. "How long before those B-52s are over the target, Major?"

"Five minutes out, General."

An RPG struck the pickup truck, and the entire screen was temporarily whited out.

Couture glanced at the UAV screen for a better picture, but it was obscured as well.

"Cynthia, back that off."

The Air Force lieutenant zoomed out, and they saw that the truck was burning. Gil, Steelyard, and Crosswhite were falling back, leapfrogging north through the rocks and trees toward the dead horse, where there would be no cover at all. Two more pickup trucks loaded with fighters raced out of the village, many of the men in back firing wildly over the top of the cab as the trucks careened along over the rugged terrain.

Couture stole a glance at Captain Metcalf. "Looks like this is it, Glen. I'm sorry."

"Yes, sir." Metcalf mopped his brow with an olive drab handkerchief.

The room had fallen silent as a tomb minutes before in the instant Big Ten was struck by the RPG. No one had dared to even breathe as the huge plane slewed out of control temporarily, only to nose up again seconds later, banking left like a fighter plane to snare the balloon line and snatch Sandra from the Valley of the Shadow. Then, minutes later, the message came that she was safely aboard the gunship, and everyone in the room had shouted in triumph and disbelief, high-fiving and backslapping one another.

Admittedly, that had been the single most exciting moment of Metcalf's life.

Now—just over three minutes later—he found himself at the lowest moment of his career. He was about to watch three terribly brave men gunned down in the open without so much as a ditch for cover. Tragically, this was not an unheard-of occurrence within the Special Forces Community. Brave men—like Sean Bordeaux and his Rangers—had been caught out and shot down a number of times in Afghanistan, more times than most of the American public realized or cared to hear about, but this time Metcalf was going to lose a close personal friend.

He and Steelyard had found themselves knee-deep in the shit together more than once during the Cold War. He owed his life to Steelyard, in fact, having been shot through both legs during the First Gulf War, riding over Steelyard's shoulder for more than a mile across the desert to make their rendezvous with another SEAL unit. It sickened Metcalf, and it shamed him that he could do nothing more for his friend in return than to watch him die on television, as if it were a Tom Clancy film, from the safety of a climate-controlled office in downtown Kabul.

"At least they can go out knowing she's safe," he said, speaking as much to himself as General Couture.

The pickup trucks were rapidly approaching Steelyard and the others now, and the enemy force to the west was across the river and charging through the almond orchard. The screen was full of muzzle flashes. In a matter of seconds, it would be all over.

Couture turned away from the screen. "I don't think I care to watch, to be honest."

Metcalf's gaze never wavered, his eyes fixated on the screen. "With respect, General, you must . . . we owe it to them."

61

AFGHANISTAN,
Panjshir Valley, Bazarak

From a thousand yards farther up the road, Forogh and his uncles could hear the shooting. When they saw the balloon go up, Forogh ran for his horse, shouting for everyone to follow him. They were needed to provide cover for the extraction.

But Orzu refused to let his men ride any closer to the battle.

"We can't risk getting that close," he said. "There's no cover back there. If the HIK knows we helped the Americans, we'll be hunted. We'll never be able to go home. You said he was supposed to meet us here, at the edge of forest. Why did he change it?"

Forogh shrugged and shook his head. "You've been in battle, Uncle. You know things sometimes go wrong. Listen to the shooting. He needs our help!"

Orzu still refused to jeopardize his men. He ordered them all mounted up and ready to leave. Once they were mounted, they sat on their horses listening as the battle continued to rage a thousand meters away. Then the plane suddenly went soaring overhead for the second time, trailing the woman behind it from the end of the rope.

"There!" Orzu shouted over the roar of the engines. "She's away! He didn't need our help. We can go now."

The sound of the shooting began to intensify, and they heard the explosions of RPGs down in the pass.

Forogh reined his horse wildly around. "Listen to that!"

Orzu caught the bridle of Forogh's horse. "Stay here, Nephew. You'll be killed if you go back there."

"It's my life to lose! Let go of my horse."

"Why?" Orzu said, letting go of the bridle. "Why risk your life for a man you owe nothing?"

Forogh brought his saddle even with his uncle's and looked into his eyes, the first signs of dawn beginning to show in the east. "Because he would do it for me! Now . . . what would Massoud do if he were here?"

62

AFGHANISTAN,
Panjshir Valley, Bazarak

Gil grabbed Steelyard under one arm. Crosswhite grabbed him under the other, and the two of them dragged him as fast as they could through the trees toward the pass where the horse carcass lay.

Steelyard was hit bad in the gut, a portion of his intestine hanging out of his lower back. "Leave me!" he shouted in agony. "I'm finished."

They ignored him, increasing their pace. Gil was pumping blood from a leg wound, and he could feel that his lung had begun to collapse. He could see that Crosswhite was in great pain, too, realizing now that he'd been hurt more badly upon landing than he'd previously let on.

"Is that hip fractured?" he asked, panting heavily against the collapsing lung.

"Bet your ass it is," Crosswhite grunted. "Don't know how the fuck I'm still standing. Won't have to worry about it much longer, though. Whattaya think—this far enough?"

Gil stole a glance over his shoulder. "Good a place as any. Those fuckin' trucks'll be up our ass any time now."

They stopped and set Steelyard down against the last tree between them and the wide open spaces.

"Get the fuck outta here!" the older man said. "I'll hold 'em off."

"I hear ya, John Wayne." Crosswhite put his HK .45 in the older man's hand. "Hey, Gil, you think this is what Custer felt like?"

Gil laughed and got down on his belly beside the tree, taking shots at the enemy with an AK-47. His night-vision monocular was dead; he had no idea why. He supposed it had been struck by a bullet, but there was no time to check. He didn't know if the strobe on his helmet was still functional or not, but it hardly mattered now. They'd be dead long before their evac arrived . . . if it was even coming.

Crosswhite got down on the other side of the tree to fire his M4.

A group of eight men broke from the almond orchard, firing on the run. Gil hurled a grenade at them, blowing them off their feet. A couple of them bounced back up, but Steelyard was up on his knee, firing the pistol. He put one down, and Crosswhite killed the other. A wild firefight broke out between them, and the enemy now occupied the orchard. Steelyard took a round to the shoulder and fell over backward. There was nothing that Gil or Crosswhite could do for him but keep as low as they could and pour on the fire.

"Truck!" Gil shouted, shifting his fire as the driver hit the brakes fifty yards away. Men leapt out of the back. One with an RPG took a knee and fired. The rocket struck the ground behind them, and both men felt the shrapnel rip into them. Steelyard's body bounced off the tree and flopped over onto Gil's legs. Two more men dashed from behind the truck with RPGs and took aim.

"Reloading!" Crosswhite shouted.

"Fuck—me, too!"

Crosswhite let out a maniacal burst of laughter as he raced to beat the grenadiers. His laughter swept through Gil like a stiff morning breeze. "The only easy day was yes—ter—"

Their world was engulfed by the unholy, all-consuming roar of multiple Pratt & Whitney engines, F-15 Strike Eagles flying snake and nape over the valley, dumping their combined payloads of napalm and thousand-pounders danger close to the trio's position, obliterating the attacking forces to the front of their line.

Gil and Crosswhite were lifted from the ground, the air sucked from their lungs by the vacuum created by the exploding napalm, the blood vessels in their eyes ruptured by the thudding shock waves that hammered the earth, knocking them senseless.

In the fiery glow that shone through the blood in his eyes, Gil was crawling away from the heat on his hands and knees, feeling the burn of his shrapnel wounds, the scorching fire biting at the seat of his ass . . . and the twisting of his trachea from the tension pneumothorax. Crosswhite leapt to his feet, caught fire, and dropped back to the ground, screaming and rolling to put out the flames. Gil threw himself onto Crosswhite's head to protect his face, beating his uniform with his hands. Neither man thinking, driven by instinct alone to escape the heat, they half crawled, half dragged each other away, but it was no use. They couldn't see where they were going, and they couldn't breathe because of the petroleum fumes that filled their lungs.

63

AFGHANISTAN,
Kabul, Central Command

"Is that them?" General Couture was asking. "Is that them?" Due to the heat of the burning napalm, the infrared camera feed from the UAV was impossible to make out, so the operator had switched the feed coming in from a satellite to an unfiltered lens generally used for daytime observation. By the light of the fire, they could see two men crawling past the flames where globs of napalm had splattered the ground, partially blocking their retreat up the pass.

One of the figures jumped up to run, caught on fire, and fell back down, attempting to roll out the flames. The other figure jumped onto his head and began beating at the flames to smother them out.

"That's them, General," Metcalf said quietly, dominating the nausea he felt in his stomach. He knew that Steelyard was dead. The RPG had struck the ground right behind him. His body had probably absorbed the majority of the blast, enabling Gil and Crosswhite to survive long enough to be bombed by their own people.

"Go! Go!" Couture muttered, watching the two figures struggling along. "Get up and run! Run—don't give up!"

Something on the infrared UAV feed caught the attention of the Air Force lieutenant. She switched the view to the bigger of the two screens without asking the general. Twenty mounted horsemen were riding south from the Khawak Pass toward the wall of fire that shielded the Americans from the view of the village.

"*Now* they come!" Couture said, throwing his hands up. "A day late and a dollar short. Fucking hell—what have you people been waiting for?"

The major stood up at the back of the room, calling, "General! The president is on the line, sir."

Couture went to the back of the room and took the phone. "Yes, Mr. President?"

The president didn't waste any time coming to the point. "What's happened, General? Do we have her or not?"

"Yes, sir. She's aboard an AC-130J as we speak, bound for Bagram Air Base. She's been shot, but we've got our top surgeons standing by on the tarmac. The medic aboard the aircraft reports that her vital signs are weak but stable. It sounds like she *should* make it, Mr. President. That's all I can confidently say at this time, sir."

There was a long pause before the president spoke again. "Okay," he said with a resigned sigh. "Provided she makes it, General, this is how we're going to play it . . . for the good of all. You will prepare an operational brief within twenty-four hours detailing the plans for this operation. It will be entitled Operation Earnest Endeavor. Is that clear?"

"Yes, Mr. President." Couture was still eyeing the screen. The riders were halfway to where Gil and Crosswhite lay motionless in the road, fire burning all around them, but something was wrong, what were all of those heat signatures in the forest north of the valley sweeping down through the Khawak Pass?

The president continued, "You will submit the brief to my military advisor Tim Hagen, who will then submit it to me for my approval. I will approve the brief as of twenty-four hours ago, and *that* will be the official story of how this mission was carried off. Understood, General?"

"Cynthia!" Couture shouted into the room. "Upper right of the screen, sweeping south in the trucks! Who the hell are those people?"

"General Couture," the president said over the phone. "Did you understand what I—"

"I'm going to have to ask you to stand by a moment, Mr. President. We've got a situation developing here." He set the phone down and stepped into the com center as the aerial shot panned around to the north to show a column of more than twenty vehicles racing down from the Hindu Kush toward the Panjshir Valley loaded with men. "Oh, Jesus."

64

AFGHANISTAN,
Panjshir Valley, Bazarak

Gil felt himself borne up from the ground, hands pushing him into the air. He heard the urgent shouting of men over a very great distance. No, not distant. Close . . . but it was as though he were hearing them from beneath the water. The blood ran from his ears, and suddenly he could hear their voices clearly, chattering away in a language he did not understand. The enemy had him, and now they were carrying him over their heads as a trophy of war, shouting in glee over their victory.

He struggled to draw his pistol, but a hand caught his wrist. The orange glow of the fire receded with the heat, and he was swallowed by darkness. He felt cold air against his skin where patches of his uniform had been burned away, then came to rest again against the hard ground. Ice cold water poured over his face, washing away the blood to clear his vision.

"Gil!" someone was shouting into his face. "Gil, can you hear me?"

For the first time, he realized that his ears were ringing like church bells, but, yes, he could hear the voice. The dim face came into focus. Forogh was kneeling over him, shaking him by the shoulder, showing him the PRC-112.

"Gil! I need your authentication code! There isn't much time! Your people will shoot us!"

Gil opened his mouth to speak but found that he could not talk above a whisper, his trachea twisted. "Roll me onto my bad side," he croaked.

Forogh put his ear close to his lips. "Say it again, Gil."

"Roll me to my wounded side. Can't breathe!"

After a quick examination, Forogh found that Gil was bleeding from the right side of his back. He rolled him onto that same side to keep the blood from draining into the good lung.

Gil felt some relief at once and was able to speak with a bit more force. "Typhoon Actual," he said. "Authentication . . . Whiskey-Whiskey-X-ray-Five-Zero-Five."

"I've got it," Forogh said, preparing to key the radio.

"Find Steelyard," Gil croaked. "Steelyard!"

"We have him, Gil. I'm sorry—he's dead."

Forogh keyed the transmitter. "Hello! I am calling for Typhoon Actual . . . Whiskey-Whiskey-X-ray-Five-Zero-Five! . . . I am his interpreter! Typhoon is badly wounded and needs a medevac! Over!"

Another sortie of F-15s swept into the valley to the south. The mountains erupted in orange-black roiling pyroclastic clouds of fire, and the blasts of thousand-pound bombs echoed like thunder.

Forogh called out again, but no one answered.

His uncle Orzu appeared at his side, holding the reins of his horse as the rest of the men held their defensive perimeter. "We need to leave," his uncle said. "We're not safe here. The Americans will mistake us for the enemy."

"We have to let them know!" Forogh insisted. He spotted the kit box from the STAR system and dropped the PRC-112, running back toward the flames. Inside the box, he found a flare gun and a standard strobe light. He ran back to his uncle. "This will be enough."

His uncle gave orders for the three Americans to be brought along.

Forogh mounted up. "Put that one up here with me," he said, pointing down at Gil.

Crosswhite came to, howling in pain when they tried to sit him up on a horse, his fractured hip unable to take the strain. So he was draped over the animal's shoulders, the same as Steelyard, and they galloped north back toward the original extraction zone.

When they arrived, they put the Americans on the ground, and Forogh activated the strobe.

"Our job is done," his uncle said. "I can't risk my men being killed."

"Thank you, Uncle." Forogh offered his hand.

"You trust them?" his uncle said, jutting his chin back toward the valley, where the last of the American aircraft was flying away to the south.

Forogh shrugged. "I am in the hands of Allah, Uncle. I trust *him*."

His uncle nodded and shook his hand, turning to order his men north into the mountains. That's when they both saw for the first time the column of vehicles racing south down the pass, bristling with rifles and RPGs. Without headlights, the trucks had drawn to within two hundred yards, unseen in the dawning light. Forogh and his uncles were caught between the enemy to both the north and the south, with nowhere to run but a short box canyon to the west.

"Allah, be merciful," Forogh muttered.

"This is no time for mercy, boy." Orzu turned in the saddle, bellowing to his clan. "Ride! Put your backs to the wall! We will see if the Americans are still a friend of the Tajik!"

More than twenty horses bolted across the shallow river into the box canyon. The trucks came speeding toward them, bullets whizzing through the air and ricocheting off the rocks. An RPG exploded against a boulder, and one of Forogh's cousins was thrown dead from his horse.

Slouched in the saddle behind Forogh, struggling for every breath, Gil drew the 1911 and forced his eyes open, turning to fire at the enemy.

The horsemen rode into the box canyon and dismounted among the rocks. The firing fell off for a moment as the trucks slid to a stop on the far side of the Panjshir River and the HIK unloaded, taking up positions of their own as they began to maneuver aggressively toward the canyon.

Orzu was shouting orders to his men, putting them where he wanted them. Finally, when there were not enough rocks or positions of cover for them to fall back to, he ordered the horses formed into two separate phase lines of a dozen each. Then he ordered them all shot in place.

Gil screamed and slammed his fist against the earth, strangling against the tension pneumothorax in his chest, his blood-soaked face turning blue, lips beginning to swell.

Crosswhite and Forogh dragged him to the back of the canyon and propped him up on his knees over the belly of a dead mare.

"You're dying!" Crosswhite said, jerking the water tube from Gil's CamelBak. "I gotta drain that lung. Forogh, hold his ass down!"

A wild firefight broke out at the mouth of the canyon a hundred feet away; rockets exploded among the rocks.

"Do you know how to do this?" Forogh asked, shaking like a dog shitting a peach pit as he lay across Gil's shoulders.

"I saw it once in a cartoon," Crosswhite said, grunting against the pain of a cracked pelvis. "Be sure and hold his ass tight."

He took Gil's Ka-Bar from its sheath and cut Gil's jacket up the back to expose his sweat-soaked skin. "Hold on now!" He put the point of knife into Gil's lower back and slowly pushed it in at an upward angle toward the bottom of where he hoped the pleural cavity would be.

Gil writhed around like a fish on the end of a spear, choking blood, unable to breathe or scream. The fight raged on in the mouth of the canyon, the HIK desperate to kill them all before the next inevitable airstrike. A grenade landed in the middle of the canyon and exploded harmlessly near the first phase line of dead horses. Crosswhite pulled out the knife and stuck his finger deep into the wound, sliding the hard plastic water tube in behind it. He felt the tube slide into what he hoped was the empty space of the pleural cavity, and a few seconds later a pinkish red fluid began to drain from Gil's body.

"Got it!" he said, slapping Forogh on the shoulder. "Can you fucking believe that?"

After forty or fifty seconds Gil had begun to breathe again. "Get me a rifle," he croaked, his face contorted with pain, still smeared with gore.

Forogh gave him his AK-47, and Crosswhite took Gil's pistol and what was left of his ammo. Forogh ran to join his clan among the rocks where he knew there would soon be another available rifle.

Crosswhite took a few moments to get Gil propped comfortably in the crook of the dead horse's shoulder, careful to keep his wounded side lower than the other. "How you wanna play this?"

Gil took the last grenade from his harness and gave it to him. "Save that for us."

"Okay," Crosswhite said with a smile, tucking the smooth green orb into his jacket. "I wouldn't be able to run even if we had someplace to go."

65

AFGHANISTAN,
Kabul, Central Command

Couture went back into the office and picked up the phone. "Still there, Mr. President?"

"What the hell is going on over there?" the president demanded, very pissed at having been put on hold.

"Mr. President, one of our men on the ground is already dead. At this time, the two survivors and twenty-some of our Tajik allies are cornered in a canyon just outside the Panjshir Valley, south of the Khawak Pass in the Hindu Kush. They are surrounded by more than one hundred heavily armed Taliban and HIK fighters with hundreds more on the way. I've got two B-52s about to drop a JDAM strike, but that's only going to buy these people ten or fifteen minutes of relief. I do have a few helos on standby to extract our men—both of whom are very badly wounded. What I do *not* have, Mr. President, is the means to extract the Tajik fighters who have risked their lives on this operation to save our people."

The president cursed under his breath. "So exactly what are you asking me for, General?"

"Mr. President, I'm requesting permission to declare Winchester, sir."

The president hesitated, embarrassed to admit that he didn't immediately know what Winchester was.

"Mr. President, declaring Winchester means that I intend to call upon every single air asset at our disposal in a continuous series of sorties until I have annihilated all HIK and Taliban forces within the Panjshir Valley . . . leaving only the village of Bazarak itself untouched. This will not only eliminate the imminent threat to our personnel and our allies on the ground, but will also eliminate the expanding HIK military presence in the Panjshir Valley."

Couture looked at the major and covered the receiver with his hand, giving the go-ahead for the B-52 strikes to commence.

"Are you aware, General," the president asked, "of the parliamentary problems such a military strike against the HIK would create for President Karzai in the present political climate over there?"

"With respect, Mr. President—Mr. Karzai's political woes are not my concern. My concern at this time are the lives of our people and our allies on the ground who helped to rescue Warrant Officer Brux. What are your orders, sir?"

Couture waited as the president considered his response, pensively watching the screen as the JDAMs struck all around the mouth of the box canyon. Men and truck parts were blown across the valley floor in great sweeping explosions, leaving gaping black craters in their place.

"General Couture," the president said finally, "I'm going to grant you the authority to use every air asset we have in that hemisphere from Diego Garcia to London, England. In fact, I'm calling the chairman of the Joint Chiefs to tell him you have the tactical authority to call upon whatever you need—be it air, land, or sea. But understand me, General: if you decide to escalate this battle to that level, you had better make damn sure you can bring those people out of there alive. If you fail, I don't want to hear any excuses. Is that clear? Because I've just given you *everything* you've asked for."

"Thank you, Mr. President. Now, if you'll excuse me, sir, I have a battle to direct."

"Very well, General. Good luck."

"Sir!" Couture hung up the phone and turned to his staff. "Winchester is in effect, people! I want those A-10s in the sky right now, and get those alert B-1s off the ground in Diego Garcia—I want them supersonic all the way to the target!" He stabbed his finger at the screen. "Our priority is to bring every one of these fighters trapped in this canyon out alive! Is that clear? Every one! Now get on the phones—brief your helo crews, your flight leaders, and crew chiefs! Everybody! I don't want there to be any confusion on this! We are lifting those indigenous people *out* of the Panjshir Valley!"

Practically everyone grabbed for a phone.

Couture sat down on the edge of the table next to Captain Metcalf. "I damn near cried when they gunned down all those horses, Glen. Reminds of me of what my granddaddy had to go through on Corregidor back in '42."

Metcalf thoughtfully stroked his chin. "Your grandfather was a cavalryman?"

Couture nodded. "He was forced to eat his horse . . . and he never got over it to the day he died."

66

AFGHANISTAN,
Panjshir Valley, Bazarak

Gil was firing single shots over the open sights of the AK-47 when the JDAMs struck at the mouth of the canyon. Great shock waves reverberated off the canyon walls. He and Crosswhite took cover behind the corpses of the horses to avoid being hit by an avalanche of pineapple-size rock that came showering down. The B-52 pilots had been smart, carefully dropping their ordnance much less than danger close to avoid killing friendlies, wiping out the vast majority of HIK and Taliban fighters who had come down from the north but leaving enough of them alive that the Tajik fighters were still engaged in a dangerous firefight. At least now, however, they weren't in immediate danger of being overrun.

"I'm not sure I can walk!" Crosswhite shouted over the din. "I think my hip's dislocated."

Gil was busy flashing back to Hell Week, five and a half days of misery and pain in the cold surf during the first phase of SEAL training, a week specifically designed to determine who was cut out to endure days like today and who was not. He could see in Crosswhite's eyes that he was beginning to break down mentally and knew that time was running out. Every man had a limit. Gil had his. But even though Crosswhite's wounds were not as bad as his own overall, Gil could see that Crosswhite was now much closer to reaching his limit. No shame in that. Had it not been for Crosswhite, Gil would be dead already. This was not a matter of who was the better man. It was simply a matter of who had the deepest reserve of will. Gil would now have to impose that will upon Crosswhite to keep him from giving up so close to the goal line.

He sucked in a deep, painful breath to mostly inflate the still partially collapsed lung and forced himself to his feet. Crosswhite looked up at him wide-eyed, watching as he stepped over and offered him his hand. Both were bleeding from more than one bullet wound, and both were covered in enough blood and grime that their own mothers could not possibly have recognized them.

"Not going to let you ring the bell today," Gil said, referring to the infamous bell every SEAL knew intimately as throwing in the towel during Hell Week. "Give me your hand, brother. We're going forward to see this fight through."

Crosswhite could feel Gil's strength flowing into him as he grabbed his forearm and hauled himself to his feet. A sharp pain cut through his groin, and he screamed aloud. The joint was definitely dislocated, so Gil supported his left side as they limped past the second line of dead horses toward the mouth of the canyon, where Forogh and his uncles were still trading fire with the enemy.

"Goddamnable waste of horseflesh," Gil muttered in disgust.

Crosswhite screamed again, trying to slip free of Gil's grip to the ground, but Gil refused to release him.

"Fuck it! Put me down!"

"They can't get a chopper in here. Walk!"

"What fucking chopper?" Crosswhite howled.

Gil ignored him, dragging him forward on the good leg.

Two Cobra gunships thundered over the canyon, firing rockets and Gatling guns into the remaining HIK and Taliban forces among the rocks at the mouth. Sparks flew, and rock fragments zipped through the air as bodies exploded and men screamed in agony. The Tajiks threw themselves against the ground, horrified they were about to be annihilated as well, but the Cobras peeled off abruptly and banked out into the valley, their guns still blazing away at God knew who.

A flight of A-10 Thunderbolts flashed briefly overhead, their own Gatling guns roaring with a chainsaw sound that cut through the air in short, ripping bursts of fire.

"Winchester," Gil said, chugging along like a perforated steam engine. "They popped the fuckin' cork for us. We're gonna make it."

"Let me down!" Crosswhite gasped, crying in agony now. "They can bring me a stretcher."

They reached the front of the line. Enemy fire raked the rocks from the trees a hundred yards out across the river where the choppers hadn't been able to spot them. Gil put Crosswhite down behind a boulder, wishing like hell they still had a functioning radio.

"Thank Christ!" Crosswhite said, feeling relief sweep through his body.

Gil saw Orzu looking at him. "I'm sorry about your horses," he said in English, pointing back at the dead animals and holding out his hands in the gesture of a supplicant.

Orzu stepped forward and turned him around to see the plastic tube hanging out of his lower back. His eyebrows soared, and he patted Gil on the shoulder, saying something in Tajik that Gil hadn't a prayer of understanding, but the older man's eyes were telling him not to worry about it, that this was life, and that life was sometimes very cruel.

Forogh joined them. "My uncle asks, What should we do? We can break out now, but there's nowhere to go on foot."

"We wait for the helos," Gil said.

Forogh spoke with Orzu and shook his head with a shrug. "But what about us, he asks? That valley is still full of HIK."

They stood listening to the jets hammering the valley on the far side of the mountain.

"Not for long, I don't think," Gil said.

"They will not get them all. The caves are very deep. The HIK will wait until—"

Gil grabbed Forogh's arm. "Don't worry! Tell your uncle you're all going out with us, or I'm staying here *with you*." He looked at the old man and smiled. "Fair enough, Uncle?"

Forogh translated and the old man smiled back.

"He says, Fair enough, Nephew."

They picked up their rifles and went forward through the rocks to add their own fire to the tree line.

A pair of Night Stalker Black Hawks appeared overhead five minutes later, and three RPGs shot up from the trees after them almost instantly. Only the practiced evasive maneuvers of the pilots averted utter disaster. They banked sharply away, climbing for altitude, their door gunners pouring fire into the tree line.

Gil busted Forogh on the shoulder. "You'd better get your uncle to pull his men back. Air Force will definitely barbecue that fucking tree line now."

But even as he was speaking, fifty or more Pashtun came pouring out of the forest one hundred yards across the river in a desperate charge to finish off the Tajik traitors, every one of them bent on killing and dying for Allah in this great battle for what they considered to be the soul of Afghanistan. RPGs exploded among the rocks and against the ground as the Tajiks fell back through the canyon with no other option but to give ground rapidly.

Forogh and Orzu dragged a screaming Crosswhite between them, scrambling over the jagged terrain toward the heel of the canyon, where they took cover behind the double phase lines of horses, firing singly at the enemy on semiautomatics, many of them on their last magazine. Were it not for the machine gunners in the Night Stalker helos stationed overhead, they would have been overrun completely or blown to hell by RPGs.

Gil felt the vibration in the canyon floor even before he heard the roar of the General Electric F101 turbofans. "Get down!" he screamed, making gestures with his hands. "Get down!"

A pair of B-1B Lancers streaked through the valley past the mouth of the canyon so low that Gil could have sworn he saw the rivets on their fuselages just before he buried his face against the earth near the belly of the dead horse. When the bombs exploded, the ground shook like the very earth was coming apart at the fault lines. Rocks tumbled down into the canyon, and the Tajiks screamed for their lives until the air was sucked from their lungs in the vacuum. Gil and Crosswhite fared better than the rest, having known to expel the air from their lungs before the bombs went off.

When the explosions ceased and the roar of the Lancers receded, Gil raised up to see an entirely different landscape at the mouth of the canyon than had been there only seconds before. The rocks and the river were no longer really there. Only a moonscape of craters and rivulets of muddy water. A number of the Tajiks were badly battered by the shock wave, and still others were partially buried by the avalanche of rock, but miraculously only five of them had been killed.

Gil got to his feet and staggered forward to help as the pair of Night Stalker helos set down at the mouth of the canyon a hundred yards away. The Cobras reappeared seconds later to stand watch as two more Air Force Black Hawks arrived on station awaiting their turn.

The first Night Stalker crewman to reach Gil was a Master Sergeant that he knew well. His name was Waters, a muscular black man with a bright smile and perfect teeth.

"Master Chief, I've got orders to put you and Captain Crosswhite on the first helo out."

Gil shook his head. "Get Captain Crosswhite out of here. I'm not leaving until the last Tajik fighter is loaded up."

Waters stepped forward to take a hold of Gil's arm, not to move him, only to steady him so he wouldn't fall down. "They're going, too, Chief. The Air Force helos are responsible for them. Where's Master Chief Steelyard?"

The last Gil had seen of Steelyard's body, it was among the rocks outside the canyon. He pointed to the crater at the canyon mouth. "He's gone, Sergeant . . . just gone."

Four army medics were working their way through the canyon, tending to the Tajik fighters who needed it most. Two other medics loaded Crosswhite onto a stretcher and began to bear him out. They could still hear bombs falling in the valley beyond the mountain.

"We're safe now?" Gil asked, swaying on his feet.

"Yeah," Waters said, being patient with him, still steadying him to prevent him toppling over. "Ain't nobody gettin' back here now. You should come with me, Chief. You're bad off. I don't want you dyin' on me."

Gil looked at him. "Get those Air Force helos down here, Sergeant. These are my people, and I won't leave them." He knew that if Waters decided to pick him up and carry him out of the canyon over his shoulder, there wouldn't be jack shit he could do about it, but he was determined to use the last of his strength to see his will be done.

Waters got on the radio and requested the Air Force helos land at once.

A badly bleeding Forogh sat on the ground against a rock, a long gash in the side of his face that would take at least fifteen stitches to close. His uncle Orzu lay against him, clutching his chest with both arms, his lungs injured by the blast wave. Gil tried to smile at them and found that he couldn't, but they smiled back.

"My uncle thanks you," Forogh said.

Gil felt his eyes fill with tears. "What for?" he croaked.

"He says this battle will be told in the Panjshir for centuries. He says that you have made our clan legend . . . and that he is proud to know you as a warrior. He says to tell you that you will always be his American nephew."

Gil's legs gave out and Waters caught him, lowering him gently to the ground.

"Need another stretcher over here!"

67

WASHINGTON, DC,
The White House

Gil spent the first five weeks after Sandra Brux's rescue in physical rehabilitation for his broken ankle, the gunshot wounds to his leg, and the knife wound to his lung. His wife, Marie, flew to Maryland to be with him at Bethesda Naval Hospital, where he was treated like any other wounded combat veteran during his stay. No one over the rank of lieutenant ever came to speak with him, nor did anyone from the Judge Advocate General's Office. Upon his release from the hospital, he was given written orders telling him to report to the Training Support Center Hampton Roads at Virginia Beach, Virginia.

Upon his arrival at Hampton Roads, he was assigned a task of mundane training duties. He was told by his new commanding officer that under no circumstances was he to speak with anyone about the unauthorized rescue mission, and under no circumstances was he to attempt to contact Captain Daniel Crosswhite. He then spent the next three months cooling his heels around the training center, bored to death.

The news of Sandra's daring rescue had spread like wildfire across the United States, though very few actual details of the operation were released to the public. There were rumors around Hampton Roads of Gil's involvement, but no one ever had the poor judgment to ask him about it.

Then one afternoon, after his second month in Hampton Roads, the other shoe finally dropped. He was called before his commanding officer and given the news that he and Daniel Crosswhite were to be awarded the Medal of Honor, along with Halligan Steelyard, who would be awarded the medal posthumously. There was to be a ceremony at the White House at the end of the month, during which the president himself would present them both with the award. Gil felt his temper flare, but he maintained his military bearing, snapping to attention and stating respectfully that he intended to refuse the award.

"Oh, you can certainly refuse it," the Navy commander said, "but you might want to consider the fact that this president now stands poised to win reelection. Do you really think it's a good idea to spit in his face a second time? Your court-martial has been held in abeyance only because of his personal order."

That had settled the matter. Gil would have no choice but to accept the Medal of Honor, allowing the president to use him as a prop in his political freak show.

MASTER CHIEF GIL Shannon stood in the White House in his Navy dress whites, posing beside Captain Daniel Crosswhite before a bank of photographers. Marie sat off to the side beside Sandra Brux, who had only recently made her first public appearance. Her husband, John, sat on the other side of her. Both were in uniform, and both were smiling. Neither of them had any idea what the charade was really all about. All they knew was that two brave men were about to receive the nation's highest military award.

Sandra gave him a wink, and he nodded back, feeling like a complete chump to be accepting a medal for getting one of his best friends and seven brave Tajik fighters killed.

Crosswhite, however, was eating it up. He knew the whole thing was a charade, but he didn't care. As far he was concerned, they'd both earned the goddamn medal, and Steelyard, too. "Why let it get to you?" he'd said to Gil earlier in the day during one of the brief moments they'd been left alone. "The only thing that pisses me off is that Sandra doesn't get shit for what she went through."

Gil tried to focus on the bright side. He was still a member of DEVGRU, as far as he knew, and he had been somewhere that no other SEAL had ever been . . . Iran. Who knew how valuable such an experience might be to SOG in the future? There was also the medal itself to consider. Good or bad, right or wrong, Medal of Honor recipients enjoyed a certain status within the US Armed Forces, and Gil realized there would be ways of using that status to his advantage.

Still, there were jealousies within SOG that he would have to contend with, other operatives who might now try to edge him out of the game. Only time would tell how well he would be received by his peers in the coming months. And only time would tell how willing the Head Shed would be to put a Medal of Honor recipient back into harm's way.

The President of the United States entered the room and stood before the podium. "Good afternoon," he said with a smile. "Today, we are gathered to bestow . . ." And so the brief speech went, and after the president had finished telling the American public what gallant warriors both Gil and Crosswhite were, he stepped from behind the podium to accept the first of two medals from the secretary of defense.

He was about to slip the sky blue ribbon over Gil's head when he stopped. "You know what?" he said, turning to look toward the honored guests. "I've got a better idea. Sandra, would you mind doing the honors?"

It was an unprecedented turn of events, and neither Gil nor Crosswhite believed for a damn minute that it was as spur-of-the-moment as the president was trying to make it appear.

Sandra was smiling as she rose from her chair. "It would be my pleasure, Mr. President."

She accepted the medal and stepped over to Gil. This was the first time they had seen each other since she had gone sailing off into the night beneath the belly of the AC-130J, and when their eyes met, Gil felt it clear down in the pit of his stomach. She winked at him and smiled, then slipped the ribbon over his head, muttering "fuck it" loud enough for his ear alone and leaned to kiss him on the cheek. Every camera in the room flashed, and everyone in attendance applauded.

Gil looked at Marie and rolled his eyes, feeling his face flush. Marie smiled proudly and clapped.

Sandra accepted the second medal from the president and slipped it over Crosswhite's neck, giving him the same kiss on the cheek she had given Gil before stepping back to join in the applause. In those brief few seconds during which the president was just another person in the room and no cameras held an angle on his face, Gil caught the gaze of the commander in chief's half-lidded expression, an expression that . . . no matter how fleeting . . . was unmistakably a smirk.

EPILOGUE

MONTANA

After the award ceremony, Gil was ordered to take three months' leave while the fallout from Operation Earnest Endeavor finished blowing over. President Karzai was still having trouble with the Hezb-e Islami factions in the Afghan parliament, but it didn't look like that trouble was going to translate into much of a threat to his presidency. The US Air Force had done a pretty thorough job of reducing the Hezbi forces in the Panjshir Valley, and it was doubtful they would be able to replenish their numbers or regain their influence in and around the Hindu Kush. They had simply lost too much status, allowing Sandra Brux to be rescued and essentially transformed into a Western heroine. What was more, as a result of the HIK's slide, the Taliban had begun another resurgence.

Which of those two pseudo-political groups held the most

power in the region didn't matter to Gil. To him they were both equally violent, equally dangerous to the Afghan people. He hoped the country would begin to stabilize, that reasonable alliances could be struck with the mountain warlords to prevent them throwing in with the Taliban again, but he didn't hold much hope.

Today was the day after New Year's, and he rode Tico through the deep snow of the high country overlooking the Ferguson Valley, sitting in the saddle and thinking back on that night in the Panjshir, of the horse that had been killed beneath him in battle. As he sat reflecting on the death of his friend Halligan Steelyard and the dozen near-misses that should have taken own his life, he heard the sound of a distant bugle come echoing across the snowy linen landscape. For a moment he was reminded of the cavalry's call to arms, but a glance over his shoulder revealed the elk two hundred yards down the slope. He lowered his hand to shuck the Browning from the scabbard and reined Tico around in place, shouldering the rifle to peer through the scope at a beautiful fourteen-point bull, easily the finest looking animal he'd ever held in his crosshairs. He'd brought the travois rig along on the off chance that he would spot an animal for the freezer, but this elk was a prize well beyond the promise of food. This bull was a taxidermist's dream, and Gil had him broadside to a barn door.

Fingering the trigger, he could not help thinking again of the horse killed beneath him, of the two dozen other horses gunned down in the box canyon by their own men. He remembered Kohistani struggling for his life with the piano wire slicing through his trachea. How could he ever tell Marie about something like that? Could she possibly even stay married to a man who had done something so hideous to another human being? And what would she say if she knew how much he'd enjoyed it?

He lowered the rifle and pulled back the bolt, ejecting the round that would have killed the elk and tucking it away into the breast pocket of his Carhartt. He was finished with killing for sport.

The cell phone vibrated in his pants pocket, and he glanced across the valley, where the new telecom tower had been erected atop the far mountain the year before on Ferguson's property, gaining the old man a tidy profit from the lease. Gil did not recognize the number on the screen, but he answered it anyhow.

"Hello?"

"What's the matter?" asked a gentle-sounding male voice. "You couldn't do it? Or it just isn't the same anymore?"

Gil felt the goose bumps rise across the tops of his shoulders. "Couldn't do what?"

"Shoot the elk."

He turned his head, checking all four points of the compass and pushing the bolt forward to load another round into the battery. "Who the hell is this?"

"Look up," the voice said.

Gil looked straight up into the brilliant blue sky directly overhead, seeing absolutely nothing at all. "Pope?"

"I don't have long," the voice continued, "but I wanted to warn you."

"Warn me?"

"Whether you know it or not, you were given that medal as a punishment. I did what I could to prevent it, but the president himself wanted it to happen."

Gil recalled the smirk. "I guess I should have realized that."

"He wanted to use you for political points," the voice said. "While at the same time destroying your anonymity, knowing how much a SEAL's privacy is worth to him and his family. What I *don't* think he realized was that he was putting the mark on you—at least I hope he didn't. There's an element within the Muslim world that knows Kohistani was killed with a garrote. They're furious over it, and they think it was you who did it. The chatter I'm hearing gives me cause for concern."

"They want revenge."

"This is irrespective of sect . . . Taliban, Al Qaeda, HIK . . . they're all Muslim . . . and the brutal assassination of a Muslim cleric would be seen as a direct insult against Islam."

Gil slid the rifle into the scabbard, taking up the reins in his free hand to set Tico sauntering off toward home. "So you think they're comin' for me here."

"I believe we need to assume so—there's definitely a price on your head—but don't expect anyone from the Pentagon or the White House to give you the heads up."

"In other words, the president threw me under the bus."

"No, not him," the voice said. "The president's a banker. He knows very little about things *militaire* or the Muslim world. Unfortunately, he looks to his sycophantic military advisor when it comes to these affairs. So, it wasn't the president. It was Tim Hagen. Hagen's the guy who burned you, and so far I've got nothing on him—but don't worry. Everyone's pumping the neighbor's cat. I'll find something."

ABOUT THE AUTHORS

Scott McEwen is a trial attorney in San Diego, California, and has taught at Thomas Jefferson School of Law. He grew up in the mountains of eastern Oregon, where he became an Eagle Scout, hiking, fishing, and hunting at every opportunity presented. He obtained his undergraduate degree at Oregon State University and thereafter studied and worked extensively in London. Scott works with and provides support for several military charitable organizations, including The Navy SEAL Foundation.

Thomas Koloniar is the author of the post-apocalyptic novel *Cannibal Reign*. He holds a bachelor of arts degree in English literature from the University of Akron. A former police officer from Akron, Ohio, he currently lives in Mexico.